Lieutenant Jacob Starke and the Spanish Gunboats

Michael T. Ribble

Apalachicola Publishing—Dumfries, VA
ISBN: 978-1-7330842-2-2
Library of Congress Control Number: 2021900632
Title: *Lieutenant Jacob Stark and the Spanish Gunboats*
Author: Michael T. Ribble
Digital distribution | 2021
Paperback | 2021

This is the third book following a fictional navy officer just before the Spanish-American War; when the United States Navy and Revenue Cutter Service carried out now largely forgotten operations to prevent military supplies and fighters from illegally entering Cuba. While the coordinated effort described may not have occurred, it would have been possible. People from the period with political, military, and public roles were included and actual events inserted as accurately as possible. All fictional events and characters are wholly imaginary and any likeness to actual persons, living or deceased is coincidental. Certain long-standing institutions, firms, agencies, and government offices are included and their activities taken from historical sources, or assigned tasks that could have occurred within normal operations.

Cover photo courtesy of DeGolyer Library, Southern Methodist University. Torpedo gunboat *Nueva Espana* (Spanish Navy) from Columbian Naval Parade album of April 27, 1893.

Dedication

To:
Commander Douglas A. Thompson, USNR,
Chief Warrant Officer Donald F. Anderson, USNR,
and most especially, Baerbel, my love and muse.

Other books by Michael T. Ribble:

Lieutenant Jacob Starke and Calypso
Lieutenant Jacob Starke and the Anarchists

TABLE OF CONTENTS

CHAPTER ONE
NORFOLK

The United States Navy's steam bark *Calypso* left a St. Johns River anchorage off Florida for Newport News and sliced easily through an indulgent Atlantic. Stay and topsails, tautened by a steady wind from the port quarter, damped her rolls and softened what little pitch existed. She spent the first month of 1897 and previous six prowling the Caribbean and Gulf of Mexico to curb filibuster expeditions smuggling men and arms to Cuban insurrectos; until a coal bunker fire forced her north for repairs.

José Julián Martí Pérez, known as Martí, founded Cuban Revolutionary Party, or Junta, and since April 1895 the island reprised its last ten-year upheaval after expectations for Spain to leave following a brief revolt became interminable guerrilla war. Nearly bankrupt and hemorrhaging young conscripts, Spain's government and constitutional monarchy could not risk leaving the island even if they wanted to so Cuban insurrectos, knowing they could not defeat the several hundred thousand troops sent, resorted to destroying the island economy and creating unsustainable costs.

The Cleveland administration barely avoided entanglement in Cuba and a war with Spain while it struggled to protect American investments on the island. This dilemma would pass to the incoming McKinley administration after an election where debate centered on the gold standard and a recession caused by the 1893 financial panic. Broad public support for Cuban independence ensured little debate and the same Junta achieving this sustained insurrectos with filibuster expeditions to Cuba that smuggled supplies, weapons, ammunition, military goods, and recruits. The Navy Department's role suppressing this fell to Captain Sidney Albert, special assistant to the secretary of the navy, who coordinated with the North Atlantic Squadron for what provisional support was available. Since far more ships than that squadron would be needed to seal the coasts, he adapted the Confederate strategy that crippled Federal shipping by converting a merchant ship and assigning it to the catchall Special Service Squadron. The mission was to raise Junta costs and risks by harrying its filibusters within legal limits; and since commissioning she had stopped Junta expeditions off the Florida Keys and Yucatan Peninsula, disrupted their operations, and sown internal distrust.

The single screw bark *Calypso* cut through a darkening ocean with one of two main boilers on line. Light-gray smoke from her single stack drifted over the starboard bow before settling across undulating swells. She was designed by Starke Shipping & Shipbuilding as a merchant ship ready for conversion during war, but the bark rig was never installed. Albert discovered her while searching for a suitable ship, then arranged for conversion and modernization at the new shipyard in Newport News. The 1,150 ton wood-sheathed hull was 220 feet long with 31-foot beam, clipper bow, fantail stern, and fine lines accentuated with a bark rig. The first two masts were square-rigged; with fore-and-aft sails on mizzen, bowsprit, stays, and jibboom. Each mast's lower section was painted straw-yellow with bowsprit, upper masts, yards, booms, and gaffs blackened to match the hull. The deckhouse ran about two-thirds her length, and a varnished mahogany pilothouse rose above it. The slightly raked straw-yellow stack between fore and main masts served two Normand water-tube boilers powering a Navy-designed vertical, triple-expansion engine with three massive cylinders producing 1,227 horsepower. This steam plant was more powerful, efficient, and economical than its double-expansion predecessor because steam was reused twice at successively lower pressure. Deck space allotted for large muzzleloading pivot guns beyond the main and mizzen masts was occupied by modern 4-inch, 40 caliber breech-loading rifles. Her steam pinnaces and whaleboats rested in chocks aft of midship under two pairs of round-bar davits on either side. Two Hotchkiss 3-pounders, Gatling guns, searchlights, and an Ardois signaling system came with the conversion.

Calypso's commander was Lieutenant Jacob Jefferson Starke, nephew of Immanuel Starke, owner of the Starke Shipping & Shipbuilding. Sailing out of Baltimore, its blood-red swallowtail house flag with three interlocked black S's in a yellow circle flew above more than a dozen schooners and steamers working the East Coast and Caribbean. Lieutenant Starke's expatriated father, Jefferson Starke, lived in Rio de Janeiro and operated the Southern Caribbean and Atlantic Shipping Company. Its ships never entered American ports because he was branded a pirate by Radical Republicans whose secretary of the navy, Edwin Stanton, dismissed him and others who submitted resignations rather than fight Americans. His services went to the Confederacy after Federal troops invaded Virginia, where his wife lived on her family plantation, and he took a prize secretly carrying gold to New Orleans' banks as the Confederate government fled Richmond. Navy officers who "went South" had been treated shamefully, and often accused of piracy, but an insatiable enmity remained for Starke's father. This was returned by a man who saw his birth country vanish with secession and himself dishonored by its successor. After the war took his wife as well, he left for Brazil and never returned, even to visit his son.

That son stood on *Calypso's* flying bridge over her pilothouse in a service dress blue uniform surrounded by sea smells and coal smoke. He continuously scanned the far horizon and intermittently checked anomalies with Bausch & Lomb prismatic binoculars; paired-telescopes' prohibitively expensive successor. He was of average height and build, though wiry, and walked confidently. The short, neatly trimmed beard was sparse and failed to conceal a pleasantly roughhewn and lightly scarred countenance. His faded blue eyes were mounted beneath arcing eyebrows and when not panning a far boundary between water and sky, constantly surveyed everything until locking on whatever caught his attention. *Calypso's* commander was taciturn, determined, and disciplined with tightly compressed lips warning their owner was open but not pliable and the only hint of rebellion a lock of hair that refused to align with its fellows.

He was eager to pass between Capes Charles and Henry, enter the Chesapeake, and deliver *Calypso* to a shipyard in Newport News where her coppered hull and high pressure boilers would be attended. The dry-docking was scheduled for the Port Royal shipyard until a coal bunker fire off the St. Johns River dictated returning to her conversion yard. Starke suspected orders to a yard nearer Washington presaged some type of summons to explain his ship's role in the loss of two filibusters: *Rafael Riego* near the Yucatan Peninsula and *John Gwinn Williams* off the Florida Keys' Bahia Honda.

The lost filibusters' master was Fachtna Harler, reported lost with *Rafael Riego*. He was known in waterfronts along southern coasts as Captain Buff due to his build, demeanor, and, when young, a thick mane of black hair and matching beard. Starke disliked the skilled mariner, but the scoundrel's demise seemed unacceptable and created a void. Even more disquieting was an ongoing relationship, mostly by letter, with Katherine Ledford, a distant English cousin. Their unanticipated intimacy the night before he left Havana tweaked Starke's conscience and regularly disrupted his thoughts since he felt obligated to marry the widow. She was also the first woman he seriously saw spending a life with. His longtime confidant, Darwin Tyson, Havana correspondent for *The Sun*, warned months before that her sex viewed correspondence as commitment. Sometime later he suggested proposing but Starke refrained because she seemed distant after their lovemaking and when *Calypso* left for Newport News Katherine was at her family's London house.

CHAPTER TWO
SPECIAL CORRESPONDENTS

Darwin Tyson had returned to New York City where his life and passions centered on *The Sun*, a newspaper ruled by Charles Dana. He was more at ease in its newsroom than the rented rooming house and it was one of the few locations his silver flask remained holstered. The others being church, which he seldom attended, and Starke mansion with its well-stocked liquor cabinet and matron poised to pounce should he even consider the flask.

The Sun transformed newspapers on September 3, 1833, when its first edition sold for a penny, rather than six cents, and covered what interested a voting public. By 1897, the press was no longer a print shop byproduct but shaping public opinion with papers in relentless competition for the latest and most sensational news; aided by international cable, nascent telephone systems, and advanced printing presses. *The Sun* stood apart from sensationalist competitors by offering literate, quality reporting with stories stripped to essentials, few illustrations, and well-written headlines. Dana employed unwritten axioms to obtain accurate, clear, and brief writing published without bylines, whether by Dana or the greenest hire. Reporters also took what was assigned and were expected to file the same quality whether their specialty or something they lacked interest in. Consequently, the paper became a portal for prospective journalists who went on to other papers. Many were female and their ranks swelled with *The Evening Sun* adding more for women readers.

The paper had moved to the building once owned by Tammany Hall at Frankfort and Nassau streets before Tyson joined. This red-brick structure's first four stories varied little from its neighbors but the fifth was a gabled mansard roof sheathed in slate. Summer morning business days saw a patchwork of retractable awnings cranked out while the sidewalks were swept in front of ground level stores. Rows of tall, rectangular windows above peered over paved roadways scored by streetcar tracks and the foot, carriage, bicycle, and cart traffic's sounds and smells, punctuated by street vendors' hawking. The city hall, post office, and a landscaped park lay across the street. On pleasant days people ate lunch on the old commons that was once a prison and execution ground for colonial insurrectionists but was now sprinkled with gas streetlights and dominated by two fountains, the Bethesda, sculpted by Emma Stubbins, and the Mould.

The Sun's expansive third-floor newsroom was converted from the long, high-ceilinged meeting room with five windows opening to the street. Its wood floor was now covered by rubber matting under rows of desks with the managing editor occupying a large version at the end that controlled entry to Dana's office. Lesser editors had smaller ones aligned under windows with reporters assigned the third style that filled its interior. The newsroom was open to anyone walking up from the street, because Dana decreed the public must have access to their press, and this ambience increased when windows were raised to catch summer breezes and let in urban sounds and smells.

Tyson's desk was in the corner furthest from his managing editor's patch and crowned by the new Underwood typewriter that replaced an elongated Daugherty bought two years before. There were few typing machines about because not many individuals or small businesses could afford them; and those present in the office represented various designs and keyboards. Dana and most reporters dictated stories or wrote them in long and short hand but Tyson believed these machines a necessity and liked this one's pleasing lines, smooth action, and touted longevity.

Starke posted his friend's Havana notebooks after returning to Key West and Tyson had shifted that package from desk to floor several times since receiving it. He extracted one battered book, marked his place with a pencil, rolled sheet paper into the Underwood, made an adjustment, and began poking keys. Between clicks of the letters being impressed on paper was the space bar's tap and slap of Tyson's hand returning its carriage after each line. He occasionally paused to consider some promising angle or extract a Turkish cigarette from his silver case, tap it, light up, and quickly deposit another burnt and bent carcass in the hammered-copper ashtray near the right desk edge.

During one interlude, the thin, nearly bald correspondent spent several minutes with interlocked fingers cradling his head, observing an overhead fan-electrolier. Trusting Starke had paid off since his luggage and person were thoroughly searched in Havana's customs house and again on *Olivette* before the liner left for Key West then Port Tampa. He intended to visit Starke during that layover but a small, steel cruiser in dull white with straw-yellow stacks and masts lay at *Calypso's* anchorage. Blessed or cursed by needing little sleep, he trolled island bars and hotels where reporters schooled, but the rounds of drinks only watered dry wells in a desert of voracious supplicants hoping to obtain a seed pearl to cultivate some mostly fictitious story for demanding editors.

Before leaving Havana he dined at Saloon Brunet, a small cafe across from the Hotel Inglaterra, with Richard Harding Davis and Frederick Remington. The correspondent and artist came from the *New York Journal* with enviable salaries and expense accounts; but lingered in Key West until mid-January because the paper's press boat *Vamoose* was unable, or her master too shy, to attempt a surreptitious crossing. Tyson suspected the *New York Journal*'s publisher, William Hearst, obtained the fast boat for filibustering and inserting correspondents to meet with insurrectionists. Neither Davis nor Remington wanted that aspect discussed in a Havana café, but they were vehement about having to resort to *Olivette* and Davis did not spare the Key West correspondent mob.

This musing ended abruptly when the managing editor, Charles Lord, gestured from his large desk. Aptly named, he oversaw operations, examined applicants, and mostly promoted from within, causing some to be labeled Lord's bright boys; but dispensed opportunity, not favoritism, and was invariably proper, composed, and polite. Tyson went to him and they spoke briefly before passing through a plain wooden door into Dana's office. Their publisher was seated at a small, round table with inkwell, various desk items, and piles of paper. Dana bought the paper in 1868 as he neared fifty after a career in literature, teaching English in the German states, freelance reporting during Europe's 1848 revolutions, and serving President Lincoln as an assistant secretary during the war; assigned to accompany field armies and send back accurate information. He now set the profession's standards and become one of its legends.

Dana was bald with thick, white hair on both sides and flowing beard of similar color and texture, surrounding trademark brass spectacles bridging a large nose. He was neither thin nor heavy and often outpaced pace younger men while walking; with intellect and vigor also undiminished as eighty years approached. Dana shifted his armchair then motioned them to a pair of plain chairs with worn cane seats. Although known to appreciate art and maintain a well-appointed house and summer home, Dana believed offices should be purely functional so he worked by a tall window on the small, round table overhanging a large wicker wastebasket. The same armchair served it and veteran walnut desk where a japanned mechanical calendar was almost obscured by papers. A couch was placed against one wall and another near the fireplace and mantel below Lincoln's portrait. The other hangings, including Horace Greeley's picture, were placed wherever space permitted; and a mysterious stuffed owl that came as a gift eyed Tyson and Lord as they sat.

Dana smiled at Tyson, "Fine work on the trocha story."

Tyson knew this was not why he was summoned because Dana usually entered the newsroom to recognize exceptional results, but replied, "Thank-you, sir. It was fortunate I met Lieutenant Starke in Havana."

"Starke? Wasn't his father the traitor and pirate?"

Tyson was cornered. Despite knowing Lincoln and Martí, Dana felt as strongly against the South's attempt to secede as he supported Cuban independence. Starke offered little about his father over the years and Tyson was only acknowledging a friend's help, but a response was necessary and Dana's exceptional judgement of people, situations, and politics was buttressed by an uncanny ability to sense lies, waffling, or avoidance. Tyson braced, recalled a recent conversation, looked directly at Dana and replied, "I suppose that depends on one's view. Starke's father believes his nation died in sixty-one and has adopted Brazil. Many honorable men were accused of piracy then and after, with most charges unproven and few cases brought to trial."

"I see; and now perhaps an equally candid observation on Cuba, Darwin."

Tyson continued carefully, "The provisional government controls too many areas for Spain to retake without support, resources, and time she doesn't have; but the insurrectos can't stand against their army and the Junta doesn't speak for all Cubans. Governor-general Weyler's reconcentrado policy could end the stalemate but there's no way to care for those displaced."

"Weyler's responsible?"

With some caution, Tyson answered, "No more than Gómez who claims he'll make Cuba too costly for Spain, destroy its economy, and execute all opposition as traitors. The government won't talk unless insurrectos disarm; and they don't trust Spain."

"And it stands where?"

"Weyler's clearing out corruption and deadwood, Maceo's dead, trochas are more effective, and a Pinar del Río offensive has begun. However, the provisional government still controls Cuba's eastern provinces, except the cities, and Pinar del Río's not pacified. Less disease this time of year favors the Spanish, but Gómez will try to keep his army intact then force Weyler into the field during summer when Spanish draftees fall in droves from fevers."

"And filibuster expeditions?"

"They are illegal but boost insurrecto morale and provide military supplies; especially with the reconcentrado policy separating them from local support. However, the coordination between our Navy, Justice, and Treasury is improving."

"I believe your friend Starke sank two expeditions without trial."

"He claims the first tug blew a boiler running from *Calypso* and the second opened fire on him after attacking a Spanish gunboat."

"How well do you know him?"

"We went to the same school."

"And your evaluation?"

"Is he lying? No. Is it the whole story; probably not."

Turning to Lord, Dana gave his beard a quick stroke, "We didn't run stories on either."

"No sir. Free silver and the election took priority; besides anarchists were rumored to have been behind *Rafael Riego*."

Dana returned to Tyson, "You met Davis in Havana?"

"He's with Remington looking for accurate insurrectionist information in Havana after *Vamoose* didn't pan out."

"Interesting, but what are your thoughts on Crete?"

Tyson was surprised but answered cautiously, "Christians have received arms, encouragement, and support from Greece; whose government believes it'll gain territory in a war. The Turks, or Ottomans if you prefer, want to end the revolt and restore order, but can't govern. European powers fear any war could spread and have proposed an international blockade."

Lord looked at Tyson, "Greece is assembling an expedition so war and blockade are almost certain; and we need someone there."

Looking from Dana to Lord, Tyson heard himself reply, "What's the plan?"

Lord obtained a confirming glance from Dana, "Passage is arranged on the French Line for Le Havre, rail to Marseille, and then a liner to Athens; but you must leave on a Saturday. When can you be ready?"

"Several days to finish the Havana stories, get my affairs in order, and obtain what's needed. I'll buy some items in France."

Dana interjected, "That's agreeable. Mr. Lord will arrange letters of credit and trusted contacts. Remember, we need accurate reporting, not meddling. *The Sun* will not imitate the *World* or *Journal*."

"Yes sir.'

He then stood. With Dana framed in a tall window lit by morning sun, Tyson found himself looking directly into his publisher's steady eyes. He was wished Godspeed after a firm handshake and followed Lord through the door into the cavernous newsroom with its talking, smoking, writing, and intermittent typing.

Tyson stood at *La Gascogne*'s starboard rail in the early morning of January's last day, wrapped in heavy overcoat, hat, mufflers, and leather gloves. A horse-drawn taxi with appreciative driver brought him to Morgan Street pier the night before. He had posted a letter to Starke and a second to Cassandra Evans, the Washington reporter he assisted when she fell ill in Havana. Tyson located his first-class cabin on the main deck between her two stacks and learned he would share it during the week's transit with a young Englishman returning from visiting Foreign Service Office relatives in Washington.

La Gascogne was one of four built less than ten years earlier for Compagnie Générale Transatlantique, known as the French Line. A trifle less than 500 feet long and fifty wide, she maintained a seventeen-knot pace. Two of the original four masts had been removed, along with her sailing rig, when the triple-expansion engines were replaced by a pair of newer quadruple-expansion types. The black steel hull between her straight bow and overhanging stern accommodated near 400 first-class passengers, many more third, and relatively few second. Tyson suspected this deficit of second-class cabins forced *The Sun* to book first-class accommodations rather than any attempt to make amends for sending him to the eastern Mediterranean within days of returning from Cuba.

Tyson mixed with others at the railing outside his cabin between two round bar davits rising to the deck above. He finished a cigarette as steam tugs warped the liner from her berth, flicked it overboard then traced the butt's slow fall through the opening distance between pier and hull until landing amidst shifting flotsam. Watching the slowly dancing debris, he decided there was nothing for it but relax until they reached Le Havre then took the silver flask in a gloved hand, tilted it upwards, and felt the sharp liquid that was always reassuring in a New York winter. After replacing its cap and sliding the flask beneath his heavy coat, he took in *La Gascogne*'s departure. Once the harbor pilot judged the pier clear and large ship aligned with the channel, Tyson heard tug whistles acknowledging the order to cast off and felt the deck vibrate dully as engines received steam. The ship slowly gained speed while piers, streets, and buildings began passing as they headed downriver to the Atlantic.

Tyson's letter surprised Evans at her Georgetown relatives' house the day before an afternoon interview with Miss Clarissa Barton at Starke mansion. *The Evening Times* reporter recuperated faster than anticipated at her family's upstate home after arriving in New York City from Havana; and recently returned to the paper. Whatever the affliction, its convalescence, and her continuing recovery indelibly marked body, perspective, and spirit. The overpowering collapse and accompanying dependence was shocking, as was an unfamiliar reliance on those attending her; especially the thin, balding, correspondent with an affinity for liquor and cigarettes. Tyson contrived medical care, handled cables, and used his connections to file stories she wrote for *The Evening Times* while bedridden. He also fed and anchored her mind by describing *The Sun*, past assignments, and longtime friend, Jacob Starke; then placed her on the liner for New York City arranged by the Starke firm's agent. Havana altered the independent, self-assured, and politely condescending woman; as she was reminded daily in the mirror and different approach to work. Assignments once resisted as unsuitable were completed without complaint, she proposed rather than demanded, and the editor remarked her writing possessed greater weight, insight, and truth; while conveying more confidence and empathy. Her male colleagues were also more accepting because she earned their respect for her reconcentrado stories and, they said, having seen the elephant.

Evans stepped down from the yellow, white, and mahogany Capital Traction Company streetcar near St. Margaret's Episcopal Church, walked Florida Avenue, and then turned west. At the Romanesque mansion with red stone exterior, four stories, and two turrets she climbed its stone porch steps, pulled a mechanical brass doorbell, and was greeted by Joshua Altman, the Starke's butler. He assisted the well-bundled guest remove her wraps then guided his mistress's first visitor, with Brussels carpet bag, between double doors into the familiar parlor. Constance was sitting upright at her afternoon location in the parlor alcove formed by the large turret, where a warming sun effortlessly passed through tall windows into the room.

Constance watched Cassandra approach; noticing she lacked Katherine's practiced grace. The young guest's outer garments, left in the cloakroom, undoubtedly consisted of gloves, a dark over-frock coat rising from knee to collar with a double row of buttons, one of several hats rotated for variety, and something for the umbrella stand. Evans invariably chose a traveling suit for work and today's was a fine blue-black wool jacket with leg-of-mutton sleeves and matching full-length, flared skirt that barely revealed high-topped black leather shoes. A broad black-cotton belt encircling the wasp waist concealed where a lace-trimmed white blouse slid under the skirt. Her pale throat was slightly constricted by a long, black necktie that nearly covered the cotton blouse's bone buttons. She was noticeably thinner than last year, but still achieved a solid S-figure with light corset and modest bustle.

Constance poured steaming coffee into a semi-translucent bone china cup; certain something hot was welcome after Evans' winter excursion. Then, as her guest settled, Starke's aunt considered the woman she thought her recalcitrant nephew might develop an attachment for. Attractive, with obvious intellect, it was clear she was still recovering and Constance had known many, including her late sister-in-law, whose lives were ended or altered by similar maladies or bearing children. The sharp countenance and figure had evolved to one more drawn or experienced that seemed to enhance a natural attractiveness. Poise and movement were also more assured, with a flowing, natural quality, as though youthful exuberance was transmuted to a polished grace. New lines lightly etched a face that discarded its previous brittle tenseness; adding depth and character to the handsome countenance. What had not changed were the steady brown eyes under perfect light brown eyebrows matching a pompadour of rolling auburn hair that required long pins to anchor hats. Her cheeks were blushed from walking in late winter, she was discreetly applying eye make-up respectable ladies denied, and a light scent from lemon juice used for her complexion was discernible.

Constance welcomed her, "It's good to see you continue to improve."

"Thank you. I cannot express how much your agent's assistance meant in Havana."

"Think nothing of it. Take some coffee; it will help warm you before our guest arrives and there's cake if it appeals."

Cassandra accepted cup and saucer, added two spoons of brown sugar, stirred, and slowly sipped the warming liquid. Minutes later, they heard a carriage, horses neighing, and shuffling of shod hooves. Constance poured a second cup and placed it on the small table near a third chair while Altman assisted their latest arrival, whose entrance was announced first by noise in the entranceway then the butler ushering a short, thin, vigorous woman into the parlor. Miss Clarissa Barton, or, as she preferred, Clara, was nearing eighty but walked erect with purpose and firmness. Her center-parted hair was gray-black and pulled tight above dark eyebrows and a broad face with prominent cheeks, ears, mouth, and nose. She wore a dark, high collared leg-of-mutton sleeved blouse adorned with two vertical rows of small red flowers, one award pinned over the heart, and second medallion fastened just below her collar. Every detail was flawless, with compassion and determination jousting for primacy in her manner and deportment. Cassandra thought her host a formidable woman but Constance paled in comparison to Barton.

Clara Barton was the nation's best-known woman and beau idéal of her sex who was educated to teach, one of the patent office's first female recording clerks, and saw war as nurse. On and off American battlefields she went far beyond nursing then reprised this role during the Franco-Prussian War with the International Red Cross; despite visiting Europe to improve her health. She then founded the American Red

Cross, became its president, and oversaw several major disaster recoveries. Awarded Germany's Iron Cross and the Imperial Russian Silver Cross, she was a popular writer and speaker who enjoyed access to presidents. Since Barton returned from the Ottoman Empire and Armenia in September, Evans was assigned to interview her regarding the Red Cross moving into its new Glen Echo headquarters. Her association with the Starke family probably influenced the editor's decision because Constance and Clara's long friendship began when a very young Constance helped Barton raise money, assemble medical supplies for the front lines, and comfort thousands of wounded scattered across the city. They pair already visited several times since Barton's return and Mrs. Starke obligingly arranged this interview.

Evans sensed fire, passion, and purpose in prominent eyes peering from Barton's heavily, but not unpleasantly, lined face. After taking their seats and distributing small cakes, the afternoon passed with her asking questions that Barton would answer; then add specific Red Cross aspects she would like in print before noting a few personal items she did not. It seemed Barton was particular about appearance, her hair especially, and favored bold colors like red. She rose early then read or worked until late evening, was open about her Universalist religious beliefs, and ate meat only for sustenance or propriety having once seen an ox slaughtered. Over the years she became proficient in weaving, farm tasks, nursing, and other skills; but not dancing. Her family forbade that despite supporting every other interest, constantly urging education, and encouraging her competition with either gender. She claimed to be an excellent rider who learned bareback and sat almost every type of saddle, even the McClellan, but saw no value in sidesaddles. Her experiences included two wars, major floods, a Russian famine, and

Florida's yellow fever epidemic five years before. Barton was anxious about Negroes in southern states and spent a year helping those on the South Carolina Sea Islands recover from a hurricane. She also spoke of Frederick Douglass, Walt Whitman, and Susan B. Anthony before revealing her dislike of presiding over public meetings due to a natural shyness she learned to overcome. After encouraging Evans to become familiar with military ranks, social courtesies, and other protocols, Barton emphasized the necessity to obtain government agreement before relief work; then turned to her interviewer, "Having answered your questions, what did you learn in Cuba beyond that in print?"

Evans described Key West, Havana, her sudden illness, and Cuban hospitals as Barton silently absorbed each word and idea; weighed them for relevance, value, and credibility; then nodded. She was particularly interested in Wyler's reconcentrado policy and abject despair permeating the old men, women, children, and babies filling half-roofed warehouses, camped in open ditches, or shunted to unused grounds with little food and less sanitation. Barton did not dwell on suffering but plunged into what might be done and leveraging politics. Evans would have once replied with a barrage of opinions, but now spoke precisely about what she knew then recommended Tyson. The afternoon ended when Barton turned to Constance, "I fear this catastrophe will grow unimaginable and yet cannot be addressed unless all involved allow it."

Barton's carriage was soon brought around and she departed. Evans remained a few minutes longer to slide the notebook into her carpet bag, thank Constance, and dress before walking rapidly to the streetcar stop. While taking leave, she tested the water with Starke's aunt about getting a *Calypso* story since rumors of sea chases, anarchists, and tweaking the Junta were creating a reputation amongst junior officers that he was their generation's man of action. Constance warned Starke was unlikely to agree but half-suspected this interest went beyond a story when Evans described Key West dinners with Jacob. This was welcome if her nephew reciprocated since Katherine had returned to England with her brother, Edward Curtis, after the Starke sugar mill and plantation sale. Constance believed either woman suitable for a nephew delaying marriage overlong and showing perverse resistance that was becoming a source of constant worry. She allocated some blame to his longtime friend Darwin Tyson; a clean-shaven, thin, and bony reporter working for *The Sun* who met Starke at Jefferson Classical & Military Academy then left for a Michigan university. He was an enigma whose sole passion beyond hard liquor and Turkish cigarettes was his profession but, excluding religion, seemed to share her liberal views and appeared genuinely intellectual.

Before abandoning these thoughts to speak with Cynthia Jefferson on domestic issues, Martella Young on next week's menu, and a Center Market trip with Darius Sutton, she thought Olivia or Isabella Albert might also be suitable if neither Katherine nor Cassandra were successful. At the dinner party before Jacob left for *Calypso*, she observed the pair to be young and unpolished but intelligent and vibrant. Marriage to either was likely to quickly extend the Starke family line past Jacob; something needed more than ever with Immanuel shedding the firm's riskier assets and choosing to be more often at home than away on business. She would know by fall since the sisters were summering with her in Newport.

CHAPTER THREE
RETURN TO SEA

C aptain Albert glanced up from his desk through the tall window of his small, east wing office in the ornate State, War, and Navy Building officers referred to as the Building. He just came from standing there contemplating the morning panorama of Executive Mansion, Presidential Grounds, Treasury Building, and Lafayette Square; but rose and returned to look out, one hand cradling a warm pipe and his other resting lightly on the sill. *Calypso* and the Navy's effort to curb filibusters were at risk.

The bark was scheduled for a Newport News dry-dock during February's second week, since North Atlantic Squadron ships in various yards during the year's closing months would leave in January. Admiral Bunce intended to employ these ships for summer maneuvers off the Atlantic coast where already tenuous relations with Spain would not be exacerbated by a squadron entering the Caribbean. However, he did agree three could cruise off Florida to assist the Revenue Cutter Service if the Apprentice Training Squadron's *Essex* covered Caribbean port calls traditionally made by his ships. Albert exploited this by suggesting *Calypso* take some early spring visits *Essex* could not. This would move the bark throughout the Caribbean, increase Junta uncertainty about her role, and create pressure for *Calypso* to clear Norfolk before March; and be at sea when the new administration arrived.

Albert drew in pleasantly tart tobacco smoke, peered through the glass, and wondered if his tenure, or even filibuster coordination, would continue much beyond the March inauguration. William McKinley's choice for secretary of the navy was likely the former Massachusetts' congressman and governor, John Davis Long. The Harvard lawyer's political proclivities included women's suffrage and temperance but he was not thought an activist, spent the war at home in his state militia, and lacked naval experience. He was also close to the new president, neither warmonger nor jingo, and feuding with Senator Lodge; the ardent jingo with no military background. The greatest concern for Albert, however, was Justice. John McCook, a successful attorney, was lobbying for attorney general and would scuttle any legal action against filibusters, allow them freer passage, and provide the Junta with Department of Justice support or cover. McCook promoted Cuban independence, thrived on confrontation, saw those not sharing his views as enemies, and had little use for diplomacy. This had not changed since his teens when he eagerly enlisted as a private then rose rapidly to captain after several major actions. When a severe wound ended his war, the naturally bellicose McCook finished Harvard's law school then left for legal battlefields.

Many things would change as Washington adjusted to the fall hurricane damage and election. Back at his desk, Albert gently tapped the meerschaum pipe's cooling bowl against the ashtray then stood it alongside others in the rack as he prepared to leave work on time. Change was also coming to the Albert household. The family, or more accurately the eldest daughter Olivia, had invited Lieutenant (junior grade) Benjamin Watson for dinner. Starke said his executive officer needed time away and forcefully suggested Watson take leave while *Calypso* was in the shipyard. Although an alliance between Stark and Cupid seemed unnatural, Albert was certain *Calypso's* captain anticipated this leave would include a six-hour train ride north to Olivia.

Calypso was in dry-dock where work was now overseen by a larger and less entrepreneurial Newport News Government Department than during *Calypso's* conversion. While on blocks, marine growth was removed from her hull then copper sheathing inspected and replaced. A small stove-in section was repaired that explained the slow increase in bilge pumping frequency; but not whether the cause was collision, storm, or *Rafael Riego* debris. Around two dozen weak, suspicious, or plugged water tubes in the boilers were replaced; much to the black gang's relief since repair at sea required cooling the boiler then sliding a man on a plank inside the fire box to remove tubes and plug header openings. The coal bunker where their hot spot occurred was meticulously inspected and probable cause traced to a defective main deck bunker plate seal intermittently allowing small amounts of water down its coal chute; so inspectors agreed to replace all bunker plate seals. Exchanging the ship's black powder .45-70 rifles and Gatling guns for smokeless weapons did not occur because defective 6mm ammunition limited supplies; so priority went to new ships and the Marine Corps. This justified Lieutenant Commander Leutze's efforts to ensure *Calypso's* initial outfitting included bolt-action, magazine-fed Remington-Lee rifles rather than single-shot Remingtons.

By mid-February, *Calypso* was moored alongside the Norfolk shipyard quay-wall where she commissioned; preparing to get underway the next morning. From her pilothouse, Starke looked past red-brick industrial buildings down the Elizabeth River's southern branch and saw the Norfolk naval station's receiving ship *Franklin*; converted from an obsolete frigate. Beyond her, a Portsmouth to Berkley ferry was steaming for dark, water-stained wood pilings at its landing near the train depot. Starke's old Academy friend, Philo McGiffin, preyed on his mind. He was not offered a commission, used his severance pay to enter Chinese service, and returned home after the Yalu River battle; wounded worse than Starke realized. After a revolver ended the increasing indignities and pain, Starke regretted they had seen little of each other, but not his act; which included a note apologizing for the disruption. McGiffin's thinking of others was the same in China where his hospitality included Thanksgiving and Christmas dinners for a mixed crowd. *Calypso's* commander knew McGiffin would now join the other ghosts who intermittently returned during his sleep; beginning with Second Lieutenant William Reily, who died with Company F in Montana, several hills distant from where Starke's pack train and several cavalry companies dug in.

Starke crossed to the chart table where their navigator, Ensign Walter Dunbar and Chief Quartermaster Paul Owen plotted *Calypso's* return to her southern cruising grounds; while engineers below deck completed the lengthy procedure to raise steam in propulsion boilers. Watson was inspecting lines, boats, and sails on the main deck with Ensign Carl Martyn and Chief Boatswain's Mate Braddock Weaver. Paymaster Matthew Wiggs was securing storerooms for sea and Assistant Surgeon Sidney Conrad stalked the main deck with his camera; an interest that blossomed over the last month.

He finished the last paperwork soon after Cabin Steward Hiroyuki Yamashita cleared the supper table. There was also an awkward letter to Katherine replying to the last from her saying little more than she and Edward arrived safely in Saint Nazaire after leaving Havana, took a train to Calais, and then crossed on a channel ferry. They would be a month at the London townhouse before leaving for the family's Bridport estate. He did not write to Tyson since his friend sent a brief note warning he was overseas and mail might be held by *The Sun*. Starke also postponed a letter to his aunt until better able to frame the refusal to accept an interview with Evans. After skimming a newspaper, he killed the lights, cracked cabin windows to entice a slight breeze, and climbed into bed. A slight but sudden pressure on the wool blanket near his feet as he drifted off caused him to look down its length where bright eyes in coiled fur reflected what light remained. The gray and white cat several sailors rescued from an irate Key West bartender about to quench its life for lapping customers' whiskey had joined him. Thaddeus had been cleaned, dried out, and restricted to the ship ever since so food was now his preferred drug. He must have entered the cabin searching for table scraps then became trapped, but Starke saw no reason eject his softly purring companion from a warming bed.

He rose early the next morning, looked out his windows, and set the mechanical calendar to "FRI FEB 19 97". Yesterday's *Norfolk Virginian* beside it caught his interest. Greece landed troops on Crete and took at least one town. The Ottoman Empire was mobilizing and the European powers established an international blockade to prevent escalation. Its French commander already warned the Greeks and their insurgent allies against attacking areas on Crete controlled by the international force or Muslim civilians; so the war would be fought along the two nations' common border. Tyson was probably there. He admired his friend's alleged ability to remain detached although it might explain the self-medication.

North Atlantic Squadron exercises off Charleston were also covered. It seemed the squadron received a far different reception than the one blockading that port during the war; and before dispersing to different destinations, with *Vesuvius* and *Dolphin* steaming south on filibuster patrol, there was a large formal ball. Starke not only regretted missing it, since he enjoyed dancing and, like fencing, was skilled at it, but also the chance to be an exercise blockade runner. That honor went to *Vesuvius* after a brief flirtation with *Calypso* during several staff planning meetings on Bunce's flagship *New York*, where Starke had to emphasize his mission under the Special Service Squadron. These visits did allow him to examine the popular flagship; an armored cruiser with first-rate accommodations, excellent sea-keeping, and pleasantly impressive appearance. Her type formed the Spanish navy's backbone because they were well-armored, heavily armed, and swift enough to catch, engage, or outrun opponents; except others of the same species and a few swift liners. Backing her ram bow was over 8,000 tons of steel with three straw-yellow stacks towering over a graceful hull almost 400 feet long and sixty-five wide. She reached twenty-one knots on trials and boasted six 8-inch breech-loading rifles backed by twelve 4-inch mounts.

Starke wanted *Calypso* underway with the seven o'clock sunrise so Passed Assistant Engineer Adrian Osbourne and Assistant Engineer William O'Leary spent most of the previous day and night lighting off boilers then warming the main engine. To achieve this, small kindling fires were lit then carefully tended until boiling feedwater created steam for the engine that exhausted to a condenser where it was returned to feedwater and resent through firebox headers and tubes. As heat increased, funnel guys were adjusted to accommodate expansion, safety valves tested, and the engine turned over. Intermittent whiffs of burning coal joined the harbor bouquet soon after midnight, slipping through slightly open windows. After a breakfasted crew went to sea and anchor stations, the pilot and tug arrived just after sunrise to tow *Calypso* down the Elizabeth River into Hampton Roads.

The weather was fair, temperatures mild, and skies clear so, with an offsetting wind and her bow pointed north, *Calypso* came easily off the shipyard quay wall when mooring lines were taken in. Once away, the tug towed her placidly down the Elizabeth River's southern branch. Sailors on the forecastle watched Portsmouth's built-up waterfront of red-brick buildings, piers, and quays pass down the port side; first the small Thomas Shipyard then Union Depot and a ferry landing. The Norfolk & Southern Depot to starboard marked the Eastern Branch junction with the main river and *Calypso* began coming port as it passed abeam. The tug, having continued further into the channel, helped pull her bow around to a northwest course that left the Norfolk waterfront to starboard and cleared a peninsula to port that jutted into the main channel and contained the naval hospital. The tug and tow shifted starboard as Norfolk passed until a clear course presented, then port to pass between Craney Island and Lambert Point; where *Calypso* entered Hampton Roads.

Off Craney Island the tug broke its tow then heeled in a hard turn under billowing black smoke to approach *Calypso*'s starboard side. Starke disliked them coming against the hull's wood planking but it was necessary to drop the harbor pilot. This master was skilled and the hulls barely brushed before his passenger was aboard and the tug tooting a steam whistle while circling starboard. Osbourne slowly walked up their speed during the run north, allowing the black gang to build steam pressure as they monitored piping, valves, and machinery. He enjoyed conning since Starke was comfortable with ship and plant. Many commanders were not; having acquired little experience rising slowly through a stagnated promotion system. Those lacking shiphandling expertise in restricted waters usually excluded all but a few subordinates so junior officers did not learn and the cycle perpetuated. Starke rotated line officers and naval cadets through different evolutions, then their cadet engineers. He and Watson also tailored their assistance and evaluation, with those found wanting or having a bad day dealt with privately. No matter who was conning, the captain and executive officer appeared at ease, in control, and sensitive to situations where someone strayed beyond their depth. Starke might edge up beside the fellow to ask if they were comfortable while Watson invariably suggested some action might be worth considering.

Calypso's chief engineer paid close attention to course, traffic, and performance as the bark steamed north with her bowsprit pointed at Hampton as she neared the Fort Wool turn bearing. The tall, black bark advanced with gray-black smoke and steam rolling from her stack as the graceful cutwater below a naked bowsprit gently cleaved calm water, leaving a white wake that quickly turned dark blue before ending as a series of smooth, v-shaped rollers. A light, cool breeze flowed lengthwise over the main deck, passing gun mounts, masts, superstructure, and boats to stream the ship's commissioning pennant and national ensign astern.

Several other ships underway in Hampton Roads were closely watched by pilothouse, flying bridge, and masthead lookouts. The ferry crossing from Norfolk to Old Point Comfort passed astern, a black barkentine departed the Newport News coal docks surrounded by tugs, and small harbor tug towed its lumber barge towards the shipyard waterfront. In addition, small fishing schooners and several diminutive pleasure craft were scattered across the calm blue surface.

Osbourne brought *Calypso* to starboard once certain she would clear Fort Wool then steadied on a course to pass safely between the fort's rip-rap and Old Point Comfort. Starke said little as they gauged the James River current, which could easily set them down on large boulders girding the fort's foundation. As these passed, Starke briefly trained his binoculars on the Hygeia Hotel's pier where he walked with Katherine after dancing and resisted an overwhelming urge to embrace her. Once clear of the two forts separating Hampton Roads from Chesapeake Bay, the bark headed northeast to set up the turn that would take them between Capes Henry and Charles into the Atlantic. After the jibboom swung onto it, Starke confirmed they were on Dunbar's plotted track that had them turning east well before the Middle Ground to pass nearer Cape Henry.

Calypso's docile advance, resembling the ride of a well-sprung carriage, ended as her stem cut into the first Atlantic swell and elegant bow dipped before gracefully lifting to ride over it; then repeated the movement with little or no heel. *Calypso* and her crew begin adjusting as wind picked up and shoreline scents succumbed to the ocean's clean, brisk salt air. Capes Henry and Charles fell astern while Virginia's coast contracted to little more than a thickening at the horizon. The black bark with straw-yellow masts was at sea, steering for the southern drill ground, about twenty miles east of Cape Charles, where there would be little commercial traffic to distract from drills or restrict live firing while her crew reacquainted themselves with the ship and expunged bad habits endemic to yard periods.

Calypso entered the drill ground then steamed east and west using both main boilers, changing speed, and conducting man-overboard drills to exercise officers, black gang, and plant. The last were done under sail, steam, and both since each configuration had its own peculiarities. *Calypso's* capability to recover an overboard was limited under canvas alone so a Jacobs ladder and short grab line were rigged over the stern when sailing. It was less effective than many ships due to her overhanging counter but still possible for someone to catch hold and make it to safety; and white-canvas covered life rings mounted in outboard hull racks along either side could be tripped. Recovery was only fair in good weather when the victim was seen going over. The ship would let fly sheets or back sails then lower a ready lifeboat while coasting to a stop. Even if the victim was fortunate, able to swim to a lifebuoy, and spotted, there were sharks that trailed ships for garbage. Rescue became pure luck during heavy weather or with untrained crews; and the risk of losing other sailors while working sails or in the boats increased.

The prescribed approach under steam was to back down until the ship lost way, then lower a boat for the recovery. Weather, discipline, experience, and good fortune still predominated although steamships could usually come about and retrace or parallel the original course. Starke also trained his crew to use the ship because it improved their feel for *Calypso's* response to helm, engine, and natural elements. Conning officers were allowed to think, guess, or muddle through then Watson would gather them together and examine results. A consensus developed that coming alongside a clearly visible dummy was uncertain, since hulls and humans felt sea and wind differently, so the best approach was to steer slowly at the unfortunate, without trying to place *Calypso* alongside, and then make the recovery with lines thrown from the main deck, forward of the beam, or the ready lifeboat.

After a day's work and drill the exhausted crew took their assigned "dream sack" from bins, where these tightly rolled bundles were stowed, then swung it from assigned overhead hooks marked by stenciled numbers listed in the watch, quarter, and station bill. Once filled with mattress, pillow, and blanket, the pliable, agile, and elusive canvas made for a comfortable bed. Most occupants slept well throughout the night or until their next watch; once the surrounding smells, snoring, noise, and other distractions became reassuringly familiar. The method of climbing in depended on experience, location, and other sailors' advice. The majority grasped overhead beams to lift themselves up and in, but a few chose more acrobatic mounts. Green landsmen often provided evening and morning diversions because vacating was equally challenging, but *Calypso* had been unusually fortunate avoiding losses so there were few unskilled replacements.

Starke waited in his day cabin for Watson and Dunbar to bring the night order book for signature. The next morning would be sail practice or gunnery drill, depending on weather; then rope-yarn in the afternoon since it was Saturday. After signing the night order book and reviewing the executive officer's day order book Watson and Dunbar left for the pilothouse and Starke slid easily into bed under an open window where the calm weather and light traffic made for an unusually pleasant night's sleep.

The ship beyond his cabin was dark except for small, red interior lamps and topside running lights; red to port, green to starboard, with white at the masthead. The running lights were lit precisely at sunset then checked every watch with "all lights bright lights" reported to the officer of the deck and logged. As *Calypso* steamed slowly east through the night and midwatch reliefs called, leading seaman Doran Kearney was wakened by the shake of a starboard watch landsman, slid from his hammock, and felt bare feet touch a slightly pitching, hardly rolling, deck. He tugged trousers into place, buttoned up, pulled on the blue blouse, and squared a well-weathered work cap on his forehead. Like many, he went barefoot at sea to lessen shoe upkeep and add longevity, especially during morning watches when the decks were scrubbed with salt water.

He was under the well-liked Ensign Carl Martyn and Naval Cadet Terrence Timme in the port watch. Although regulations and custom segregated officer and enlisted worlds, the extent was influenced by ship size, wardroom, and specialty; with engineering officers having more republican tendencies than line. Executive officers molded culture and carried out the routine their commander set since captains resembled hermit priests due to regulations, tradition, and, too often, inclination. They also ate alone and were looked after by their own cabin steward; on *Calypso* this was Yamashita, a Japanese sailor whose taciturn nature equaled his charge. Kearney was admittedly biased in Starke's favor but thought their captain was gaining the crew's loyalty despite his introversion and strict observance of custom; while Watson provided an effective bridge. In any case, *Calypso* was a home.

After visiting the head, with acrid-salty atmosphere from seawater flushing its steel trough's contents overboard through scuppers, Kearney worked past a dozen or more sausage-shaped gray bundles swaying gently from overhead hooks. He moved deliberate and careful through the moist, dark below-deck, ensuring every movement retained balance and avoided white light that would destroy night vision. Kearney favored these watches because there were few people about with the crew asleep and the ship felt isolated from the human universe. Nights with uninterrupted hours of dark sea and stars were best; and *Calypso* was away from coastal shipping lanes tonight so passing ships were likely to be no more than intermittent light looms. With few distractions beyond the throbbing engine, smell of burning coal, and water sliding along the wood hull, night was ripe for conversation on every imaginable topic, or solitary contemplation.

Kearney stepped onto the main deck and greeted a shimmering black sea with small white-crested waves and somewhat darker heavens sprinkled with bright stars. He climbed to the flying bridge over the pilothouse, where forward lookouts were stationed at night if not in the ship's eyes near her anchors. He began scanning the horizon and picked out a solitary light loom from some well-lit ship far astern, perhaps a passenger liner moving up the Atlantic Coast. Nearby, Landsman Mallory Hawk remained in the port watch because Watson practiced consistency and avoided shuffling sections in Norfolk. Kearney watched over the young man and discovered he fled an Indiana farm's monotony; unlike his own sudden departure from New York City around the same age after battering a tough from one of the street gangs.

Hawk showed promise and might be one of the few landsmen who became continuous service men by reenlisting. Most sailors and boy apprentices left when or before their obligation expired due to the work, treatment ashore, and, unlike soldiers, discovering a long career brought no pension. Kearney would have done the same but the Navy provided steady pay, helped curtail a compulsion for hard liquor, and allowed him some savings. Results varied between ships with those more indulgent seeing him waste what money he kept back on a single bender while dryer commands with temperance officers like Paymaster Wiggs kept him sober and respected. Consequently, he remained on board until it became unbearable because every trip ashore was a risk. This was partly because he was unable to slip ashore alone, uniforms were required off-ship, and most establishments did not serve sailors. This concentrated them in small areas and specific establishments where the custom was to exchange drinks until all funds vanished. Even when he returned without trouble and his inebriation overlooked or undetected, several days were always spent sick, disgusted, and broke. When fate was less kind, he had been disrated and came within an eyelash of dismissal several times; and recently only just avoided a relapse in Newport News and Norfolk. The sailor was adamant this would not occur on *Calypso* because she was a home and Starke her captain.

Kearney scanned the horizon then looked aloft to thousands of bright stars sparkling unevenly over the Atlantic sky beyond a waning moon. The bow effortlessly rose up then over each wave creating a firm but gentle motion. Several in his watch were still adjusting and relieved at the sea's kindness. Most did not experience the constant and complete debilitation visited on a landsman they left in Key West but everyone needed readjusting after several weeks in port. He suspected they best enjoy it since the sea air's smell, increasing closeness, light chill, and *Calypso's* changing motion as she slid through the darkness meant a storm in the offing and the next few days promised to be rough.

Dawn was still just a promise when Ensign Gideon Blair's section relieved Martyn's after four uneventful hours. Later, with twilight approaching, the clock's black hands jerked towards six when turn-to, sweepers, and hoisting ashes would be called. Sunrise arrived near seven, accompanied by calls to unrig hammocks and issue water rations. At the precise time calculated and called for in the night order book by Dunbar, running lights were extinguished, lookouts climbed weather shrouds to the foretop, and the reddish-yellow orb emerged from an eastern horizon to transform a light gray morning sky into hues of red-streaked pink clouds.

Breakfast, officers' call, sick call, and other activities continued until nine-thirty quarters when, standing in ranks by division, the crew learned their morning would be spent at 4-inch gun practice while the black gang repacked a donkey boiler's leaking stop valve. Confirmation their afternoon would be rope-yarn, except for the obligatory fire drill, was received more enthusiastically, especially by those regaining sea legs. Later, as they steadied on a westerly course, *Calypso*'s port watch returned to station and two sailors went aft with the taffrail-type patent log. Its predecessor was exchanged in Norfolk after proving so inaccurate Dunbar stopped deploying it and resorted to a traditional chip log. Once they finished, the readings were compared to screw revolutions provided by engineering and used to update dead reckoning calculations.

The 4-inch gun crews went to numbered positions around their long-barreled, black and brass mounts on schedule; with every item required to load and fire precisely arranged on the deck beside them. The crews began by gaining rhythm with dummy rounds then competing for time with Ensign Blair intermittently declaring a misfire or other casualty. Gun captain Theodore Grier's forward mount prevailed over Beauregard Kirby's aft crew on timing but no one doubted which team shot just a hair better. Watson stepped from reviewing the navigator's proposed course in the pilothouse to watch this; finding it difficult to accept less than six months ago those guns shattered the filibuster *Rafael Riego*.

Paymaster Wiggs' sermon the next day came from Isaiah and spoke of the Lord giving power to the weak, and the weary receiving strength from Him. The Baptist deacon was articulate, sincere, and tolerant within excusable limits, which was critical with *Calypso*'s various faiths, agnostics, and unbelievers attending Sunday sermons. Starke disliked dogma and lacked faith but embraced sound moral principles and logic so Wiggs was a godsend. This sermon concentrating on youth stumbling was doubtless inspired by their Saturday fire drill, and more forgiving than the executive officer's response. Starke saw overconfidence as the fiasco's root cause but communications were poor, equipment missing, and some did not reach their revised watch, quarter, and station bill assignments. Watson was beside himself, even after Starke reminded him it was valuable to surface problems during drill and the crew's collective embarrassment could prove useful to build from. Wiggs then led a cappella hymns, services ended, and the regulars drifted off to hear Coxswain Clement Melvin's mandolin at the fantail. While there was still light, Conrad snapped a photo with the new camera then left his subjects singing enthusiastically.

Watson knocked before entering the captain's cabin for a supper of boiled cabbage, potatoes, corned beef, and warm cider. The ship was growing lively so Yamashita rigged the spider, a light framework that corralled items on the table. After the meal, he cleared off, retreated to the pantry, and left them alone. Starke retrieved a pipe then, looking over white porcelain tableware displaying embossed light-blue anchors and silver coffee server with protruding black pouring handle, considered his executive officer. It did not seem a year had passed since Captain Albert offered him *Calypso* at the same time he was considering resignation or another leave of absence. A lot had happened since, and much of their success due to Watson, an officer he nearly rejected because of malicious correspondence from his previous commander. Starke yielded to Albert, mostly because Watson was otherwise the best candidate, but he proved an excellent shiphandler and administrator who was equally capable of dealing with the crew or sensitive seniors. Unaware of his captain's thoughts, Watson watched Starke prepare his pipe, thinking him enigmatic at the best of times, before inquiring, "What next Captain? Dunbar's worked up the track for Charleston."

"I'm afraid he'll have to do another for Bermuda since the Junta probably heard we were going to Charleston and a revenue cutter's already off that port."

Starke offered what passed for a smile, continuing, "A coded message came from Albert before we left Norfolk. The *Bermuda*, with British registry and American owners, might use Hamilton or St George, and European filibusters could be stopping there during their crossing; but none will fly American colors so we've no authority. Instead, we'll enter port, remain long enough for the Junta to hear we're there, and then head south."

"For where; Captain?"

Starke, having finished loading his pipe, passed a match over its bowl while sucking the yellow flame down through its tobacco, replied, "The Caribbean. Albert wants to take advantage of the rumors we hunt filibusters. Britain fortified Bermuda, built a dockyard, and rotate their North America and West Indies Station between there and Halifax because it covers our coast and the Caribbean. A submarine cable was laid between there and Halifax six years ago so our arrival and departure should reach the Junta immediately, but they won't know where we'll surface afterwards. It could be Europe, along our Atlantic Coast, the Caribbean, or even Gulf of Mexico if we rounded Jamaica then passed through the Yucatan Channel unseen. Until then, every Junta expedition must look out for us."

"So Albert's gambling ignorance of our location complicates Junta planning and uses their intelligence organization against them."

"Exactly; and with our ships and cutters patrolling the Straits of Florida and Gulf Coast some expeditions might be delayed or caught from miscalculation."

"Captain Albert seems a good sort, and helped me, but is certainly more devious than he appears."

Starke emitted what Watson knew sufficed for a grin, "Something to consider if things go well between you and Olivia."

The quip was Watson's opening for a more personal topic; Starke's views on his officers marrying. He visited the Alberts during his Washington leave and a brief interlude alone with the older daughter, Olivia, changed everything. While she appeared less vivacious than her younger sister Isabella, neither was reserved and he concluded the primary differences between Olivia and her more openly extraverted sister were the muted, dark reddish-brown hair, scant freckling, and absence of translucent skin. Closer scrutiny that first evening also revealed the elder daughter boasted a fuller figure and more grace; which could hardly be overlooked since her snugly laced corset was suggestively strained while the mother and sister wore loose-fitting tea dresses.

The elder daughter was more striking than he remembered from the Starke dinner party when she wore a red satin dress with scalloped black lace trim hemmed to ride just over the floor with the belt forcing a Swiss waist. As if trying to stimulate those memories, her hair was pulled back and rolled to a bun with a tuft left free above very brown eyes and the long, loose hair of a child abandoned and worn up for the remainder of her life; except for the bedroom. He noticed her father seemed cautiously amused and mother anticipatory when his eyes chanced to leave her. The understanding that took root through their correspondence bloomed while they walked the mall extending from Capitol to river. Olivia's inclinations also cast her as the modern woman extolled in press and magazines since she eagerly ventured beyond her home for long walks and donned bloomers to go wheeling with him. Three days convinced him she was the one he would pass through life with and she discarded plans to enter university.

Starke sensed Watson wished to broach something personal but allowed him space by nursing his pipe. Finally, the lieutenant leaned forward, shifting slightly with the ship's movement, "Olivia Albert and I have an understanding, Captain."

Starke tapped his pipe against the ashtray's side, releasing a small mass of smoldering, singed, and burnt tobacco, "She seems a fine woman and marriage would help your career. Take what leave you require when we're in port. Dunbar can cover if there's a short underway; it'll do him good."

Watson realized he had leaned forward and sat back in the chair while their captain refilled his warm pipe. Starke was considering his assignation with Katherine and regretted not proposing immediately after bedding the widow; not out of responsibility or duty but because their unintended tryst vanquished his hesitancy. Taking another pull on the meerschaum, he acknowledged the failure to act came from habitually avoiding or resisting what Watson and Albert's eldest daughter embraced. That solitary night with the widow Ledford seemed more bursting passion than any calculated affair but sparked a desire to be with her that continued to grow despite her obvious distaste for the States and clear religious differences.

Monday gunnery drills took Starke's full attention, beginning with the 4-inch mount sub-caliber practice then followed by shooting at improvised targets. Landsman Hawk was equally interested as he studied the forward 4-inch mount, with cloth-plugged ears held fast by a worn kerchief improvisation. It seemed a long time from the muzzle's yellow-white blast until a thirty-pound projectile struck the surface over a half-mile off to cause a single vertical water column; or skip across the surface striking one, two, or three times. It was little different from throwing stones at wood chips floating on the mill pond.

Dunbar and Owen were on the flying bridge honing their expertise determining range with the Fiske stadimeter; an instrument designed by a fellow officer that was not routinely issued and had to be coerced from the Bureau of Equipment. These produced range readings using a target's known or estimated height, which was today a tall pole with red flag. Their Gatling guns were unlimbered after the Hotchkiss 3-pounders. Firing at about half the 1,000 to 1,300 yards used for the main battery, each run produced earsplitting staccatos of .45-70 rounds with the engaged side wreathed in fine, gray-white gunsmoke and a distinct odor permeating ship, clothing, and person.

After gunnery practice, every boat was inspected for condition and equipment then lowered and maneuvered near the ship to soak wood hulls with salt water and operate the steam pinnaces' machinery. Besides raising, lowering, towing and sail exercises, the boats raced under oars or a sliding gunter rig. According to rules Watson devised, the crews would move off then make for the ship and re-stow their boat alongside; with the first to pass inspection declared winner. Meanwhile, Paymaster Wiggs tried to sniff out surreptitious wagering, enlisted their master-at-arms, never found proof, and later heard Osbourne lost two dollars to Conrad when Melvin's pinnace developed a steam leak.

Calypso banked her main boilers for sail drills and the crew picked up Chief Weaver's enthusiasm as courses and topsails were bent, unbent, reefed, unreefed, and then shifted singly or simultaneously. Each officer, under Watson's critical eye, tacked and jibed the bark then backed sails to halt it. These maneuvers also allowed officers to feel *Calypso*'s different reaction to port and starboard turns under sail with a windmilling screw pulling to one side.

Navy ships were required to contribute to fleet landing parties so sailors were selected in Norfolk. *Calypso*'s rate required they supply a naval infantry company in two sections, one carriage-mounted Gatling gun, and stretcher-bearer party. Since they lacked line lieutenants, Ensign Blair was given company officer duties until a landing party was formed, then he would become Lieutenant Watson's second. Today's exercise was mustering in full gear which included haversack, knapsack, rubber blanket, canteen, and overcoat. Each sailor also wore leggings and carried a lanyard knife. Officers and chief petty officers' load was lighter but included a belted sword or cutlass. A landing force wore regulation white or blue uniforms, but Starke already decided to use their white cotton uniforms, dyed to tan using coffee, for any extended operation and accept flagship objections.

Calypso's sailors were armed with Remington-Lee .45-70 bolt action rifles designed for ammunition clips along with a tan, webbed cartridge belt supported by leather braces. The harness included four, five-round clip pockets, single loops for twenty-five rounds, and spike bayonet scabbard. Everyone carried a double-action .38 caliber model 1895 Colt revolver since it was standard issue and ammunition readily available from Army or Navy stores. Starke had no control over that, but for his own use brought a single-action Colt Army, flap holster, and dozen boxes of .45 caliber ammunition. The Navy revolver was more modern, loaded faster, and allowed users to carry more rounds but he had less confidence in small bullets after Montana and Alexandria. Any sidearm was useless at distance and carried for self-defense; so when his life could turn on a single round Starke wanted it large enough to stop rather than wound, even mortally. Besides, good infantry officers concentrated on tactics and ranges.

After pistols were discharged off the stern, *Calypso* went dead in the water about 100 yards from an improvised target for each member, sailor or engineer, to fire five rounds and gain familiarity with their clip-fed bolt-action rifles; although Kirby placed all .45-70 rounds in the thick wood target. Spike bayonets were then fixed and practiced with. After drills finished the guns, especially rifles since black powder badly fouled them, were thoroughly cleaned and oiled. Meanwhile, Conrad had stretcher bearers rehearsing procedures and inventorying equipment. Blair energetically exercised the ship's thirty-man company and meticulously inspected their equipment, but Starke was uneasy about sending him ashore without Watson since he could not forget having survived years before only because a white-haired captain chose to dig in on high Montana ground rather search out their aggressive commander.

Calypso spent a week drilling. Officers, chiefs, and men not assigned particular events trained in their specialties and completed maintenance. Along with ship exercises, Osbourne inserted improvised casualty drills, quartermasters practiced with navigation equipment, Wiggs inventoried storerooms, and the medical department walked through potential medical scenarios.

CHAPTER FOUR
BERMUDA BOUND

The drill ground offered few distractions since it was away from shipping routes and the North Atlantic Squadron lay in Charleston, excepting ships on independent assignment. *Calypso* did board a freighter on Wednesday that flew the Starke Shipping & Shipbuilding's blood-red swallowtail house flag with three interlocked black "S"s. They were closing the northbound ship as an impromptu exercise when Starke spotted the family's house flag through binoculars.

It was *Eveleth*, a steamer the firm recently obtained a controlling share of and sailed as a company ship. The 2,000 ton iron-hulled, single-screw steamer could bend gaff-rigged fore and aft sails to both masts, supplemented by jib and staysails; for steadying, reduced coal consumption, or providing a few knots should the engine fail. The English shipbuilder Charles Mitchell & Company launched her in 1881 to British shipbuilding laws then sold several times before becoming the firm's largest ship. As her port bow approached, Starke examined the black, straight-stemmed hull with stockless anchor flukes protruding from hawseholes, orange masts, and white superstructure. A monkey walk crossed from her forecastle and ended under the bridge spanning her beam. Two lifeboats in davits were outboard of a single stack with orange ventilators sprouting from the forecastle and over the midship superstructure. As she steamed north, cooling or flushing water jetted from a large scupper with its lips guiding the shimmering stream clear. She was riding too low to be in ballast, but not overly deep, so Starke guessed a light, bulky cargo.

Dunbar broke out the Navy Department's *International Code of Signals*. Although employed like the Navy signal book, its flags and pennants were understood by foreign warships and merchantmen. Quartermaster Third Class Jason Smithers raised a B, M, W, and R flag-hoist, *Calypso*'s designation, so any ship or shore station with an updated version could identify her. When *Eveleth* continued steaming without dipping the national ensign, Starke knew Stede Schumacher was master.

He sailed under his father and was chief mate on Starke's first ship, a three-masted schooner built for a coal trade then bought by the firm when larger ships with more masts made her less competitive. After an overhaul at their small West Point shipyard, she carried whatever was available between ports along the East Coast and throughout the Caribbean. Schumacher eventually commanded her before she was left to settle and rot in a Chesapeake marsh. He was given a small steamer and eventually became the firm's senior captain. Many masters were reluctant to exchange flag-hoists with any navy ship unless they wanted news or to confirm position, but Schumacher never saluted American warships, a courtesy extended by most merchant ships passing close aboard. He only explained once, years before, following an unusual night of serious drinking. After serving Jefferson Starke as bosun, Schumacher returned to find his home burned, Federal troops occupying the state, and father unable to pay Republican taxes because secessionist states were forbidden to honor war bonds. A wealthy Massachusetts man who paid the bounty to avoid fighting then profited from the war wanted a winter cottage and bought it for taxes owed. Many other homes, businesses, and properties went to similar types descending on the battered states. Schumacher hoped to avoid this with a merchant berth but found shipowners refused to sign ex-Confederate sailors, their officers were banned by law, and most American ships were lost or put under foreign flags during the war. The Starke firm took him in and, despite losing the home, was unswervingly loyal to them; but not the government and refused to salute its ships even after Reconstruction.

Starke turned to Dunbar, "Signal that ship to heave to. Let's speak with him."

Calypso's navigator acknowledged, paged through the book, selected flags, then advised, "QH, Captain? 'Stop or heave to, I have something to communicate'."

"Very well; make your signal, Mr. Dunbar."

Petty officer Smithers raised the distinctive code pennant with five vertical red and white strips above the Q and H flags. Starke's binoculars remained on *Eveleth* until certain the hoist was clearly ignored. He turned to the watch officer, "Mr. Martyn, go alongside to starboard at 500 yards and run parallel. I want to be able to turn away without risking our stern. Mr. Dunbar, have Chief Owen break out the stadimeter; it may be for gunnery, but range is range."

Calypso came right trailing a long smoke plume, heeled slightly, then eased alongside the northbound *Eveleth* as Owen called out ranges. When pacing the freighter at a little over 500 yards, *Eveleth* raised the code pennant over B, N, and K flags.

Dunbar confirmed the meaning before stating, "It reads, 'Unless your communication is very important, I must be excused,' Captain."

Starke lifted his worn pipe from the commander's shelf then slipped it in his mouth. It was pure Schumacher. Martyn waited patiently beside his captain, having no desire to interrupt when there was an unlit pipe in his teeth. Dunbar warned Smithers to stand by as Owen reported they were just beyond 500 yards. Starke extracted the worn pipestem, "Mr. Martyn, please request Mr. Watson come to the bridge and assemble the boarding crew. Use the ready lifeboat. Mr. Blair is boarding officer and I'll accompany. Mr. Dunbar, please signal that gentleman to heave to and add my last name."

Dunbar wrote some lines on a scrap of paper, "Recommend BNJ. That's 'Heave to, I will send boat,' then PSD, CFMR and CFJL. It reads, 'I am Stark' without an e."

Flags rose smartly up the halyards as two lines of sailors pulled the ready lifeboat's falls, lifting the keel from its chocks. Although monitoring their boat crew and boarding party, Martyn noticed his commander's sardonic grin and heard, "Excellent Mr. Dunbar. Mr. Martyn, the freighter should slow directly, be ready to match him."

Starke seldom delayed merchant ships, but this was one of his family's, the crew had not boarded another ship at sea, it was some time since speaking with his old chief mate, and twisting Schumacher's tail appealed. *Eveleth* replied with the code pennant for affirmative then slowed once *Calypso*'s hoist closed up. Watson entered the pilothouse to find Starke, pipe in hand, studying the looming freighter; with both ships maintaining just enough way to hold course and run boats.

Starke walked aft to the bulwark's open gangway, leaving *Calypso* to Watson. The whaleboat floated easily alongside, riding to a sea painter wrapped around its inboard bow cleat. A short Jacob's ladder was rigged to pad eyes and stabilized with wood strips extending from either side to prevent crushed fingers. Some ships had steel rods protruding from their hull, but both required caution and agility to enter a lively boat with dignity. The sea painter was cast off once he settled on the thwart's varnished wood and they were off.

Calypso came to full stop once the boat was away, *Eveleth* reciprocated, and both fell off their respective headings. Rowing the 500-yard gap was enough for Stark to recall how boats' insignificance and vulnerability were revealed when contrasted with a ship's sudden immensity and nothing else in sight but sea and sky. The coxswain made his approach then landed at a cavernous rectangular cargo port in the towering black hull just above her waterline and red-orange anti-fouling paint below. Starke was first through with Ensign Blair and a petty officer close behind. His boarding party was kitted out in their best uniforms, web belts, and .38 Colt pistols filling leather flap-holsters. Schumacher grinned broadly as his powerful hand shot out, "Welcome, Captain. Wasn't sure you'd keep *Calypso* after sinking two of the Junta's best."

He appeared older and different. Once clean-shaven with longish hair, the leather bill of a dark blue soft cap now covered his close-cropped head, accompanied by a respectable mustache. Schumacher had adopted the newer grooming style while Starke, with short beard and moderate length hair, had not. His girth also increased, judging from the peacoat, but he remained formidable and the distinct walk was unchanged; a pugilist face seemingly thrust forward, dragging the body along and creating the impression of someone eager to engage whatever waited. A plain blue-flannel shirt was tucked into solid work trousers beneath the long coat; accompanied by thick leather braces, broad belt, and sheath knife he was never without. The heavy boots rising well over the ankles almost certainly concealed thick wool or cotton socks.

Turning to Blair, Schumacher issued an invitation that suggested acceptance mere formality, "With your captain's permission young fella, follow us to my cabin. My bosun'll care for your men."

Starke nodded and they trailed *Eveleth's* autocrat to her great cabin under the bridge. Before leaving, Blair confirmed the freighter's bosun was boarding the whaleboat's crew since it tempted fate to leave them in a small boat alongside, even if barely moving. Once in the cabin, Schumacher removed his cap to reveal short-clipped hair and baldness advancing towards the crown from both temples.

"Rum, Captain? Thought you'd join the company; not command a Yankee."

"No thanks, Captain. *Calypso's* dry, so I won't drink at sea."

"Same for the young'n, I suppose?"

Starke felt the ship wallow less as *Eveleth* returned to bare steerageway then replied with a slight smile, "Yes, I'm sure he wants to set an example."

Blair looked at Starke. He was willing not to since the rum would be welcome and it certainly fit the moment. Besides, the thick web belt with heavy and ungainly revolver made sitting uncomfortable; and the leather holster's boot oil was staining his white uniform. The master glanced at this fidgeting, "Your ensign needs a shoulder holster to lug that hardware. Now, to what do I owe the honor? Your uncle won't carry Junta goods, although I would if he asked and the price right."

Schumacher's essentials were unchanged. He would join Captain Buff running guns to Cuba except run for loyalty to the firm and *Eveleth*. That benefited Spain and deprived the Junta since he was as formidable as Captain Buff but craftier and an accomplished deepwater sailor.

Turning to Blair, the master laughed, "Your captain ever mention saving my ass in Veracruz? Two boys mistook me for a crimp that shanghaied 'em. Hit me from behind. I was down and about to get the boot when Mr. Starke, about your age then, brained the first with a bottle, pulled a Colt on the second, and explained they made an understandable mistake but the next would be fatal. Bastards even bought a round."

Starke quickly changed topics, "*Calypso* needed boarding experience, I've not seen *Eveleth* up close, and wanted to speak with you anyway."

"Well, speak away, Captain."

"Where're you coming from?"

"San Juan. Which reminds; a small Don gunboat hailed us going in. Came alongside and confirmed the house flag was Starke shipping then couldn't do enough; even helped with customs."

"Teniente Emiliano Mendoza. *Rafael Riego* shot up his gunboat last fall."

"Thought it was something like that. You've a friend there; and those folks don't forget. Anyway, we're New York bound with sugar, tobacco goods, and whatever else was available. It's to your uncle after that unless something turns up while offloading."

"Did you hear anything in Puerto Rico?"

"Nothing you probably don't know. They expect autonomy this year. There's another gunboat in port, *General Concha*, but most have been sent to Cuba; and there's a lot of revenge talk after insurgents got *Relampago* in the Cauto River with some sort of torpedo, shot six survivors swimming to safety, and wounded others. There's also talk our consul-general in Havana might go if the new administration wants their man, although most think Lee's doing well. Williams did a good job before him but was played out."

Starke did not want to hold Schumacher longer than necessary so discussion wrapped up a few minutes later. *Eveleth* was barely moving and the whaleboat manned when they reached the cargo port. While rowing for *Calypso* with the seas again lifting then lowering the light craft, Starke turned at the sound of a long blast from the freighter's steam whistle to see frothing white water under the counter signal her return to a course and speed that would soon raise New York. Blair quietly asked if Schumacher's story was true during the crossing and Starke responded it was embellished and preferred it went no further; but knew that was hopeless with the boat crew straining to pick up whatever their officers said.

On March 1, 1897, Starke put *Calypso* on an east-southeast course for the British naval base near Hamilton, Bermuda; 600 miles distant with difficult approaches. He also agreed to Dunbar and Owen's request to plot a great circle route for the archipelago rather than more convenient rhumb line. The earth's curvature on flat maps made a rhumb line course, which plotted as a straight line, longer than the shorter great circle route requiring a series of small course adjustments. Great circle navigation was seldom employed under sail or for short distances, but necessary for long voyages due to coal and cost. Starke agreed to it for honing their quartermasters' skills but ensured it was understood they might spend time under canvas where wind and current meant adjustments.

Blockade runners packed Bermuda during the war but Starke knew filibusters were unlikely now and he could do nothing if one was there. Arriving as a ship commander also meant salutes, courtesy calls, and liberty issues along with the challenge of anchoring off a shipyard encircled by wreck-littered reefs. The archipelago, once heavily forested, was a rough circle of reefs and islands formed by the peak of an extinct underwater volcano. What land rose above water resembled a fishhook with the Royal Navy shipyard at the barb's tip but it could not be approached directly because ten or twelve miles of reefs and shoal water lay to the north; elsewhere it was deep water almost to shore. The narrow channel serving several anchorages just above the hook's eye must be followed precisely and straying from it or next leg to the yard meant piling the ship on sand, rock, or coral. The almanac suggested they'd have favorable weather with the islands just leaving their coolest months, temperatures in the sixties, showers most days, and rising humidity soon after sunrise. Dunbar calculated two and a half days travel making ten knots good, possibly longer under canvas, so they would arrive during the inauguration of McKinley on March 4, 1897. Course and speed would also require adjusting for a morning or early afternoon arrival since anything later meant standing off until it was light enough to enter the treacherous approach then transit a long internal channel.

Calypso steamed west through the night on one boiler until early morning when Starke, Watson, Dunbar, and others gathered on the flying bridge for morning sights. Once these were taken, reduced, and compared; their position was established, the set north due to the Gulf Stream calculated, and speed estimated to be slightly better than eleven knots for ten over ground. *Calypso* then turned east-southeast for Bermuda and kept to the great circle route for next day while seas built, barometer fell, and normal underway routine of cleaning, eating, drills, and maintenance continued; except Starke delayed shifting to sails.

Stokers below decks fed the boiler with coal supplied by passers after trimmers wrestled it from hot, dark bunkers. Near its searing face, water tenders stood by a polished brass panel filled with temperature and pressure gauges; gingerly working valves to balance heat, steam, and feedwater. Men in the engine room just aft also endured fatiguing humidity and temperatures well beyond 100 degrees as they monitored two small brass gauge panels with a large bell guide-plate stating, "1 BELL, AHEAD SLOW; 2 BELLS, STOP; 3 BELLS, BACK; 4 BELLS, AHEAD FAST" in black letters on white-painted steel. A smaller black sign warned repeating any signal emphasized that action's meaning since *Calypso*'s engine, unlike her rudder, had no direct pilothouse connection besides operators communicating through an engine order telegraph, or EOT; which signaled and confirmed desired shaft direction and revolutions. Steam valves that controlled the engine were scattered about the enervating space and operated by men who considered their lot relatively pleasant compared to the boiler room. Very limited relief came from outside air scooped up by broad-mouthed ventilators as the ship moved forward then forced it below deck through a tube which also slightly pressurized engineering.

Berth-deck cooks prepared their mess' food for heating then brought it to the galley where other cooks used a combination stove and oven. While this went on, individual messes lowered tables from the overhead and broke out personal mess gear; mostly white enamelware embossed with "U.S.N." and trimmed in dark blue. Besides ground coffee dumped in boiling water, each mess had the standard ration plus whatever their berth-deck cook bought. This meant variety and quality rested on individual preference and cook. Paymaster Wiggs constantly pressed Starke to establish a single enlisted mess that combined funds paid directly to sailors but he resisted because the crew liked having control, sailors resented change, and *Calypso* was not configured for it.

Starke enjoyed a steamed fish Yamashita caught during the slow overnight run before turning for Bermuda. Today's was a northern species, firm with a strong taste, served alongside rice and canned vegetables. After coffee, the afternoon was spent wading through correspondence and reports Yeoman First Class Samuel Pond piled in sorting baskets. He possessed a stork-like appearance, being thin and balding with a large nose, and clearly changed his name several times since birth; although to the Navy he was an American with naturalization papers. Pond was also habitually reticent, a useful trait for captain's writer or yeoman, and spoke precise but heavy English due to his first language being a Polish dialect, achieving fluency in French, and capable of nearly conversational German. Later, while waiting for the night order book, Starke finished a letter to Katherine for posting in Bermuda. Only one from her arrived after December so he surmised she had not received others he sent. A second letter to his aunt and uncle mentioned *Eveleth* and her master.

Swells increased throughout the day to become waves with white caps and some spindrift by early evening. Watson spent the afternoon ensuring spaces below deck were secured for heavy weather then enlisted Martyn and Weaver to inspect topside preparations. He left the pair forward with several sailors adding more stoppers to both anchors. The storm broke suddenly during the night when Blair had the pilothouse and delayed summoning Starke; but Watson's preparations ensured no harm was done beyond increasing concern about the ensign's reluctance to call his captain. *Calypso* was riding up one wave then plunging down its far side until most of the bow submerged under dark water. When she rose, or her wood hull struck a large or unruly wave, the tall bark would shudder as white water exploded over bulwarks, buried the main deck, then raced aft, spewing overboard through every opening. Wind came in bursts separated by sheets of rain as the pilothouse watch completed tasks with one hand grasping a solid fixture; and slid across the deck with flailing limbs if not anchored during a plunging roll. Raising jib and staysails might have dampened her movement but the storm's suddenness meant doing this now required sending people on deck when Starke wanted them inside the bark's skin.

Throughout Blair's watch, then Martyn's, Starke was in his sea cabin or the pilothouse. Heading and speed were constantly adjusted to ease their ride, avoid being caught broadside in a trough, or pooped from astern. Strong northwest winds gradually forced *Calypso* to northerly headings and reduce speed to avoid being driven too far off course. Their engine added to the wind and rain's tumultuous noise by racing madly each time her screw raised from the sea then subsided when it submerged and bit. A direct shaft was the culprit, and would be eliminated if heavily geared steam turbines became practical, although any screw arrangement was infinitely preferable to the paddle wheels heavy seas often damaged and pulled side-to-side in calm water. Steam was more than a convenience and losing it during a storm crippled ships without sails while forcing those with them to risk sending sailors aloft or lie-to on a sea anchor. Osbourne requested permission to place their second boiler on line earlier in the day for that reason, although it increased coal consumption, work, and temperature below deck. Roving watches also checked on Thaddeus throughout the night and included his status during turnover. The gray and white tomcat spent his first storm in a lifeless stupor. Since then, he grew anxious as one approached then went low in the ship to wait it out; and once ensconced required no attention except to ensure an urge to escape did not spark an attempt to slip past secured doors and port-lights to the weather deck.

The wind veered northwest by morning, becoming strong and steady. *Calypso* took these unsettled seas well, steaming east-southeast until her position could be updated and accurate course plotted. Her topside sprouted peacoats since the slight chill made for a clear and brisk morning. Starke also needed to review the binnacle list since severe storms usually drove a sick bay customer upsurge. He already heard one stoker fell against a boiler face, pushed off with his hands, and was severely burned; while a landsman launched from his hammock landed on his head. There were probably other minor cases but *Calypso* was fortunate regarding disease and accidents. Storms invariably exposed poorly secured items so re-stowing was the day's work; including two of Paymaster Wiggs' spaces that needed restocking and some dry stores condemned. An overhead line storage rod came loose in one of Weaver's lockers and was being addressed, along with the bins and small cabinets it damaged. The pilothouse was more orderly because watches maintained it throughout the night, but Starke thought it best not to ask about the wardroom, officers' staterooms, and his own pantry.

The day offered near perfect sailing with a strong and steady wind from astern over calming seas so *Calypso* began raising sails after breakfast. Under Watson's direction, topsail, then main course gaskets, were untied, allowing damp sheets to fall free from the yards until the billowing canvas, flapping forward with flat cracks, was brought to heel by sheets. When each sail caught the wind, it could be felt in the deck as the ship heeled, steadied from the press of sails, then cut the waves as pitch moderated and roll vanished. Once square sails were drawing well, her jib, aft jib, staysails, and mizzen were raised; steering shifted aft, propeller shaft disconnected, and fires banked in the main boilers. Dunbar sent two men aft with the patent log while Watson and Weaver ensured sails were tuned. The fantail was soon reporting just over eight knots, very fast for feathering a large screw.

Weaver liked his commander when they met years ago and did still. He never strived for popularity and was not known for favors or platitudes, but respected despite being stricter than many. His fair and consistent demeanor was seldom unresponsive or defensive when new or rewarmed ideas were put forward. At least that's what Weaver wrote home the previous night when he, like others, finished their letters ahead of the storm. Correspondence went to his Newport News row house at every opportunity since anything could happen at sea and he was acutely aware of his good fortune marrying Patience, an exceptional, though never comely, woman endowed with intelligence, kindness, and the ability to gently encourage.

Intermittent spray veils plumed thinly into the air forward then drifted aft to settle on Grier and his forward gun crew trying to clean, preserve, and lubricate their 4-inch rifle; while consuming too much deck space for Weaver's liking. Besides the gunners and men working sails, others found reasons to come on deck after the rough night. Dylan Jones, the Welsh Pennsylvania miner, and Delmar Kemp, a Negro farmer from Virginia, stood like white and black pawns at the port side waist; looking to sea with elbows on the cap rail. On deck and below were British, French, and Germans mixed with lesser numbers of Swedes, Hispanics, Caribbean Islanders, and others. Resting, working or moving about along *Calypso*'s length, most congregated by mess, but today there were also small clusters of Irish, Negroes, and Japanese. Some were born in the States but many obtained naturalization papers, chose not to, or for some Asians and others were unable. The majority enlisted for a paid berth and planned to leave when their time was up, if not before, but sailed under American colors and were loyal to *Calypso*.

The main boilers remained off-line and sails drawing well when Dunbar's fixes and dead reckoning projected an easy run under steam would raise Bermuda early on the fourth so *Calypso* resumed steaming and ran true until morning. Once the islands appeared off their bow to the southeast, they still had to circumvent the extended maze of reefs and shallows north of the dockyard before entering a fleet anchorage between Ireland Island and Spanish Point. This included the Narrows, a constricted channel bounded by reefs and shallows, followed by a long inner channel to Grassy Bay anchorage off the dockyard. *Calypso* kept well west of the islands until able to come about and steam safely along their southern coasts. Buildings, barracks, and fortifications were clearly visible through binoculars from the port railing, but even without them, the bark's sailors studied a blurred panorama of fields, trees, buildings, and homes.

Calypso slowed to board a weathered, taciturn pilot with strong African features off St. David's Island then regained speed, manned the rails, and slowly steamed along the northeast coast past St. George City until clearing Fort Saint Catherine's batteries where she turned southwest to thread through the half-dozen sail and steam merchant ships in Murray's Anchorage. A gray-black smoke plume marked her cautious advance down the north coast through shimmering, translucent turquoise water; interspersed with light tan, dark green, and black patches marking a plethora of shoals, reefs, and small islands that rose just far enough above salt water to sustain vegetation and emphasize how shallow these areas were. As always, Starke extracted local information from the pilot while evaluating his comfort with the ship. This one was from the islands, knew his trade, and found *Calypso* less challenging than British cruisers.

As they approached the Royal Navy Dockyard on Ireland Island, the barb in Bermuda's fishhook shape, *Calypso* bled off way until barely advancing towards a huge breakwater protecting the waterfront. Starke spotted the massive floating dry-dock towed from Great Britain and, on a hill behind the waterfront, white stone dockyard buildings, large barracks, and protecting fortifications. As *Calypso* ghosted through Grassy Bay she was met by a steam pinnace with spotless canvas and varnished wood that glistened in the same sun reflecting from a brass stack. Its young officer in a spotless uniform boarded, was greeted by Watson, and taken to the flying bridge while Starke observed the Royal Navy pinnace with oversized White Ensign take station alongside. The pinnace's coxswain was signaled once introductions were complete and port instructions received; and instantly spurted ahead with practiced ease to mark an anchorage directly in line with a tall clock tower ashore and parallel to the massive breakwater. After Weaver dropped their black anchor through near crystal-clear water, causing its tackle to erupt with cacophony of rattling, hammering, and banging amidst clouds of red and black dust; *Calypso* backed down to set it as gun salutes were exchanged.

CHAPTER FIVE
INAUGURATION

William McKinley's inauguration occurred 800 miles north and west of the Bermuda dockyard, with Captain Sidney Albert standing in front of the Capitol's east face for the ceremony. He was briefly at the Building before crossing to the Executive Mansion with a small party making the Navy Department's last call on President Cleveland.

Washington sprouted uniforms, with most foreign officers and diplomats especially resplendent. The Americans, and particularly their Navy, contributed less to this bloom since most lacked equal plumage of medals, stars, sashes, and other accoutrements; but they were not without gold epaulettes and striping. There were almost no Congressional Medals visible and only a handful of enlisted sailors received the Medal of Honor since the war; although several approved awards from foreign nations and military societies could be spotted. Albert wore sword, cocked hat, and Brooks Brothers special full dress uniform that had been let out. No uniform looked as well after such attention but new regulations planned for midsummer argued against replacing it.

He accompanied Rear Admiral Brown's party with the flag aide, Lieutenant (junior grade) Alexander Sharp, because the Navy's senior admiral and Norfolk commandant asked Albert to represent the secretary's office. He could not decline this unsought function since it was a last opportunity to repay the admiral for several favors, provided an intimate view of the ceremony, allowed early exposure to incoming officials, and included inauguration ball invitations. Whether the last was a benefit remained to be seen since its preparations plunged his red-brick row house into pandemonium.

The ceremony came off reasonably well under clear skies with temperatures just north of forty degrees. McKinley passed by President Garfield's plaque in the Baltimore & Potomac station, avoided crowds, met with the inaugural committee, and spent his evening at the Ebbitt House; a six-story hotel with mansard roof and servants' quarters. He attended morning service at St. John's Episcopal Church after a quiet night shielded by his third floor suite's curtains and Venetian blinds then rode to the Executive Mansion to meet President Cleveland.

The president spent the day before, and late into the evening, signing legislation he judged complete, setting aside some that was not, and deferring several agency funding bills. After speaking with the president-elect, they left the Executive Mansion in black frock coats and silk top hats, with McKinley on the left, for a waiting black victoria pulled by four horses. Their carriage was escorted by the Ohio militia's plumed Black Horse Cavalry and the inauguration procession led by the same Colored police officer filling that role since President Grant's second ceremony. The tradition began when he arrested the president for speeding. Grant paid the fine, saw he was promoted, and had him lead the next inaugural procession.

The incoming vice president, Garret Hobart, took his oath in the Capitol's old Senate chamber alongside cabinet members turning over offices. The future Navy secretary, John D. Long was not there, however, and rumor had it Cleveland and Onley from State were at odds over Consul-General Lee's resignation telegram. Lee released it and Onley wanted him removed but Cleveland refused because the consul-general managed to favor Cuban independence and maintain good relations with Spanish officials.

Albert agreed with the president since losing Lee risked one of Senator Lodge's jingoes going to Havana. The strident ones sought foreign interventions, expansion, and Hawaiian annexation. Albert not only believed them dangerous but was apprehensive they might gather momentum over the next two months as the new administration and Navy Department filled vacant positions. Every turnover brought a deluge of nominees, appointments, or hires; with most having infinitely less experience than enthusiasm, and sometimes neither, which disrupted painstakingly developed and groomed relationships. His Revenue Cutter Service contacts would probably suffer least, but Clarence Newcomb at State could not survive, and the Justice collaborators might remain in limbo. Every customs collector would change since these were political, powerful, and lucrative positions. Transitions and the spoils system caused Albert to dislike civilians controlling the Navy; although these regular changes no longer reached down to shipyard trades. That practice had caused ships to be unfit for sea after long and costly yard periods with complaints of poor management, shoddy work, incompetence, corruption, or some combination treated as a political issue. After serving in the Building, at sea, and ashore, however, he adapted and saw mastering its politics as a skill to hone rather than become blindly partisan like the recently retired Admiral Meade.

The incoming secretary of the navy lacked naval experience but rumored to be a competent administrator who would rely on the staff. This fit Albert's inclinations but might also encourage bureau chiefs to behave like powerful, independent vassals and worsen an already precarious situation. Long was also against war with Spain and he hoped the secretary's legal background would favor law enforcement activities and support the project to disrupt Junta filibusters.

An afternoon parade to the Executive Mansion followed the inauguration ceremony, speeches, and congressional luncheon. President McKinley took the victoria's right side and Cleveland its left, with the Black Horse Cavalry replaced by regular army troopers. Although a horse slipped on the asphalt and landed haunch-first in its traces, the procession continued smoothly to a glass-enclosed viewing stand. Hired detectives walked alongside to thwart any anarchist assassination attempt, which many saw as insulting, but it failed to lessen the cheering; except when passing pockets of Bryan supporters and populists. The avenue was a sea of dark dresses, sack and frock coats, top hats, bowlers, caps, foreign costumes, and uniforms. The military was mostly army but *New York* contributed a blue-jacket formation with its goat mascot. Following by state, came militias, high school students, bands, and various organizations including the Grand Army of the Republic, a multiracial stalwart whose reconstruction focus had transformed to Northern veteran pension issues. Foreign nations were distinguished by national dress and the deposed Sandwich Island monarch, Queen Liliuokalani, came from The Cairo Hotel to observe with mixed emotions since Cleveland blocked her kingdom's annexation, even if he did not restore her throne. Some men were cranking boxes that produced moving pictures but most, including Cassandra Evans, captured the celebration with notebooks and drawing pads.

Inauguration balls commenced at the National Museum and Pension Building that evening then continued until early morning. The Albert tickets were for the Pension Building, a massive red-brick structure with a seven-story, fully roofed center courtyard surrounded by rows of arches on its lower levels leading to naturally lit and ventilated offices. Only three stories were visible that night because several light, fine awnings were spread to diffuse electric lighting. The walls beneath were trimmed by flowers and evergreen boughs; with a large center court fountain dressed by flowers, ferns, and floating water plants. Four large columns towards each end of the large rectangular courtyard were painted to resemble marble; and decorative even without the greenery. Musician stands against the court's center walls were across from its fountain and supper rooms established just off one end. An overhead banner consisted of stars on a blue field, and separate cloak rooms for men and women flanked the Fifth Street entrance.

The Albert family arrived just after seven in a hired cab because they did not own a carriage, renting was impossible, and the drivers knew best how to navigate foot, horse, and carriage traffic swirling about the building and approaches. Albert presented their tickets then entered with Abigail's hand resting lightly on his crooked arm. Her attire was a serviceable veteran of previous Washington balls. Olivia and Isabella trailed in new empire-style gowns that were a trifle more revealing and caused Albert to balk at the expense. Abigail seized the opening to warn her husband their daughters would develop rapidly and pass through several sizes over the next few years. He relented with a good-natured quip about marrying them off before the poorhouse that caused his wife to laugh then deliver a telling blow about the cost of weddings dwarfing gowns before leaving for the dressmaker with their excited daughters. Abigail took a quick glance over her shoulder. Olivia and Isabella were flashing between dumbstruck and overstimulated while fiddling with souvenir dance cards on their left wrists. The sisters spoke incessantly about the best strategy to populate it during the ride while their mother plotted to fill her own with one captain.

Evans approached them almost immediately. She arrived early to capture guests and their attire for the morning edition but later pulled Olivia and Isabella away, promising to find them young officers and gentlemen. The parents began working the congested court and spoke first with Admiral Walker, whose wife wore a dark, velvet gown and was well-versed in protocol. There was also the Spanish minister, Enrique Dupuy de Lôme, a career diplomat nearly five years in Washington. The balding man possessed a pleasant face, neatly trimmed beard, and wore an ornate court dress uniform with orders and medals. Albert was puzzled the minister recognized him and introduced his consort, a tall woman in white satin set off by diamond jewelry and fluent in five languages. After speaking about Parisian society, de Lôme mentioned *Calypso* aiding *Francisco de Montejo* and disrupting filibusters. Albert appreciated the compliment but realized it meant Spain's interest in his operations equaled the Junta's.

The Alberts passed between congressmen, senators, counts, countesses, barons, baronesses, governors, diplomats, generals, admirals, and a sprinkling of writers and reporters. The president's party arrived later to an inauguration march composed for the occasion. Albert heard there was some delay when the entourage grew larger than planned and additional carriages needed. The new president and first lady passed through the same entrance as the Alberts, greeting people as they entered. McKinley wore evening dress and his wife, Ida McKinley, an ivory silk gown with Venetian lace, high collar, long train, and gold-trimmed waist; and there were rumors it concealed blue slippers the First Lady crocheted from wool. She later fainted during a march, supposedly brought on by heat, press of people, and exhaustion, but her health was said to be poor and such episodes common because she often pushed herself to the limit. Abigail observed that trait in the determined jaw line set in a roundish face under center-parted hair. She was also well-educated, once worked in a bank, toured Europe, was widowed, and familiar with Executive Mansion customs from a previous administration; so it was not surprising she encouraged her husband to open more federal jobs to her sex. They were said to be a loving and devoted couple although Ida refused to attend church after their two daughters died young. When Abigail heard that she looked for Olivia and Isabella then reflexively gave her husband's arm a squeeze he failed to understand. New revelers were still entering at eleven when the Alberts slipped off to a supper room and buffet of oysters, chicken, sweetbreads, turtle, ham, turkey, and other dishes.

They met Immanuel and Constance Starke in the queue then shared a table where Olivia and Isabella found them. Under Evans' tutelage, the sisters merged with a large covey of young single women, including daughters of the incoming Secretary of the Army, Postmaster General, and General of the Army, then filled their cards for the serious dancing that would come after midnight when those with less stamina departed and the floor cleared. Albert and Abigail would have left with the Starkes but wanted to prolong their daughters' evening; which allowed Abigail to coax a husband, amenable from several stiff drinks, onto the dance floor.

Rich food, strong drinks, brilliant fireworks, and dancing left them near exhaustion by early morning when the daughters were collected and they left for home. Once through the Fifth Street entrance, Albert gave his number to a man who summoned their yellow Herdic cab and they were soon off for the city's west side, rolling past rows of darkened, red-brick buildings. The horse shied while passing one of its species left on the street after dying in harness, but their trip ended in front of the row house without further mishap. While the animal shifted nervously, impatient for stall, hay, and oats, Albert settled with the driver as his family climbed their home's low concrete stairs. He remained outside for a moment in the early morning twilight, watching the cab return to well-lit streets, tallying costs, and concluding the outlay was well worth a special evening for his daughters and Abigail's favor.

Captain Albert often began a day at sea after little or no sleep so he shrugged off the morning as any other while Abigail forced herself awake to see him off. The daughters' room was finally silent after a discussion, interspersed with giggling, that continued nearly until dawn; and Albert passed by wondering how much of the evening would find its way into their letters to *Calypso*.

CHAPTER SIX
ATLANTIC DERELICT

Albert stood in the Building, studying traffic passing above and below Lafayette Square. A dozen blocks east, the Pension Building decorations remained in place for public concerts. Admiral Ramsay was attending Navy performances and the secretary not expected. Albert considered spending the day at home but anticipated a cable from *Calypso*; which he welcomed because Abigail, Olivia, and Isabella would spend the day reliving the night and comparing it to *The Morning Times* description that was probably Evans' work. Olivia and Isabella were taken with the reporter and listened intently while she recounted her interview with Queen Liliuokalani about the foreign planters' coup d'état.

An older paper laying open on the desk reported the filibuster *Laurada* evaded a trailing cutter that blew two boiler tubes; and rumor had it she left Baltimore for Cuba on Friday after loading men, weapons, and military stores offshore. It was almost certain she did the same in late December since her voyage from Gibraltar to Norfolk took twenty-one days when fifteen was normal. Reclining, he gazed at the distant, off-white ceiling and its solitary light fixture, suspended some feet towards the wood floor. It was unlikely *Calypso* could intercept *Laurada* but the large ship usually mothered smaller tugs and boats that made the runs in; and the Junta would know that news of her departure reached Havana so they

67

might delay offloading. If so, there was an outside chance for *Calypso* to intercept by steaming from Bermuda to Jamaica's Port Antonio, then sweeping north up Old Bahama Channel to Florida.

Albert selected the meerschaum pipe, carefully packed its bowl, passed a blueish-yellow flame over the mouth, and leaned back in his chair. Within minutes, a clerk bringing a yellow cablegram envelope knocked on the door. He slit its seal with a mother-of-pearl penknife and read, "Arrived Bermuda 4 March. Await instructions." Starke was reporting in, as regulations required, so Building, Junta, and world would soon read about it in newspapers that routinely announced arrivals and departures.

Orders to ships were issued through the secretary and Herbert already turned over to Long, who caught the office off guard by arriving in the Building sooner than expected. *Calypso* required immediate orders or *Laurada* was home free; besides, Albert might not even retain his current role or position a day longer. Lines formed across his forehead as teeth pressed into the pipestem. With Ramsay attending the concert and secretary's office in turmoil there was no way to force new orders through fast enough; however Starke's existing set established Albert's coded cablegrams as advice. He decided *Laurada* was worth the risk and Friday might be his last day anyway so he drafted a coded response, "*Laurada* for Cuba last week. Port Antonio then sweep Old Bahama Channel from south?"

Abigail often remarked on Starke's buccaneer inclinations and Albert relied on them now since this placed himself and *Calypso*'s commander at risk. He allowed a half-hour to reconsider then summoned a clerk and the message went to Halifax, Nova Scotia for retransmission to Bermuda. When it reached *Calypso* late Saturday morning, Watson was quickly called to the captain's day cabin and given it to read before Starke asked, "Well, XO?"

Watson lowered the yellow form to the table, "His cables are usually precise, Captain; this one's not so I suspect that's by intent."

"I agree XO. If we act, it means approaching Cuba north of Haiti then following the coast towards Florida. There's also no indication how reliable the source is so this could be a Junta diversion. *Laurada*'s well-known so reports she's headed south might pull patrols from the coast and away from a real expedition. If *Laurada* is making a run and we left now, *Calypso*'s lost to the Junta until we make Port Antonio and might not be warned in time if we went up Old Bahama Channel immediately."

Watson paused; cap in hand, "That's the plan, Captain?"

"Have Osbourne put both boilers on line, recall our liberty party, then signal for a pilot; preferably the one who brought us in. Those ashore should be nearby, unless they've ignored the limits and are in Hamilton. We'll get underway when engineering's ready, liberty party's back, and pilot on board. Word'll be out we left in a hurry so have the coxswain let slip we're for Florida or Key West."

Calypso boarded a pilot, raised anchor, and retraced her path out with sailors losing out on liberty complaining slightly more bitterly than those missing a rope-yarn. She passed Murray's Anchorage and the Narrows, dropped her pilot, turned southwest, and drove the inviting green islands under a picturesque horizon. *Calypso* came to a more southerly course when confident no one could see; slicing through the Atlantic for Puerto Rico and the Leeward Islands.

The evening watch looked to the next afternoon's rope-yarn that would follow the first Sunday's muster, full-dress inspection, *Articles of War* reading, and church service that included a sermon warning of demon rum and fornication's evils to a congregation that had anticipated liberty, not a week at sea. Ensign Martyn and Naval Cadet Hamilton Caldwell's port watch relieved at midnight with *Calypso* steaming south by west. Both boilers would remain on line until early morning when the port one would come off; as stipulated in the night order book and engineer's orders. Martyn was almost relaxed as he scanned forward, making periodic sweeps of the entire horizon. He learned to search with his eyes for an anomaly before investigation with binoculars, although the urge to constantly stare through them remained. The black instrument swung from his neck as he observed there would be no separation between sea and sky if not for the half-moon passing between gray clouds.

Landsman Hawk peered forward into an undulating black ocean from the ship's eyes, a spot between upraised stocks of recently blackened anchors, then beneath the bowsprit where *Calypso*'s prow opened the water's skin to a gurgling stream of white froth fading rapidly as it slid along her coppered bottom and wood-sheathed hull. Remaining awake would be challenging as the bark gently raised then settled into passing water making only a little noise and that barely audible against the stack's low panting. The running rigging did fret somewhat and when a sharp slap from loose canvas disturbed the calm he looked up and prophesied the foremast captain would catch hell from Weaver that morning.

Hawk periodically gulped cool salt air and slid bare hands under the peacoat's armpits since he forgot to bring gloves. Seaman Kearney should be with him but the older sailor was off to the head for business requiring more than the small tube and funnel rigged by the port anchor. His own unsettled stomach caused him to suspect their cook added something unclean or spoiled to supper; which happened even with one as capable and sober as their own. There were also the lost opportunities left astern in Bermuda that first beckoned while surveying the green coast they ran down to reach the dockyard. Because of that, Hawk was musing aft when he glimpsed a light arc across what little horizon existed. It was faint, not in his sector, and might be a shooting star; besides calling out a sighting astern, especially if mistaken, could land him and the aft lookout in trouble. However, Martyn was more tolerant than Blair and the captain's orders were to wake him if in doubt. A second occurrence, with nothing heard aft, spurred him to cup his hands, "Pilothouse, forward lookout, blue rocket; port quarter."

Martyn's satisfaction of a quiet watch, impending relief by Blair, and waiting bunk vanished. Although the forward lookout was a landsman and the sighting outside his sector, he nodded to Caldwell who yelled, "Very well, Hawk. We'll look for it, but keep your eyes forward."

Hawk was pleased Caldwell knew his name, although the admonition chaffed his ego. But if that was the only kick, he would accept it since Martyn and Caldwell were not abusive. While chewing this over, a third occurrence brought, "Pilothouse, aft lookout; blue flare or rocket, port quarter."

A third, faint flare meant the aft watch would be explaining why he missed the first two and it would not go well if the quiet night and ship's gentle rocking lulled him to sleep. Kearney more or less trained all lookouts and invariably stressed that those forward watched over the ship but any man aft was the only hope for someone going over; then vividly described floating alone, waiting to drown or for a shark, after being left by your ship due to a slack watch. Few would show mercy for tonight.

Martyn studied the third blue or bluish-white flare arc, faint and low on the horizon, while Caldwell responded to the hail.

71

He was surprised Hawk noticed, but it was now to him so he sent for the captain and had Caldwell confirm a flare's meaning under the 1890 nautical rules that became effective in January. The cadet found a paragraph describing distress signals; with one option being, "Rockets or shells bursting in the air with a loud report, and throwing stars of any color or description, fired one at a time at short intervals." His recollection that color had no bearing was confirmed and these were clearly regular.

Entering the pilothouse, Starke went to his binoculars, retrieved them, and walked out the door with Martyn in tow. Scanning astern, he quietly inquired, "You reported rockets or flares off the port quarter?"

Still unwilling to fully commit, Martyn responded, "I believe so, Captain."

Starke observed the officer fingering his binoculars while watching the horizon, decided he was nervous and apprehensive, then interjected, "Mr. Martyn. Say what you think. If you're wrong, it happens, but . . . ;" interrupted by a flickering spark on the horizon, Starke quickly raised his binoculars to witness a light arc skyward then burst into an umbrella shape that descended in small sparkling tails. It was difficult to determine whether blue or white, but a few minutes or miles further on and the display would have been too far off to be noticed. Starke lowered his binoculars then, with tightening jaws showing through the thin beard, turned to the ensign, "You are correct, Mr. Martyn. Come about and make for the rockets. Walk her up to full speed and wake Mr. Dunbar."

Responding to Caldwell's rudder orders, the helmsman spun his large, brass helm using its thin spokes to start, then regain control by grasping the rim to slow its spin before their rudder reached the stops. Slowly, then with ship increasing speed and heeling, the indistinct horizon and a half moon moved past *Calypso*'s bowsprit while sucking, slushy, slapping sounds came from the forefoot. Another flare, now off the port bow, gave Caldwell a magnetic course to steer. *Calypso* steadied northeast with full speed ordered through the EOT. The increasing revolutions were soon noticeable and a cooling topside breeze created. Below decks, a few still up felt the change and experienced hands wakened. Starke ordered the searchlight on either side of the pilothouse powered up and cone-like beams were sent up into the sky, apprising the distressed ship they were coming. Martyn hesitantly asked, "Set general quarters, Captain?"

Taking his eyes from ahead, Starke replied, "No, Mr. Martyn. Let the crew sleep; they may go without later."

"Yes sir."

The pilothouse watch and Hawk saw the light loom appear just as Kearney returned. It continued brightening until becoming discrete lights against the vague outline of a ship's port beam through binoculars. A single line of portholes angling to the water told Starke it was a small passenger liner, or troopship. Although rockets ceased, indicating they sighted *Calypso*, frenetic steam whistle blasts suddenly shattered the ocean's gentler sounds. Since they were running full out Starke thought the ship must be foundering, and turned to order general quarters; then saw a shape just as Kearney yelled, "Ship close aboard off the starboard bow; Gawd dammit, ship off starboard bow!"

Martyn reacted instinctively, "I have the conn. Starboard your helm. Starboard your helm hard, dammit."

The appropriate response, especially from their most hesitant ensign, caused Starke to silently walk to him. Confusion from multiple orders made helmsmen hesitate and seconds would decide *Calypso*'s fate. The port turn began infuriatingly slow then the dark hulk began inching right of bowsprit, jibboom, and foremast; partially obscuring the well-lit liner beyond. Starke's hand squeezed his binocular's black body as pilothouse tension grew palpable. Ship, crew, and career hinged on the next few minutes, but he retained control, grateful for darkness hiding white knuckles. After deciding the ensign's initial response correct, Starke knew Martyn might later face something similar without his presence and began coaching. The ensign was shocked his captain did not take over but acting as if this was another exercise.

As the amorphous shape took a hull-like appearance, Starke spoke in a conversational tone, "Maintain speed and don't set general quarters. Let's not have everyone running about if we strike. Backing's no good. We're too close, rudder's over, and it'd only slow the turn."

"Yes sir; should I have held course and backed?"

It amazed Starke how time could slow as he parroted his uncle, "No second guesses, Mr. Martyn. Decision's made; play it out."

Swinging to port with her rudder hard over, timing the next maneuver became critical. As her bow opened the drifting hulk, the stern closed. Starke calculated the odds of hitting or missing about even, but kept silent, let the binoculars swing from his neck, then slid a battered pipe kept in the pilothouse between his teeth. Caldwell took over the searchlights; lighting the derelict hull with one beam while the second scanned ahead for anything else floating half-submerged. Starke made a note to add a favorable comment to the cadet's journal then removed his pipe and turned to Martyn. His orders were intentionally loud, to alert the helmsman, "When the bow clears, shift your rudder to kick the stern away from the wreck, steady, then steer for the liner."

Martyn acknowledged, despite a dry mouth and wishing the captain would take over, while Starke waited for the moment, prepared to prevent the ensign from succumbing to the temptation of an early turn that would send their bow back into the wreck. Others in the pilothouse were amazed Starke did not take the conn but instead looked calmly ahead, fingering an unlit pipe. Their captain retained command of his own fear, uncertainty, and apprehension as a searchlight beam illuminated the waterlogged carcass then played along its length, creating a surreal aura by turning pilothouse, main deck, and everything forward into a starkly bright macabre universe of blacks, whites, and grays.

The hulk was probably a lumber schooner out of Nova Scotia, or other northern port, bound for the Caribbean. These floating wrecks were common according to the Navy Hydrographer, Commander Sigsbee, who estimated hundreds at sea during a six-year period. Some settled to the bottom, ocean currents carried others hundreds of miles, and a number were trapped in the Sargasso Sea. The ocean would eventually claim most, storms destroy others, and a few drift ashore. Most were small ships, but this one was perhaps 150 feet long and 500 tons. Illuminated by searchlight he could tell she was once schooner-rigged, the deck structures were washed overboard leaving only splintered mast stumps, and they would pass close aboard or strike its stern.

Calypso's hull pivoted below the pilothouse so, as bowsprit and jibboom cleared the wreck and separation increased, her aft two-thirds winched towards the hulk. Martyn felt panic, wondering if the captain was waiting on him, then, as the pilothouse was about past the derelict's stern, heard, "I suggest you shift your rudder, Mr. Martyn"

The ensign turned instantly to the helmsman, "Port your helm; hard."

Several long seconds later, the bowsprit and jibboom slowed, ceased sliding to port, paused, and began inching starboard towards the passing hulk and open sea beyond. Heeling now to port and her stern movement reversed; those on deck watched the wreck's half-vanished, half-bleached, taffrail shoot down *Calypso*'s side so close the vanished rudder's rusting and bent pintles, flanked by two lumber ports, were visible without the searchlight. Once the stern would miss, Starke continued, "Hold her steady until clear, Mr. Martyn, then steer for the liner. Also, pipe stow hammocks then set general quarters when complete. You and the watch did well."

Caldwell resumed the conn as *Calypso* plowed forward more slowly; probing ahead with searchlights. Watson and Dunbar arrived as boatswains' pipes called the crew to stations, with a slightly more disheveled Dunbar showing greater anxiety than Watson and checking himself from pushing past the executive officer. Watson reached the ladder's top then walked to Starke, whose abused and unlit pipe was clenched between teeth. Saluting, he ventured, "Good morning Captain, below deck's a mess, and there's some bruising. I heard a steam whistle, everything canted, then we heeled twice. Woke up thinking we'd be swimming."

Starke extracted the mangled pipestem with a relieved grin, "There's a ship in distress ahead, XO, and derelict lumber schooner astern. We missed the wreck but I suspect the liner didn't and is flooding forward. Prepare to lower boats. You'll lead. Take Osbourne, Conrad, and a boarding party; rifles and bayonets. They make a better impression than revolvers if there's panic."

"Live rounds, Captain?"

"Yes, but don't load clips unless necessary."

Calypso approached the liner's port side, bow towards her midsection, then halted 100 yards off; with searchlights playing back and forth across the separation. Whaleboats went first, led by Watson and his party. The first was soon riding smartly at the open cargo port while the second stood off, waiting for the steam pinnaces. Climbing through the large port was awkward with the ship down by the head, but her chief mate and a deck officer waited patiently. After eyeing the armed boarders with forced casualness, suggesting apprehension and relief, the senior officer extended his hand, "Welcome abroad, lieutenant. Your artillery's not yet required, but we've over a 150 passengers who are a bit excited."

Watson learned RMS *Gamma* was a Royal Mail Ship chartered to the Halifax & West Indian Steamship Company. The firm ran between Halifax and Jamaica, with port calls at Bermuda and Grand Turk Island. She was bridging a gap created by selling their old steamer *Alpha*, then discovering the other steamer, *Beta*, required repairs. To fill it, this liner, resembling *Alpha*, was chartered and renamed *Gamma*. She was over twenty-five years old and received few upgrades during the last ten years. Her 220-foot iron hull was painted black with an outside strake in white and prow that curved up and out under a truncated bowsprit. The two masts no longer spread sails but supported navigation lights and booms serving the forward and aft holds. Her pine pilothouse, with curved bridge-wings, was incorporated into the boat deck and a single black stack protruded from her white deckhouse. She accommodated twenty-five first-class passengers in main-deck staterooms under an overhanging boat deck, and 150 third-class passengers in small cabins behind the row of portholes along the hull.

Gamma departed Halifax on the fifteenth of every month and struck this derelict without warning on her return leg. The collision crushed her lower stem, probably shifted machinery foundations, and caused flooding to the collision bulkhead. Water was leaking into spaces aft of it so her pumps could just hold the flooding; leaving *Gamma* unable to steam without aggravating her predicament. Knowing this could only worsen, her master gambled firing rockets with no one in sight.

Trailing her chief mate through first-class passengers milling about the weather decks, Watson saw *Calypso* standing off, bow on and looking spectral with her rigging and eye-like pilothouse. Both searchlights played brilliant beams across dark water to *Gamma*'s waterline, but not above. Standing on the bridge-wing facing *Calypso*, Watson found a solid man in blue master's uniform who reminded him of Captain Gibson Fischer with the Revenue Cutter Service. The leathered face hosted a nose crisscrossed by blue-veins that, like his manner, came from a lifetime plying the trade routes. Turning, he introduced himself as Captain Kent Salack, then, "Our deliverance is owed to what ship, lieutenant? American, I presume?"

"United States warship *Calypso*, Captain, and I believe we're returning the favor.

"Yes, our whistle, the only choice with no flares left or searchlights. Your ship heeled well over. Did you strike hard?"

"Captain Starke came hard away with the bow then shifted rudder at speed. That caused her heeling. I was told the hulk cleared by less than thirty yards, although our crew swears thirty feet."

"We struck just aft of the derelict's bow. Shouldered it off somewhat but still felt like going hard aground so it must be waterlogged with cargo."

His calm evaluation told of a master who experienced similar events over a long career. Watson immediately asked, "How can we assist? I've about thirty men coming, along with our chief engineer and surgeon."

The chief mate smiled, "Including a boarding party nicely kitted out; rifles and bayonets."

The master looked into Watson's eyes, "You've a prudent captain."

"Yes sir. His family runs the Starke shipping line and he's sailed merchant and navy."

"As have many in the Royal Navy. My lads are nearly spent sorting out passengers and shoring up since we struck so the assistance is welcome. Number One will get our chief engineer with yours. If your surgeon could set up shop, I rather expect there'll be trade. Bones says some guests lost their footing, several stokers were burned, and the chap forward accumulated some wood splinters."

Watson returned to the cargo door and boarding party with *Gamma*'s chief mate, waved all four boats alongside, left the pinnaces crewed for running between ships, and stationed armed sailors at the entrance to the cargo port space. Conrad went directly to sickbay with the ship's doctor while Osbourne waited for *Gamma*'s engineer. His opposite could have been Salack's brother, cousin, or fraternal twin, except for the clothing, light coating of dirt, and a Scottish or Geordie accent. The hand lifting his worn cap's black leather visor was creased and battered from years of hard labor that left dark stains in deep crevices. Watson observed he was skeptical about the much younger Osbourne at first but that changed quickly as each took the other's technical measure; a notable achievement since one spoke with a heavily accented brogue and the other a slower, almost laconic, Southern drawl.

Gamma's engineer stood to one side as Osbourne quietly explained to Watson, "Their engineer believes the damage's not yet mortal but she could sink. Stem's forced aft from orlop deck to forefoot and the keel could be warped."

Osbourne continued as *Gamma*'s engineer joined them, "Ship's designed to the 1854 British standard so there's watertight bulkheads on either end of the engine room, a small one around parts of the shaft, and the collision bulkhead forward that's keeping her afloat. The fore peak tank's open to the sea. The orlop deck above isn't watertight but the peak tank entrance hatch is in the overhead and was secured when they struck. It's holding but water's entering the next compartment aft. There's about a foot, but if it floods the forward cargo hold could fill and the next watertight bulkhead is at the engine room. Both holds are nearly empty on return trips so she'll go quickly if they fill and could capsize."

"What do you recommend?"

"Well, XO," he drawled contemplatively, "Their chief mate agrees she can't steam or be towed without opening up forward and the pumps could fail or flooding get worse. Best bet's to shore the orlop deck and hatch, do the same for her collision bulkhead, and pump out what we can. Depending on what's there; cement the leaks, brace her bow, and try for Bermuda. Jettisoning ground tackle would lighten her forward, but might cause damage coming out and she couldn't anchor. Their chief mate will speak with the master but it'll be a slow trip back and she can't be left alone."

Watson considered this momentarily before adding, "We might risk bringing the portable hand pump over. It's not much, but everything helps."

As was his habit, Watson then sprang from apparent lethargy to action, "Send a pinnace for it and our carpenters. We should also be able to bring shoring across, given time; anything else?"

"Not on my end. I'll take the engineers and get started."

"Take as many of the others as you need."

"Yes sir."

Osbourne and *Gamma*'s engineer walked off like old friends unraveling a riddle, as the chief mate turned to Watson, "Must speak with the Old Man about our passengers and would appreciate your thoughts."

Transferring passengers entailed as much risk as not. *Gamma* could founder with *Calypso* a few hundred yards off but it was not yet daylight and all 300 passengers would have to go or there would be panic, especially if first-class, or cabin, passengers went first. It would also mean lowering and crewing *Gamma*'s five large whaler-style boats, two less capable ones, and still require *Calypso*'s sailors and boats. That meant pulling men off damage control. Either way, should the forward hold flood, survivors could only come from the sea. It was the master's call but Watson expected he would continue efforts to save *Gamma* since a well-manned ship was standing by, the situation uncertain, and abandoned ships sometimes refused to sink.

Salack decided to delay until daylight and continue repairs. This released *Calypso*'s pinnaces to shuttle relief parties, lumber, and cement. The materials were added to the liner's wood shoring, tables, mattresses, and anything suitable to shore the collision bulkhead, then orlop deck above her forepeak tank. Meanwhile, Salack used rudder and screw to work the ship around and keep the liner's stern to the sea as her pumps and a portable from *Calypso* began to halt the rising water then slowly lower it. Chief Weaver was also permitted to fother the bow. Placing a rough canvas bandage over broken and twisted iron was uncertain and unorthodox, but they now had enough people and it might buy time or make other work easier.

Salack agreed to jettisoning anchors so Weaver and the bosun removed weak links fastening anchor chain bitter ends to the locker before easing out her starboard stocked anchor until fully suspended below the keel on a chain stopper. When released, it plummeted to the seabed trailing fathoms of chain, creating an ear-battering din, and whipping its bitter end over the forecastle in a cloud of red rust and dirt. The port followed, with an additional crash as its chain slapped an already mangled bow. Storm canvas from *Calypso* was then draped over the wound and secured with lines. With that poultice in place, pumps at work, and two crews using rags, oakum, wood, or whatever fit to plug wet compartments and voids, the receding water began revealing her wounds. Once plates above *Gamma*'s bent keel became visible, cement was worked into the irregular spaces like batter until *Gamma* and *Calypso*'s supplies were exhausted. The peak tank was completed by afternoon, uncertainty lessened, *Gamma*'s master felt repairs would hold, and boats began ferrying men and equipment back to *Calypso*; where the inevitable cleanup and inventory began. The two engineers retreated to a large cabin where they rechecked calculations and Osbourne accepted a glass of Scotch whiskey in the interest of international relations. After Watson returned to *Calypso*, it occurred that Starke allowed him free rein, although the fothering suggestion was probably not exclusively Weaver's.

Starke's first impulse had been to play a greater role but forced himself to trust the officer in charge, support him, and ensure he received credit. Meanwhile, their Sunday events, including church service, were rescheduled for Monday, with

Paymaster Wiggs' observation that accomplishing Lord's work on His day was a blessing; and personal relief he gained enough time for a new sermon. There was also the task of accounting for every canvas scrap, spar, cement sack, and other article taken from stores. They would not only need replacing, but every item lost, used, or damaged required a survey or explanation for audit clerks in safe, comfortable offices shielded by sleeve protectors and green eyeshades. Watson would review an initial list that evening and the process play out over the next few days. He expected some items claimed would have been used or lost before meeting *Gamma*; so the more egregious cases must be exposed then rejected. Watson decided Navy regulations forbidding cadets to be detailed as clerks did not apply to a specific task and drafted Caldwell to update the ship's boarding book, which he believed was not only part of a cadet's education but a window into the administration lurking in his future. Caldwell threw himself into it without complaint.

Salack began the limp to Bermuda by slowly easing her around while the cement was still setting. Osbourne, Timme, and a small *Calypso* party remained aboard while their ship went to hunt the derelict. Starke attempted it only to report he had since they could not leave *Gamma* for an exhaustive search and even if they found the old lumber schooner there was little to be done because of its buoyant cargo. The best option was beaching but *Calypso* was not set up for towing and needed to stand by *Gamma*. The 4-inch mounts would probably cause nothing more than dust, splinters, and depleted magazines. *Calypso* did not carry torpedoes, which were more expensive and probably have as little effect. A boarding party might place charges low, near the keel, but the wreck's cargo could shift or it might sink without warning so Starke would not ask that of anyone. Setting her alight was already tried if the charred hull was any indication and another go could leave the hulk a greater hazard by lowering the silhouette. Ramming was sometimes attempted but *Calypso* was more likely to cripple herself and *Gamma* colliding with it might already have initiated a journey to the bottom that could last months.

Calypso completed her cursory search, came about, and made for the retreating liner which remained in danger. Among those aboard was the third-class passenger Manuel Valencia y Gomis, architect of a filibuster expedition the bark intercepted off the Yucatan Peninsula. Although the Italian anarchist Niccolo Salvaggi supplanted him before *Rafael Riego's* massive detonation destroyed the revolutionary's planned propaganda of the deed, Valencia still saw his eyes; dark orbs lit by hate that allowed neither tolerance nor mercy for those obstructing a better world; and vaguely remembered Captain Buff shoving him over the fantail as *Calypso's* Gatling guns began tearing apart those fleeing aft,.

Surfacing once the wake released him, choking on saltwater, seeing the tug disintegrate, and feeling its shock wave pummeled his body he waved at and cursed the departing American. Salvaggi was gone and Valencia's own thoughts jumbled, but his commitment to anarchism had been consecrated. He had struggled to stay alive and avoid swallowing saltwater while clinging to a packing crate the swells lifted then lowered. Burned by the sun and blinded by its reflection, early evening found him near delirium and hoarsely repeating, "Long live anarchy," when he was roughly yanked over a white whaleboat's gunnels. When strength returned he looked up to a raised sail flapping gently and mast pirouetting against a clear sky. Fresh water burned cracked lips as he recognized Captain Buff, two battered insurrectos, and an artillerist. The soldier of fortune had the boat's first three occupants row far enough away to avoid being seen then used its compass to steer towards the explosion. They located Captain Buff, holding *Rafael Riego's* log, and then searched long enough to recover Valencia, who apparently lacked sufficient blood scent to lure sharks from more pungent remains. Captain Buff sailed their fully equipped whaleboat to Arrecife Alacranes where they spent the day masquerading as a fishing boat then left for Puerto Progresso, slipped past an American revenue cutter, and landed down the coast. Locals supporting Cuban insurrectos ensured *Vanguard* received the log, whaleboat, and no information. Captain Buff left for Key West, but Valencia went to Jamaica, obtained forged identity papers, and booked passage on *Gamma* as the first leg of his return to Europe.

The experience convinced him violent anarchy was the way forward. Even so, he experienced a fleeting relapse when passengers seemed ready to panic after ramming the derelict; and then *Calypso's* arrival quelled them with order, assistance, and subtle threat of bayonets. She twice saved his life, since it was her whaleboat in the Gulf of Mexico, but left him with recurring nightmares; and seeing this nemesis again stoked an already increasing radical hatred for government oppression.

CHAPTER SEVEN
PLANS AND DILEMMAS

*C*alypso stood by while two tugs made up to *Gamma* just off Bermuda's main channel. Informants might use the rescue location or sailors' gossip to project *Calypso's* track but Starke decided his best course was press on as before so he left a cable with the pilot then steamed west over the horizon before turning south. Albert added it to a brief on the Spanish war plan and filibustering status for the new secretary of the navy, John D. Long.

The secretary listened amiably then shuffled across the room with arm extended and feet more hindrance than help. He preferred short presentations, crisp summations, and the required decision clearly stated; but grew fatigued if inundated with minutiae, especially technical details. Long understood administration, the broad canvas, did not plumb unfamiliar waters deeper than required, and never portrayed himself as an expert through meandering monologues.

The assistant secretary was still unnamed a month after inauguration so Albert briefed McAdoo, whose last day was April 18, 1897, then returned from the high-ceilinged suite on the second floor in a pensive mood. He was pleased with the secretary and familiar with Captain Arent Crowninshield, the new Bureau of Navigation chief, but McAdoo's successor was still uncertain and three times lucky was unnatural. Albert took up a fresh pipe, charged it, slid into his chair, leaned back, and accepted the inevitable delay. There was no solace in rumors the current New York City police commissioner, Theodore Roosevelt, was lobbying hard and supported by Speaker Reed, the politically connected Commander Charles Davis, and others.

Captain Crowninshield had turned over *Maine* to the recently promoted Captain Charles Sigsbee. Before Rear Admiral Ramsay retired he explained Albert's reputation, ability, and contacts were needed with the new administration and volatile Spanish situation. This violated the admiral's axiom about unique officers but he was notoriously honest so Albert mostly accepted the explanation. He was still unpersuaded Sigsbee's orders upon promotion to captain were not partly due to a powerful clique built on familial, political, and philosophical ties that included the chief intelligence officer, Commander Davis, and others. It was necessary to politick for billets, but this group advocated, with some justification, removing or shunting aside older officers; which also included any who disagreed. Albert was uneasy with their unswerving adherence to retired Captain Alfred Mahan's writings although agreeing a far more capable navy was needed. He smiled, drew from his pipe and watched its pungent smoke waft to the ceiling. Perhaps it was also distaste for a captain who avoided sea duty emerging as the press' darling for naval matters. He never disparaged writing, academics, or even the Naval War College, as many did, but saw any captain reluctant to command at sea an anathema. Ramsay apparently shared that opinion and packed Mahan off to sea in a choice command despite his protests. There was also the time Albert spent with Starke, who slightly favored the French Jeune École and claimed the proposed pace, technology, and fleet composition unbalanced.

Albert's portfolio also fattened under the new administration with the Spanish war plan being continued, Ramsay involving him in various tasks for Long, and the filibuster project expanding with the new administration supporting his proposal for involved departments to intensify activities beginning in April. Justice and Treasury would concentrate on the prime offenders of New York City, Key West, and Jacksonville while the Revenue Cutter Service planned to prioritize their anti-filibuster role and assign *Calypso*'s alter ego, *Vanguard*, to patrol the Straits of Florida and further into the Atlantic than cutters limited to one district. More navy ships would take up filibuster patrols and any transiting the East Coast encouraged to act. Although the protected cruiser *Newark* came north in March for overhaul and sailing rig removal, two torpedo boats, a monitor, the dynamite cruiser *Vesuvius*, and dispatch boat *Dolphin* were made available. Albert's ferret, *Calypso*, was also coming from Nassau and a coded cable brought her up the Atlantic Coast to New York City, further offshore than *Vanguard*, to coal at the Brooklyn Navy Yard then patrol south towards Cuba.

The overall effort was close-held because correspondents, Junta sources, and jingoes were active but what did slip was done knowing it would reach the Junta's Washington or New York office. Albert's sources, although sparse, confirmed they hoped to gain traction during the administration's transition and increase expeditions because the reconcentrado policy and government offensives since December had severely weakened Pinar del Río insurrectionists. April and May were the favored months to prepare for the rainy season so Albert intended to constrict filibuster traffic from the States using these additional patrols. His efforts over the last year already reduced the number of safe havens, raised interception risk, and increased prosecutions. There were also rumors of growing distrust between the Junta's disparate factions. Although this was primarily due to Pinkerton agents infiltrating filibuster expeditions then informing or testifying, their numbers never reached the level portrayed by the press. Even so, the Junta had begun to suspect they had organized saboteurs, informants, and traitors; encouraged by *Laurada*'s Port Antonio damage, *Commodore*'s sinking, and *Calypso*'s destruction of *John Gwinn Williams* then *Rafael Riego*.

The captain drew from his briar pipe, then slowly exhaled as floating dust specks were illuminated by the sun's rays passing through window panes. He had also become Long's advisor on Crete. It was not a national interest for the States but equaled or exceeded Cuba on front pages; with missionary organizations demanding action and the inevitable squadron. While Britain, France, Russia, and Italy were adding territory from Sudan to China, Greek leaders, buoyed by Athens' 1896 Olympics, planned to absorb Ottoman territories containing Greek Christians and began with Crete; which forced major European nations to take sides. Island Christians formed irregular forces and a Greek army arrived in January, triggering Ottoman reinforcements, so by February the European powers were facing cooperation or war. They established a blockade in mid-March and demands for the adversaries to stand down were anticipated before May. The States was not involved and possessed little leverage with its three-ship European Squadron and domestic pressure for it to support Armenian Christians. The squadron was no longer composed of obsolete curiosities, but their number made them irrelevant for either mission. That would not improve unless the fleet was sent; which the British, French, or Italians could easily outmatch without coaling limitations.

Albert watched a British fleet pummel Alexandria, Egypt twelve years before from his elegant but impotent steam sloop with muzzleloaders; part of a squadron that could only offer refuge for those loosely interpreted as citizens then land sailors and marines to offer some order. When Long learned of this, Albert was assigned to assemble Office of Naval Intelligence information, internal files, ship reports, and attaché assessments on the eastern Mediterranean into a regular brief. This strained an already ambivalent relationship with the chief intelligence officer since Wainwright believed this task belonged to his office. Albert acknowledged his concerns, ensured sufficient credit flowed in that direction, and obtained the lieutenant commander's acquiescence; which he suspected resulted from a reduced working staff with more clerks than officers.

Albert was also spending more time than prudent parrying the Junta, jingoes, and their fellow travelers; even with assistance from the Machiavellian lawyer-clerk Maximilian Falk y Machado working for Arliss Spencer at Justice. Son of an Austrian engineer and lady from Cadiz who married in Havana then immigrated to New York, he proved adept at Washington maneuvering, understood Spanish politics, and was familiar with various Cuban factions. His counsel and Albert's access to the secretary on the Crete issue prevented *Calypso*'s exile to the European Squadron but Junta efforts to remove the only Navy ship dedicated to disrupting filibuster expeditions continued. One congressman's staff even pushed for *Calypso* to represent the nation at Queen Victoria's Diamond Jubilee, rescheduled for June, by arguing *Gamma*'s rescue guaranteed a favorable reception. Crowninshield, Albert, and State explained an obsolete, minimally crewed bark under the Navy's most junior commander would be insulting; so the armored cruiser *Brooklyn* went under a flag officer.

Albert's adversaries proved more successful orchestrating June testimony in the House Committee on Foreign Relations during a special session of the Fifty-fifth Congress on March 4,

1897; held the day after its predecessor closed. Albert always felt betrayed when Congress exposed individuals enforcing its laws to one-sided, theatrical displays while praising those violating them. Falk, however, accepted this as just another approach to impede anti-filibuster activities despite *Rafael Riego* being the stated topic; and repeatedly reminded him that most senators and congressmen were attuned to public pressure, supported the Junta, or both. A minority, including Speaker Reed, opposed risking war with Spain by supporting the Junta, but every legislator felt pressure from the Cuban Leagues, lobbyists, sympathy meetings, and newspapers.

These were coordinated in varying degrees by Estrada Palma's Junta. Ostensibly an arm of the provisional Cuban government in eastern Cuba, it was headquartered in New York City, sent filibuster expeditions to supply and reinforce General Maximo Gómez's forces, published *La Patria*, held daily press conferences, and fielded an effective legal section under Horatio Rubens. Its Washington lobbying group, informally called the Cuban Legation, operated under Gonzalo de Quesada from a Raleigh Hotel suite. Falk believed Quesada's subtle push for a summer hearing gained momentum in mid-February when the *New York Journal* printed a short Richard Harding Davis story under a sketch of two male Spaniards strip-searching a woman on *Olivette*; which was false in this instance.

The press emphasized Governor-general Don Valeriano Weyler y Nicolau's contribution to Cuba's wretched state while ignoring the Gómez strategy. It also portrayed minor skirmishes as major rebel victories while downplaying defeats like the surrender of Maceo's successor, Juan Rius Rivera, at Cabezedas that Weyler used to declare Pinar del Río pacified. Albert's efforts also surfaced in one or another paper as brief stories. Two navy ships foiled *Bermuda*'s rendezvous with a tug and tow at sea then *Colfax,* one of the side-wheel cutters used along coasts, intercepted her near Fernandina. Apalachicola's paper claimed a filibuster expedition was delayed, presumably because *Calypso* was reported lurking off their coast while the bark was actually in Nassau preparing to come north through Old Bahama Channel.

CHAPTER EIGHT
DANCING THE LION

*C*alypso's sweep for *Laurada* proved worthwhile despite the large filibuster's escape. Information and dates varied slightly, but the expedition departed an East Coast port in early March to transport fruit then, according to the Pinkertons, took men and munitions aboard at sea off New Jersey. A British ship spotted her nine days later near the Bahamas' Watlings Island.

Starke cabled from Nassau to report arrival and sighting a small westbound freighter in the Atlantic. It turned south after being spotted, but not before the lookout, Kearney, spotted her maneuver. Starke boarded despite a British mercantile flag to check documents; which had her leaving Liverpool with agricultural and mining machinery for Caracas, Venezuela. The master, with a New York accent, claimed the sudden turn was to pass between Hispaniola and Puerto Rico; while vigorously protesting boarding and delay of a British ship. Ensign Blair, the boarding officer, accepted his proffered documentation at face value but left convinced she was a filibuster. Starke suspected the southeast course concealed a destination laying east or north, so he steamed just west of the freighter. Speed changes to create impatience or test the bark's limits failed because *Calypso* was generally headed in that direction; forcing the suspected filibuster to continue towards Caracas, outrun the bark, or lead it to some rendezvous. When *Calypso* finally turned west for Old

Bahama Channel, the clock had been run out for any planned filibuster scheme and no destination remained but Caracas.

Boarding was a potential legal transgression that risked an international incident, especially with Britain, so Starke only checked papers then shadowed; discourteous but not illegal. Albert speculated *Laurada* waited off Watlings Island for this additional cargo then finally made the run to Cuba without. The overall expedition seemed exceptionally large and critical since reports arrived that insurrectionists offloaded a ship in Banes with canvas-covered name boards on March 21, 1897; a major Junta gamble. Additional information allowed Albert to estimate the cargo Starke diverted by various discrepancies. Some sources claimed 6,000 rifles and others 2,500. Three dynamite guns were expected but only one off-loaded and large small arms cartridge disparities existed. A trio of Hotchkiss guns, thirty tons of dynamite, and 5,000 machetes were also unaccounted for, along with material, clothing, and medicines. Consequently, *Laurada* apparently made Cuba but *Calypso*'s sudden appearance and extemporaneous action diverted some cargo and seven days after leaving the island customs officers boarded her off Delaware to detain the master, Samuel Hughes.

Calypso anchored off Nassau for a week to rest, wait for instructions, and let the Junta see her poised to cruise the Old Bahama Channel, off east Florida, Straits of Florida, or along the East Coast. This did not concern Landsman Hawk who sat on the fantail studying a clear Bahamian evening sky and enjoying Melvin's renditions of *Aura Lee* and *Barbara Allen*. They were just north of Hogfish Bank, east of Silver Cay, and west of the thin breakwater peninsula jutting from Hog Island. Obscured by the bulwark were long, rolling waves that slid up the Hog Island peninsula's white beaches then retreated from its lighthouse and sand hill backbone;

backdropped by the busy port. The view was better from the tops, and more solitude, so he spent several evenings there. Kearney sometimes joined him with a long glass borrowed from their quartermasters who explained the sheltered bay's shifting white sand bottom added to depth concerns that forced *Calypso* to anchor off the entrance then run steam pinnaces to the waterfront. Several large ships anchored nearby to deliver or take on cargo used launches towed by small tugs. The peninsula's lighthouse signaled when enough water covered the bar for ships to leave or enter but those that did drew less than *Calypso* and her neighbors.

Their Newfoundland mariner, Marius Moreau, was in the pilothouse watching a broad bay's translucent emerald water turn light green as it shoaled over fine sand to end in a white fringe licking the beach. Sheltered by Hog Island peninsula, shallow water, and several small cays; the shoreline from west to east saw a long inner beach yield to an abandoned gray fortress then bustling waterfront with its seawalls, landings, and piers partly obscured by sponge schooners and other craft. Small boats, with bronzed men standing in the stern using a single oar to scull and steer, flittered below the ancient pirate fortress rising from the beach just south of *Calypso*. According to Coxswain Melvin it was to be replaced by a hotel, with harbor defense left to Fort Charlotte further up the slope and the oddly shaped Fort Fincastle above town center.

Some arriving ships would board a pilot, cross the bar, close Nassau's waterfront, and anchor just off shore. One was the black and white side-wheel steamer *City of Monticello* Henry Flagler chartered to bring hotel guests from Miami three times each week. Moreau heard Dunbar tell Blair she was built during the 1860s and before joining the Bahama tourist trade operated mostly off Nova Scotia. Her 230-foot, 450-ton iron hull contained forty staterooms in addition to dormitory accommodations Dunbar derided as troopship berthing. A trail of black smoke billowed from the single stack centered between two raked masts while her black walking beam thrust up and down behind white paddle boxes. Moreau also noticed *Calypso*'s officers often accumulated in the pilothouse for each arrival to scan her crowded decks with binoculars for female passengers they might later see at the Flagler hotel bar.

Tourists, island natives, soldiers, and locals mingled along the waterfront and several blocks inland so British soldiers and *Calypso* sailors frequented the same bars. Friction was inevitable, but one donnybrook left a sailor facing the next year or so in prison. Chief Weaver believed the most accurate account came from a suspected participant. It seemed Matthew Parnell, a young New Yorker with Irish parents, went ashore with several Irish sailors from his starboard watch. After leaving the pinnace for a rumored watering hole before pursuing other delights ashore they prudently chose a small bar just off the waterfront; after bypassing an establishment filled with merchant seamen, watermen, and spongers reputed to be a notorious crimp's hunting ground. When a roughly equal party of soldiers saw the sailors enter with capital they began sharing rounds until resources dried up and convention demanded a detailed accounting to ensure no one was holding back. This played out with inebriation's effects dulling the merrymakers' decorum and discretion. Dialogue became philosophical, grew insinuating, devolved to accusations, and finally achieved mutual animosity. When several slightly less drunk peacemakers had nearly persuaded everyone to part ways, regain sobriety, and curse the injustice, Parnell spoke up. Being the youngest with the least Irish bona fides, he contributed a final insult to ameliorate empty jumper pockets and enhance future retelling. It began by prodding shortest soldier's chest with his finger while announcing a single Irishmen could whip six British soldiers; twice that number if Irish traitors. The colorful soliloquy continued unabated until a blow landed squarely under his jaw. Inebriated, infuriated, and stunned, he backed into a sailor who stepped forward to roundhouse the soldier; whose mates joined the affray.

Other patrons stood aside as the publican moved expertly to shield the bottle-laden bar with his custom cudgel, an oar shortened to just over a foot, which dropped the second sailor then a soldier. The district constable was summoned and he sent for a back-up squad of uniformed Bermudians. Well aware these troubleshooters served under British officers, the soldiers retrieved their fallen comrade and rushed the rear door. Most sailors concluded the soldiers were not bolting from defeat and followed with their stunned shipmate. Parnell, still thinking his back covered, continued to harangue the Colored constable who quietly fondled his worn nightstick, comfortably aware reinforcement would arrive in seconds. Parnell's increasingly virulent verbal barrage about British generally and constable in particular continued until, smarting from a sore jaw, the landsman raised his fist and was smoothly dispatched by a well-oiled, oak baton.

He regained consciousness in a police holding area with Ensign Blair, Chief Weaver, and a British officer conversing nearby. His captors were willing to surrender him to *Calypso* if the sailor paid damages, but Parnell's head hurt, he was not yet sober, and Blair was negotiating with foreigners. This brought forth a barrage of colorful invectives about the ensign that ended when Chief Weaver forcefully twisted the handcuffs.

An unapologetic Parnell sullenly passed into *Calypso*'s brig that evening; sick, sore, defiant, and demanding an audience with the captain. Watson sent word the next morning this would take place once Starke returned from formally apologizing at Government House. There was no sympathy from Parnell's shipmates, since all shore leave ended, so his only comfort was the ship's gray feline. Thaddeus found steel rods no bar to a cool, comfortable spot for naps, grooming, and extensive stroking from a human with little else to do; causing the master-at-arms to remark it would be a fine thing if their mouser gave four-legged rats equal attention.

Starke stepped to the quay from a steam pinnace serving as captain's gig, boarded the small carriage, and settled in its seat. The light rig's compact horse pulled it up a road bordered by brick and wood buildings with living quarters above street-level shops and offices. He had an excellent view of town and bay when the driver turned in to Government House on a hill overlooking Nassau. *Calypso* was floating off the bay entrance with her dark hull standing proud over translucent, blue-green water ringed by restless white breakers with the blue sea beyond. Two smart sentries stood by large, brick pillars flanking the roadway and Starke wondered how their crispness would survive a nearly cool morning giving way to the rising Caribbean sun.

He left early for Government House where he hoped to make some overture even if the governor was unable to receive him. Minor incidents pricking national honor could fade away with little notice or become a cause célèbre. The United States and Britain were still involved with the South American boundary dispute they faced off over less than two years before and Speaker Reed narrowly averted war with Chile after sailors on liberty were killed; by pointing out the Navy's deficiencies and potential for a general South American war since Argentina was eager to help for a slice of Chilean territory.

Starke walked under a veranda, through the main entrance, and was immediately ushered into the governor's office. Their previous meeting went well but Starke was still surprised to be seen on such short notice. Sir William Frederick Haynes Smith was a career diplomat who came from the same position in Britain's Leeward Islands colony of Antigua and Barbuda. From Starke's courtesy call and minimal exposure with British titles he knew the governor was Knight Commander of the Most Distinguished Order of Saint Michael and Saint George so he addressed him as Sir Smith. The governor offered him a chair then opened with, "To what do I owe this pleasure, Captain?"

"Please forgive the lack of notice, Sir Smith, but I wish to extend my personal apology and that of my government for last night's disturbance and any improper actions by my crew."

Sir Smith's facial features relaxed, "Some lemonade, or perhaps tea, Captain?"

The change told Starke that Sir Smith anticipated a formal protest but now wished to extend their conversation without appearing to. He chose tea, which quickly arrived in the bright, airy room by way of a neatly dressed servant before the governor resumed, "I was apprised of yesterday's unpleasantness. The army's here redesigning batteries so we must anticipate some high spirits and I believe our soldiers were equally keen. They'll be brought to book despite some creative explanations, yours too I shouldn't wonder, so dropping this matter seems most appropriate and convenient since all parties seem little worse for wear."

"That's appreciated, Sir Smith."

"It serves everyone's interests, Captain. Tourist season ends this month and there's a great deal of American investment by

Mr. Flagler and others, so it seems a poverty to jeopardize this over fisticuffs."

He then changed subjects, "You may find it of interest to learn a British master submitted a complaint in Kingston about your boarding to confirm registry but appeared more agitated about *Calypso* sailing in company and blocking his way north. Since Mona Passage is the preferred route to Caracas our man was suspicious."

The governor lowered his tea to the table, "More questions produced progressively less satisfactory answers. There was also an exchange of coded cables with New York City rather than Britain before their conversation so our excisemen chose to examine her cargo. While not at liberty to divulge more; that particular variety of agricultural and mining equipment would find no employment in Caracas."

With that, his servant reentered and Starke sensed a scheduled appointment in the anteroom so he mentioned *Calypso* would depart the following day and took his leave. The waiting carriage rolled slowly forward from what shade a nearby tree afforded as he crossed the verandah and paused to look beyond the city to his black bark with furled sails floating serenely below. When the driver called out, "Walk on," they started with a slight jerk and were soon rolling easily downhill, slowed by occasional brake applications. On the way, Starke retrieved Dunbar from the port office and they passed through the city then along the waterfront to quay and pinnace. Dunbar sat quietly facing his captain in the carriage, then beside him in the gig, while Starke absorbed the working waterfront's sights, competing odors, and gentle, salt-laden breeze.

Watson produced Parnell that evening but there was no way to avoid court-martial since Blair filed charges. Martyn or Dunbar might have dismissed the rant as that of a drunk but *Calypso* must take precedence over the landsman. Blair was correct, given audience and circumstance, but if Weaver had retrieved Parnell alone it would likely have been resolved by a short detour during their return. Instead, a sailor Weaver claimed worked hard and got along well with messmates was going to prison; although the chief persuaded a reluctant Starke to restore Parnell's freedom until trial and support a recommendation the court-martial forego prison if Parnell performed well. Starke also told the young man he could easily have been killed before returning him to his mess; as Watson mused about a gratuitous fight costing the sailor time as a convict, dismissal from the service, and loss of several rights due citizens.

Starke left for the wardroom to review their next morning's underway as the bark swayed smooth and easy on incoming rollers slipping past to claw up the beach or expire in the bay's calm waters. Chief Owen spread and weighted charts on the long table. On top was the sailing chart and below those covering increasingly smaller areas then ports. Alongside them lay two *Coast Pilot* books with one describing the Atlantic shore from New York City to Chesapeake Bay, and the other from there to Key West. Starke began once everyone was seated and door closed, "Gentlemen, as some of you already know, we're for New York City. *Calypso*'s design incorporated her use as an open ocean raider so she's longer and has deeper draft than many gunboats and revenue cutters. This constricts us near ports or shallow water so our role is to cruise well offshore. Better suited ships will work the coast and harbors, along with transiting warships, while *Vanguard* patrols between them and us."

Starke paused, then continued, "Cuba's rainy season's coming, which means tropical storms and hurricanes, so the Junta will ship all they can. New York or New Jersey will supply the bulk so Navy, Justice, and Treasury hope to pressure expeditions from these areas over the next few months. We will head north, board suspicious ships, make ourselves known, and disrupt filibuster activities."

Possible boardings fired Blair's imagination, Martyn calculated risks, and Watson moved beside Starke, who continued, "We'll head for Brooklyn, coal, and then return south. Mr. Dunbar?"

Their navigator lightly traced the proposed course using his dividers, "There are two routes out; the Northwest Providence Channel towards Jupiter Inlet or the Northeast Providence Channel for Bermuda. We'll be taking the northwest channel. It's approximately 160 miles before the turn north, and then we stay about sixty miles off the coast. The other ships will work inshore, with *Vanguard* roughly thirty miles out."

Ensign Blair looked up, "What speed?"

Dunbar glanced at Osbourne and O'Leary, then responded, "I'm estimating nine knots over ground to maintain track but riding the Gulf Stream means one boiler should suffice along the coast."

Naval cadets Caldwell and Timme were silent so Martyn asked, "Lighthouses and currents coming out of Nassau?"

Dunbar realized Martyn asked for their benefit, "We'll pass several Bahama lighthouses but visibility, time of day, and lookout height will determine most sightings. Leaving Nassau, the Hog Island Light is dead astern for our northern leg. At the turn northwest, Hole-in-the-Wall Light may be visible to starboard, but Great Stirrup Cay Light should be to port before and after. Since we just clear Great Bahama Island, we'll pass Eight Mile Rock Light to starboard and use it for a fix. On the western leg, we stay well north of Great Isaac Cay and that light, so we're well off course if it's seen. Shallows to the north and Grand Bahama Island are our primary concern since the ship will be set north. However, the Gulf Current works to our advantage once clear of the islands; especially if we keep to its center."

Blair followed Martyn's lead, "What can we expect on the run north?"

Dunbar looked to Watson, "I doubt we'll see many ships under sail before Charleston but that could increase afterwards with ships leaving the Southern Route from Europe joining those outbound from the Straits of Magellan. They usually steer north and west of the Bahamas until clear then close the coast, while steamships headed further up the East Coast or to Halifax cut through the Bahama passages; so the heaviest traffic should be early on then near New York."

Watson cautioned, "So, gentlemen, keep a tight watch and be extra vigilant at night. Fog's not likely but storms are, even if it's early for hurricanes, so look for any barometer change. Don't forget *Gamma* hitting a hulk; there's plenty still about. Mr. Dunbar will update course and speed during the day, watch officers will find everything in the night order book, and our naval cadets will shoot morning and evening stars as well as sun lines to fatten their personal logs."

Cadets Caldwell and Timme were not happy. Taking sights and standing watch meant little or no sleep the next several days. Their evil eye fell on Watson but Starke wanted to stretch them while there was little risk, and improve their chances of a commission.

Calypso raised anchor in the early morning of Saturday, April 17, 1897, came about in a sweeping turn, placed Hog Island Light astern, and worked up to speed. The tall bark steamed north under a broad, lingering plume of grayish smoke as still indistinct figures on a nearby pair of steamers and three-masted schooner watched until the black stern shrank to a spot on the horizon. Fifteen minutes before noon,

Starke was eating sea turtle soup at his day cabin table when the messenger of the watch brought midday reports and requested permission to strike eight bells on time. He considered going to the pilothouse after lunch for their turn into Northwest Providence Channel, then chose to show confidence in the executive officer, navigator, and Blair. Once on the western leg, they would hold course until about midnight then come north when Grand Bahama Island would safely clear.

The flying bridge lookout reported a flickering light off the starboard bow just before two bells of the first watch. As *Calypso* ghosted forward with a full moon illuminating calm, black seas, several weaker lights appeared nearby and the flicker became a distinct series of light and dark periods. The lookout called out the sequence just before Blair and Dunbar confirmed it was Eight Mile Rock Lighthouse, using night order information taken from the *Admiralty List of Lights*. Starke was asleep in the at-sea cabin but went to the pilothouse and found Dunbar holding *Calypso* slightly north of track steering west-northwest and a half west. He recommended west-northwest to Starke, who agreed after examining their dead reckoning plot and glassing the bright, intermittent light off their starboard beam. *Calypso* shifted easily to port with few asleep below noticing. The bark steadied on this new course with her curved prow slicing calm seas with little more than a gurgle, lines slapping above deck, the stack's constant dull panting, and ever-present vibration from three pistons spinning a single shaft.

After passing the Eight Mile Rock Light, Dunbar calculated they were running safely off Grand Bahama Island and a little over three hours to the turn north, so Starke left for the sea cabin behind the pilothouse. He managed an hour's sleep before the messenger brought him back to the pilothouse where an agitated Blair reported a small fishing boat running without lights went unnoticed until there was no time to act and *Calypso* flashed past about twenty yards off. Some sailors swore it as more like twenty feet but the boat was roughly handled then left bobbing astern. Dunbar surmised its crew fell asleep and let an untended lantern go out since a light quickly appeared astern. *Calypso* was lucky, and the unlit fishermen even more so since those nearly run down were not waving a light or showing other distress signals. Blair was sufficiently shaken so Starke confirmed the incident was logged then left an exceptionally vigilant watch for his sea cabin.

Calypso turned gently starboard then steadied due north under a full moon soon after the port section assumed their middle watch. Starke had delayed the turn for them to settle in and gain sea room for passing by shallows to the east. He was summoned later when Martyn sighted a flickering white light on the horizon without bearing drift and felt the ships would meet not quite head-on but close aboard. This was confirmed when the masthead light split slightly to reveal an aft range light. The illusion of speed increasing as they closed became obvious about the same time her red and green running lights appeared. Lowering his binoculars, the ensign said, "Looks like a liner, Captain. Coming fast and holding course."

"What do you propose?"

"I believe we'll pass close down her port side; so come starboard, when we're closer."

"You believe?"

"Yes sir."

"If a liner; she's running a set course and maintaining schedule with little incentive to alter either unless forced."

"Turn away?"

"Not yet, dodging ships could take us off track or into extremis."

Martyn checked *Calypso*'s running lights as the closing ship's two white orbs rose over her sidelights. He watched, waited, fidgeted, then turned to Starke, "Captain, I'd like to come starboard and open the distance."

Starke pulled the unlit pipe from his beard, "Wouldn't have waited much longer for you. Turn boldly so they see what we're about but don't disturb those sleeping or take us too far off track."

Martyn spoke to Caldwell, who had the conn, and their helmsman worked the brass wheel. *Calypso*'s jibboom and bowsprit slipped smoothly across the northern horizon, separating from the foremast and opening their view ahead. A scattered pattern of white lights spread across the liner's port side with the red one just visible amongst them as her green running light vanished. Caldwell held their new course long enough to clear then brought *Calypso* back to the original heading.

The New York and Cuba Mail Steamship Company's *City of Washington*, running hard for Havana, flashed past at little more than 500 yards. Her master was about to come right when the ship bearing down on them clearly maneuvered, saving time and money. The firm, popularly called the Ward Line, ran a tight schedule from its New York City Pier 15. After entering Havana late in the day, she would remain overnight then make for Veracruz and Panama before returning to New York. The mate logged their passing close aboard a bark-rigged steam warship after spotting gun mounts under canvas in the moonlight. At 500 yards, the liner's portholes, windows, and open doors reflecting light from the dark water made her 300-foot hull appear to be alongside *Calypso*. Starke recognized *City of Washington* from the single stack amidship, straight stem, extended counter, conspicuous rudder, and row of rectangular ports beneath the main deck.

Sunday routine began with sweeping, hoisting ashes, and a saltwater wash-down before full-dress uniforms came out for inspection. Paymaster Wiggs selected Romans 16:17 for a congregation of Protestants, Catholics, agnostics, atheists, and sprinkling of less common religions; great and small. During afternoon rope-yarn Starke began a letter to Katherine while the regulars' ballads, hymns, and drinking songs on the fantail drifted through an open window. The accompaniment for Coxswain Melvin's mandolin had more passion than harmony but created a mood of belonging.

Calypso cleared Little Bahama Bank to starboard as Washington's morning sidewalks were swept and washed. Albert stood at his window, faded white-china cup in hand, looking north through a gap between the Building and Executive Mansion to Lafayette Square. He contemplated the people and horses until, like every weekday, a yellow, white and mahogany Capital Traction Company car squealed to a halt and gray canvas bags were transferred to a horse-drawn vehicle and passengers stepped down. More than a year passed since he waited there to offer Starke *Calypso*. The office entered as a senior commander was most comfortable in April and May when he watched a morning sun rise over the city. The window could also be opened to encourage a light, refreshing draft, if the door was left ajar, and its red and white striped awning ensured afternoon shade. Whatever season, his desk remained a plateau of organized clutter, below the brass gas lamp suspended from an ornate ceiling medallion, which included a pipe rack, letter boxes, mechanical calendar updated to "MON APR 19 97", and surrounding blanket of memorandums, letters, and reports already in flux.

The pale yellow cane wastebasket beneath it contained Good Friday's *The Times*. That edition and two papers he read over the weekend were unusually informative. One reported impregnated cloth could stop bullets and another that some foreign power seized the Sandwich Islands, now the Republic of Hawaii. The Emancipation Day parade was described; Colored students' Annapolis experiences noted; a cigar-shaped airship had been constructed in Texas, and Navy civil engineer, Robert Peary, was preparing his North Pole attempt. The administration transition continued, despite election returns from Kentucky being disputed, with more Colored appointees anticipated and difficult committee assignment negotiations underway. Albert took note of the last because it suggested his testifying could be delayed, then extracted his pipe and loosed a blueish smoke cloud. The Republicans also planned to reinstate "old soldiers" pried from War Department positions by the Civil Service Act. While they excluded those expelled for criminal acts; incompetence and negligence were not crimes so his contacts there anticipated several extremely unsavory or unscrupulous characters.

There were also items affecting his portfolio. The Eastern Mediterranean war had begun with Turkish troops driving out Greek irregulars that entered the Ottoman Empire and new American minister to Constantinople claiming he was promised a ship. Another article lamented the Navy's absence off Honduras, where revolution was a political staple. Albert made a note to see if either was an attempt redirect *Calypso* as he passed through accounts of Spain's failures, atrocities, and reconcentrado. Despite what was printed, his sources still placed roughly equal blame on the warring parties with individual atrocities usually tracking back to guerrilleros or insurrectionists. There was less about filibusters, but a British master did report an unidentified American warship circled his ship then left.

Albert's chair creaked from his weight and movement as another bowl was prepared then lit. The newly appointed assistant secretary of the navy, Theodore Roosevelt, was also due. He was roughly Starke's age and rumored a cauldron of energy, belligerency, and intelligence; also a professed naval reformer without active military service and avowed jingo. Albert began work as another cloud of smoke floated upward past the gas lamp.

CHAPTER NINE
NASSAU TO NEW YORK

Sunday passed under clear skies with an Atlantic coast beyond the horizon and *Calypso* making well over what a serene five-knot bow wave suggested, thanks to the Gulf Stream. Dunbar and Owen's three daily fixes and dead reckoning placed them north of Jupiter Inlet on Florida's east coast with Matanilla Reef at Little Bahama Bank's northern tip astern to starboard. They came north-northwest after noon sight reduction to angle across the current towards Port Royal and would turn again some miles off the coast.

Starke prolonged the transit by taking a main boiler off line since the few extra knots using both cost dearly in wear and coal; besides Osbourne was monitoring several water tubes. The sedate pace was also useful crossing routes filibusters favored, even if a sighting was unlikely. With an eye to deterring or delaying expeditions rather than apprehending any specific one, *Calypso* approached candidates, visually examined them, and ensured she was recognized as a warship. Those closing from ahead watched *Calypso* increase speed as she passed, circle back, and cross astern to log name and homeport; but if overtaken were examined by the bark briefly falling in astern. The oceangoing tugs and small, nondescript steamers were of particular interest because one type could leave port without exit papers and the other often served as mother ships. Starke seldom boarded since there was little value accumulating protests, even taking *Laurada* would initiate months of legal wrangling that would hobble *Calypso* more than the Junta, but every contact encouraged reports she was stalking filibuster routes.

Starke joined Watson, Dunbar and Owen on the flying bridge during morning twilight to shoot stars in crisp sea air. Using personal or Navy sextants, each observer slowly moved its arm then twisted a tangent screw until the star or planet brushed a faint horizon in the telescope's split-view. As readings were called, quartermaster Moreau matched them to times picked from a pocket chronometer synchronized to the ship's. Yeoman Pond, balancing a worn clipboard in the crook of his arm, then penciled each result on small paper sheets. During this ritual, two dolphins appeared alongside, one slightly exceeding the second in bulk. Darting contemptuously forward, they crossed the bow, briefly amused themselves under the jibboom, and sped off through calm seas sprinkled with brown and green sargassum patches bound for the Irish coast. These minuscule rafts shaded schools of small fish and supported birds that refused to leave until their soggy mats were going under *Calypso*'s foot; then rose excitedly, gathered speed just above the surface, climbed out, and leveled with the mainmast before gliding in loose spirals to an inviting replacement.

After evening stars were reduced and placed them just over sixty miles southwest of Port Royal, *Calypso* came leisurely northeast, with shadows shifting on deck and her curving lackluster wake the only indications. They would remain about sixty miles offshore for 340 miles, passing Frying Pan and Cape Lookout shoals, then Cape Hatteras, to port. The track along the coast to New York required several offshore legs to parallel the land's inward curvature south of Hatteras and two capes with shallows jutting miles into the Atlantic. These worked with the Gulf Stream's relentless thrust north to channel legitimate Caribbean-bound shipping and *Calypso's* prey into a narrow area.

The crew's primary interest was a New York City port call while Conrad's was presenting a clean bill of health to avoid quarantine. Although their Bahama visit left no significant diseases, health officials would board in the port's approaches and any yellow fever cases, or other potentially contagious disease, meant the quarantine anchorage off New Jersey or returning to sea. Quarantine laws were non-negotiable under Navy regulations and Starke agreed; any ship could bring disease and this prevented thousands dying from a single infected arrival.

The black gang had no interest beyond their underway existence dictated by boilers and engine. Delmar Kemp's dark features glistened from exertion, heat, and humidity while he orchestrated the port section's rhythm of filling steel shovels, cracking one of three portals, and spreading coal evenly over a glowing red, orange, and yellow bed before its heavy door clanged shut. Proper firing required more than feeding shovelfuls of coal. Lumps were broken to the best size then carried to the boiler flat where stokers slid flat blades between coal and deck at the exact angle to collect smaller bits without snagging, or riding up and over. Levering with knees and taking advantage of ship motion, the precise amount passed through heavy steel doors that allowed only a few seconds to evenly spread it over an intense, glowing bed. Endurance, skill, and practice sustained this pace over the four-hour watch that would end when Dylan Jones' starboard team arrived. These were usually smooth turnovers since both men taught, encouraged, and pushed trimmers, passers, and stokers to excel in their subterranean arena. Once relieved, the off-going section would half stumble into a stokers' shower where soap alleged to lather with saltwater waited. When complaining began, older hands reminded any grousers that *Calypso*'s accommodations compared well to most, especially those with only a spot on deck and pail.

The ship slid lethargically north through sargassum patches with Yamashita fishing off the stern. When a translucent, green and yellow dolphin, shading below one, struck his lure, Yamashita's club completed the fatal mistake, its colors quickly faded, and the steward split the catch between Starke's supper and his own. While he cleaned and sectioned, Thaddeus crouched nearby holding down long, stringy, wet entrails with two front paws while attacking the red mass with needle-sharp teeth and intermittently lifting his head to check for lurking interlopers.

Calypso's passage was occasionally disrupted for short excursions to examine coastal freighters and oceangoing tugs without tows. Chief Weaver also quizzed his men on several passing sailing ships' rigs. Although most were schooners or barkentines, a ship-rigged collier in ballast came near enough to see a small white bow wave. He guessed it was bound for the coal docks at Newport News and thought about his family waiting there in a row house. Parnell was swabbing the gently moving deck with seawater, a routine early morning evolution to clean and preserve the oak. Weaver breathed deep, pulling salt-laden air into his lungs, and looked up through the mainmast rigging to its truck. The thin red, white, and blue commissioning pennant tethered to its pigstick would stream briefly, go limp, and then regain life. Feeling *Calypso* pierce then shoulder through the thrusting ocean before twisting easily down into the trough, he considered suggesting more canvas to steady the ship as well as lessen coal and steam fragrances supplementing the sea's bouquet.

Cape Hatteras was rounded during early morning then they steadied north by northeast in clear, nearly benign weather Weaver expected would hold for the next 280 miles; before coming to north by west for the final sixty. He often passed through the area and knew its unpredictability, gales, and hurricanes populated the North Carolina coast and seabed west of *Calypso* with wrecks, debris, and graves. The passing ocean was also transforming from green or deep blue hues to shades of gray, or blue-gray, trimmed with thin, broken, white streaks. Flying fish were absent and fewer dolphins raced along the hull before disappearing in bursts of speed. Their replacement was an aged, gray, shark that preferred filling its dirty-white belly with garbage floating in a ship's wake over hunting.

Coxswain Melvin was restowing equipment and untangling rope falls in the port steam pinnace when he looked up, spied Chief Weaver, and used the opportunity to request help. The chief turned to Hawk, blacking an anchor, but Parnell yelled, "I'll help him, Chief." The landsman looked up, raised grimy hands, and grinned. Working boats was infinitely preferable but he disliked interrupting a task; particularly one that spotted his uniform and skin with a heavy black paste Melvin would not want in his boat. Weaver nodded and motioned to Parnell, who went aft at a trot, climbed a short ladder to the pinnace, and slid over its gunwales. Melvin waved to the chief then put the landsman to work untangling the aft boat-falls.

Weaver suppressed a weakness for the Parnells he met over the years. They strove to be the worst when running with a bad lot but dedicated equal effort towards being the best when working with good shipmates. Invariably caught, often to the benefit of their instigators, few escaped cycling from splendid to sordid performance. It was impossible to predict the small number who would succeed, but he still persuaded the captain to release Parnell from the brig then paired him with Hawk. His performance improved and the young man regained popularity with a crew that sensed the landsman would suffer for Nassau while those he refused to name avoided formal retribution. This was not lost on the chief. He volunteered the miscreants for every dirty or unpleasant task; which became so obvious Watson circumvented Ensign Martyn and approached the chief. Weaver expected the executive officer to end his seasoned thumb's pressure on the scales of justice but argued the unfairness of Parnell facing prison while his accomplices walked hurt morale. Few officers really grasped the sailors' world, beyond Academy summer cruises, and most executive officers were more concerned about completing their tour with the least vexation possible. Watson seldom overreacted or sought crew popularity, the breed's common failings, but Weaver was still surprised when he only suggested greater circumspection, took the suspects' names, and then dropped their liberty class to the lowest level. The crew observed and understood but was unable to explain how their executive officer divined the offenders; leaving Watson with a percipient reputation and Weaver convinced that he, like Starke, understood enlisted society. It would not keep Parnell from court-martial, which might have been avoided except for the young landsman's dark cloud and Ensign Blair. Starke or Watson, when ensigns, would have let their chief deal with a drunk but the gunnery officer exhibited sundowner tendencies and should Watson's maturing efforts fail, Weaver would place Blair high on the list of officers he would move heaven and earth to avoid sailing with.

A small, gray feline shape noiselessly rounding the deckhouse then padding silently aft distracted him. Thaddeus was creeping cautiously along the superstructure on his way to the fantail and potential fish offal. He placed food far above loyalty, as evidenced by an expanding girth since his Key West rescue, and was particular about those he took up with. The tom stayed well away from the deck edge and sea beyond but Weaver wanted it taken below and Parnell was the best suited since Thaddeus seemed attached to him after sharing the brig; and when not stalking meals sometimes trailed the young sailor about or napped where he could watch over him.

Weaver decided to wait for Parnell to untangle the aft boat fall, where its three-strand line was jammed in the block. Wedged between sheave and cheek, fiber lines could be worked free but usually required disassembling the block since pounding them with mallets or prying, even using wood fids, always damaged something. The chief's attention had returned to the cat when Melvin paused inventorying the boat-box and glanced aft to see Parnell's growing impatience tightening the jam, but decided to give him a few moments more before intervening. Unexpectedly, the landsman grabbed a marlinspike and stood precariously on the pinnace's sternsheets to get a better purchase. Melvin yelled he was coming since it would seriously damage the line, but this only intensified the landsman's effort to resolve the tangle alone. He stepped up on the transom, grasping the block in one hand while the other probed the recalcitrant manila with the marlinspike. Melvin called out, "Dammit, Parnell, git . . . ," as *Calypso* struck a large swell then heeled and shuddered rather than slice through. The coxswain upended into bilges forward of the black boiler, heard the marlinspike clatter into the cockpit, regained his footing, realized he was alone, checked the deck, and then cupped his hands to yell, "Man overboard, port side, man overboard."

Weaver repeated the alarm in a booming voice that brought Ensign Blair onto one of the collapsible bridge-wings jutting from the mahogany pilothouse to scan their wake with binoculars. Timme gave orders to the lee helmsman, who worked the EOT back and forth before leaving it the back full position. The sweating steam whistle bellowed each time its chain was pulled. Engineers in the boiler and engine rooms jumped to well-practiced emergency measures. Firing and feedwater were adjusted while key valves spun to slow then halt massive pistons driving the shaft. After they stopped with a loud sigh, there was a brief silence before other valves whirled open to rotate pistons and shaft in the opposite direction. For a few moments, no one knew whether the emergency backing bell was a man overboard or collision.

Starke left for the pilothouse and Watson reached the boat deck as vibrations from their screw's struggle to resist 1,100 tons of forward momentum spread through the hull while sailors assigned to launch and man the lifeboat raced to station. Those uninvolved fell into ranks for muster as Starke entered the pilothouse, checked the horizon, and turned to Ensign Blair, "Report."

"Man overboard, Captain. Ship's backing and lookouts are searching astern."

"Very well, Mr. Blair, lower the whaleboat once we've lost way. It's your recovery."

Blair looked aft where two columns formed to man boat falls as the lifeboat crew settled in; then, just before *Calypso* stopped, he ordered dead slow ahead and put the rudder hard right. This brought the ship about to slowly parallel her wake as the duty lifeboat was lowered into water smoothed from the turn, rode briefly to its sea painter, and then cast off to begin searching. The steam pinnaces were also lowered to ride on sea painters until reaching operating pressure. When they were away, Starke recalled the whaleboat. Flanked by a pinnace fifty yards off either beam, *Calypso* slowly backtracked until Blair paused alongside a large white life ring the Swede released from its hull rack when Melvin yelled; and their pinnaces began making ever-widening circles near the heavily rolling ship. Mustering confirmed only Parnell was unaccounted for and other casualties consisted of minor scrapes and burns below decks; rope burns and abrasions above. Starke allowed the search to continue until early afternoon since the weather was conducive and schedule flexible, but nothing came of it.

The pinnaces were finally retrieved and they continued north under a cloud. Parnell's personal effects were collected, statements taken, and log entries made. Starke knew steamship crews required more time to accept sudden death than sailing ships where storms reaped a rich harvest. Steam also complicated any decision to stop searching when no body was recovered since crews, especially landsmen, often saw it as abandoning a shipmate miles from land. He also wanted to ensure the roughhewn Chief Weaver did not feel responsible. The chief had obtained Parnell's release and taken him under his wing; otherwise, the landsman would have been safe in the brig. The fault was Parnell's, but even Starke sensed the landsman would join his own set of dead friends, foes, lovers, adversaries, acquaintances, and others who visited during dreams ashore or when events summoned. Watson arranged a burial service that Wiggs accomplished with one unusually small mourner. Thaddeus emitted low squeals throughout the ceremony and several days after when confronting a closed space as he searched the ship.

Captain Albert would not learn of the loss until *Calypso* reached New York City; besides, his overriding concern was the assistant secretary. Roosevelt paused to retrieve a specific desk from storage then began sending daily memorandums to the secretary. Long not only mostly controlled "Theodore" but damped his jingoism and insurrectionist sympathies then walled off the filibuster project from his assistant's direct control. Albert thought this strange until catching Long immediately after one of many imbroglios his pugnacious understudy initiated with those not sharing his views. It must have been notable since an unusual burst of exasperation revealed his concern Roosevelt would expose project details during a midday Metropolitan Club tiff or one of the recurring verbal altercations. Unfortunately, he also began routing the daily memorandums through Albert; rightly assuming the captain would coordinate with the appropriate bureau chiefs, especially Crowninshield. Inclination and necessity forced him to work these when time permitted, unless the secretary was interested.

Albert increasingly viewed his office overlooking the Executive Mansion and Lafayette Square as a sanctuary since Roosevelt's inexhaustible energy proved less ordered than his predecessor's reasoned sophistication. McAdoo possessed experience chairing the navy and militia committees before taking the assistant secretary position and was at various times a lawyer, reporter, assemblyman, and congressman. Roosevelt's maritime or naval experience was limited to writing an 1812 naval history and speaking with the retired Mahan. His government background was equally meager: state government and a Civil Service Commission position. The assistant secretaries' only commonality was an inclination to preserve some tracts of land in a natural state.

A glance at the clock told Albert it was approaching noon so the l'enfant terrible would be holding court at the Metropolitan Club; one of the clubs, hotels, and restaurants where more well-off inmates of the Building, Treasury

Building, and Executive Mansion took dinner. Those less flush ate at desks or, on pleasant days such as this, nearby parks. Albert did both, but was resolved to spend today enjoying his cinnamon-brown meerschaum pipe while leaning back in the wooden swivel chair. He began comparing Roosevelt and Starke as gray-bottomed white pipe smoke drifted past the window. Theodore worked to expand and improve the Navy through research, reason, and bombast while Starke, perhaps more knowledgeable and experienced, seemed irresolute, eschewed national politics, and was never a vocal advocate. Both were from wealthy, but not exceptionally rich, families with links to the Confederacy as well as solid business and political connections; yet Roosevelt squandered money on a ranch while Starke's financial state appeared prudently managed but an enigma to outsiders. Their time in the territories left Starke with a hardness and cynicism while Roosevelt's self-confident optimism swelled from it.

Someone passed outside the door then continued down the corridor's black and white checked floor. Albert repositioned himself and realized he knew more about Roosevelt than his protégé since Starke was naturally reticent while Roosevelt effused stories of ranch life, fisticuffs, police, and other experiences. A slight arthritic twinge in Albert's knees caused him to shift again. This was unusual during stable weather but the last few days were an exception and made him envious of the pair since they seemed in excellent condition, frequented gyms, and were horsemen. Roosevelt rode local trails and hunted fox, while Starke trained at a military school where he was immersed in tactics, logistics, classics, grammar, and mathematics. Starke never married and seemed overly polite and circumspect around the opposite sex. Abigail even considered matchmaking until learning his aunt was already engaged, with little success. Roosevelt already buried one wife, remarried, fathered more children, and was devoted to his family. He dominated rooms with unbounded enthusiasm and passion for a host of topics. The assistant secretary invariably pummeled the air when making points and even walked leaning forward with chin jutting out. Although Starke possessed command presence, he still seemed one of life's tourists and an almost passive observer at social events. Albert viewed Roosevelt as the romantic adventurer while Starke seemed more calculating and potentially deadlier. Another small pipe-smoke wisp was released. Roosevelt was already attracting young officers who welcomed his drive, energy, demand for change, and enthusiasm for technology; while many of the same men were enticed by *Calypso's* reputation for action and weary of retold anecdotes about a war they barely remembered, if at all.

Albert concluded by thinking it best to keep them apart, cleaned the pipe, racked it, and combed his desk for *Calypso's* last cablegram. It was beneath some of Roosevelt's daily memorandums relegated to the desk's far corner. He also retrieved a draft assessment of fighting in Greece. Once that was briefed to Long, he would leave for home early, enjoy an early night with Abigail, and depart for New York the next morning. This most recent new assignment slithered across his desk because the president chose a Marine captain for his naval aide. Navy officers saw this position as their preserve and refused to serve under a Marine; while their counterparts took it as support for keeping marines on ships rather than guarding bases and shipyards. Albert's good relations with all parties made him the president's ersatz naval aide and unwilling tinker's dam between department tribes for the dedication of Grant's Tomb and review of the North Atlantic Squadron.

CHAPTER TEN
THE DEDICATION

It was Dunbar's first New York trip as navigator so he rose long before the horizon lit to review the track and prepare for morning twilight. His speed recommendations were calculated to place *Calypso* southeast of the Scotland station lightship at dawn Monday. The station, just off shallows near the sandy coast, was named for a nearby 1870's wreck, long since removed; and lightships took the name of their station. His apprehension was assuaged somewhat by their captain's familiarity with the approaches from previous visits and executive officer during a coast survey tours. The perpetually cheerful Chief Quartermaster Owen even seemed to enjoy himself so Dunbar sighed; lifted his personal sextant from its wooden case with green felt padding, filters, and lenses; examined condition and settings; then climbed to the flying bridge for morning sights.

Starke and Watson tolerated a slightly less formal pilothouse than many so the surgeon went there after a rejuvenating night's sleep. He peered through freshly cleaned glass while *Calypso* sliced the light surface chop towards the lightship *Scotland* with a steady slapping at her forefoot. He savored the clear, brisk morning with crisp salt air, slightly gusty winds, and temperatures promising something between forty and sixty degrees. A bright sun in the east edged above an increasingly distinct horizon as the shoreline to their west flickered from its rays. Scattered about were several sailing ship types, steamships, tugboats, and a few large liners with European immigrants gathered at their rails as they jockeyed to enter East Channel, north of *Calypso*. Outbound was a single tug with low, flat superstructure, steaming slowly southeast trailing a dark plume. The large barge towing astern was blanketed with birds that circled, dived, or landed until scattered by men clambering about its overflowing cargo.

Their captain entered, spoke briefly with Dunbar then turned to him, "Good morning, Mr. Conrad. You've an interest in garbage scows? Take my binoculars, but don't change settings." Conrad was astonished. Dunbar once mentioned he never let others touch them, even for cleaning, to ensure they stayed adjusted to him; and understood why after struggling not to twist the adjusting knob once he held them. The tug was soon obscured as it shortened the tow while *Calypso* passed astern. Small figures began shoveling refuse over the barge's grime-encrusted sides and fighting off flocks of birds; with grey-white gulls proving particularly tenacious. Starke interrupted, "A friend who writes for *The Sun* did a garbage story last year," then retrieved his customary unlit pipe, placed it briefly in his mouth, returned it to the right palm, and then lowered it, "It's been illegal to dump in oceans or navigable waterways since last June, but still goes on out here; less since Waring redid New York's sanitation department two years ago. Dead animals, ash, and trash collected on every street except wealthy sections. Pigs were even loosed to tackle the more digestible bits. Now there're street cleaners in white uniforms and laws forcing everyone to separate what they discard."

"Yes sir."

"Most trash is reused now, but when they were dumping in the river and out here, these approaches looked like a debris field. Those men shoveling are called trimmers, same as ours, so that's an old barge. The newer dump scows have hoppers with trapdoors."

Feeling more at ease, Conrad, returned the binoculars, "New York sanitation did come up in medical school because cholera and typhoid seem to thrive in less clean cities. The British have a new vaccine for typhoid and . . ."

Starke looped the binoculars around his neck, looked forward, placed the pipe between his teeth, and said quietly, "A good thing Mr. Conrad. My mother died of it." *Calypso's* surgeon knew their brief interlude had passed.

Alongside Starke, Dunbar, and the watch, Conrad scanned shimmering gray waters with sparkling white borders off port and starboard bows as everyone competed to sight one Sandy Hook lightship or the other. Their track passed closer to the wood-hulled lightship *Scotland*; schooner-rigged with an obsolete spencer mast and no bowsprit. Her white hull was less than 100 feet long with bow and stern rising from midship, name painted in black letters along her sides, and each mast crowned with a large oil lantern and round day-shape. *Sandy Hook* was moored on station just over two years before. Her steel hull was painted red with the station name in large white letters. Owen mentioned the pencil-thin stack between two schooner-rigged masts was from a boiler powering electric beacons, the service's first. Two black boats, ready for lowering, swung from midship davits for errands, rescue, and escape; since lightships moored where storms or collisions were the primary disruptions visited on their tedious routine of watch, maintenance, and idleness.

A lead line being set up on the forecastle next attracted Conrad's interest. Their leadsman in heavy tarpaulin apron anchored his breast band to the starboard fore chains while the lazy leadsman laid out thirty fathoms of line in a series of loops to allow free running. This morning it was a hand lead rather than the heavier coasting or deep sea types, but even this light rig, marked by leather and rag bits, demanded skill and practice. Its ten-pound pyramidal-shaped lead pendant took the line to the seabed where it also obtained bottom samples using a depression armed with tallow in its base. Once entering water where twenty fathoms was likely, the leadsman extended his torso out and away from the fore chains by leaning into the breast band then paid out sufficient line to swing the pendant just above the passing water like a pendulum with each cycle higher than the last. When the line appeared ready to collapse on itself, it was released to curve out and up, plunge into the sea ahead, and peel off line from the deck until up and down. The marked line was then read and reported before tending astern. The morning's first heave resulted in "No bottom" reported to the pilothouse as the line was retrieved and readied for another heave.

The pilot boarded *Calypso* just east of Scotland station after a pair of fast schooners with large numbers on their mainsails dueled for the privilege. There was no second place so once one established a clear lead her opponent sheered off for other inbound customers. Watson explained both would have come alongside in the past, touting their man, but a common pilot boat commissioning that fall would end the practice. Today's winner left a weathered, well-dressed pilot who conned *Calypso* north, keeping Sandy Hook to port until a lighthouse at its northern tip, uncompleted fortifications, and Fort Hancock were almost due east. After pointing out the Gedney Channel sea buoy to starboard, he took *Calypso* towards the passage. They entered using that buoy and *Sandy Hook* for the turn then steered west-northwest and a quarter west between small channel buoys bobbing easily in a seemingly, broad, open bay.

Calypso's large brass helm was expertly handled by a dark, wiry seaman whose eyes kept to the steering compass. Marius Moreau relieved the helm after breakfast when they went to sea and anchor detail south of the Scotland station. His height was average and distinguishing feature a pronounced black mustache. This younger and thinner version of Owen displayed similar optimism and skill; especially as helmsman. He was superb under steam, sail, or both, never chased the compass, maintained every course with frugal helm movement, and held to procedure. Owen made every quartermaster stand a trick at the helm when maneuvering was restricted so he more often assisted with piloting unless the situation was unique or tight.

Moreau regularly reminded shipmates he was from New Foundland, not Canada, using his second language; which was clear but slightly accented English. A French dialect often surfaced when he mumbled or cursed since fishing and smuggling brought his family to the New World from Brittany almost 200 years earlier. Moreau abandoned their tradition of cod-fishing the Grand Banks, chose merchant ships, and was stranded in Norfolk between berths when Watson's recruiting party offered higher pay, better conditions, and opportunity. Weaver lost out to Owen, and Moreau was soon reading manuals and using the library to expand and refine what he learned growing up in a fishing town then at sea. He quickly became expert with charts, compass, protractor, and dividers but proficiency using the wig-wag system to communicate with two flags eluded him. His sending and translating were awkward at best, often causing the exasperated chief to shake his head, grin, and opine, "They're flags not flyswatters, Moreau," which was accepted with good humor after overhearing their senior petty officer being told, "Smithers, drunks spit tobacco with more accuracy than that five-finger fix."

Calypso cut a straight wake up Gedney Channel with more than fifteen feet of water under her keel. Four sets of small buoys, red to right and black to left, marked their passage through broad, open water concealing shoals and deeps where ships grounded without warning. Once through, the bark came right, entered Swash Channel, and went north to the quarantine and boarding station. As Conrad escorted the health officer to sick bay, *Calypso* steadied on northeast and a quarter east to clear a line of black buoys; Swinburne Hospital Island, where diseased immigrants were once detained; Hoffman Island; and finally Craven Shoals. The traffic was exceptionally light due to the Grant's Tomb dedication, but their weather deteriorated as each new fix was called out. *Calypso* came slightly port after Craven Shoals to center her bowsprit on The Narrows's southern mouth with its entrance guarded by Fort Tompkins to port complimented by Fort Lafayette just offshore to starboard, supported by the larger Fort Hamilton on Long Island. *Calypso* held course through The Narrows to enter a deserted Upper Bay naval anchorage off Tompkinsville where she would remain until receiving permission to enter Brooklyn Navy Yard.

Two drenched sailors quickly stowed the lead line after Watson used a speaking trumpet to tell Weaver it was no longer needed as men made for the large black anchor suspended from its davit and ready for dropping. Dunbar picked out prominent landmarks to fix position then offered recommendations as the bronze screw ceased spinning and ship coasted to a stop. Weaver assessed forward movement by small bits of floating debris, waited for the pilothouse order, and then tripped the chain stopper. The marking buoy spun on the surface as its line was unreeled by a stocked anchor plummeting through murky river water, trailing heavy links, battering the chain pipe, creating deafening noise, and raising clouds of red dust. After striking bottom the anchor was dragged downriver, rolling until a fluke buried and brake briefly applied then released set it in the mud. The brake was set again when enough scope was out, causing the chain to straightened and anchor plow deeper still. Starke gave permission to set the watch, stow gear, and clean ship once they settled and anchor bearings taken.

The North Atlantic Squadron, under Commodore Bunce, had left for the ceremony and moored upstream off Riverside Park with foreign warships, revenue cutters, lighthouse tenders, and merchant ships. The dedication not only involved thousands of participants and spectators but closed the navy yard until the next day so it was decided Osbourne and Wiggs would take the steam pinnace over in the morning to report their arrival, arrange for repairs, requisition stores, and prepare to coal pierside rather than in the stream from a barge.

That evening, a procession of warships, most white-hulled, came downriver past Staten Island to anchor near *Calypso* or continue south through The Narrows into the Atlantic. The foreigners came first, led by HMS *Talbot*, a new British cruiser built for the North America and West Indies Station. Well-handled and close astern of the twin-stacked, steel cruiser was Spain's armored cruiser *Maria Teresa* and her barkentine consort, *Infanta Isabel*. The Italian cruiser *Dogali* that Starke recognized from Rio de Janeiro and the Brazilian Naval Revolt came next. The North Atlantic Squadron was close astern of the last foreign warship, a French cruiser. *New York* led, with three tall stacks, two masts, and six 8-inch guns. Large, fast, and powerful, this armored cruiser was a favorite of admirals and sailors due to her appearance, generous space, and easy ride. Behind came the battleships *Maine*, *Indiana*, and *Texas*; followed by two cruisers, *Raleigh* and *Columbia*, then monitors *Amphitrite* and *Terror*. Flirting about like a sheepdog was the bottle-green torpedo boat *Porter*. The dispatch cruiser *Dolphin* remained upriver flying the president's flag since she, like *Calypso*, was assigned to the Special Service Squadron. A lighthouse tender and revenue cutters trailed the squadron, including First Lieutenant Boyd Hunter's *Vanguard* then, in no discernable formation, the tugs, yachts, press boats, and police launches.

Commodore Bunce, a rear admiral while commanding the squadron, was senior officer present so Starke anticipated *New York*'s flag-hoist summoning him. As the reply broke from *Calypso*'s signal halyard, her steam pinnace, serving as captain's gig, left with Coxswain Melvin at the helm and cadet Timme the boat officer. Melvin laid his pinnace smoothly alongside the armored cruiser's lower accommodation ladder platform after a rough crossing. Starke boarded in a single, smooth motion, keeping extremities clear, climbed to the top, saluted the flag, and was piped aboard.

A white-haired captain with matching mustache, French Ensor Chadwick, stretched his hand across spotless deck planks to greet him. He had just taken command and Starke knew him from the Building when the captain was Bureau of Equipment chief during *Calypso*'s fitting out; and long before from the Alexandria bombardment where he was an observer with the Royal Navy. Chadwick commanded the steel gunboat *Yorktown*, possessed strong academic inclinations, often published articles, was considered a naval reformer, had been one of the first naval attachés, and served as chief intelligence officer. They went immediately to the flag quarters where Rear Admiral Bunce greeted Starke and revealed he and Rear Admiral Montgomery Sicard would relieve each other within hours since Sicard commanded Bunce's next duty station, the New York Naval Station that included the Brooklyn Navy Yard on East River.

The topic, as with all flag officers, was what had the admiral's attention; and today it was Bunce's final squadron mission. The Grant's Tomb dedication included over 50,000 people from every imaginable organization and what seemed a million observers. Included were warships anchored in two columns on the river that sent contingents despite an ebb tide and westerly winds that made landing sailors and marines difficult. The naval review consisted of *Dolphin*, led by *Porter* and flying the president's flag, passing between full-dressed ships rendering honors. There were also more than a hundred civilian ships, yachts, and spectator boats. Many dipped colors when passing warships so additional sailors were stationed to acknowledge these constant salutes. The next topics were the two filibuster tugs' demise, Starke's recent Havana visit, and finally Captain Albert serving as the president's ersatz naval aide for the ceremony. Their tight schedule ended the session with Bunce offering assistance once he reached the new command and Chadwick returning Starke to the accommodation ladder. Coxswain Melvin was lying to some yards off to avoid chaffing his pinnace but close enough to hear the accommodation ladder lower platform's steel frame maintain a sucking sound as it pumped through choppy water. He was quickly alongside, Starke boarded, and the gig plowed back through agitated gray water to *Calypso*.

Captain Albert passed *Maine* on his way to *Calypso* the next morning, accompanied by First Lieutenant Hunter of the Revenue Cutter Service. Starke was waiting at the bulwark gangway then took them to his day cabin where Yamashita set up coffee before returning to the pantry. Hunter, traveling closer inshore and ahead of *Calypso*, found *Vanguard* drafted into the Riverside Park ceremony and sent to moor up the Hudson River with other ships. Albert was more involved with the parade, dignitaries, and protocol but both echoed the pilot's description of overfull social clubs and hotels. Albert also described organized chaos at the diminutive 129th street pier assigned to the warships' boats. Grinning, as he probed his pipe, Albert claimed the only humor since arriving had been the presidential entourage's passage to *Dolphin* taking place in the lighthouse tender launch *Daisy*. With the naval review complete, McKinley departed for Washington and he was released from unsought liaison duties accomplished with no more minor catastrophes than expected. *Amphitrite* was dealing with a sailor whose arraignment became local news, but her captain now owned it. *Calypso*'s Nassau incident was too recent for Starke to see the same humor so Albert sensed something and lowered his pipe, "How long before you're back at sea, Captain?"

Starke considered work requested, estimated completion times, and added margin to cajole shipyard hierarchy. Reprovisioning, a full day coaling, and another half day clean up would also be needed. He responded, "No less than a week and a half, but two's more likely. That assumes no docking or major work beyond water tubes and two gate valves. The valves might require overhauling if replacements aren't here and Osbourne expects to find more water tube issues once the boiler's open since they seem to erode faster than advertised. At least two weeks after work starts, Captain."

"That's probably optimistic. Water tubes are a challenge but worth it. Besides, the crew's missed several holidays and due for a long run ashore. *Vanguard* can take the offshore patrol for now and Pinkerton operatives are hearing rumors more than one black bark is at sea; thanks to your false name boards."

Hunter smiled, "*Calypso*'s making Junta expeditions more costly. They also confuse our ships so often that what *Vanguard* does is often blamed on *Calypso*."

Albert looked at Starke, "You're under the Junta's nose here so let's convince them this work and provisioning's to join the European Squadron. It might distract certain parties back in Washington and prevent any local attempt to cripple the ship. *Rafael Riego* proved Junta anarchists are not benign."

Starke stoked his sparse beard, "We've taken steps, Captain. Topside watches will be doubled when pierside to deal with that and the East River pirates but I'll request shipyard marines add an additional watch on the coal barge and watch for coal torpedoes."

Albert fiddled with a pencil that once lay undisturbed near his open notebook then added, "Wyler's reconcentration is hurting insurrectos' indigenous support so Junta filibuster expeditions have become more important. He's also pushing hard before the rainy season ends campaigning; but the insurrectos are convinced independence is near and gaining public support here from reconcentrado stories and concern the diseases will come north.

Starke understood but another ship covering for *Calypso* did not sit well, even if it was *Vanguard* and Hunter amenable. Albert picked up on this, adding, "Admiral Sicard will want the squadron to exercise together this year, so the Apprentice Training Squadron will carry out most Caribbean courtesy visits. *Essex* is on for Barbados, La Guaira, and Kingston. I'm considering offering *Calypso* for Puerto Rico, Port au Prince, or Veracruz before you're dragooned; but send your thoughts."

Albert saw no reason to further discomfort Starke by mentioning he nearly became the new assistant secretary's aide. Commander Goodrich, the European Squadron's chief of staff at Alexandria and current Naval War College president, recommended Starke to Crowninshield and Roosevelt. Albert disagreed, certain Starke would resign rather than accept, but Roosevelt wanted Admiral Brown's flag aide, Lieutenant Alexander Sharp, and was willing to wait until the admiral retired in June. Albert judged Sharp, or Sandy to his intimates, the more qualified but believed the overriding factor was the pair meeting during inauguration ceremonies and finding themselves simpatico.

Starke wanted time alone with both captains but the ad hoc planning session finished just before noon. A friendship developed with Hunter during the *Rafael Riego* pursuit, making him a welcome partner for taking in the city with Tyson still in Greece; and Albert alluded to a congressional committee summons before leaving, which required detailed preparation and a strategy session before testifying

He also left a thin bundle of letters. Most were from Katherine, now at Curtis estate near Bridport, England, but one came from Aunt Constance who apparently got on well with Albert's wife Abigail. Thinking his aunt must be intrigued by letters from the widow she subtly put forward as a match, Starke sat at the table that evening, wishing for a snifter of whiskey, to sort and combine these with those already received. The chain ran from late December into March with Katherine's distinct feminine hand bordering on art; but having different shades of ink within the bodies meant each was written over several days. He charged a pipe and began with the December letter. There were numerous thoughts and observations but mention of social functions had nearly vanished and she was now living in a Brydian Grange cottage that sounded more like a modest house. Earlier letters spoke to a slight, lingering, stomach complaint that seemed to have passed while some possessed a sharper edge than those written before Havana. One seemed unusually emotional, without explanation, and the rest inconsistent in this aspect; and she asked how he dealt with nightmares like the one she witnessed in Havana. Starke slid the bundle into a drawer when Osbourne entered to discuss their shift to the navy yard.

Due to the dedication and Saturday's change of command, *Calypso* was told to arrive in the Brooklyn Navy Yard on Friday. Starke woke from a deep, dreamless sleep that day to a cool cabin with windows open to night breezes and muted rattle of a sailing ship at anchor. Closed rooms were healthier but he slept best in the sea air beyond shore-based pests' operating range. Although not at sea, the crisp, clear morning brought a sense of renewal and good spirits; easing his burden and evoking a fondness for ship, crew, and situation.

After a pilot familiar with transitions to the yard boarded, permission was requested from *New York* to proceed. *Calypso* acknowledged and replied to the flag hoist on the cruiser's yardarm before the black-hulled bark with straw-yellow masts got underway with water frothing below her counter before threading east though the squadron then Upper Bay. With the pilot conning and Dunbar calling out position, *Calypso* gained speed, turned north, and steamed into the flat expanse. She soon passed Bedloe's Island, with its Statue of Liberty, and Governors Island before coming slightly east to leave the Ellis Island Immigration Station's wooden buildings and pier to port.

Before reaching the Hudson River's piers, wharfs, and docks, *Calypso* turned starboard smartly, south of Castle Gardens, into the East River and its powerful current. More turns were put on as Starke closely observed the downriver traffic of ships, barges, ferries, and boats; anticipating some would maneuver with a logic clear only to their masters. As the bark pushed upriver, two towering, neo-gothic granite towers of what locals called the Brooklyn Bridge grew larger until its suspended deck passed slowly overhead; much to the relief of sailors in the tops. The unexperienced feared they would be swept to the water below or crushed when topmasts struck, but instead had a spectacular view of the bridge and its orderly arrangement of horse-drawn vehicles under the pedestrian and bicycle walkway, crossing alongside railroad and streetcar tracks. Once clear, they had a birds-eye view of the shipyard off the starboard bow.

The bark lined up its approach, with just enough way to counter current and ease forward, as the yard tugs *Nina* and *Narkeeta*, sporadically belching black smoke, eased *Calypso* against battered crush poles protecting the quay that fronted a road running along piers and wharfs. Heaving then mooring lines went over; to be replaced by chains in a day or two. Once *Calypso* settled, her polished brass EOT with its round, white face and black commands signaled the pilothouse was finished with the engine and their black gang begin shutting down boilers, drawing fires, and cooling the plant. A heavy brow came across with requisite cursing as the watch shifted to the quarterdeck.

CHAPTER ELEVEN
NEW YORK CITY

*C*alypso's officers and men worked maintenance or small repairs while shipyard trades saw to major or specialized ones such as replacing water tubes. Osbourne and O'Leary pushed to keep the ship spotless and maintain pace, believing civilians worked best on clean ships and lost schedule was never regained. Starke wanted their water tube issues resolved since boiler explosions cost lives and ships; but also leave on time. Besides resuming their mission, he knew morale, energy, and proficiency would erode if overlong in the yard; especially with New York City's opportunities, diversions, and perils just over the river. It was one of several reasons ships were decommissioned for major work.

Meanwhile, surgeon Conrad was at Navy medicine's nexus because the walled compound adjoining the yard contained a hospital, laboratory, and medical board; with large city facilities and United States Marine Hospital on Staten Island just across the river. His first courtesy call was on *Vermont*, an old ship-of-the-line outfitted as a receiving ship. Her surgeon, Howard Wells, received him warmly and offered an introduction to the Naval Hospital's director so they walked across the shipyard through an impressive gatehouse into the medical compound.

The three-story naval hospital began as a rectangular building with its roof pierced by tall, brick chimneys and faced by gray granite from local quarries. Two rear wings in the same Greek revival style came later. Its main entrance was a recessed portico with wooden doors under glass transoms leading to an off-white world of long corridors, high-ceilings, white piping, and varnished wood bannisters under glass skylights. Some consulting rooms even contained off-white brick fireplaces; albeit far more utilitarian than the large ornate version found in the medical director's office.

Thomas Penrose, medical director by rank and commodore by courtesy, raised his bulk from behind the desk in greeting. His mustache and goatee contrasted with a balding head that matched the build, and what hair populated its curving surface was clipped short. Conrad learned Penrose would retire in June after serving since the war, and his relationships with the laboratory and Marine Rendezvous, but the twenty minutes was primarily devoted to probing *Calypso*'s medical state and Conrad's informal study of Caribbean afflictions. Before passing him to Surgeon Phillip Leach for a short tour of wards, consulting rooms, and operating theater; Conrad was invited to an evening social at the director's quarters. After the tour, Conrad found Wells' business complete so he left his card then walked back with the receiving ship's surgeon.

The director's quarters lay inside the compound and overlooked the East River. Walking towards the two-story stone house with mansard roof pierced by several attic dormers, Conrad noticed a large stable to one side. Granite steps rose to a double door and its smallish front porch was flanked by two pairs of tall, rectangular windows under dark, protruding lintels. Five duplicates were equally spaced across the second floor while the eastern wing contained a three-sided bay window-alcove that matched another in the west wing servants' quarters. Maggie Penrose greeted him at the door with an Irish maid who took him down a short hallway's lacquered floors then left into the parlor. On one side, an oriental carpet runner snaked up wood stairs climbing the side wall beyond polished bannisters curving from sight near the top. Wallpaper was hung throughout, except where a varnished chair rail cap crowned matching veneer panels. The parlor's off-white, high ceiling with crystal electroliers hanging from ornate medallions rounded to the wall in a graceful curve. Deep casings of its two draped windows concealed louvered privacy shutters while allowing enough light to create a pleasant room.

The occupants' uniforms alerted Conrad he was the most junior guest and should join their conversation cautiously. It was also clear this insular group gathered regularly so he answered questions about practicing at sea, tropical diseases, and shipboard accidents until conversation reverted to well-honed, unilateral debates over the necessity for line officer grade equivalency and a medical corps. Conrad felt his medical degree and assistant surgeon designation sufficient, but was more receptive to better organization after slogging through the *Instructions for Medical Officers of the United States Navy*'s pages of text, forms, and charts preparing for the Navy board. Their practiced agenda then shifted to establishing Navy training hospitals or infiltrating those in the city. Conrad could not speak to the first but thought the second delusional since medical school graduates fought for city hospital spots and Harvard Medical School controlled New York City's.

The evening left Conrad with mixed feelings. His seniors were impressive but the climb to medical director seemed uncertain and opportunities fewer as he advanced. To rise from assistant surgeon required promotion through passed assistant surgeon, surgeon, and medical inspector before reaching medical director; above which was only the Navy's surgeon general. That meant spending years at sea or foreign service when he could easily return to some Michigan town, associate with a local hospital, perhaps add a railroad surgeon contract, and quickly reach Penrose's situation with fewer tribulations. It would have been an easy decision except the short *Calypso* tenure already provided more adventure than his previous life and the travel amplified this narcotic effect.

Work limited the excursions Starke, Watson, Osbourne, O'Leary, and Wiggs made to the city, but some refrained by choice. Kearney knew its temptations and pitfalls, especially around his family. Yamashita's liberty hinged on his captain's needs but he politely declined several offers Starke made until Watson recommended shifting the onus to his steward after Weaver overheard an Italian sailor returning from Little Italy suggest Yamashita visit Chinatown. The habitually taciturn steward loosed a singularly colorful barrage of mixed English and Japanese emphasizing he was not Chinese and had no wish to go ashore.

Starke was at his desk when a most unexpected visitor was announced. He anticipated a politician or police official bearing the inevitable complaint whenever fire hoses were turned on constituents from one of the East River pirate clans out for an innocent cruise. Pirates were still active across the globe, but this variety favored the river with its easy access to stationary shipping. Yard marines had orders to shoot if a warning failed to halt thieves on federal property so incursions usually came from the river; and a punt of brigands recently made a run at the steam pinnace moored alongside while its crew was at dinner. The raiders were hosed down with odious East River water and nearly capsized so he braced for a local ward healer's half-hour harangue. Instead, *The Times* reporter, Miss Cassandra Evans was ushered in.

He last saw her in Key West, en route to Havana and some undetermined affliction. Starke rose then invited her to sit as Yamashita brought coffee and small cakes. Her noticeably more worn Brussels carpet bag was placed on the floor while performing the necessary contortions to gracefully sit while constrained by a light corset and modest bustle. Then, displaying unusual familiarity, she reached up and unpinned the boater that topped a well-tailored traveling dress consisting of a fine blue-black wool jacket with leg-of-mutton sleeves and matching full-length, flared skirt. It lifted slightly as she sat to reveal tight-laced, high-topped black leather shoes with lightly stained soles from the yard. A black-cotton belt cinched her waist to form a wasp-like figure and conceal where a lace-trimmed white blouse slid below the skirt. Her throat was obscured by a frilled collar and encircling long, black necktie that fell down, out, and over the blouse's bone buttons.

The smooth auburn hair, tight pompadour, distinctive eyes, and deportment he first noticed months earlier on a Washington streetcar remained unchanged. Flawless eyebrows revealed she still surreptitiously applied eye makeup, but a noticeable alteration occurred since their Key West dinner with Tyson. Layered clothing and gloves could not conceal the leaner figure and pale complexion his aunt mentioned in a letter; with the once unmarked countenance now including light lines in strategic places as she spoke or smiled, and a slight scent replacing more proper lemon juice. He was considering how affliction and recovery sculpted character and maturity into this attractive woman surveying his cabin with the professional scrutiny he recalled from Washington and Key West, when she conjured an intriguing smile, "It's been awhile Jacob, or should I say Captain?"

"It has Miss Evans. What brings you to New York?"

"The dedication; but I'm also visiting friends who took me in after Havana and approaching *The Sun* about a position."

Starke saw long, smooth fingers worry the coffee cup handle in the same manner she caressed a wine glass stem in Key West as her eyes settled on pipes reclining in their desk rack, "Please smoke if you've a mind. The smell of a good pipe is quite pleasant."

"Later perhaps."

She smiled, "My assignment's complete and I'm not after a story. Have you heard from Mr. Tyson? They wouldn't say much at the paper."

Starke was curious since few besides Aunt Constance were interested in his thin, balding friend with silver flask and gold-trimmed, jade cigarette case, "Two letters arrived from Greece. Crete was blockaded so he went to Athens then left for Volo in Thessaly."

"So he's well?"

Starke stifled a remark that Tyson's alcohol intake cleansed any wound and drove away all disease when he detected something in her eyes, "I've heard nothing to the contrary. You've recovered?"

"Due to your family's agent and Darwin; he managed everything and even sent my work to the Washington paper."

Starke sensed more than gratitude and suspected they were together long enough for her to see through Tyson's pretense. Starke was considering this when her eyes lifted in a momentary flash of defiance or resolve, "I'm bored with evenings alone or at home with friends and even resorted to Delmonico's room for unescorted women."

It was a bold invitation and Watson mentioned remaining on board to complete a report so Starke persuaded himself to act after several pregnant seconds. Evans waited uneasily with eyes demanding a response until Starke ventured, "If you're available, perhaps we might attend Herald Square Theater tomorrow, *The Girl from Paris* is playing, then breach Delmonico's front door."

The humor fell flat but she accepted, prepared to depart, and allowed him to escort her through the yard to the main gate. Evans hailed a hansom cab for her friends' home and, as the bay moved out at a brisk pace, reflected on her impulse to visit Starke after learning *Calypso* was at the shipyard. There was no justification, although she admired his aunt, who once arranged for him to escort her to a Starke mansion dinner party. He was financially well-off and promised to become wealthy, only fools ignored that, but married women who stayed with the profession wrote from home, their topics were constrained, and they did not run with the pack. She, and probably others, found him attractive but not handsome; yet there was something in eyes and manner she could feel more than define. His almost too proper courtesy and civility appeared to mask emotional depth and menace that created an unsettling air of mystery. She also sensed he might be moved, but not manipulated, and capable of whatever violence the situation required. Settling in the seat, she admitted feeling uncomfortable but secure around him. She had no idea what brought her to *Calypso* then brazenly solicit an invitation.

Starke enjoyed having Evans on his arm at the theater then Delmonico's. While seated at a small white-clothed table overlooking street and passing traffic he noticed her scent was a touch stronger than when she moved about his cabin. The eventful year added fluidity and poise, polished her hard edges, and added a patina endowing her with an undefined, but potent, physical and emotional allure. Evans' thoughts, positions, and passions also seemed to be created then held with greater confidence and less demand for others to embrace them. After studying this singularly impressive creature throughout the evening and now across the table, he realized, as she touched a cloth napkin gently to her lips, that Evans assimilated Tyson's better qualities. How and to what extent remained a mystery, but he suspected her visiting reconcentrados, recent affliction, and strangers' kindness tempered a natural confidence. However, while returning the reporter to her lodgings, he abandoned plans for another sortie, this time for dancing, after she mentioned leaving for Washington the next day. His return to the ship was under a canopy of stars spread across the night's clear sky; weighing their New York evening against the shared passion Katherine generated in Havana. Evans' emotions appeared less volatile than the widow's explosive display in Havana but promised equal intensity. He could only describe it like black and smokeless gunpowder; one exploded and the other burned powerfully.

The wine's effects faded with the stars and the next morning found Starke inundated with monthly reports and correspondence. Watson briefly interrupted just before midday to report Conrad was examining three men reporting from the receiving ship. Desertion, disease, and injury losses had been unusually low but seasickness and drowning took two from an already limited crew so *Vermont*'s executive officer, Lieutenant Commander Nazro, allowed them to sift through candidates. Watson and Weaver returned with an Italian sailor, complete with violin; a German wearing the figure eight apprenticeship insignia; and a landsman claiming to be Wampanoag.

Calypso maintained Starke's projected completion date by postponing several nonessential tasks to focus on replacing suspect water tubes after discovering a half-dozen more than estimated; even as Osbourne and O'Leary struggled against yard inertia worsened by post-election personnel shifts and change of command. A newly completed dry-dock also took priority since it was not only unusable but the Navy's solitary East Coast dock capable of taking the new battleships. Despite these and other perturbations a coal barge was alongside early in May's third week and they coaled on the eighteenth.

A hand-delivered dispatch from Albert also arrived. *Vanguard* would continue coastal patrols while *Calypso* was to steam east, or nearly so, swing south past Bermuda to the Mona Passage between Puerto Rico and Santo Domingo, and then make for Jamaica's Port Antonio. Heading due east would place *Calypso* on a route sailing ships favored so Junta observers would see she was not going south to meet *Vanguard* and could be bound for Gibraltar, Africa, or around either cape. Starke was to salt the waterfront with rumors to encourage this but *Calypso* would swing around Bermuda to the southwest then approach popular filibuster routes from an unanticipated quarter. Unexpectedly appearing off the Jamaican port would disrupt Junta expeditions, especially those preparing for sea, since she could leave there and steam north along either Cuban coast to Florida, return to the Gulf of Mexico, or join the training ship *Essex* in making port calls. He proposed Martinique but Albert wanted him cruising north along the Cuban coast.

Starke inquired about Delmonico's private dining rooms while there with Evans and decided to host the wardroom. They invited him several times, and two or three officers at a time would join him for supper, but more was needed. The restaurant's intimacy and privacy would be costly in a city whose residents found cabs too expensive but he enjoyed a private income and had yet to hold any social functions since taking command. Dinner parties were traditionally held in private homes, like his aunt's a year before. For that, his options were the West Point plantation house or Starke mansion in Washington, but distance and *Calypso's* gypsy-like existence meant neither was suitable. Other venues were limited. Boarding houses, hotels, and gentlemen's clubs furnished evening meals while social clubs, hotel dining rooms, and drinking establishments provided a midday fare so restaurants were unusual in most cities; but dining out was growing fashionable in New York for those who could afford Delmonico's or an imitator.

He approached Commodore Bunce and the North Atlantic Squadron commander, Rear Admiral Sicard, for permission to leave *Calypso* with an experienced senior staff officer for the evening. The proposed event would be less formal than a dining-out with its uniforms and protocols. He participated in those over the years and, where different ships attended, friction and camaraderie were often about equal. This caused enough angst during the century's first years that the Navy forbade dueling, but participants were still offended and often extracted less sanguinary satisfaction. Civilian attire would not only promote a more congenial atmosphere, but ensure officers owned presentable ensembles so future events would not force the wardroom to combine resources in order field one or two suitably dressed. This sent more than one to a tailor; another New York advantage.

A private room at Delmonico's on South William Street was reserved. The building vaguely resembled a pillared ship's prow and was nicknamed The Citadel. Completed six years earlier after fire wrecked its predecessor, the first and second floors contained the restaurant wine storage, dining sections, two private rooms, and unaccompanied ladies' area. The five levels above were leased offices and top floor occupied by kitchens. Laid out as a right-trapezoid constrained to its lot, the short side faced Williams Street and longer one, Beaver Street. Its main entrance was the rounded corner at their convergence with several floors above having false balconies and tall pillars. The first two stories were dark stone and the remainder a brownish-red brick. The Williams Street face incorporated a huge archway with stairs and side entrance while tall rectangular windows under large, jutting shades overlooked Beaver Street. Small basement apertures rose inches above a sidewalk with grated building vents opening to red-brick streets bounded by cement curbs below two gaslights near the convergence, with a fire hydrant on Williams.

A lieutenant commander from Sicard's staff met Weaver, Owen, and their other chiefs then assumed the watch. Starke's party crossed Brooklyn's bridge in carriages and was soon entering Delmonico's between the pillars flanking its main doorway. Following a uniformed host to their second floor room required snaking through a public area with deep-dished white ceilings lit by ornate electroliers over lines of rectangular, square, and round tables draped with white linen and set with polished silverware. The walls were papered in rich, intricate patterns or clad with dark wood panels; except for tall and deep windows trimmed with long drapes that overlooked Beaver Street. The floors were carpet, tile, or varnished wood and the private room's entrance was off an open staircase with its intricate cast iron baluster capped by varnished wood handrails. A sliding door opened to high-ceilings, faux baroque wallpaper, electrolier wall sconces, short-pile carpet, and pair of draped windows overlooking Beaver Street. Its center was occupied by a large rectangular table under a white tablecloth, silver service, and two small glass lamps. The surrounding dark-wood chairs were plain, nicely varnished, and had padded seats for comfort.

Thirteen were attending but deference to superstition required fourteen place-settings so one end chair would be unoccupied. That position was traditionally taken by the most junior while Starke sat at the table's head and others assigned by seniority. Different officer types with their equivalent ranks made determining seniority a thorny issue but civilian attire helped, as did a department growing less inflexible about assigning everything, including staterooms, by rank; driven by numerous cases requiring the secretary of the navy to resolve what most often was the Marine and chaplain contesting who bunked with warrant officers. For this evening, Watson seated himself, Passed Assistant Engineer O'Leary, Ensign Martyn, Ensign Blair, Naval Cadet (engineer) James Thomas, and Naval Cadet Timme to Starke's right; with Passed Assistant Engineer Osbourne, Passed Assistant Paymaster Wiggs, Ensign Dunbar, Assistant Surgeon Conrad, Naval Cadet (engineer) Harold Duke, and Naval Cadet Caldwell to his captain's left.

The evening began with guests standing behind chairs waiting for Starke's, "Gentlemen, please be seated," then one attendant in long, white apron served water and an oyster tray while another offered the French menus common in quality restaurants. A garden consommé was followed by a lobster timbale hors d'oeuvre that preceded their fish, beef, or chicken main course. Most, including Starke, selected the restaurant's trademark steak, but Conrad and Wiggs chose a salmon and potato entrée. Sherbet followed then cold meat with the final course being a fruit and cream meringue dessert. After dinner coffee came once the table was cleared.

Starke managed reasonably well, having experienced many such affairs. Hosting them required a quick eye, agility, and concentration because success depended on encouraging dialogue while restraining those inclined to dominate, direct, or diminish conversation. When someone, usually a junior, appeared neglected, he would elicit their thoughts on the current topic or raise one they were familiar with. For Conrad it was medical school, mystery novels, and photography. The four cadets contributed their Academy years and midshipman cruises. Osbourne fielded questions about West Coast squadrons and ports. Wiggs was unique in being a superb paymaster and effective orator, but bore watching since his interests were almost exclusively regulations and theology. Watson avoided discussing *Winston A. Capps* and her demise, but proved effusive describing his family's ranch above Gunnison, cattle, and range anecdotes.

Many restaurants forbid smoking so Starke's pipe remained pocketed, but cognac and wine more than compensated. After dispatching a respectable amount, the evening ended when Watson, seeing their captain nod, proposed a closing toast. Starke was also pleased to see their moderately tipsy cadets corralled before leaving, placed under Paymaster Wiggs' control, and sent back to *Calypso*. While it might be thought draconian to exclude them from the vibrant city's attractions, naval cadets competed for line commissions after graduation, and their steam engineering brethren were just starting out, so this avoided a drink-inspired event ending years of work. Even so, Starke also acknowledged their boyhood was over and by their age he already fought in a major battle and faced down foreign rioters.

Starke and Watson shared a cab for the trip back over the river while Osbourne, Dunbar, O'Leary, Blair, Martyn, and Conrad remained in the city. Starke suspected their objective was the Haymarket, a large tenderloin dancehall where social elite and general population intermingled. Single women were not charged so the respectable seeking an adventurous evening or dancing, along with a reliable ladies-of-the-evening cadre, were in good supply. Starke watched their officers board a streetcar that squealed to a halt on rails embedded in the red-brick street then reclined in the cab's velour seat, extracted a pipe, and relived dancing with Katherine at the Hygeia, their exchange on its pier, and that confused night at Hotel Inglaterra.

It was delightful rolling through city streets with windows down so he finally risked a matchbook to light his pipe and safely completed the task without igniting every match by striking one; a common occurrence. With the first draw he concluded this had been an agreeable New York visit. Besides Herald Square Theater and Delmonico's with Evans, there was an evening at Hoyt's Theatre, attending *The Man from Mexico* with a classmate stationed on *Vermont*. He also resolved to include everything in the next letter to Katherine despite her dislike of the city; including the evening with Evans since the women were formally introduced at his aunt's dinner party. Satiated, relaxed, and more at ease than any commander had a right, they passed through Irish Town. As Watson nodded off, Starke wondered if Osbourne would recount the Haymarket evening in his next letter to Albert's daughter, Isabella.

They soon reached the yard's wrought-iron gates that swung inward from gray stone gateposts below the red-brick Sand Street gatehouse's crenellated towers. Marine sentries briefly detained them under a single, tall streetlight before they passed through a silent industrial area to the waterfront. Fleeting ghostlike shapes prowled between buildings, equipment, and material. A foreman overseeing water tube repair explained to Osbourne these were feral cats; protected now but nearly trapped to extermination in years past. This resulted in a burgeoning mouse and rat population that destroyed canvas, line, packaging, and other stock so cats were now enticed by milk and other inducements to establish territory in departments competing for their favor. Visiting ships like *Maine* often made off with cats or kittens as the population multiplied; or their feline mascots jumped ship for a new life ashore. Consequently, Thaddeus was confined in ignorance below deck enjoying more food than was good for him.

The lieutenant commander, Weaver, and master-at-arms met Starke at the quarterdeck where Watson relieved what proved a quiet watch. Starke had concerns about fire or flooding, especially in a shipyard. An East River pirate raid was also possible because sentries were forbidden to pursue thieves beyond the fence line where local politicians were infinitely more concerned with votes than stealing from the Navy, and Weaver already lost two blocks left to dry after oiling. A hundred things could have made the arrangement seem ill-judged but none occurred so *Calypso's* commander slid gratefully into his wooden berth enclosed by rectangular drawers and storage compartment doors. Across the cabin, his father's sword rested on wall pegs and the night breeze passing through created a blended scent of river and industry. He fell asleep immediately and slept undisturbed until morning.

CHAPTER TWELVE
CARIBBEAN RETURN

Osbourne and the black gang worked through the night bringing boilers on line so the ship was ready to get underway before Yamashita brought Starke a Friday morning breakfast of coffee, bacon, eggs, and toast. Intermittent rain and a southwesterly wind belied *The Sun* prediction of clear weather. That paper eschewed bylines, but Starke suspected Tyson wrote its article reporting an armistice between the Ottoman Empire and retreating Greeks that was forced on the combatants to prevent a general European war. He also wondered if his friend would stay for negotiations. Another reported a belligerency bill about to pass the Senate that the president was unlikely to sign; but *Calypso* would be blindsided if he did while she was at sea.

His immediate concern when *Calypso* left the Brooklyn yard was a current created by the confluence of East River and the Hudson. Even a standing tide would see the bark faster downriver with less control than during their arrival; and facing heavier traffic. Leaving New York City was never comfortable regardless of the pilot's skills, so Starke and Watson concealed their anxiety. Today's conned the ship downriver, across upper bay, and through The Narrows; then took the East Channel, passing south of Coney Island light towards the open Atlantic. Their egress was completed with no more than normal drama: crossed signals with an approaching tug, yachts coming too close, and four inbound liners. A small freighter followed almost to Gedney Channel before turning southeast for a coastal port or the Caribbean. The pilot was dropped in the eastern approaches where his schooner loitered. While they slowed for the transfer, Starke caught a whiff of greasy smoke; an unusual occurrence since their galley exhausted high up the stack rather than through a lower Charlie Noble.

Weaver and his mast captains dropped sails and shifted yards in a southwest wind with drizzle punctuated by brief showers. When it veered west, yards were trimmed and sails sheeted home. As the bark steadied and speed increased, Starke considered seeing what she could do under steam and sail with a soldier's wind but kept to plan so *Calypso* slowed as one main boiler came off line. When her second followed, the deck ceased vibrating as *Calypso* slipped forward under sail, using her donkey boilers for distillers, winches, and dynamos. Running before the wind with square sails thrust forward, a ship-rigged merchantman confirmed they were on the sail route into the open Atlantic towards a junction where ships swung south for Cape Horn, turned northeast for Britain, or chose another route set by prevailing winds. Starke wished for a longer voyage; one where the ship became its own world for weeks or months and making a good passage his solitary concern.

Starke and Watson remained until steering shifted aft where there was a better feel for the ship under canvas alone. Ensign Blair desired their departure sooner but accepted what was and placed his binoculars on their ship-rigged companion ahead, trying pick a name off her transom for the log. He also eyed what seemed a Grand Banks fishing schooner that closed then ran parallel and astern. Although well-handled and staying clear, it was sailing wing-on-wing and clearly struggling with the wind nearly dead astern of the square-rigged bark having a much easier time of it. Excepting the unusual effort to pace *Calypso*, Starke saw nothing suspicious through binoculars; then she came about smartly to begin a series of long leisurely tacks into the wind for New York. Ensign Blair noted her departure in the deck log.

The route was a primary sailing passage to Europe and the Mediterranean but intersected another major southeast route for ships bound for Africa and the Far East. Depending on season, prevailing wind, and currents it swung several hundred miles east of steamship routes converging on Bermuda for coal or fixing position. Sea lanes met, crossed, or split into tributaries across the globe with some flowing in one direction and others both, having evolved from centuries of experience and improving knowledge of geography, ocean currents, and prevailing winds. Most favored steam or sail, but some served both and they were as familiar to mariners as turnpikes, roads, and paths to teamsters; with intersections, choke points, and destinations well-known to warships and others. Dunbar's track took *Calypso* well into the Atlantic before curving southeast, passing 360 miles northeast of Bermuda before settling on a nearly due south heading. Remaining under canvas, they would intersect a secondary branch of the Southern Route, an all-season sail passage that looped southwest from the English Channel to the Western Hemisphere where it split on the Americas' side. After that, a northern leg swung northwest for United States' ports, but *Calypso* would continue south then west into the Caribbean.

The bark showed an excellent turn of speed with yards and sails requiring only occasional trimming. One was lowered briefly for repair, but otherwise it was an easy transit. With little chance of meeting ships, and crossing traffic mostly found on the New York to Bermuda leg, Starke slept strong, well, and deep while being gently caressed by a breeze passing through open cabin windows; except some dirty weather that briefly pummeled the ship then passed within hours. A slow, steady shift in wind direction was anticipated as they approached the Southern Route fork; nine days and just under 2,000 miles out of New York. Starke's sailing report showed *Calypso* making eleven knots good and proving her compromise design was swift under canvas, regardless of the south and west legs' favorable ocean currents. Unfortunately, it also meant Junta filibusters and choosing the best passage through islands and reefs forming the Caribbean's eastern boundary now required attention. Albert suggested using Mona Passage to reach Port Antonio; taking them north of Puerto Rico before heading south. They could also cut through archipelagos and reefs west of Puerto Rico using the narrower Virgin Passage or nearby Anegada Passage then follow the large island's southern coasts and Santo Domingo's.

While working a report at half-past nine one morning, he heard the drill call that followed quarters, decided against Mona Passage, donned the blue uniform cap, and went on deck. The rhythmic clicking of singlestick practice beyond open windows had disturbed the rigging's rustle and sails' occasional slapping as their warm breeze from astern wavered slightly or paused. The armory's singlesticks consisted of a round, yard-long blade of ash, oak, or hickory with its lathed grip shielded by a leather basket hilt secured to the base with a large screw. They were once issued for cutlass training, and *Calypso* carried those as well, but now used primarily for exercise. The crew preferred singlestick over monkey drills, but their enthusiasm required discipline since a solid strike could break bones, incapacitate, or kill. Sailors would form two facing rows with right foot forward and left ninety degrees to it, then exchange blows with their left hand behind the back and right engaging the opponent. Starke made a note to speak with Watson about their southpaws. Trying to force left-handers into a right-hand form not only frustrated them but reduced the advantage they enjoyed due to the different perspective. Their lives might never depend on this skill, but right-handers also needed to experience this factor in training should the occasion arise.

Yamashita was exchanging blows with a Chinese steward struggling equally to prevent animus from seeping into their practice due to atrocity stories emerging from the recent war. Their loyalty to *Calypso* and Weaver, the instructor, were likely the only barriers to a far more spirited contest. Yamashita's opponent preferred kendo, like many Chinese, while the captain's steward had greater expertise with another blade and style. Shipmates might question edged weapons' usefulness, but Yamashita agreed with Starke when he overheard their captain tell Watson the shock of a cutlass, bayonet, machete, short spear, lance, or bolo could be paralyzing; as many Spanish troops in Cuba were learning. Wardroom participation was required but line and steam engineering officers only went through the motions. Conrad was extremely enthusiastic, which Watson attributed to Sherlock Holmes partiality towards singlestick, but surgeons, paymasters, and others did not spend hours practicing at the Academy. Starke would have enjoyed joining in, and Conrad intimated some officers were interested in cane lessons from him, but thought it inappropriate as their captain and kept to daily mainmast climbs for exercise.

Ensign Blair and First Class Gunner's Mate Stefan Poniatowski drilled the landing party a day before. Their division respected and feared the future chief gunner's mate in roughly equal measures due to his physical features, language, and demeanor. The square-shaped head incorporated a flowing black mustache, powerful jaws and facial expressions that were threatening and unforgiving whatever the mood; and his English colored by several other languages since first learning to speak a Polish dialect. His banking family moved from Berdychiv to Odessa after the petty officer's 1850s birth; which made it convenient to escape Russian conscription on a shorthanded French merchantman to Marseilles where he jumped ship for a British barkentine bound for New York. American citizenship freed him from the Czar, its navy provided a home, and reenlistment brought the Washington Navy Yard gunners course and diver qualification. He approached Weaver while between ships in Norfolk after learning *Calypso* was commissioning without a chief gunners' mate and her gun division' latest model 4-inch mounts would be a first class petty officer's fiefdom.

Landing party drills saw Poniatowski, Grier, and Kirby supervise kitting out, assigning weapons, and mounting two Gatling guns on carriages. The Gatlings were assembled, dry fired, broken down, and reassembled but not live fired. Rifles and revolvers were, but the chief persuaded Blair to limit the number since a full day or more was needed to clean weapons and reorder magazines to his satisfaction. Wood blocks were tossed over for sailors to shoot at and, as they worked the M1885 bolt action rifle and its box magazine, blue-white smoke from .45-70 rounds wreathed the area. Their volume of fire demonstrated the Remington-Lee's improvement over trapdoor Springfields but these were still inferior to the Spanish Mauser's smokeless powder, smooth action, and strip cartridges. Their .38 Colt M1895 double-action pistols did use smokeless powder and reloaded faster than the .45 caliber single-action Army Colt, but Poniatowski favored the older weapon since pistols were often a last resort and larger rounds gave an edge. As Poniatowski passed down the line behind each shooter, pausing to adjust an arm or offer advice, he thought Starke must agree since the captain's personal weapon was an old Colt; but could not understand why he also had a .45-70 Sharps trapdoor with telescopic sight. Finally, before shifting to other equipment, gun captains Grier and Kirby were coaxed into an impromptu match and emptied rifles at wood chips. Starke thought Kirby had the best of it but without a target to mark both gun crews claimed their champion shot slightly better.

Starke surveyed the horizon, confirmed the sails were set and drawing well then left for his day, or in-port, cabin to review reports. The morning brought a clear day with *Calypso* heeling slightly starboard under a press of canvas, rocking slowly as it sliced through long, low swells; and driven forward by the warm, pungent breeze breaching his window. He never mentioned his decision not to reenter the Caribbean through Mona Passage and wanted to test his thinking so Watson, Dunbar, and Owen were summoned when drills ended that afternoon.

Chief Owen accompanied the three officers, with results from noon sights and several long rolls under his arm, then spread these charts across the table and weighted their corners with brass pieces. Starke began, "Gentlemen, Captain Albert's direction was to ride the trades west under canvas as long as feasible, but consider using Mona Passage to reenter the Caribbean between Santo Domingo and Puerto Rico; so we have latitude. Passing north of the Puerto Rico takes us across routes from the United States and Europe into San Juan but filibuster traffic between San Juan and Cuba is constrained by Spanish gunboat patrols. We could continue past Puerto Rico, then north of Haiti and Santo Domingo to the Windward Passage between Cuba and Haiti but this alters his intent so let's consider passages through the Leeward Islands east of Puerto Rico."

He retrieved a pipe from the rack then dredged it through a worn tobacco pouch; partly because lighting a bowl pleased him but also to let his officers consider the chart. He began with Chief Owen, as was customary to avoid pressure from seniors, although the chief was seldom reticent about navigation and piloting. The quartermaster shifted a chart to the top of the pile, repositioned three brass weights, smoothed the paper with both hands, and began, using his pencil as a pointer, "We've three options, Captain. The Virgin Passage between Culebra and the Virgin Islands is used by sailing ships and steamers making for Caribbean and South American ports. Anegada Passage to its west is also deep and fairly wide, but it lacks traffic and Anegada Island's a lot like Arrecife Alacranes; not much above sea level, encircled by reefs and shipwrecks, and sits in a west current. There are passages west and south along the Leeward Islands, including one north of Antigua sailing ships favor, but I can't recommend them."

"Mr. Dunbar?"

"I agree. Entering through the Leeward Islands by any route but the Virgin or Anegada Passage only adds time and risk. I suggest the Virgin Passage if we want to announce our presence?"

"XO?"

"I'm inclined to go with Mr. Dunbar and Chief Owen, sir. Taking the Virgin Passage will allow us to intercept traffic from Europe into the Caribbean, between the Leeward Islands and Puerto Rico, out of Ponce and Guayama on the south coast, and cover the Windward Passage."

Starke had hoped the officers' thoughts would confirm his decision so he set the pipe aside, "Very well. Mr. Dunbar; let's adjust our track to enter the Virgin Passage with enough daylight so we don't join any of the wrecks Chief Owen pointed out. Once the track's ready, get with the XO and Mr. Osbourne about the best place to begin steaming," then Starke ended the session by rising with, "Well, gentlemen, if there's nothing else?"

CHAPTER THIRTEEN
CROSSING SWORDS

Captain Albert shifted uneasily on a wood bench outside the Senate's Naval Affairs Committee Room in the Capitol. It was on the top floor, just off the east elevator, which he initially thought a mistake since these sessions had been held in a suitably decorated basement room near the west elevator. Falk, sitting easily beside him, explained it was the Senate Printing Committee's room until Hale outmaneuvered Lodge for the Naval Affairs Committee chair and kept this better sited and less dungeon-like room. He also confirmed the president nominated Joseph McKenna, appeals court judge and ex-congressman, for attorney general rather than McCook, a Junta advocate. McKenna was Irish Catholic and Albert wary of Rome, but the captain was less anti-papist than many and the California moderate seemed willing to enforce laws against filibusters.

Falk also orchestrated, through several moves and countermoves, to improve their position regarding his testifying about *Calypso* dispatching the filibusters *John Gwinn Williams* and *Rafael Riego*. The master stroke was scheduling Albert's testimony to coincide with George Rea's appearance before a different committee. That respected correspondent wrote *Facts and Fakes About Cuba*, so this forced Senators and press to choose between an authority on the insurrection or probing past issues that could expose anarchist participation in the Junta, publicize filibusters attacking a Spanish gunboat, or unmask *Rafael Riego*'s funding.

Albert adjusted the dress blue uniform while his companion added to a small notebook he was seldom without. Falk was confident attendance would be poor and examination cursory, although they prepared for the worst. The hearing began minutes later with Albert noting *Calypso* was at sea, inserted Starke's report in the record, and clarified several ambiguous passages. Falk also learned two unrelated questions would be asked so they were prepared for. The Spanish cruiser, *Reina Mercedes*, put a round off the American steamship *Valencia*'s bow two weeks before after being ignored by the well-known liner on her regular route but not flying an American flag. The participants displayed poor judgement but the press was portraying it as an attack and national insult while conveniently ignoring attacks on Spanish patrol boats by *Rafael Riego* and another American filibuster. Albert's rehearsed response was a dry recitation of international law and custom. The second was more closely related to the topic and Albert's portfolio. The unarmored cruiser *Marblehead* approached Mullet Key from an unexpected quarter one evening to find the filibuster *Biscayne* rafted with *Dauntless* and busily transferring insurrecto recruits and military stores. Both filibusters fled in different directions with the cruiser chasing *Dauntless* and using searchlights to maintain contact. When *Marblehead*'s whistle and blanks failed, three live rounds landed near enough for *Dauntless*' master to understand it was not a sporting event; especially considering *Calypso*'s recent actions. After the tug coasted to a stop, was boarded, and a prize crew detailed, the cruiser entered New River and took *Biscayne* along with thirty unexplainable Cubans, despite her having jettisoned or landed the cargo. *Marblehead* and prizes were not welcomed in Key West and Junta supporters were especially agitated. Albert's response was again the bare facts, along with *Marblehead's* report. The inquisitors were equally circumspect about delving into the effect *Calypso*, *Marblehead*, and others were having on the Junta since rumors of Pinkerton agents and informers within the organization were apparently disrupting operations and accomplishing what Albert hoped to achieve through coordination and his ferret.

Evans approached Albert and Falk as they left the room and began threading through people loitering in the hallway. Albert was introduced to the reporter at a Starke dinner party then she befriended his daughters at the inauguration ball and recently met Starke in New York City. The last became a concern because she was intelligent, polite, and attractive, could be hard-edged at times and exploited a spinster's freedom; while Starke was single, wealthy, eligible and, thankfully, circumspect by nature. Evans mentioned her colleagues were covering Rea's hearing while she was assigned his. They passed several minutes in conversation while Falk nervously hovered a few paces off. Albert evaded questions about *Calypso's* whereabouts and offered no more information than the committee received, but respected her polite doggedness. After parting, she entered an elevator to the rotunda and later boarded a yellow, white, and mahogany Capital Traction Company streetcar that ran along the Capitol's west and south sides then passed north of the Building; with Albert sitting at the opposite end. She failed to notice him and seemed deep in thought with her Brussels carpet bag held bottom-forward like a shield.

He debarked at Lafayette Square, went to the office, and began clearing his desk for the weekend. There were more newspapers bound for the wicker wastebasket than usual due to compiling morning notes to Long on the Greco-Turkish imbroglio. The papers' topics, perspectives, and accuracy varied to reflect publisher and readers but most predicted a European war over eastern Mediterranean events. Another reported the Army had been summoned to place Montana's White and Red protagonists in their respective corners after an off-reservation killing. Coverage of the Cuba fighting was also increasing and it appeared yellow fever was sending thousands of Spanish soldiers to hospitals, home, or worse; while reconcentrados found death their most common escape from starvation and disease. Most papers saw ejecting Weyler as the solution, with every edition demanding his recall or predicting imminent downfall. When the governor-general and Spain ignored them; eyewitness reports of Spanish soldiers attacking hospitals, raping nurses, killing patients, drowning pacificos, burning people alive, and drag-hanging men increased; although horsewhipping women was currently favored. New York, Key West, and Tampa created most of the material, which failed to note genuine atrocities were usually down to guerrilleros and insurrectos.

General Gómez saw destroying Cuba's value and bleeding Spain as the only way forward and would accept nothing less than independence while that country's conservative government was equally intransigent, determined to retain their western empire's remnants and protect Cuban loyalists. This forced Weyler into an unfunded strategy exacting exorbitant costs for small gains while insurgent forces increasingly relied on actual and moral support from the States; with loyalists increasingly blaming Americans for the starvation, disease, and death.

Cuban suffering became so appalling Congress appropriated $50,000 to ostensibly aid American citizens living there but the States had its problems. Despite McKinley winning the first popular vote since Grant, the effects of a war forty years past lingered and recovery from the 1893 panic remained slow.

Cycling from boom to bust was expected, so Albert was cautiously optimistic but Reconstruction aftereffects were bringing changes that could infect the Navy. It seemed a Negro sailor on *Indiana* argued with messmates, there was a fight, and he vanished but was unable or unwilling to leave the ship and finally shot himself. Albert was neither one way nor the other about Colored sailors, and thought the Irish more troublesome, but suspected the changing civilian climate played a role.

Building life was also tumultuous lately. Rear Admiral Crowninshield could not be swayed into giving him a sea command, claiming his greater value lay in the Building. Since Long also valued his services, he remained on the forming war board in addition to the daily Greco-Turkish briefs. Gazing through the office window, Albert hoped his testimony would play better with the secretary than Theodore's Naval War College speech. Roosevelt thundered through a twenty-two page soliloquy arguing for a vast battleship fleet, extolling a warrior society, and exalting jingoism. The infuriated McKinley and Long were left to deal with the aftershocks but Albert believed they should have been anticipated something along those lines since duplicity was not a Theodore shortcoming. The episode did, however, reaffirm the secretary's decision to keep the filibuster project off-limits to this energetic soul. When Albert did leave the office, he was looking forward to taking his family to a Marine Band concert on the Executive Mansion grounds at five-thirty and invigorated by walking home through a warm, breezy, late afternoon. He could also take comfort in Rear Admiral Brown's retirement freeing Lieutenant Sharp to become Roosevelt's aide and perhaps inject some restraint. Besides, despite losing *Maine* and Building tribulations, life ashore with Abigail, Olivia, and Isabella had grown more desirable than another command.

Calypso had cleared the Virgin Passage and was off Puerto Rico, west of Ponce. When she approached their chosen entrance to the Caribbean, one boiler was brought on line and the other lit off as several sails were clewed and brailed; forcing the black gang to regain their rhythm after tending donkey boilers since New York. The azure sea lit by a brilliant tropical sun revealed green, brown, and crystal patches near reefs and islands while gulls examined *Calypso*, silver flying fish began skipping past, and three dolphins raced the ship for several miles, proved their supremacy, then left. When the sea ahead regained deep water's single color, *Calypso* was in the Caribbean, gliding forward under steam and canvas. After passing Vieques Island she turned to follow Puerto Rico's south coast with its mountains blurred gray against the horizon. Fishing boats with single sails would appear off the ports and small fishing villages, or the occasional coastal steamer closer in. With Ponce and Guayama astern, the bark was below Mona Island, just south of Mona Passage, in waters between Puerto Rico and Santo Domingo that saw heavy traffic from ships serving Mayaguez and Santo Domingo or passing between Atlantic and Caribbean.

Calypso's sails were furled to ease maneuvering in this traffic and the pilothouse's wood exterior burned bare skin. Inside was oven-like and flooded by intense light with the only amelioration a warm breeze passing through open windows. Ensign Martyn glanced at mushroom-like ventilator cowls rising from coamings with their bell-mouths swung forward to gather air and push it below; thinking topside was endurable compared with the engine and fire rooms' humid hell. His port section was on watch, Chief Weaver's sailors were working in small groups, and Poniatowski was instructing gun captains standing around the forward 4-inch rifle. Its open breechblock's raw steel stood out from the black mount with polished brass fittings and hand wheels attached to greased gears that pointed and trained the gun. Tightly furled sails stood out against a cloudless blue sky and the national ensign would stream aft then hang limp.

The Irish seaman Kearney was in the fore top, scanning his sector's horizon and examining what caught his attention with paired-telescopes. An anomaly appeared to their northwest that first appeared as a sail but was quickly joined by a faint smoke plume. He nearly reported it as a small steamer with canvas steadying her passage except smoke should have been visible before sails so he just called down a sighting. When a steamship appeared astern of the schooner, he hailed Caldwell who acknowledged with a wave then trained his binoculars where Kearney gestured. The steamship was further back than she appeared, probably due to poor coal creating clouds of black smoke rather than the light-gray settling off *Calypso's* wake. The schooner was on a beam reach, her fastest point of sail, with a strong, steady east wind and well clear of any island wind shadow or shore breeze. As they continued closing and bearings drifted slowly down *Calypso's* starboard side, Kearney thought the sailing ship resembled a pilot boat, but the steamer was nearly bow-on and indistinct. He was about to rescan his sector when white smoke blossomed from the steamer followed seconds later by a faint, dull crack. He cupped both hands to his mouth, "Pilothouse; forward lookout. Ship astern of schooner has fired on her."

Martyn had grown more comfortable with his section and their enigmatic superior after months of tutelage. He turned to his assistant, "Mr. Caldwell. Kearney's up there?"

"Yes sir."

With that, Martyn set general quarters and the ship exploded from its heat-induced calm with voices and boatswain pipes as the main deck filled with the crew going to station. The fireroom off-watch slid down ladders as the second boiler's coals were spread then fuel and feedwater added. Water tenders stared at gauges and worked valves as boiler steam pressure slowly climbed towards its consort's. Osbourne left the fire and engine rooms to O'Leary then walked quickly to the pilothouse. Starke stopped reviewing Conrad's binnacle list, retrieved his blue cap from its wall peg, handed the magazine keys to their gunner, and climbed to the pilothouse with as much decorum as possible. The pilothouse setting general quarters unexpectedly was gut-wrenching for any commander but more so when done by Martyn; the more hesitant of their two watch officers. Starke struggled to appear the dispassionate captain preparing to fight his ship as he scanned the horizon, entered the pilothouse, saw a brace of distant ships to starboard, and watched Martyn approach anxiously. Osbourne already had the conn and stood forward of the helm with binoculars laying against his broad chest and tugging the solid neck.

"Report, Mr. Martyn."

"Small steamer pursuing a schooner to starboard, Captain; I set general quarters when the lookout reported gunfire."

After listening, Starke saw there was time, despite the atmosphere, then walked to his binoculars and worn pipe, responding, "Very well, Mr. Martyn. Well done. Please shift the watch to the flying bridge, hoist the large ensign, and report manned and ready."

Turning to Osbourne, Starke asked, "Second boiler's coming on line?"

"Yes sir. No more than a half hour."

Before easing the unlit pipe through his sparse, carefully trimmed, beard, Starke looked at his chief engineer, "Very well. Slow to bare steerageway and maintain course."

Orders were given and relayed to the engine room by EOT as Starke walked to the chart table where Dunbar and Owen pointed out their estimated position. On impulse, he left his pipe and cap, went to the main deck, and began climbing to the foretop. Without thinking, he went out and over the futtock shrouds rather than through the lubber's hole; at the cost of several sticky tar streaks on his uniform. The lookout was peering north through paired-telescopes when *Calypso's* captain stood, grasped a standing rigging section absent of grease or blacking, and asked, "How certain, Kearney?"

"Long way off, Captain, and nothing since; but what looked like gunsmoke came from the second fellow. Heard what could have been a blank charge or live round."

"Very well; let's see what develops?"

"Aye, aye; Captain."

The steamer was attempting without success to pin its quarry against Puerto Rico's coast but the schooner enjoyed sea room and a fair wind; although that could change with any weather shift or equipment failure. Neither's colors were visible but Starke suspected the pursuer was a Spanish gunboat and pursued a filibuster or smuggler. Dunbar held *Calypso* in Mona Passage's southern approaches but well clear of Spanish waters so Starke calculated they could reverse course to cut the schooner off or let it pass astern unmolested since his orders did not include working with Spain's navy or interfering with ships under foreign flags.

Starke remained aloft until that view became no better than on the flying bridge, left the tops, and descended through the lubber's hole. Looking down on foreshortened figures around the two 4-inch guns, he could see their crews cycling through training and pointing arcs. Case ammunition was coming up from the magazine where their gunner took every precaution to avoid accidental explosions; and he was again thankful their main battery did not use bag ammunition. After rejoining Martyn and Osbourne on the flying bridge, Starke heard Blair on the main deck chastising sailors trying to bet on what came next and decided to let this play out astern when Martyn exclaimed, "She's turning, Mr. Osbourne!"

The schooner had come right and was close-hauled on a port tack that would take her just past *Calypso*'s bow and uncomfortably close to the jibboom rather than comfortably astern. Starke held course and speed as schooner's bearing drift slowed, paused, and then shifted left, walking towards the bow. *Calypso* lacked twin-screw maneuverability so he waited until the schooner was committed then had Osbourne put the rudder hard left and briefly increase speed. The maneuver muscled a port turn that brought *Calypso* in line with, and ahead of, the schooner. As *Calypso*'s bow fell off to port, the schooner lacked time to adjust and was forced to pass down either side, but not cross the bark's bow or stern. This ensured the 4-inch rifles and Gatling guns covering the schooner remained clear of superstructure, masts, and rigging.

The schooner heeled well to port as a gracefully curved prow below her pronounced bowsprit sliced through the swells, causing Starke to suspect she was a refitted pilot boat designed by George Steers or some imitator. He guessed her to be about a 100 feet long with a beam of perhaps twenty-five and approaching 150 tons. She was swift and well-handled with the fore-and-aft sails on two masts spread and drawing perfectly. The gunboat slowed and turned with the schooner; leaving her some distance off *Calypso*'s stern with a clear shot at *Calypso*, but Starke wanted the schooner covered until she passed.

The 45-star American flag streamed to starboard from the schooner's main mast as she went down *Calypso*'s starboard side then pulled ahead. Whether it had been obscured by the sails or just hoisted was unclear but any intent to remain an observer became impossible. The man looking coldly up from the schooner's round tiller well as she slid past close aboard was probably the master. There was also something familiar despite the distance and his features obscured by a cap's leather brim. He was powerfully built and above average in height with a large head securely affixed to broad shoulders by a thick neck. The master, almost certainly a filibuster, must have closed *Calypso* for a reason since the odds were better than even his schooner would have outrun her pursuer.

The stern identified her as *Astraea* out of New York while passing and once clear, before being ordered to heave to, she hauled off to port then coasted to a stop facing east, stern to *Calypso*'s port side. Osbourne stopped their engine, leaving both ships rolling on a crestless blue sea with a strong east breeze while the third ship closed with a white mustache under her bow and trailing a thick smoke plume. Before she was close aboard, Starke gave orders positioning the bark to cover the gunboat and prevent the schooner from bolting. The crew responded well despite the unorthodoxy, perhaps due to the last weeks under sail. With frigate precision, *Calypso*'s mizzen and mizzen topmast staysails were run up, then the spanker. Imitating a wind-vane aided by the rudder and judicious engine turns, her bow slowly shifted towards the schooner and beam left facing the gunboat. With general quarters set and steam to maneuver, she could ease forward, swing the bow starboard, and smother the schooner with Hotchkiss 3-pounders and Gatlings or bring 4-inch rifles to bear on the Spaniard. This still bought time only since failure to protect an American ship, even a filibuster, might create a reputation for shyness or rumors of cowardice.

Martyn went to the flying bridge's outboard side where, clear of mainmast, bowsprit, and rigging, he watched the schooner lower a whaleboat. As swells rolled both ships, he double-checked the black transom's gold leaf dancing in the binoculars' lenses then returned to the boat and called out, "She's *Astraea*, Captain; and looks like her boat's boarding passengers."

Astraea's lines reminded Starke of the well-handled schooner that trailed them briefly off New York as he replied, "Very well, Mr. Martyn. Enter it in the log."

Calypso controlled the tactical situation but not the coming moves. The gunboat continued closing as *Astraea*'s whaleboat rowed towards *Calypso*, rising and dropping with the swells. Tension was building on the flying bridge and Starke expected the same for their gun crews so the next minutes would test discipline and training. The schooner-rigged, flush-decked gunboat turned left somewhat over 200 yards off their starboard side and stopped with ram-bow pointed into the wind, then raised the mainsail and sheeted it home on centerline. It was *Francisco de Montejo*, the gunboat attacked by *Rafael Riego*, an anarchist filibuster *Calypso* destroyed. Since *Calypso* and *Vanguard* assisted the wounded gunboat, Starke knew her triple-expansion engine could push the 156-foot steel hull and 295 tons to nearly fifteen knots on good coal, which was seldom available, and the main battery consisted of two 57mm Hotchkiss quick-firing guns that were no match for *Calypso*'s 4-inch mounts. Her secondary 22mm twin-barreled Nordenfelt guns would fare worse against the bark's 3-pounders and Gatlings. A white-uniformed captain stood on her small bridge and Starke wondered if Teniente de Navío Emiliano Mendoza y Aguilar still commanded.

Mendoza entertained similar thoughts as his Zeiss binoculars moved between *Calypso*, *Astraea*, and the small boat. He recognized that tall bark and, should Starke still command, did not doubt the man's honor and propriety. Their brief acquaintance in Havana also suggested the American's capacity for decisiveness, duty, intellect, initiative, and nonconformity mirrored Capitán de Navío Antonio Eulate y Fery who commanded that city's naval arsenal before given *Vizcaya*, one of Spain's best armored cruisers. While Starke supported him at the *Rafael Riego* inquiry, Eulate forced *Francisco de Montejo*'s repairs through an almost nonexistent yard. In appreciation, he carried presents from the captain to his wife, Julia Sanjurio, in Puerto Rico and daughters María and Carmela. The mother was a gracious host, María an excellent painter, and Carmela not only a popular author but active in some women's rights group. He found Carmela particularly intriguing but her intellect and frankness unnerving.

Returning to the present, Mendoza knew *Astraea*'s whaleboat carried three passengers who were undoubtedly the fugitives he was sent to apprehend. They were involved with two late-March attacks on Yauco designed to replicate the Cuban insurrection but their scheme failed when Governor-general Sabas Marín y González was warned and the instigators captured or exiled, except this trio. They remained at large because the same island politics that alerted the governor-general concealed then them. When Mendoza arrived in Puerto Rico, he discovered anyone not a loyalist fell into three roughly equal camps: autonomists wanting self-rule; annexationists seeking to join the States; and those favoring independence.

The independence faction concealed this trio while the New York Junta's Puerto Rican faction arranged passage from

Mayaguez to Santo Domingo and information predictably reached the government that an unknown schooner would divert from its declared itinerary, enter Mayaguez, pick them up, and leave immediately for Santo Domingo, some eighty miles across Mona Passage. Once they were put ashore by small boat, the vagaries of sail would be used to account for the schedule aberration after Mayaguez. Governor-general Marín's military staff persuaded him to apprehend the fugitives at sea, away from any crowd, with one of the ships at his disposal. Once *Francisco de Montejo* was chosen from two unprotected cruisers, a destroyer, and three small gunboats, Mendoza was ordered to leave San Juan, patrol off Mayaguez, board an unidentified schooner in or near Mona Passage after she left port, and bring her to San Juan with the fugitives. He thought these orders as flawed as those sending him after *Rafael Riego* and received no opportunity to point out that Mona Passage was not only a major sailing route to the Caribbean with strong winds, treacherous seas, coral reefs, and shifting sand coastline; but the ship might not be a schooner or even Spanish. Nevertheless, he sailed with these reservations to begin loitering just beyond reefs protecting the port's harbor. *Astraea* was clearly from the Junta and, as he anticipated before leaving San Juan, flew American colors so boarding and bringing her to a Spanish port would resurrect the *Virginius* Affair of twenty years earlier, rekindle the more recent outrage over the filibuster schooner *Competitor*, and fuel American papers' demands for action after *Reina Mercedes* fired across *Valencia*'s bow.

Mendoza also believed taking *Astraea* could increase the American public's support for Cuban insurgents and provoke a war Spain was ill-prepared to fight at sea so he planned to intercept the schooner leaving port while still in Spanish waters. Unfortunately, her master proved a virtuoso under sail, knew the offshore reefs, and was favored by the wind. If *Francisco de Montejo* was in the condition she left her Scottish builder's yard, and not crippled by the poor support available to the Spanish navy in Puerto Rico, *Astraea* would have been quickly overhauled; but the Cortes' inability or reluctance to fund operations, maintenance, and ammunition meant the major repairs required after rough handling by *Rafael Riego*'s dynamite gun were not accomplished and her worn boilers received coal that reliably produced mostly rich, dark smoke and clinkers.

This allowed *Astraea* to race through the night for Santo Domingo; hugging the coast and skirting shallow areas to elude *Francisco de Montejo*. She entered international waters with the gunboat astern and favorable winds just when Mendoza calculated a warning shot would fall beyond her bow. He gambled, fired, and watched an American flag break at the mainmast as *Astraea* turned and made for a ship on the horizon. It seemed likely this maneuver was to obtain a witness until he recognized *Calypso* and realized facing the more powerful ship could not be avoided; all because San Juan's military staff tried to avoid publicity. Mendoza was resigned to play out the hand, ordered the gig launched, changed to his best uniform, and left to place a weak case before *Calypso*'s commander.

When Starke saw *Francisco de Montejo*'s gig being lowered he brought Watson to the flying bridge then left for his cabin to change. *Astraea*'s contingent arrived first and offered conveniently common Puerto Rican names: Señors González, Morales, and Camacho. During the customary long Spanish introduction, their recent transport ignored directions and raced back to the schooner. The resulting commotion and hails cued the eldest to hold a broad hat at his waist and state, in precise English, "We are United States citizens from an

American ship threatened by Spain, Comandante, and request protection."

Cubans often claimed citizenship, and some were, but he also intimated the Spanish gunboat was interfering with an American ship. This resurrected Admiral Brown's warning about State's fickle nature; and the new secretary's public antipathy towards Spain was well-known. His assistant, William R. Day, was said to be pragmatic and allegedly ran the department since his aged boss, General Sherman's younger brother, suffered poor health; but this only added unpredictability and limited Starke to established practice, custom, and courtesy as stated in Navy regulations.

When a hail revealed *Francisco de Montejo*'s gig was making its approach, Starke excused himself, had Naval Cadet Timme escort their uninvited visitors to the wardroom, and was standing at *Calypso*'s gangway to welcome the gunboat commander. After the appropriate honors, Starke apologized for not rigging the accommodation ladder, although rolling in a seaway at general quarters clearly made it impractical, before stating it was an honor to welcome *Francisco de Montejo*'s captain. In the day cabin, Yamashita served coffee despite the wallowing ship. Preliminaries continued until disrupted by a speaking trumpet hailing *Astraea*; followed by a long burst that brought both captains to the main deck. Watson stood at the flying bridge's port railing, partly obscured by its white canvas windscreen, speaking trumpet in hand and the acrid smell of .45-70 black powder hanging in the air.

The schooner's sails were coming down at the run as Starke looked up, "XO?"

"*Astraea* tried to run for it, Captain, so I ordered a burst across her bow."

"Well done, XO. Detail an armed boarding party under Mr. Blair to take command of the schooner."

Since *Francisco de Montejo* would have heard, he turned to Mendoza, "Perhaps you would like to signal your ship, Captain?"

Mendoza shrugged in resignation, "Thank you, Captain, but it is unnecessary. We know you and *Calypso*; besides my segundo comandante has orders to respond only if attacked and preserve the ship above all else."

"Then shall we return to the cabin?"

They heard Blair's directions, followed by the rattle of harnesses, rifles, and bayonets as they reentered the cabin where Starke apologized for lack of wine. Mendoza knew there were few options with the schooner flying an American flag and the fugitives claiming protection as citizens. He still explained the situation, challenged their false claims, and made the expected formal demands. Starke listened without interruption, knowing the Spaniard must report going through these motions; although both were well aware surrendering any American ship, even filibusters, to a Spanish gunboat while in international waters would be indefensible publicly and within the Navy Department. Despite dubious citizenship claims, Starke was equally unable to surrender the trio to Mendoza or deliver them to the American consul in San Juan; but landing them in Santo Domingo would bring accusations of aiding fugitives, or even anarchists, and Spain's press equaled its American brethren in venom and creativity. The warning shot was especially contentious so he judiciously avoided mentioning it. Starke willingly followed his lead since Kearney was the only actual witness on board.

While preparing to command *Calypso* and periodically since, Starke studied the half dozen applicable Navy regulations articles and saw their ambiguity. Force could be used to defend national honor, American citizens, and their possessions outside other nations' territorial waters, but within them required overwhelming justification; and the ships were not in Spanish waters. Another article required him to protect American ships engaged in lawful trade and *Astraea* was not technically filibustering since she entered and departed Mayaguez legally. The same black book allowed political refugees to receive temporary shelter if threatened in a third country so long as it did not disrupt the mission or favor any side; but all three claimed American citizenship so they were not refugees. The only unambiguous article read, ". . . and take such steps as the gravity of the case demands . . . . The responsibility for any action taken by a naval force, however, rests wholly upon the commanding officer thereof."

Mendoza soon left for *Francisco de Montejo*, confident little was achievable without provoking war and losing his command. Starke watched from *Calypso*'s gangway until he reached the gunboat, her gig was retrieved, the mainsail lowered, and she began steaming back through Mona Passage for San Juan trailing a long cloud of black smoke. Mendoza's report would say *Calypso* prevented *Francisco de Montejo* from apprehending the three fugitives on *Astraea* but Starke promised to deliver them and the schooner to authorities in an American port. Although not part of the discussion, Starke had intended obtain the parole of *Astraea*'s master to surrender himself and schooner in Key West; until Blair sent word he was Fachtna Harler, a man better known as Captain Buff and assumed lost with *Rafael Riego*.

CHAPTER FOURTEEN
INTO THE BREACH

S tarke finished the last sips of morning coffee before leaving his cabin sanctuary for the pilothouse. *Calypso* had been under sail escorting *Astraea* to Key West since *Francisco de Montejo* steamed off ten days earlier. They trailed the schooner almost due west, passing south of the large island shared uneasily by Haiti and Santo Domingo, then a large peninsula jutting from the Jamaican coast west of Kingston. That port was bypassed because leaving *Astraea* alone at sea was chancy and taking her in risked British involvement. He instead paid a pilot boat's master in Mexican dollars to carry a coded message to the American consul. There was no guarantee it would get through but Albert needed to know why they were not at Port Antonio and now sailing north off Cuba's south coast for Key West; especially with Mendoza's report, or selected parts, likely to be presented at State, accompanied by a protest from Dupuy de Lôme, Spain's minister in Washington. Dunbar's roughly northwest track from Jamaica took them past the Cayman Islands into the Gulf of Mexico then through the Yucatan Channel. Once clear of Cabo San Antonio and before coming northeast for Key West they briefly rode the current flowing out through the Straits of Florida to the Gulf Stream. They had fair weather and a steady wind from astern, which was unsurprising since square-riggers favored the route, but the journey was not pleasant.

Captain Buff remained *Astraea*'s master because Starke had no grounds to remove him and he could handle schooner and a crew. Unlike their master, who could expect a favorable outcome in court, some of his twenty-something men might be desperate to escape. Filibuster pay doubled what most crews received, with a $1,000 bonus for successful crossings, but its high risk tended to attract hard-cases along with the desperate and adventurous. That made for a tough crowd and Captain Buff knew how to maintain order; but for insurance Starke had *Astraea*'s documents removed to *Calypso*, a rotating an armed guard of six under an ensign or naval cadet placed on board, one 4-inch mount standing by, and large boarding party kept ready to counter any escape attempt at night or during squalls.

Calypso had her own trials. The three passengers had been all but restricted to the wardroom after the youngest, Señor Camacho, began proselytizing sailors that appeared to come from Spain or the Caribbean. Watson was unable to politely muzzle him so Starke told González the next incident would see the gentleman residing in their brig. González had just enjoyed supper and evening conversation with Starke where several subtle inquiries convinced him their unwilling host did not traffic in idle threats. The same discussion led Starke to suspect González was the Puerto Rican equivalent of Herminio Gonzales y Ochoa, president of a Key West Cuban Club and well-connected insurrecto supporter. Starke also learned his guest was born in Puerto Rico of a Spanish father and studied at the Universidad de Salamanca. His precise speech and manners suggested some stripe of lawyer or editor, but he never said and facing American authorities in Key West appeared to cause no apprehension. He was more candid regarding Puerto Rico and provided Starke, probably

179

intentionally, with enough information to justify a letter to the intelligence office.

Forced to remain constantly vigilant, Starke began experiencing transient musings of summer nights with a whiskey in The Cairo's rooftop garden overlooking Washington or riding Gemini on Sunday mornings after a chinwag with the ex-cavalryman Darius Sutton. Several Building tasks like the torpedo boat analysis even evoked wistful memories; likely because June meant *Plunger*, a submersible version, was nearing completion and launch. As *Calypso*'s sails were furled for entering port, he speculated how Mendoza's report explaining their chance meeting was playing in San Juan, Havana, or Madrid. He doubted it was well-received since the gunboat's commander obviously considered these orders as distasteful as those sending him after *Rafael Riego*.

A thickening and darkening northern horizon announced *Calypso* was nearing Key West as a gray-white gull glided smoothly past the flying bridge with cocked head and orange beak squawking its piercing welcome. A distinct horizon encircling the bark separated endless azure skies brushed by patches and trails of cirrus clouds from the gentle surface rolls of slowly greening water. *Calypso* made for Southwest Channel with main boilers on line and harbor-furled canvas. Sea and anchor detail was set before Satan Shoal passed to starboard with the ship holding a northeast and a quarter east bearing to Key West light house. The Middle Ground and other shoals slipped safely astern as they corrected for set and drift; then two subsequent course changes to port lined them up on Whitehead Point and Fort Taylor. Without requesting pilots, both ships made for *Calypso*'s usual anchorage, clear of water flushed from the port. The graceful schooner was impeccably handled and dropped anchor under sail minutes before *Calypso*'s plummeted to the hard sand bottom, trailing a vibrating chain that spewed clouds of reddish surface rust. The quarantine boat flying its yellow flag was hailed while making for *Astraea* and changed course for *Calypso* where the ship's papers lay on Starke's desk. He half-expected to be quarantined since Mendoza stated *Astraea* entered Mayaguez where there was no American consular official to issue a Bill of Health and *Calypso*'s three passengers were from that port. The Collector of Customs might also be interested in the undeclared Mayaguez stop, but Junta lawyers would offer a plausible explanation to pliable recipients. Meanwhile, Starke used binoculars to confirm Blair posted a guard on *Astraea*'s forecastle, stern, and sides. Heavy Remington-Lee rifles straining leather slings confirmed the schooner was off limits and prevented her crew from melting into the waterfront. Seeing bayonets were not fixed, Starke allowed himself a grin; it was not like Blair to pass up such an opportunity. Sweeping further up-channel, he saw a tug leave the customs house wharf and make for *Calypso* at what seemed best speed. Since the anchor was set and a proper rode out, he went to his day cabin to receive visitors and, thanks to a New York tailor, greet them in undress blues that complied with newly revised uniform regulations.

First up the accommodation ladder was Ramon Alvarez, Special Deputy Collector of Customs and local *New York Herald* correspondent, trailed by Brian Fields from Justice, a United States Marshal, and the quarantine officer. Starke rose from his desk as they entered; outwardly enjoying a pipe and approving reports required from Navy ships returning to port. Alvarez introduced the marshal and quarantine officer before disclosing the Democrats' Collector of Customs, Jefferson Browne, would leave and a Republican replacement, anticipated to be George Allen, would be nominated in July.

Their discussion immediately revealed *Astraea*'s Key West arrival was viewed as inconvenient but the collector's office and United States District Court would enforce the law. Alvarez cut off the quarantine officer, and suggested an apology was in order, after he quipped that the waterfront was surprised *Calypso* delivered an intact filibuster.

Fields reported State received Spain's diplomatic note soon after the incident off Puerto Rico and, perhaps forewarned by the Kingston cable, displayed unusual discipline in telling the press little more than talks with the Spanish minister were ongoing; which was true for all foreign legations. Starke never fully trusted Clarence Newcomb, the Diplomatic Bureau clerk he met after accepting *Calypso* and who would leave with the outgoing administration; but suspected he and Albert had a hand in this and his first impression too severe. The Navy said only that *Calypso* was bringing the schooner to an American port for Justice Department inquiries; and that department issued a bland statement their work would not commence until then. Alvarez produced a Treasury cable, with Justice and Navy concurrence, transferring *Astraea*, crew, and passengers to the Collector of Customs at the first port *Calypso* entered. The United States Attorney was to libel the schooner then address passengers and crew. Starke expected little, but *Calypso* was released, probably due to Albert's machinations, and the episode over except for a hearing and outstanding mess bill. As wardroom mess treasurer, Timme charged their guests at a profitable rate with little hope for payment after Wiggs advised it depended on accountants deeming them prisoners, detainees, or guests.

Once everyone left, Starke took a steam pinnace to make the required courtesy call on Commander Forsyth since Commander Theodore Jewell and his *Marblehead* were at sea hunting *Dauntless*; reported to again be filibustering. Once the marshal assumed control of *Astraea*, her crew and passengers went ashore and Blair's guard detail returned. This did not please the ensign who hoped she would become *Calypso's* tender, with him in charge; or those in the crew believing their sea lawyers' prize money predictions. When the second steam pinnace returned from taking Wiggs for supplies and Yeoman Pond to transmit arrival cables, sailors on special liberty stepped from the accommodation ladder in personalized uniforms for a hot noon run to the station pier then local saloons, bars, and other island attractions.

Starke dedicated the next day to his official report and preparing for a hearing at the custom house, just visible through an open starboard window. A letter to Katherine was completed during his midday break but nothing from Bridport was waiting in Key West. It was not surprising since her letters must cross the Atlantic then linger at the Navy Department or his uncle's mansion until forwarded. He began another to Tyson but was in no hurry since *The Sun* correspondent might be in Great Britain for the Queen's Diamond Jubilee rather than home from the Greek assignment. Starke intermittently looked up through the window in thought or lifted a brown pipe cradled in the ashtray for a draw before dipping the pen to write in bursts. He paused during early afternoon to watch *Astraea* sail to the customs house pier in a series of short tacks and graceful turns. He competed under sail and her handling confirmed his opinion that Captain Buff may be one bastard of the first water but also a superb shiphandler. He also felt the afternoon heat that forced Watson to lighten workload and reschedule drills. Yamashita left his pantry to fish placidly near *Calypso's* stern; below gulls and terns circling for discarded offal the dozing gray cat concealed by an equipment box shadow saw as his.

Watson joined Starke for supper that evening and arrived when wardroom dinner call was piped at six twenty-five. They were well into it when the duty officer, Ensign Martyn, and boat officer, Naval Cadet Caldwell, interrupted. Both hesitated and briefly eyed each other, so it was not good news. Starke prodded, "Gentlemen, to what do we owe the pleasure?"

Martyn looked at Watson, Starke, then Caldwell, "You go; I would just be repeating it."

"Yes sir. There were rumors earlier, Captain, but it seems a riot's starting in town."

"Are our sailors involved?"

"Not so far. The deputy looking for Commander Forsyth saw our boat and came over. A Negro was being tried for assaulting some White woman who's supposedly in a bad way when a local swell, Mr. Pendleton, apparently demanded a lynching and solicited volunteers. This was about four. When some in the gallery agreed, the Blacks and Whites squared off. Once outside, several Blacks demanded Pendleton's lynching but he escaped in a carriage as the fighting started."

Turning to Watson, Starke mused, "The courthouse is five or six blocks up Whitehead Street from the naval station."

"Yes, sir; and there're no marines assigned."

"Please continue, Mr. Caldwell."

"Sheriff Knight tried to deputize people and has his prisoner in jail but that building, armory, and court house are surrounded by armed Blacks and Coloreds. They've sworn there'll be no lynching but Whites are also gathering. There's been gunfire near Pendleton's house as well. Deputy said it serves the bastard right."

Starke studied Martyn, "Find out who's ashore and secure liberty; no one leaves without permission."

"Yes sir."

Shifting to Caldwell, Starke revealed a barely discernible sardonic grin under his thin beard, "Maintain boat runs and contact with the naval station but ensure it's safe to land before approaching. Get a pistol from the gunner and ask Weaver for an armed sailor; rifle and clips."

As he turned to leave Starke added, "Mr. Martyn; issue cutlasses to the boat crew."

Watson looked puzzled, "Cutlasses?"

"They'll sober up a mob that might press past a man with a rifle and there may be machetes about. It'll give the men a sense of security. Have the order logged; our crew comes before any rioter."

Looking at ensign and cadet, Starke saw determination build as they prepared for action so he added, "Remember, don't take chances or overreact. You've described a tinderbox that's a local matter. *Calypso*'s not to be drawn in."

After they left, Starke looked over his half-eaten fish, "Well, XO, I was looking forward to a night's rest but suspect we'll be up."

Watson felt uneasy, dabbed his mouth with a napkin, and responded, "I'd better assist Mr. Martyn; anything else, Captain?"

"Have Mr. Osbourne prepare the second boiler. Unless the governor requests our help and president authorizes it, becoming involved is probably illegal for us and definitely for the Fort Taylor garrison. However, we must be ready to protect federal property since Knight can't have more than a half-dozen officers."

"Yes sir. In the meantime, I won't change ship's routine."

Starke slowly laid his white cloth napkin on the table as Watson rose to leave, "So much for a quiet supper, XO."

Watson nodded and left. The executive officer felt obliged to act but Starke's exposure to mobs came in Egypt and he found they had a collective consciousness that might be influenced but could instantly take them to or from sanity. *Calypso* could do little for now so he finished the steamed fish Yamashita colluded with the engineers to produce. As muster was piped, the steam whistle blasted recall, and their pinnaces left for the naval station, Starke glanced at the half-finished plate across the table; Thaddeus would fare better than anyone this evening.

Caldwell reconnoitered the station boundary after their steam pinnaces were secured to the metal pier. Watson later chastised him for doing it but those passing said tension was rising as more armed Blacks returned to Jackson Square and strengthened the line encircling jail, courthouse, and armory. This prevented Key West's militia from arming but a large group of Whites began organizing at the town's north side with their weapons. Cubans mostly stood clear, but some African-Cubans went to the barricades.

Watson reported roughly half the liberty party failed to return, including Conrad, Thomas, Kirby, and Jones, so Starke had him silently set general quarters before *Taps* sounded at nine and dispatch an armed detail to the pier with orders not to leave. No one would benefit if *Calypso* sailors made it a three-sided brawl by searching the city for their missing comrades but Forsyth needed support to stiffen what civilian watchmen and staff were available to protect the station. Blair was desperate to lead the detail and the other two ensigns required to carry out Starke's scheme, so their quixotic officer got his wish, explicit orders to avoid aggressive acts, and the steadying influence of Chief Weaver who volunteered his services.

Melvin coxswained the steam pinnace towing a packed whaleboat carrying the landing party. They left *Calypso* floating in the moonlight slightly before midnight with the city relatively quiet, except for an occasional spurt of shouting. Across the ship channel were few lights, mostly at the town's northern end, and darkened buildings. The Marine Hospital and Fort Taylor were showing more lights than normal but otherwise quiet. The few clouds had dispersed, leaving a dark sky with hundreds of bright stars. Along *Calypso*'s waterline, the gulf lapped gently at wood sheathing below slapping rigging and humming machinery. There was also the intermittent cough or shifting position of sailors napping on station.

Starke was thinking he overreacted when a rumbling in Jackson Square reached the anchored ship followed by the flat cracks of rifles interspersed with large bore pistol detonations. The ragged fusillade quickly subsided to intermittent shooting. Heavy firing briefly resumed after thirty minutes then tailed off into what sounded like sniping and nuisance shooting. Starke also spotted running lights making for the ship that could only be their steam pinnace with Cadet Caldwell standing impatiently in its sternsheets. Melvin made a perfect landing on the accommodation ladder's lower platform, the cadet boarded, and pinnace quickly backed away to avoid chaffing. Caldwell hurried to the pilothouse and Starke where he saluted, passed his captain a folded message, with Watson and Dunbar looking on, adding, "Commander Forsyth requested I wait for a reply."

Starke looked at the excited cadet with flapped leather holster swinging heavy against a white uniform, now somewhat worse for wear. The note read, "Could a larger detail be spared to guard station perimeter? Forsyth."

Its author had watched the pinnace pass down a shimmering, dark channel then ease alongside the accommodation ladder. The note's genesis was Caldwell speaking earlier with a passerby coming from the barricades. It was early morning, there was intermittent firing, and the man's light duster hardly concealed a distinct bulge at his waist. He claimed the fighting still centered on Jackson Square, five blocks away, where Blacks repulsed two attempts to take the jail and its prisoner, Sylvanus Johnson. Belligerents apparently allowed the sheriff to send and receive telegrams but refused to stand down for the fifty men he deputized. As threats, taunts, and insults were exchanged, mixed with the occasional round, he heard some Blacks, most likely Cuba veterans, threaten to kill every White while their opposites assured them that meant no quarter. He knew nothing of Black or Colored casualties but a White had been killed and several wounded before he left to defend his home.

That persuaded Forsyth to request assistance from Starke. Each faction could number between fifty and 500 so the city's small police force could be easily overwhelmed. His station lay between Front Street and the harbor with businesses along one side, customs house grounds the other, no walls, and indefensible compared to Fort Taylor or the barracks. Should either mob come for weapons, Ensign Blair's eight-man detail, even with spike bayonets fixed on heavy, quick-firing rifles, would be overwhelmed and he would be forced to abandon naval station and tugs or use its storehouse as a redoubt where many would die before any soldiers arrived; if they lasted that long. The tugs were cold iron so sending the pinnace was a calculated risk because there was no escape while it was away; but abandoning Federal property was not an option.

His anxiety increased with sporadic gunfire continuing a few blocks away while *Calypso* remained peacefully at anchor with no sign Starke was sending reinforcements. He began to wish *Marblehead* was still in port with her larger crew and marines; then the bark's running lights were lit followed by two searchlights. The port light's brilliant beam cut through the dark, moving buoy to buoy while the starboard walked up the shore from hospital to naval station. As it reached him, Forsyth covered his eyes to retain night vision and sensed more than witnessed the blinding illumination. Once it passed, *Calypso*'s green running light, below her white masthead light and just off the water, gave way to a red port running light. The single screw bark was underway without a pilot and ghosting up Key West's ship channel through early morning dark. He felt relief and dread. Bringing the entire ship was a bold and effective gesture since ten, fifteen, or twenty more sailors might not intimidate either large mob but more than a hundred shielded by bulwarks and backed with Gatling guns at the pier's head was different. It would be insanity to attempt forcing the pier once *Calypso* was in position and the station would be covered, but that assumed a mob believed the sailors would fire, which was better than even odds given *Calypso*'s waterfront reputation, but some might not. Then there was Starke. He was risking ship and crew by taking her up the channel at night and should either swarm force the issue, dozens would be dead or wounded; along with Forsyth's long career and Starke's shorter one.

Calypso's anchor rose from the seabed with Starke calculating his approach on the large pier fronting the naval station's largest building. Taking the single-screw bark through a narrow channel at night required precise handling to compensate for wind and current, avoid being set down on *Astraea* at the customs pier, or overshooting into the commercial waterfront and marine railway. Engine and rudder orders must be given and executed perfectly, while accounting for the lag time necessary to manipulate valves or stop the engine before reversing, and precision line handling became critical alongside the pier. Two or three tugs normally made up to ships like his in the channel, helped get them through, then pressed their hulls against the pier and held them until mooring lines were secure. While station tugs could not assist tonight, none were moored at the pier's head so there was enough room but no more.

The mostly dark station and customs house seemed tranquil enough despite spasmodic yelling near Jackson Square accompanied by the intermittent discharge of a rifle, pistol, or shotgun. Forsyth's attention returned to *Calypso*. She cleared Buoy C15 like a phantom then began coming left to enter the main channel. Starke was aiming just north of the pier where Blair and Weaver stationed one sentry while their men stacked rifles in two corn-shock affairs, with the spike bayonets interlocked, and then fell in along the pier. Forsyth sensed the deep-rooted bond between Starke and his roughhewn chief boatswain as Weaver told sailors how their captain would send fore and aft spring lines over first then use them to work the ship in.

The advancing silhouette grew larger and better defined until *Calypso*'s bulk, masts, and spars thickened by harbor furled canvas dominated the channel. Forsyth thought Starke had too much angle on the pier, especially with a weak current easing her bow starboard, but just as she seemed about to ram its north end, her rudder was put hard left, the backing engine raised mounds of white water beneath her stern, and she started to slowly swing. The jibboom, thrusting out from a classic bow to protrude over the pier, began twisting away as lines went over and Starke's voice came through a speaking trumpet to take their fore and aft spring lines to cleats. With her forward spring line over a cleat and held, momentum snugged *Calypso* against the pier while other lines were worked, adjusted, and secured. At the same time, her starboard searchlight beam illuminated naval station and custom house then harshly probed streets around the perimeter. Blair's detail retrieved weapons and advanced to the pier's foot in a line backed by shipmates behind wood bulwark armed with rifles, Gatling guns, a 3-pounder, and 4-inch rifles. Not only could lethal .45-70 rounds blanket the station but anyone sniping from a building or similar cover faced weapons that did not rely on a direct hit.

The short silence ended with the port bulwark gangway opening and sailors rigging an impromptu drawbridge to the pier using thick, rough planks as the panting warship released a nearly imperceptible plume of smoke and sigh of steam. Forsyth crossed and climbed to the flying bridge where Starke shook his hand and grinned through a tightly clenched jaw, "My apologies about the lack of honors, Commander."

"Excellent shiphandling, Captain."

"Good ship and crew, sir. Shall we go to my cabin? I'm due a pipe and the XO can handle things; right, Mr. Watson?"

"Yes sir."

Once in his cabin, Starke selected a pipe from the rack then dredged it through the dark leather pouch, trying not to betray his relief, "I knew you wouldn't ask unless it was tight, sir."

"How did you get steam up so quickly?"

"We set general quarters at *Taps* but didn't make a show."

"Your entrance made up for it."

"It sometimes pays to advertise. What next?"

"Wait for morning; unless there's a telegram from the Department."

"Or we're attacked."

"Or we're attacked."

"I'm concerned about the liberty party. We've ten ashore, including two officers, that didn't answer recall."

"They've probably gone to ground but there's nothing to do before morning."

"And we don't know where to look. You're welcome to my sea cabin in the meantime."

Key West's odd-looking overlord thanked Starke but ambled off to set perimeter patrols using *Calypso* sailors to augment his sparse staff. Starke moved between station and ship to speak with their sailors since sporadic shooting increased the risk that nerves might trigger a loaded weapon. Starke resolved before raising anchor that none of *Calypso's* sailors would face a mob unarmed to avoid later censure by those at safe distances. During late morning the gunfire faded and liberty party remnants began straggling through the perimeter. Later, Forsyth requested Starke visit so *Calypso's* commander walked the pier to the main building. The day was warming fast and Forsyth daubed his forehead before offering a chair, "Good morning, Captain. Thought you should know Knight deputized seventy armed men and restored order. So far, it seems a White named Gardner was killed near Jackson Square. It's anyone's guess who shot him and I doubt it will be explored deeply. There may be more, and some were wounded, but the sheriff thinks it's over and locals trust him. The deputy bringing the word thinks *Calypso* encouraged the stand-down with her waterfront reputation, heavy weapons, and searchlight probing the streets."

"I see, sir."

"Perhaps not all, Captain. It seems the president refused to commit Federal troops without the governor's request, which he could not do and remain in office, but the deputy's convinced both factions worried *Calypso* might shell Jackson Square and other places anyway."

"I can't control what people think. What about the prisoner?"

"Deputy says the young man's safe but certain to hang."

"So it's over."

"That depends on the press."

"Then, I'll stand the ship down."

"I suggest *Calypso* remain at the pier until Tuesday. Weekend liberty would be more convenient and people might believe it was an ordinary shift pierside made at first light."

Watson reported everyone accounted for that evening. Conrad and Thomas were in civilian clothes visiting a doctor acquaintance at his home and remained until it seemed order was restored. The enlisted crew was not allowed on liberty except in uniform so most went to ground in the nearby drinking and social concerns along and off Front Street. Kirby, Jones, and six others did not report back with this group because, unlike those who turned immediately left on Front Street, they went to examine Fort Taylor, which lay some distance south of the Marine Hospital and beyond Jackson Square. The fort's duty officer decided, without technically having the authority, this mixed group was safer with the soldiers and held them until late morning. Although last to return, they had the commanding major's note and Watson already decided to accept any excuse for ignoring the recall signal. Besides, spending the night comfortably asleep in the fort's guardroom was a yarn with legs that was certain to be embellished.

Calypso was still pierside Monday morning when Starke appeared in court. After pausing at Forsyth's office, he walked next door to the customs house, just off a small triangular park. The familiar red-brick building trimmed using stone and terra cotta had a large rear yard sloping down to water and piers. Its interior was unchanged since the meetings in one of the first floor's postal service and customs offices that determined Captain Buff would escape prosecution for his *John Gwinn Williams'* filibuster expedition; and planning in a third floor room to intercept *Rafael Riego*. Today, he was testifying in the second floor's federal courtroom.

Under oath from a witness chair, Starke answered questions about *Francisco de Montejo* and *Astraea*, precisely conveyed Mendoza's claims, and explained his actions were supported by Navy regulations. Junta lawyers representing Captain Buff relied on two points that ultimately swayed the judge. They argued the schooner was in ballast with no military cargo; no surprise since Captain Buff intended to enter a Spanish port to board the three men. The second was lack of solid evidence *Astraea* was part of a military organization or involved in hostile acts towards another nation. Mendoza and Spain would disagree but this well-practiced Junta defense was the reason filibuster expeditions usually loaded at sea or secluded spots and separated cargos from recruits until starting out. The approach's most recent success was freeing *Dauntless*, a filibuster apprehended with military cargo only. Since *Astraea*'s passengers had not been formally charged by Spanish authorities, Mendoza's claim they were fugitives also failed. Captain Buff boarded the three passengers during an unscheduled visit but this was legal and his claim the papers would have been revised at the next port unchallengeable. *Astraea*'s libel was removed and charges against her crew dropped. Captain Buff's fate was less clear due to *Rafael Riego*, but Starke expected Junta lawyers would also prevail there since the tug's recovered log documented his removal as master before *Francisco de Montejo* was attacked. In addition, her insurrectos and military cargo vanished in the massive detonation and left only the agricultural equipment manifest.

Although not discussed, the *Astraea* passengers claiming American citizenship that and taken into custody by the Treasury Department's Commissioner for Immigration were also released. Señor González returned to *Calypso* the next day with the Cuban Club president Herminio Gonzales to thank Starke for his consideration and pay their mess bill. Over Yamashita's lemonade in Starke's cabin they also related, to their amusement more than Starke's, there were rumors that *Calypso* fought the Spanish cruiser *Reina Mercedes* or *Alfonso XII* to save *Astraea*. The visit also confirmed Starke's suspicion that González belonged to the Junta's Puerto Rican Committee since they mentioned he was already booked on the old side-wheel paddle steamer for the growing town of Miami, Florida; East Coast Railroad to Jacksonville; and then north for New York City.

CHAPTER FIFTEEN
A NEWPORT SEASON

Tedium returned with *Calypso* at anchor west of the main ship channel; away from city effluent and the Keys' dark insect clouds. *Reveille* and *Taps* followed the naval station or another ship since Starke was invariably junior. Each clear, bright day's transient morning coolness passed quickly through warm to hot, punctuated by the brief rainstorms Key West's cisterns relied on. Since the channel current flowing south past Fort Taylor did not change direction and passed well clear, the ship swung very little on her tether; pointing north to several small keys with her starboard side opposite the white Marine Hospital building's long pier and port overlooking some diminutive keys before opening to the distant Gulf of Mexico horizon.

Starke sleep strong and well under clear skies with open windows as the bark rocked gently on small swells or passing ship's wake. Many times, a tropical breeze laden with the sea's bouquet or nearby keys' fragrance would gently caress whatever part of his body escaped the covers. Some sailors obtained Watson's permission to escape their close quarters below by slinging hammocks or rolling out mattresses topside. Canvas awnings spread above the main deck sheltered them from passing night showers, although their intended purpose was to keep metal fixtures touchable during the day and help ventilators, airports, windsails, and wood sheathing maintain below deck somewhat bearable.

There were few diversions. *Mascotte* and *City of Key West* passed several times each week, but interest in these transits vanished by mid-July; as with small sponge schooners, their twins carrying cargo between keys, and slightly larger versions rushing perishable cargoes as far north as New York. Life compressed to what transpired within her bulwarks and sanity preserved through daily routine, maintenance, training, and short runs ashore. Besides pleasant evenings with Forsyth, Starke concentrated on never-ending inspections and administrative tasks. He often climbed a mast in the early morning for exercise and, if small nurse sharks were absent, swam west of the ship in crystal green water over a sand bottom. Yamashita was always in attendance since he went ashore only for supplies and Starke ceased suggesting he go on liberty.

Osbourne and O'Leary tuned their steam plant while Blair's men inspected ammunition for deterioration and ministered the weapons exposed to salt air. Martyn and Weaver's deck department touched up sides. Dunbar's quartermasters updated and inventoried charts while officers studied the new rules of the road. *Calypso's* rigging regularly blossomed with drying white hammocks or underwear, blue pants, jumpers, and blouses; causing Conrad to remark during one bloom that their ship resembled elderberry bushes on a key.

Saturdays brought morning work, rope-yarn afternoons, and liberty ashore for the fortunate while Sunday required full dress uniform inspection, an *Articles of War* reading, Wiggs' sermon, then rope-yarn. For those not ashore drinking or pursuing other passions afterwards, the fantail sessions' popularity increased when Melvin was joined by the Irish violin player who proved equally proficient with a tin whistle, or flageolet, and read sheet music; adding *Shenandoah, Barbara*

Allen, *Soldier's Joy*, *Goober Peas*, and *Foggy Dew* to the gathering's repertoire.

A singlestick match or baseball game was arranged when other Navy ships were in port. *Calypso* did well with singlestick since arming the pinnace crew with cutlasses gave purpose to what had been a substitute for calisthenics, or monkey drills. Baseball was another matter, although the team lost less badly over time. *Maine* gave them a solid drubbing but the worst loss was a game arranged by Herminio Gonzales. *Calypso's* sailors were blissfully unaware the Cuban passion for baseball so exceeded cockfighting and bullfights Spain feared banning the games and insurrectos would not disrupt them. Consequently, its outcome was decided during the first inning with sailors hitting the ball and Cubans placing it, but the team played on, gained respect for their opponents, and learned.

Conrad regularly visited the white, three-story Marine Hospital to check two consumption cases and learn more of yellow and dengue fevers since Michigan had mostly malaria, typhoid, and cholera. The port was vulnerable because ships regularly crossed the ninety-miles to Cuba where soldiers, voluntarios, guerrilleros, pacificos, reconcentrados, and insurrectionists were dying in numbers beyond anything the island previously experienced; to the point coffins became so scarce that mass burials and bonfires became commonplace. Yellow fever predominated from June through August and was not confined to Cuba. Cities from Washington south, and northern port cities, feared its arrival. Starke remained anxious and Conrad understood why after several hospital conferences. Some patients survived without long-term effects, but others became invalids, and many died. Those coming from Europe or a northern state seemed more vulnerable than most native to yellow fever areas; with many believing Coloreds, and especially Negroes, were naturally immune. His captain did not share that view and voiced similar skepticism about cards certifying the bearer immune after surviving a bout or living ten years in an afflicted region. Its arrival also brought local quarantines and their associated violence. Disinfecting was so popular that mail from afflicted regions was often delivered with fumigation holes. Suspect ships went to quarantine anchorages or returned to sea until deemed safe or free of the disease since yellow fever required an autopsy to diagnose. Starke alluded to a voyage partly spent burying shipmates and waiting to see who would be next, but would not tell Conrad more.

With time to write, Starke posted a second letter to Tyson, three to Katherine, and one to his aunt and uncle summering in Newport with Albert's daughters. A letter from his aunt mentioned reconcentrado discussions with Clara Barton, Evans' departure for Havana, Newman Pearce's running of Starke's Oxen Grove plantation, and the *Eveleth* master's feigned complaints about *Calypso*'s boarding. She also added that nothing had been heard from Katherine or the distant British relatives.

In Washington, Captain Albert found his Building office close and particularly disagreeable. He was sweating, his white cotton uniform confining, and the open window offering no relief despite the extended striped awning, southern breeze, and slight promise of rain. The summer exodus to escape muggy heat, malaria, and yellow fever increased markedly after Congress adjourned on July 24, 1897. The president would be in upstate New York by month's end; among those fleeing to northern residences or high ground northwest of the city. Long would follow during August's first week and leave the assistant secretary without his gentle restraint; but Lieutenant Sharp just left the flag lieutenant billet to become Roosevelt's naval aid so Albert hoped he might damp the man's unpredictability and jingo inclinations. Still, he remained concerned the assistant secretary might interfere with his latest filibuster initiative and wanted orders out before August 2, 1897, when local oversight temporarily fell to the fervent Theodore.

These orders sent *Calypso* on a Gulf of Mexico sweep in response to the press and other sources reporting small Junta schooners moving material and men to sheltered locations along the Gulf Coast for transshipment to large tugs. Spain apparently saw the same activity and sent a gunboat to loiter off Tampico then enter that port. The resulting brawls involving her sailors were not only with Mexican insurrecto supporters but one Texas party that required a Mexican army detachment to quell. While Albert's ferret was occupied, North Atlantic Squadron ships would cover the East Coast and Straits of Florida; augmenting the district revenue cutters Captain Fischer was arranging. It was also arranged for *Vanguard* to accompany *Calypso* since their commanders' coordination was successful with the anarchist filibuster *Rafael Riego* and the ships' capabilities complemented each other.

Despite explaining *Calypso*'s recent actions off Puerto Rico and ensuring Department support for her recent Key West involvement, Albert gained enough time to complete the sweep's planning when three impediments faded away. House interest in testimony regarding the filibusters' demise died with the Senate hearing and Falk ensuring other committee chairs knew of the anarchist link; daily briefings on the Greek and Ottoman imbroglio ended when fighting was supplanted by diplomacy, blatant strong-arming, and threats; and Roosevelt began a Midwest tour promoting the Navy and naval militia. Additionally, press interest did not immediately return to Cuba after the Greco-Turkish War because gold was discovered around mid-month in the Canadian territories then Alaska. Promised riches and a poor economy sucked thousands north; filling papers with stories of ill-equipped men and women leaving jobs and families. Even third place fell to the Swedish balloon that left for the North Pole and Lieutenant Peary's unending struggle to start out. Although press coverage of filibuster expeditions was muted, despairing accounts of reconcentrados fueled demands for Congress to fund relief and Weyler's recall became a constant theme also taken up by liberal Spanish papers as draftee casualties and reconcentrado deaths climbed. With Albert's filibuster project attracting less interest, he was able to complete the sweep's planning and arrangements then send orders to Starke using an officer reporting to another ship at Key West. *Calypso* would leave in August, cruise the Gulf's American coast, visit Veracruz, return along Cuba's north shore, transit the Straits of Florida, and finish in Port Royal or Norfolk.

The *Rafael Riego* expedition's anarchist architect and survivor, Manuel Valencia y Gomis, also had August plans; having agreed at a Barcelona affair given by Ramón Emeterio Betances in July to help Michele Angiolillo assassinate Spain's prime minister, Antonio Cánovas del Castillo. Their Puerto Rican host was dedicated to independence and most of his guests were convinced the conservative prime minister's removal would free Cuba and Puerto Rico since he refused negotiations until fighting ended, supported Weyler, and would send more troops. The Italian anarchist explained to Valencia the assassination would be a historic propaganda of the deed and fair revenge for the Inquisition of Montjuich. Angiolillo's intensity rivaled that of Niccolo Salvaggi, rotting off the Yucatan Peninsula with *Rafael Riego*. Valencia saw supporting this assassination as partial atonement for deserting Salvaggi; a cowardly act that created the recurring nightmare of a spectral black bark's approach or Salvaggi cursing him as a traitor. He actually remembered little about the tug's final moments except trying to assert himself with Captain Buff on the fantail, swallowing salt water, and the American's inexorable grip dragging him aboard a small boat. Valencia agreed to announce the assassin's justification at Sachs' Café in New York and elsewhere; but after Angiolillo shot Cánovas in front of his wife at Mondragón on August 8, 1897, anarchists celebrated without Valencia. He was challenged by a border patrol while fleeing Barcelona for France just as *Calypso* prepared to leave Key West. A Carabinero's single 7mm Mauser round entered his back, barely missed the heart, and tore out through the chest. He felt surprise, slight pain, and overwhelming weariness; then, unable to stand, collapsed. Valencia remained conscious long enough to know he was dying, look up at the Carabineros, and then pass away silently as he struggled to yell, "Long live anarchy."

Meanwhile, Constance Starke was guiding Albert's two daughters through a Newport season in the Rhode Island city and adjusting to a different summer at their cottage than that spent with Katherine. The widow had been reserved, pensive, self-controlled, and often lost in thought while Olivia and Isabella burned with exuberant dynamism and soaked experience like dry sponges. A year had passed since they attended her Washington dinner party and she found Olivia still slightly more reserved; with the same muted dark brown hair, matching eyes, and complexion largely free of the freckles spread across her younger sister's translucent skin. Isabella still favored their mother, with flashing green eyes, rebellious springy red hair, and vivid features that made it unlikely she would ever be considered a beauty. While also lacking Olivia's grace, she would doubtless burn through life like a flare. With bust-lines dropping and hips expanding neither could be considered a girl, especially after the inauguration ball, so their long hair was worn up.

Constance sometimes played croquet with them on the cottage's broad lawns then recovered by spending evenings in a canvas chair overlooking the shimmering harbor festooned with lights; and this year was exceptional with Immanuel away less often on business. Rhode Island winters could be harsh, cold, and dark but Newport summers were glorious with constant events and society; and August 3, 1897, would see the North Atlantic Squadron arrive for fete days. She arranged a picnic lunch for that morning and took her charges to Castle Hill Lighthouse, overlooking Narraganset Bay's mouth. After setting up folding canvas recliners under squawking white-gray gulls gliding overhead or strutting nearby in a constant quest for food, Olivia and Isabella grew impatient and clambered over jumbled gray boulders above the gray Atlantic that slapped and sucked at their base. The slippery rocks were coated with sea life where crevices sheltered it from the probing saltwater and the girls' exuberance matched the ocean's energy.

Gray shapes slowly emerging from the southwest beyond Point Judith light became six or seven distinct ships in line ahead and nearly bows on, before turning in succession to follow their leader from a white-capped gray ocean into the bay's placid blue water. Parading past Cape Breton Point and Castle Hill, the squadron entered East Passage for Newport Harbor trailing plumes of light gray smoke that stained a clear blue sky over undulating wakes overlapping as though braiding the water. Leading, with national ensign and blue rear admiral's flags streaming astern, was *New York*, a large armored cruiser with ram bow, fine lines, and silhouette that displayed her balance of speed, firepower, and aesthetics.

Brooklyn, close astern, appeared French with a pronounced tumblehome, fighting masts, and three tall stacks. Four battleships followed. The two sisters, *Massachusetts* and *Indiana*, had short stacks, low freeboard, a fighting mast, and massive 13-inch turrets. Behind came *Iowa*, an improved version with raised forecastle and tall stacks. The last was *Maine*, an experimental aberration with offset turrets, followed by *Puritan*, the 6,000-ton monitor with a single mast, large stack, and two turrets housing 12-inch rifles. Powerful, well-armored, and riding low, she was formidable in calm water but plowed through almost any sea half-submerged so her crew was eager to enter the placid bay.

The Navy Ball came six days later at Newport Casino, a large, shingled structure just off the waterfront with expansive rear grounds. A hundred bright lights lit the perfect summer evening and masked a clear sky freckled with flickering stars. Hydrangeas and roses surrounded the dance floor and huge striped-marquee was erected for serving food to 500 guests. Among navy officers, local notables, New York wealthy, and others were the Albert sisters wearing their inauguration ball gowns. Neither garment left storage during the intervening five months while Olivia and Isabella's developing figures made them unusable except by tight corseting and punctilious movement. Constance was relieved to see they filled dance cards and required little guidance regarding behavior or propriety; with longtime friends, business acquaintances, and social necessities demanding her attention. Equally welcome was Immanuel claiming more dances than usual, along with an increased appetite for various other activities since restructuring the firm; so she felt this foretold a special summer as they returned to the summer cottage.

Squadron ships were also opened to the public, a ten-oared cutter race took place, and large parade held. The harbor came alive every sunset with warships and yachts turning on electric lights and, when not at a social event, the sisters watched from their shared room or cottage lawn with Immanuel and Constance. The young ladies' social life was not diminished when the squadron left to work north along the coast because invitations to chaperoned events arrived regularly. Besides several wealthy young men, they enjoyed the attentions of officers from Fort Adams, the naval station, and Naval War College. This appeared to reduce Isabella's correspondence to *Calypso* while increasing Olivia's. The elder daughter compared officers mixing social events and exercises with Watson's descriptions of fights, yellow fever, gun runners, and a Cuban war to find her attraction for him growing, gaining greater appreciation for their mother, and becoming more understanding of her father's absences.

Other distractions included ocean bathing, the country club, a golf club, several polo matches, and near continuous sail races. A national championship tennis tournament was also played on the Newport Casino's grass courts during August, but the pair was disappointed about women's matches taking place in Philadelphia; especially since Juliette Atkinson faced her nemesis, Elisabeth Moore. Constance arranged for lessons but it was obvious the sisters' passion exceeded skill and the Atkinson sisters safe. To Constance, it was a summer with daughters she never had and even the taciturn Cynthia adjusted to their flittering about and quizzing everyone from Immanuel to the gardener about whatever interested them; although she still thought it improper.

Cynthia especially looked forward to the Newport season since the once major slave port was even less segregated than Washington, with races sharing schools, neighborhoods, and business districts. She especially enjoyed Mary Dickerson's Bellevue Avenue dress shop, where Constance ordered new gowns for her young guests; and became more accepted by locals each year.

The ship chandler Aron Sharett, a regular summer visitor, called as well. He came to circulate through Newport's small Hebrew community, attend Touro Synagogue, and pay respects at the local Jewish cemetery. One or more evenings was always spent with the Starkes, although these were primarily dedicated to business dealings. He was friendly and courteous to Constance but she never felt completely at ease since he seldom spoke of his Odessa childhood or family life; and this summer included a strange evening sequestered with her husband in the windowed porch set aside for work. She refused to listen in but heard *Calypso*, Gulf of Mexico, and Zionist Congress spoken while they enjoyed vodka; liquor Immanuel drank only with Sharett.

CHAPTER SIXTEEN
GULF OF MEXICO

*C*alypso steamed southwest from Key West to clear the shallows then due west through a rolling blue and green sea until past Loggerhead Key. During the midwatch she came to almost north by east for Port Tampa and raised the sea buoy near midmorning Wednesday. The Tampa Bay pilot boarded off Egmont Key at the North Passage entrance then came to the flying bridge. He was soon standing beside the conning officer, Ensign Martyn, offering suggestions as they slipped past St. Petersburg over the glasslike surface towards Port Tampa with channel buoys, day-marks, small fishing craft, and flocks of birds passing down either side. Intermittently, a small ripple patch erupted where voracious predators sliced through schools of panicked fish. Starke watched a dark-gray pelican roll into a dive, fix half-extended swept-back wings, then drive its pointed orange beak through the surface to skewer unsuspecting prey.

Plant's expansive Port Tampa pier system stood apart from shore vegetation, light sand beaches, and occasional small port or landing. *Calypso* would coal there since her bunkers were not filled in Key West; to encourage reports she was headed for the Port Royal shipyard and make room for anthracite coal in Port Tampa. Combined with the bituminous supply already on board, Starke could choose more power or less smoke while in the Gulf. The chandler Aron Sharett made arrangements for this visit and others, including Veracruz, using the Starke firm as cover to avoid advertising their itinerary. He not only enjoyed a reputation for performance and discretion among shipping firms but possessed an unexplained bond with Starke's uncle the captain never understood despite enjoying their infrequent discussions and always feeling welcome.

The agent was a local man fluent in Spanish so he explained Tampa mostly favored insurrectionists but many saw Spain as their mother country and remembered Cubans driving them from Key West cigar factories over politics and wages. The city's Cubans were more anarchistic than those in Key West because a labor strike forced them off that island; so workers with Spanish or African ancestors rolled cigars together in Ybor City factories while lectors read books and what newspaper they requested. *Patria* favored independence and *La Doctrina* promoted broad social change. Although rival groups were energetic fundraisers, a Junta tax was voluntarily extracted in factories supporting independence so Weyler responded by ending tobacco leaf shipments; damaging what little popularity he enjoyed locally.

The black-hulled bark with tall straw-yellow masts, black yards, and harbor furled sails moored easily without fanfare just past a large bend in the huge pier south of a small customs house. Two fish processing shacks on the pier south of their mooring proved aromatic neighbors, as did a large phosphate loading dock to the north. Near *Calypso* and the customs house, two railroad buffer stops served as the Plant System's west coast terminus. Trains rolled slowly from them, passed the Tampa Inn Annex and Tampa Inn, left the pier for Port Tampa, and then crossed nine miles of swamp and sand to Tampa where rail connections to Jacksonville took them anywhere in North America.

The coal lighter alongside early the next day meant hours of filthy, backbreaking work under the broiling sun before sweeping, cleaning, and washing down; but mugs of fresh, foamy beer arrived on the pier afterwards for sailors foregoing or ineligible for liberty. Those leaving for Port Tampa and Tampa received a warm reception since summer heat and yellow fever's specter ended their November through March tourist season when trains arrived filled with them and winter refugees. Most businesses were closed, including the Tampa Bay Hotel, but those open appreciated sailors flush with pay so celebrants often returned late, drunk, or both to the inevitable extra duty and liberty class reduction. *Calypso* also experienced her first desertions, two landsmen and a seaman bolted for the Alaskan or Canadian goldfields. Starke was not surprised with gleaming rail crowns beckoning a few feet from the brow, newspapers filled with gold rush stories since mid-July, and people across the nation leaving everything behind to join the rush. Watson was particularly infuriated the pair carried out a complex plan requiring they gain the necessary liberty class; acquire civilian clothes, tickets, and a stake; then conceal everything until reaching a port like Tampa. Starke declared them deserters but personally wished them well; recalling his own impetuous journey to Montana where he first saw the elephant.

The agent mentioned during one visit that the tobacco grapevine believed *Calypso* was in port to hunt any filibuster expeditions operating near Ft. Myers or Cedar Key. Confederate blockade runners had used the first port during the war, but it lacked a railhead and the Caloosahatchee River had several limitations. The second was still struggling to recover from a catastrophic hurricane and uncharted wrecks left in its wake. Since these rumors would reach the Junta in New York, he suggested the agent subtly add credence. A week later the bark steamed due west from Egmont Key until the Florida coast went below the horizon then turned for Apalachicola on a track Dunbar laid out using charts and the *United States Coast Pilot*.

They steamed the roughly 180 miles to Apalachicola Bay's barrier islands at six knots and raised them late afternoon the next day. *Calypso* took care to avoid sand shoals to their south and made for the bay's West Pass entrance. Merchant ships preferred the deeper East Pass channel but it required a long transit to Apalachicola's piers most deep draft ships could not make; so most loaded from or delivered to lighters near the entrance. Starke chose to anchor just off the shallower West Pass channel to place *Calypso* near the town and visible to small boats using it to fish, gather oysters, or hook sponges; but would remain only long enough to create local rumors since the nearest rail line was at Carrabelle, a port connected to Apalachicola by paddlewheel steamer.

They spent two days within sight of Cape Saint George lighthouse, floating calmly off blinding white beaches near a black and white striped West Pass Bar Buoy marred by bird droppings. Watson and Weaver launched all boats to let them ride at the booms for seawater to preserve wood and swell seams, but sent steam pinnaces on runs ashore to advertise *Calypso*'s presence and gather information. There was no liberty so the crew was more than ready when the black anchor broke surface, was swung inboard by its davit, and secured. Martyn took them from the anchorage with skill and confidence that reflected Watson's tutelage. Their cadets' notebooks were equally promising, the wardroom appeared to lead rather than coerce, and conning officers grasped the need to drive rather than react. The split between line officers and steam engineers was also negligible; perhaps because Osbourne sent cadet engineers to stand intermittent pilothouse watches and their line brethren to fire and engine rooms.

Starke remained on the flying bridge while their engineers walked up the speed, clamped his teeth on an unlit pipe, and watched a small schooner with patched sails come down the channel then turn southeast for some favored sponging ground. He understood and appreciated Albert's plan to disrupt the Junta's Gulf operations but it took time, required visibly fruitless port visits that risked yellow fever, and might take *Calypso* and *Vanguard* away from filibusters. Their destination, the dormant navy yard in Warrington, lay at the entrance to Pensacola's bay. Once there, sailors could go ashore, he could telegraph Albert, and there would be yellow fever news.

They steamed west with the coast shrinking to a thickened horizon as Starke extracted his unlit pipe and breathed the sea air. Under the bark's jibboom, beyond foremast and forecastle, her stem thrust aside languid gulf waters to generate easy green mounds that slid down the hull. In twenty miles they changed course for the Pensacola sea buoy then keep a west-northwest heading under cloudless skies remaining throughout the night. Cape San Blas, with its shoal extending miles south into the Gulf, would receive an unusually wide berth since Dunbar learned the cape lacked any beacon while a less exposed replacement lighthouse was completed.

Starke was seldom called to the pilothouse so he slept strong and well during the night on a benign summer gulf with cabin windows open. After waking to an ephemeral coolness, however, the stifling summer heat soon made varnished wood painful to touch and steel unbearable. The slow speed and absent breeze also forced less air below so engineering watches became a humid hell, causing Conrad to set up a relief station aft under the limp canvas awning fashioned by their sailmaker. Beneath it, he worked with the apothecary and baymen to tend engineers carried or ordered topside once beyond endurance. After rest and tepid water, most patients hoped to avoid derision by a rapid return to stifling humidity and temperatures surpassing 120 degrees.

On Friday morning the foretop lookout, Landsman Hawk, spotted a thickening horizon off their starboard bow that soon transformed into blazing white sand beaches fronting green foliage. Beyond lay an immense bay, with Pensacola, several small towns, and sprinkling of villages around its shore creating a railroad, river steamboat, and ocean shipping hub. It could easily shelter a fleet so there were often more than fifty ships and always scores of fishing boats. Most queued for bituminous coal loadouts or to exchange cargoes between riverboat and rail connections. Liners also connected the port with Havana and other cities so it offered a useful haven for filibusters should Florida and East Coast patrols force them west.

Heaving the lead began once sea and anchor detail was set and the plan was to pause a mile west of the sea buoy, labeled Whistle Buoy on their charts, where an eager pilot boat luffed sails. Most deep-draft ships anchored off the city to load or discharge cargo, and the best holding grounds and depths were distant from the bay's entrance, but the water alongside the navy yard quay would easily take *Calypso*. Mooring there, however, required Starke ensure available pier space, the yard would take them, and local quarantine status. He planned to send a steam pinnace to find out then, depending on the response, moor at the shipyard or remain anchored until *Vanguard* arrived to join the cruise west.

While Hawk searched for the sea buoy or bay entrance, Starke easily located the passage using binoculars and familiarity with the coast profile. Santa Rosa Island lay east of the channel, where broad, white-sand beaches lay seaward of tall dunes sprinkled with clusters of green and dark brown foliage; then miles of pine forests inland. To its west lay a thick forest coming nearly to the water's edge and only a ribbon of sand beach. This disparity extended into the Gulf where the channel separated different bottoms and depths until becoming notoriously unpredictable shifting sand shoals. Three large shoals ringed the channel entrance so Dunbar selected deeper water just south of Caucus Shoal for their extemporaneous anchorage.

The port anchor was dropped using the Pensacola lighthouse and Whistle Buoy for cross bearings. After *Calypso* backed down to set it in the hard sand bottom and lay a short scope of chain, her steam pinnaces were launched and started out for the entrance under Ensign Dunbar. Besides the lighthouse, Fort Pickens sat landward with one imposing brick face dominating the channel's east side while Fort McRee's shattered remains lay to the west across hot, glassy water. The ship channel began at the sand bar's south end and was marked with buoys to the three-quarter mile wide entrance where it turned right before a third brick fort then continued east past the yard into the bay where numerous masts could be seen east of Fort Pickens beyond Santa Rosa Island; using binoculars.

The scouting expedition soon reported *Calypso* could berth at the shipyard quay in twenty-two feet of water, a flood tide was approaching, ship traffic had been light, line-handlers would be stationed once they passed Middle Shoal, and a quarantine officer was standing by at the yard rather than Santa Rosa station. Starke ordered their steam pinnaces astern, reset sea and anchor detail, and hoisted the code pennant above two square flags, one blue with a white center and the second red, white, and blue vertical stripes. In short order, a schooner loitering east of the buoy came about, delivered a pilot, and then pulled smoothly away.

The diminutive figure bounding to the flying bridge with Ensign Martyn in tow displayed a face and neck of dark bronze with thick, leather-like skin crisscrossed by lines that resisted flexing. An unlit corncob pipe extended from his mouth and broad-brimmed felt hat shielded bare skin left by a vanishing hairline, while scarred and discolored hands spoke to a past on freighters or fishing schooners. He coached Ensign Blair as they made for the entrance while carrying on a discussion with Starke. It seemed a cut was being dredged through Caucus Shoals, but *Calypso* would keep them to port, stay in the main channel, and leave East Bank and Middle shoals to starboard. They came port as the whistle buoy closed then steadied northwest by north using the range; a large marker on Pensacola's lighthouse and another on a short building-like white beacon with black sides. As they turned left onto Fort McRee range, just past East Bank, the pilot extracted his corncob pipe to caution Blair that strong currents and hard right turn at the leg's end often proved challenging. Starke nodded imperceptibly, extracted his unlit briar pipe from a thin beard, and scanned the broad expanse of surrounding water that appeared benign but was extremely shallow outside the black and red buoys. As Middle Shoal passed unseen to starboard and the black buoy ahead drew closer, their pilot nodded and Blair began the hard right turn that placed *Calypso* roughly parallel to three red buoys at the Middle Ground's western edge. This short leg, separating Pensacola Bay from the Gulf of Mexico, took them between Fort McRee's jumbled remains sinking into the sand spit to port and Fort Pickens' faded red bulk on Santa Rosa Island's western tip to starboard.

Shortly after turning right, red-brick industrial buildings filled the north shore and a broad, blue-green bay with anchored ships lay beyond the channel mouth. Most were immobile, whether waiting to work cargoes, held in quarantine, or queuing for the private shipyard; but one tug with black smoke billowing from her single stack was towing a four-masted schooner to the gulf. *Calypso*'s pilot pointed his pipe's damp stem at them, "Collier under tow. She looks good to cross the bar. They leave during high tide unless in ballast. Anyway Captain, yard's ready and your tug's standing by; port side to?"

"Yes, Captain, let's keep her bow upstream."

"Port side to it is, Captain."

Their pilot walked Blair through a competent landing against the long, brick and granite wharf near a large wet basin at the yard's eastern boundary. Starke resisted interfering throughout since he wanted officers exposed to different techniques, but his unlit pipe paid the price as orders went to helm, engine, lines, and tug. Finally, the engine was shut down, both main boilers taken off line, and mooring lines doubled. Once the bark settled these fiber lines would be replaced by wire rope since they would be longer in Pensacola than Port Tampa.

The station deputy, Lieutenant James Bull, was waiting on the wharf with an invitation for early supper at the commandant's quarters. Starke ensured Yeoman Pound took an arrival report and coded message for Albert to the yard telegraph, then changed uniforms and joined Bull in a small Studebaker stanhope. Its oiled leather top was down so he felt the late afternoon heat and absent breeze as they rolled through the oppressive stillness of deserted industrial buildings lining red-brick and packed sand streets. Starke's escort briefly mentioned the yard's commandant, Commander

William Reisinger, was on leave awaiting orders after commanding the side-wheel gunboat *Monocacy* in China when his predecessor was relieved unexpectedly less than two months earlier.

Distracted by their mare managing a lethargic swish of the tail, body shake, and toss of the head to disturb some small tormentor, Bull said little more but Starke suspected the cause was drink brought about by absolutely still industrial structures on deserted streets edged with tufts of grass. Leaving the wharf and its waterfront service building, their carriage rolled undisturbed past a red-brick carpenter shop and storehouse, maintenance shops, and ordnance workshop. These differed little from those in Norfolk, New York, Port Royal, and Newport News except for an absence of life. Bull explained the year's only activity, besides maintaining buildings, tools, and inventory, was overhauling their steam launches. Starke recalled most navy yards resembled this when he was a cadet but now had work or were closed; and mused it was even money whether a ship in ordinary or deserted shipyard was more depressing. This industrial purgatory also included a naval hospital laid up and maintained for future emergencies. Located on the solitary rise and encircled by a tall brick wall, its roof was scheduled to be repaired and interior repainted this year. Bull speculated it was kept ready because the port was regularly visited by ships working the Caribbean and connected to New Orleans by rail; both yellow fever sources every summer. He also advised Starke any repairs must be done by the crew or a civilian shipyard since the navy yard employed only a few watchmen and small administrative staff. The commandant's Navy core was limited to surgeon, paymaster, acting boatswain, clerk, two writers, and one mail messenger;

although there were rumors a small Marine detachment might reopen their vacant barracks.

Their carriage's final turn came where the foundry's tall brick stack looked down on the old armory, an octagonal building across the street encircled by a porch. Quarters A was north of the spectral industrial area near the bachelor officer quarters; two more vacant buildings. It was red-brick capped with a large windowed white cupola matching the broad wooden veranda encircling both stories. A respectable lawn separated it from the street and park-like area to the rear ended at two elongated red-brick stables with more stalls than horses. A servant stood at the door to guide them to the rear where they turned left into its library and were greeted by Commander Reisinger, "Welcome to the yard, Captain; and save your card, we're not New York or Washington."

As they waited by the seldom-used fireplace before crossing the hall to supper in the formal dining room, Reisinger continued, "I've expected *Calypso* since your correspondence began arriving; and heard you were in China for the war. You'll find Warrington dull but there's a regular street car to Pensacola and our prospective Lieutenant Commander Bull can brief your XO on what is available."

After finishing supper they returned briefly to the library for brandy and cigars. Starke left his pipe on the ship so he accepted a Cuban. Reisinger and Bull were interested in *Calypso*'s history, filibuster expeditions, and anarchists but also wanted to discuss the Spanish prime minister's murder, its effect on Spanish policy, and Governor-general Weyler. Starke returned late to be informed the station surgeon, Hatton Harris, and paymaster Henry Jewett visited. Arriving ship's officers customarily made the courtesy call but he suspected their monotonous daily routines accounted for dispensing with protocol. Watson also mentioned the unarmored cruiser *Marblehead* was four days in port during March and her sister ship, *Montgomery*, spent a week anchored in the bay during March, May, and June to train reserves and dissuade filibusters. Otherwise, with the year over half gone, only the cutter *William H. Seward* at Ship Island, supporting the Marine Hospital Ship *Surgeon*, offered companionship to the yard's exiles.

CHAPTER SEVENTEEN
HAVANA RETURN

C*alypso* entered Pensacola just as *The Sun* correspondent Darwin Tyson returned to New York City from Greece. His paper's red-brick, five-story building with gabled mansard roof was unaltered and awnings over its first floor stores still cranked in and out every business day but Charles Dana became ill in early June and was not expected to live. *The Sun*'s soul would pass with its publisher and change Tyson's world but there was more. Lord, the managing editor, saw United Press news service fading, disliked Associated Press coverage, and decided *The Sun* would start its own; with Tyson heading the Havana office.

It was an impossible proposal to consider while sitting at his corner desk, crowned by the new Underwood typewriter and suitably distant from the managing editor; so Tyson left the elongated, high-ceilinged, third-floor newsroom with five windows, rows of desks, and rubber mat flooring for a park across Frankfort Street. Finding an open bench near the Bethesda Fountain, he extracted his silver flask, took a quick shot, looked about, and downed another. The hot afternoon sun hammered city and park into a shimmering, sultry semi-stillness as he surveyed the landscaped grounds and patrons on wrought iron benches near black streetlights. This redoubt near the soothing fountain was less noisy than the periphery where a cacophony of foot, carriage, bicycle, and cart traffic competed with street vendors; and its semi-bucolic bouquet only intermittently disrupted by a fitful breeze imbued with the city's scent after flowing through streets between buildings.

Tyson closed the flask, extracted a Turkish cigarette from his case, tapped it against the edge, and lit up. Acceptance meant foregoing local assignments he used to recuperate after undertakings like Cuba and Greece. Except for lost weight, he avoided this latest war's maladies but spirit, closet, cigarette, and liquor stocks needed replenishment. He was not a climber so editor, manager, or publisher was never his goal; and the favored desk lost if he left for Havana. Thin legs extended from the park bench as Tyson took a long, slow drag. Looking up, he studied several buildings towering above *The Sun*. His tenure with this paper could end should he decline promotion and there were offers from competing papers in those offices above the treetops so he wavered between loyalty, fatalism, and common sense before resolving to accept and ride it out.

Lord already purchased tickets for the Southern Railroad's daily express to Jacksonville and St. Augustine, a less well-appointed Florida East Coast coach to Miami, that line's steamship to Key West, then a Plant Line steamer to Havana. Tyson knew the express stopped in Washington so he tilted the silver flask, took a biting sip, and decided to negotiate for several days in the capital. Starke was with *Calypso* and the family summering in Newport but a stopover would establish and refresh contacts, including Evans. Her intriguing letter lay with his friend's correspondence and revealed she had returned to work at the Times newspapers and was recently in the city covering its Grant's Tomb dedication. Starke was also in New York, where he invited her to Delmonico's and an evening's entertainment. Tyson recalled their time together in a Key West restaurant and regretted missing out.

Tyson accepted Lord's proposition and later that evening finished a letter to Starke; but delayed its posting until visiting the Navy Department since *Calypso*'s movements were not in the East Coast newspapers, unlike other ships. Writing to Evans proved more difficult. He tried describing the heady days in Greece before their army was crushed by a better trained, equipped, and led Ottoman force. There was also a missing cable that would have added the British celebration to his itinerary. He finally set it aside and resolved to approach her in Washington.

August's last days found Tyson stepping from a Southern Railroad express train to the platform of Washington's Baltimore & Potomac station. It was almost noon before he retrieved what luggage was needed for his stopover and left through the B Street entrance. Pausing under its canopy to light a cigarette, he briefly studied the Center Market building then took a Herdic cab to Ebbitt House, one of the few hotels open during summer. After he registered, unpacked, and lunched in its bar, Tyson boarded a streetcar to reacquaint himself. A bare Executive Mansion flagpole revealed the president was not in residence. Most senior officials and civil servants whose thirty days leave must be taken during summer already joined the exodus and those remaining dealt with routine matters, prepared priority documents for senior officials' brief visits, and forwarded critical ones. There were also noticeably fewer tourists and reporters stalking streets, buildings, and monuments; which would not change until cooler months made life agreeable and risk of disease lessened.

Tyson invariably unearthed opportunities during these doldrums since practitioners tended to lower their guard; and began with the State, War, and Navy Building across from the Executive Mansion. He hoped for an appointment or two but was directed to a captain working for the absent Navy secretary who proposed meeting in a Treasury Building conference room then order lunch from its small upper floor restaurant. This had apparently become popular when the incoming Treasury secretary, Lyman Gage, began to regularly invite his three assistants for a working lunch ordered from the restaurant. Tyson walked through the manicured park south of the Executive Mansion to the Treasury Building with Captain Albert to be met by a Revenue Cutter Service captain, Gibson Fischer, and State Department civilian, Maximilian Falk. Tyson never relied on first impressions but always took them into account. He initially marked Albert for one of those Army and Navy officers who inhabited departments waiting for mandatory retirement but found him a unique seaman-bureaucrat. Fischer seemed out of a Marryat novel and his element, but the facade concealed a quick and agile mind. Falk was clearly one of many midlevel politicos working the city but possessed superior intelligence, insight, and agility. All three knew the game and hoped to extract or insert information, as did he.

Tyson suspected his acquaintance with Starke and recent Havana posting played a role in this unusual attention. He was surprised to learn the revenue cutter *Vanguard* was with *Calypso* sweeping the Gulf of Mexico for filibusters; leaving other ships and cutters covering the East Coast, Bahama Islands, and Straits of Florida. Since Jacob concealed this coordinated effort, Tyson knew they now wanted it publicized and, in exchange, he offered observations on the eastern Mediterranean. While waiting for a streetcar to the Capitol afterward, he considered the change in relationships this new position seemed to entail. After dexterously lighting a single match without igniting its book, he touched it to a Turkish cigarette then tossed the charred carcass aside. Nearby was a uniformed street cleaner working the sidewalk and curb. This southern variant of Waring's New York City model was no immigrant but a Negro who knew it was nonsensical to wear a buttoned white blouse during Washington's summer. The Capitol yielded a few more contacts and background information before his first day concluded in the Ebbitt House's wood-paneled bar.

Early next morning, while visiting Hutchins Building offices, Tyson invited Evans' to midday dinner. She accepted and a few hours later he waited in the Ebbitt House lobby. As the ornate floor clock's skeletal hands inched towards the agreed time he instinctively reached beneath his coat and realized the silver flask lay on the bureau. He lit a cigarette instead then leaned back, feet across an ottoman, watching light gray smoke float towards the ceiling, two stories above. Four tall columns flanked the dark walnut reception desk with cream-colored marble top while a dozen rugs lay under the maze of walnut and dark oak furniture populating the marble floor between it and a front wall dominated by large windows opening to a bustling street.

The distance from Evans' Georgetown lodgings precluded any midday clothes change so she entered the lobby dressed for work and caught him comparing his silver pocket watch to the floor clock. Looking up, Tyson noticed a few wisps of chestnut hair had slipped their binding, she was recovering from her Havana illness, and some weight was returning. The figure remained slightly less full than he remembered from Key West but more robust than when he put her, weak and pale, on a liner for New York. Whatever she contracted from Havana's open soil drains, noxious bay, endemic diseases, or reconcentrado encampments left her with a seasoned appearance subtly enhanced by a traveling dress over corset and bustle. Evans turned towards him without breaking stride or overt display of recognition. He sheathed the watch, rose, and found her familiar deep-brown eyes now inhabited a less tense but pleasantly lined face; with the short walk through summer's heat adding a faint sheen of fine perspiration.

The dining room soared two stories above its white marble floor to a frescoed ceiling and, where it faced the street, tall windows spanned most of the distance between the wall's top and bottom with passing horse-drawn vehicles, streetcars, and pedestrians of various hues beyond the glass. At their small table draped with white linen, Tyson carefully slid the chair under Evans as she positioned herself with corset and bustle encumbrances. Once seated, Tyson ordered wine, tasted the sample, and rued the necessity to drink it unfortified by the silver flask as the waiter filled their glasses. Although he listened attentively to her describe the New York trip and visiting Starke on *Calypso*, Tyson was drawn to flawless eyebrows that seemed unaffected in Havana while the eyes below flickered as her body struggled to survive. She was also wearing scent; another change. Once engaged, Tyson contributed information, opinions, and evaluations he normally shared only with Starke. After the table was cleared, she lifted a white cup slowly to her lips, took a tentative sip of hot coffee, and lowered it with her mouth's corners raised slightly in an inquisitive smile, "Your flask is missing."

"As is your carpet bag."

Before Havana she would have been offended or defensive, but he instead received a gentle smile as the cooling coffee rose a second time; and so resorted to honesty, "I left it on the bureau without thinking," then changed the subject, "How are you faring at the paper?"

It was a curious departure from Tyson's past behavior, so she returned cup and saucer to the table, "It's been sold."

"*The Sun's* not been peddled yet but without Dana it will be."

"How is he? It's rumored there's little time."

The discussion turned instantly professional; perhaps encouraged by the Ebbitt House bordering newspaper row. Tyson finally looked across the white linen, fumbled an unlit cigarette, then spoke, "I've a proposition, Miss Evans."

She looked quizzically and directly into his eyes, "Yes, Mr. Tyson?"

"Are you interested in another go at Havana? I'll understand if you aren't."

She perhaps anticipated something different but replied quietly, "I've approached Lord before about a position."

"*The Sun's* hiring women. Cuba's a tough sell but you've experience, familiarity, and perhaps some immunity."

"I'll require time to consider, Darwin."

"Wire me when you decide. Nothing's certain. I'll contact Lord but it could require another interrogation."

Evan's reaction puzzled Tyson. She seemed willing before he finished explaining but now wanted time to consider. He understood after his reaction to Lord's offer a few days before; especially since no one would be carried and returning far from certain with the disease and fighting.

"Will you be there?"

"To stand up the wire service office then I'm not certain. My New York lodgings and desk were forfeit and what happens after Dana is anyone's guess. I'll understand if you pass."

"I'll have an answer before you leave."

Cassandra looked across the table to her thin, balding, and bony Havana benefactor with an overwhelming urge to accept, but the fever burned away any naivety preceding that first Havana expedition. Her professional goal was working on a large New York paper but she had earned respect in Washington and the physical toll exacted a year earlier was not fully paid. On the other hand, something about Tyson had taken root in her since Havana and grown steadily; without the apprehension Starke engendered.

They walked slowly past Franklin's statue to the Hutchins Building then agreed to meet again before she waved and passed through its doors. On a streetcar to the Capitol, he watched government buildings, hotels, and stores pass down one side and noticed the large grassy mall on the other was marked by circular spots of thin grass where the hurricane claimed trees. That evening, he spent several hours in the paneled bar below the Ebbitt House dining room, gently interrogating other patrons for information and taking the edge off before retiring for the few hours of sleep he required.

CHAPTER EIGHTEEN
VANGUARD

Tyson and Evans enjoyed a second Ebbitt House dinner at the same time Starke hosted two uneasy cadets with *Calypso* cutting through the Gulf of Mexico. The sweep yielded little tangible but word was spreading a fast ship with sanguine reputation prowled the filibuster routes. *Calypso's* range, speed, endurance, and weapons perturbed Junta expeditions, reduced waterfront enthusiasm, and increased costs; especially with *Vanguard* in company. Starke was amazed Albert obtained the cutter since *United States Revised Statutes 2757* needed presidential approval and the departments' agreement. His relationship with Captain Fischer almost certainly contributed to her avoiding a district assignment then being ordered to accompany *Calypso*; although charging costs to the Navy sweetened the request.

Vanguard was easily handled, versatile and designed as a cutter. The 170-foot steel hull began with a straight stem, had a line of portholes just above the waterline, and finished with an overhanging fantail. Two 800 horsepower triple-expansion engines powering twin screws took her to fifteen knots, equaling most filibusters, and less than nine feet of draft allowed access to areas closed to *Calypso*. The main deck included a working area aft and single-level deckhouse with her 3-inch deck gun and ground tackle forward. A slightly raised forecastle bulwark anchored lifelines, dense with snaking, that carried aft. Her pilothouse perched on the deckhouse, just forward of two large ventilator cowls at its rear corners. Aft of the flying bridge's white canvas windscreens was a slightly raked stack with two large rotary davit pairs on either side for whaleboats; near two midship 6-pounders. Her complement included nearly fifty experienced cuttermen.

Vanguard's arrival ended *Calypso*'s Pensacola stay just as the Navy crew's initial enthusiasm began fading. For nearly three weeks their ship had been manacled to a lifeless quay and the oppressive stillness of vacant buildings lining deserted streets proved wearing. The city's large religious community did offer priests or preachers to Catholics and Protestants, and a rabbi for Paymaster Clerk Matthias Eberhardt. Navy regulations also required everyone be allowed time off the ship, even the lowest liberty class; and many took advantage with predictable results including a number returning late or drunk. A few were arrested for minor infractions occasioning some contribution to city coffers, an escort from the police station, and reduction to the lowest liberty class if not there already. Conrad also treated additional minor lacerations and venereal disease cases at sick call, accompanied by creative explanations.

Thaddeus' nocturnal French leave caused the greatest disruption because his sortie sparked overnight arguments between watches regarding responsibility; with most turning on whether he escaped by brow or mooring wire. However, the next morning he limped through the same gangway as his shipmates, sank to the deck, and mewed pathetically. The gray tom apparently breached another's territory, was less lean and mean after life aboard, and paid the price. Whether he emerged victorious or placed equal hurt on his adversary was debatable but Conrad stitched his lacerations the same as any other sailor.

The wardroom made several Pensacola excursions by streetcar but Starke left only on business or for an evening at Quarters A with Commander Reisinger; until offered the use of a chestnut gelding. He rode some evenings and Sundays afterwards but his mount proved a barnstormer that resisted anything above a reluctant canter. Starke dealt with both but creating energy and interest proved impossible; the horse suffered through too many different riders and saw outings as little more than a short, hot escape from far too many flies and other pests in a confining stall.

Starke and Watson had observed *Vanguard* thread the channel to Pensacola from *Calypso's* starboard side. She rounded Santa Rosa Island, lined up on the yard's southeast corner like *Calypso*, then made a sharp port turn into the wide, brick and granite wet basin forward of the bark's mooring; where Weaver's working party waited to drop mooring lines over large cleats. Once the cutter settled and resumed an in-port routine, Starke and Watson went on board to be met by Hunter and the executive officer, Second Lieutenant Earnest Duke.

Calypso's senior officers were successful due to similar natures and *Vanguard's* through their differences. Duke was a Charleston political family's youngest son; which did not hurt his ability to obtain merchant ship berths then enter the Revenue Cutter Service's two-year School of Instruction in Bedford, Massachusetts. Shorter and stockier than Hunter, he was powerful, clean-shaven, agile, and quick; with a round face under closely clipped hair. His near perpetual grin and outgoing nature masked a steel constitution backed by stubby-fingered fists. Hunter once mentioned it was difficult to curtail his junior's inclination for direct involvement and their engineer complained more than once he must dissuade their executive officer from joining stokers and passers, then challenging all-comers to a contest. This was even more frustrating on deck because his seamanship and shiphandling were superb. Although only competent at navigation, he was popular with the crew; being considered capable, fair, and consistent.

Starke invited them for a roast beef supper on *Calypso* that justified departure from Yamashita's usual fresh seafood and preserved meats. The evening also provided an opportunity to flesh out Albert's sweep. Hunter thought it overdue since the western Gulf ports and Mexico's east coast received little attention beyond local cutters and *Texas* visiting New Orleans then Galveston that February. They agreed to operate like their patrols off the Atlantic Coast with *Calypso* offshore and *Vanguard* working close in. After Pensacola, they would briefly loiter off Mobile then head west past the barrier islands of Mississippi Sound to the great river's delta where *Vanguard* might go up to New Orleans while *Calypso* covered its approaches. Galveston, Corpus Christi, and Tampico would receive similar attention then into Veracruz for coaling before steaming east towards Arrecife Alacranes. Near that great reef they would turn south for the Puerto Progresso anchorage. From there, *Calypso* would continue east, cross the Yucatan Channel, parallel Cuba's north coast past Havana, and transit the Straits of Florida. This freed *Vanguard* to make for the Dry Tortugas then work her way up the Florida Keys and cover the straits' north side.

They also considered the hurricanes and yellow fever endemic to Caribbean summers and early fall, with yellow fever the greater threat. It was already in Havana, a perennial source and victim, with American cities from Pensacola to Sabine Pass, Texas reporting outbreaks. Mississippi was in denial until autopsies ruled out dengue fever and the same position taken by Louisiana until Ocean Springs and other coastal towns New Orleans' wealthy used for sanctuary were hit. Even filibuster expeditions were affected since they were among those accused of ignoring quarantines; so to avoid exposure, quarantines, fumigation, and other impediments, Starke and Hunter agreed to bypass ports where the contagion was reported unless there was an overwhelming reason to enter; including those Albert suggested they visit.

The starting date was set for September 11, 1897, to give the cuttermen a run ashore and *Calypso*'s engineers time to finish condenser and boiler cleaning. The day before, with all systems cycled, checked, or adjusted, *Calypso*'s main boilers were lit with oil-soaked wood and coal, brought on line for the next morning, and stood ready when the pilot who brought them in arrived with a tug. Three weeks had not altered the man's lined, dark bronze skin or eroded his confidence, which was needed with *Calypso*'s bow pointed into a strong current flowing out from the bay. Ensign Martyn was to conn and expected the pilot would steam into the bay, reverse course, and reenter the channel but instead chose to use the tug and pivot just off the quay; after consulting Starke. A speaking trumpet replaced their pilot's corncob pipe then, with an intermittent sea breeze flexing his gray felt hat's brim, *Calypso* was coaxed out and forward. When her stern would clear the brick and stone quay, he let current force the bow around, pivoting on the tug. When the bowsprit pointed seaward their tug was cast off and a maelstrom of gray, brown, blue, and white frothed beneath *Calypso*'s counter.

The black gang balanced feedwater and fuel to increase turns and achieve steerageway before the sharp turn out through the bay's mouth. Starke, Martyn, and their pilot stood on the flying bridge as *Calypso* left Caucus Shoals to starboard and East Bank and Middle shoals passed to port. Martyn followed the pilot's instructions explicitly since the current amplified speed and affected their helm. Traffic was light so they soon closed the sea buoy where a schooner loitering nearby heeled, made for their port side, and retrieved the pilot. After resuming course and speed, they ran thirty minutes then began incremental increases. Osbourne's practice was to slowly walk up their speed after extended stays pierside to monitor machinery, ease into full operation, and let the metal plant readjust to its malleable wood surroundings. Fort Pickens was disappearing into the shoreline astern when *Vanguard* reached the sea buoy.

Starke sensed their future might soon depend on the steam plant as an ominous atmosphere enveloped the ship. The air grew close, an expectant quiet descended, all sea life left the surface, birds vanished, and he suspected Thaddeus had gone to ground low in the hull. *Calypso* slowly lifted, rode over, then sank into deep troughs between long, gentle swells beneath rows of high, light gray cirrocumulus clouds floating in the blue sky. A tropical storm was reported in the Straits of Florida the day before leaving Pensacola and the filibuster schooner *Briggs*, carrying ammunition for General Garcia, reportedly missed its rendezvous with *Dauntless*. The press claimed sabotage but it was more likely a storm near the Bahama Islands that strengthened then moved north and west past Rebecca Shoals lighthouse, Dry Tortugas, and Marquesas Keys before entering the Gulf. Starke believed this drove the falling barometer, increasing swells, and gathering clouds so he ordered the ship rigged for heavy weather, bent on the storm staysails, and had Watson send people scouring the ship for the poorly stowed gear that was always plentiful after leaving port.

Hunter, astern in *Vanguard*, also considered his options since the cutter was less docile in heavy weather. These were to continue west with *Calypso* then clear Mobile and the

Mississippi Sound's barrier islands, or turn back to ride out the tempest at Pensacola. *Vanguard*'s shallow draft ensured rough handling and possible damage. Engine failure could leave her on a lee shore without sails and *Calypso* possessed no viable tow capability. However, rapidly building seas meant the cutter might not beat this storm to Pensacola Bay, undoubtedly thick with anchored ships. He opted to remain on station astern, rig for heavy weather, and monitor the barometer.

The storm matured to a hurricane before roaring past some miles southwest; further off than the one *Calypso* survived west of Jamaica but no less unsettling for the night watches. Eighty-mile an hour winds slammed confused seas against the wood-sheathed hull to elicit creaks, groans, and occasional dull explosions. The storm card calculations using barometer readings matched to wind direction and force placed them in the hurricane's dangerous semicircle but away from its eye. *Calypso* steamed as fast as her hull could stand, kept the wind just off her starboard bow, and followed as it veered. Stem and a length of keel often extended out over the troughs before plunging into a seething ocean differentiated from sky only by shades of dark gray and black. During the starboard watch, Naval Cadet Timme only intermittently glimpsed *Vanguard*'s masthead light because force and volume of wind, rain, and spray caused the pilothouse windows' shuddering glass to lose transparency. If he did not see the immense rollers engulf bowsprit, anchor, foremast, and sometimes deckhouse, he felt the crash then flood surging aft down the main deck, seeking escape to the sea. Throughout, one hand always grasped something solid, legs became shock absorbers, and the watch fought to remain upright in dark, stuffy dampness or wedged themselves between equipment and furnishings. Timme grasped useless binoculars to control their unruly pendulum-like swing across his chest then turned to check the helmsman. He was lashed in place, spinning the brass wheel right then left to control their steam steering engine and counteract a sea bent on forcing the ship off course by pressing her bow and lifting the stern.

Lookouts were pulled inside to stand watch behind semitransparent windows. For those in the deckhouse and below, the turbulent night forced a constant struggle to eke out some snippet of stability in a twisting, bucking universe; whether resting, working, moving through passageways, or using the head. Stokers in the fireroom deftly spread coal over the glowing bed as firebox doors snapped open then slammed shut; timing each move to the steel deck's thrusts, rolls, and cants. Water tenders beside them deftly turned valves to precisely balance feedwater levels with one hand while committing the other to remaining upright and away from searing steel surfaces. Their eyes remained fixed on gage needles and sight glass levels unless responding to Osbourne, O'Leary, or the chief. In the engine room, where three pistons thrust up and down within their two-level frame, machinists with red rags worked carefully throughout the space; operating, oiling, and wiping machinery as connecting rods flashed in and out of a dark pit. Besides the constant numbing din, each time *Calypso*'s bows plowed under and her screw lifted, power became speed and the engine screamed as though tearing itself apart. In other spaces, sailors careened slowly through the humid ship; sounding bilges to ensure water entering through the working hull was not excessive and pumps were dealing with it. Those off watch or without one endured the constant dull clatter of moveable items and occasional rumble of something larger that slipped its bindings. The more fatalistic on board accepted it and did what they could while the rest placed their futures in fortune, fate, or, Paymaster Wiggs' Almighty. Souls like Ensign Blair thrived on the tempest's power and challenge but many were more or less incapacitated from seasickness.

Starke sucked hard candy for sustenance and to prevent seasickness since he carried the burden of command. There were shoals to their north and the Mississippi River delta to avoid so he held *Calypso* on a southeast heading into the wind, using staysails and engine. Everyone was kept from the main deck until this constant battering raised the starboard anchor from its bed and in danger of getting loose on the deck or going overboard with its chain. Weaver and four deckhands entered the forecastle at first light after two attempts to emerge from a forward hatch. They were repeatedly inundated while trying to restrain a blackened anchor that rocked, bounced, and shuddered. Gripping anything solid and each other, they finally gained control with a jury-rig lashing but Starke saw all five submerge twice as bow, bowsprit, and most of the jibboom plunged into the sea; adding more indentations to the battered pipestem each time he counted heads.

Sunday breakfast was cold meat and hot black coffee, so Starke greeted the day with a mug delivered by Yamashita; the Japanese steward who, like Sharett, possessed an obscure past but unquestioned competence and loyalty. Starke also postponed church service and rope-yarn, although this heavy weather was departing for the western gulf coast. The storm faded slowly as the day matured and wind veered until Martyn and Caldwell's port section relieved Blair and Timme. Lookouts returned to day stations with clearing weather and abating seas; including Kearney who saw Starke as he prepared to climb the tarred foremast shrouds, saluted, and then added, "Lively night; Captain."

Starke returned the salute, "It was that Kearney. Slept well I trust?"

He grinned, "Like a baby, Captain, like a baby."

Watson observed their exchange. He never adjusted to his captain casually addressing individuals, despite Starke's rock-solid reputation for neither currying favor nor tolerating favorites. Sailors were inveterate schemers and never lacked an angle. Not one captain in a thousand could pull it off, but Starke would not change and somehow made it work. He then continued to the disordered chart table where Dunbar, Owen, and Petty Officer Smithers were conferring.

Vanguard was a mile astern after coming through unexpectedly well despite her shallow draft and lack of storm staysails. The exceptionally lively night almost convinced Buck his ship took perverse pleasure agitating her contents. A number of the crew suffered cuts, bruises, burns, or some combination but, except for weather deck openings allowing in more water than normal, her steel hull remained watertight and no equipment casualties occurred. He steadied himself with the steel railing and watched *Calypso* extend nearly a third of her keel out over larger swells then curtsey into the next as her stem cut down and forward into the seas before shaking them off. She reminded him of an immense sailfish and wondered how her watch saw *Vanguard*'s kaleidoscope of movements.

The hurricane left them astern to rampage through the northern Gulf of Mexico then go ashore south of Beaumont, Texas. That city was hard hit but the storm surge rolled over Port Arthur and Sabine Pass, with its recently dredged channel. In its aftermath, ships caught at sea tried to fix location and those able to steam or sail made for their original destination or closest port. The rest rolled, pitched, and yawed until repairs were complete, rescue arrived, or they sank. *Calypso* and *Vanguard*'s noon sights were unreliable so speed was reduced and a southerly course taken to ensure they would clear the Mississippi Sound and river delta. Lingering cloud cover also precluded evening twilight observations.

Starke, and most on *Calypso*, slept strong and deep the next night, aided by exhaustion and relief. For Tuesday morning twilight, Starke, Watson, Dunbar, Yeoman Pond along, with Chief Owen, trailed by petty officers Smithers and Moreau, filled the flying bridge as three sextants shot celestial bodies then recorded results and times. *Vanguard* did the same and late that morning the results compared by flag hoists. The Mississippi Sound lay to their northwest, Pensacola about seventy miles north, and the Mississippi River's South Pass entrance west and slightly south. They set course for Mobile to regain the original plan.

CHAPTER NINETEEN
PORTUNUS

*C*alypso sliced through a clear morning's low swells, heeling slightly, as gulls, terns, and dolphins returned. Seaman Kearney on her foremast was scanning the horizon when a flash and smudge astern caught his attention. He thought waves were reflecting the rising sun but placed his paired-telescopes on the bearing and waited. When it came again he hailed Martyn, standing by Starke on the collapsible bridge-wing, "Pilothouse, forward lookout, possible flares to the southwest."

Starke extracted a battered pipestem as Martyn turned towards him. Although most likely a reflection, ships would be in extremis after the storm; and they were slightly north of steamship routes from Europe, northwest of those from the Yucatan Channel, and near the approaches to New Orleans and other coastal cities. Deciding it was easier living with a wild goose chase than ignoring a ship in distress, and since Kearney made the sighting, he turned to the ensign in a conversational tone, "Mr. Martyn. Signal *Vanguard* we've spotted distress signals, give the bearing, and ring up full speed. Let's see what one boiler can do."

Vanguard watched her consort's masts tilt as she turned southwest under a darkening smoke plume, then saw the code pennant break, followed by flags and pennants for "CWQ" and a bearing. As the bark's stern became her port side, *Vanguard*'s conning officer started his own turn to follow in

Calypso's wake and passed the word for Hunter; who was already making for the bridge with Buck on his heels. *Vanguard* turned with less grace, breasting through rolling blue-green swells, but soon steadied astern of *Calypso*. Hunter reached the pilothouse to find the bark approaching eleven knots and his cutter struggling so he replied to the flaghoist, spread fires on her second Babcock & Wilcox boiler, and attempted to see beyond *Calypso*.

The steamship's funnel smoke and flares were undeniable in ten minutes and her silhouette visible in thirty. The liner *Portunus* carrying 300 Sicilian immigrants from Palermo to New Orleans had been adrift nearly twelve hours. The storm overtook her shortly after turning northwest into the gulf; unable to turn into the seas, she ran with them throughout the night. Her stern was hammered and when the propeller shaft fractured the master was forced to lock it or see bearings wiped and stuffing box disintegrate. He was skeptical about lying to during hurricanes but allowed the liner to passively accept what wind, sea, and storm hurled against her. She pitched and rolled viciously while mostly sick passengers and an exhausted crew groped through the ship or retreated to bunk rooms, main deck cabins, and watch stations. His chief engineer examined their shaft when the weather moderated and determined any turns put on it would spread the fracture, wipe bearings, and open the stern tube to the sea but no repair was possible without dry-docking so they were condemned to roll lethargically with every capability intact except to steam the final miles of an Atlantic crossing.

The 3,500 ton British liner was 370 feet long, with a thirty-nine-foot beam and twenty-one-foot draft. She was designed for first and second-class cabin travelers, steerage passengers, and freight so her original staterooms were piped for steam heat or cold water cooling and contained two berths, with the lower folding into the wall during daytime. The interior woodwork had been maple, black maple, French walnut, birds-eye maple, and satin wood; although the steerage passengers in open berthing were excluded from these common areas. She was shunted to short routes or charters as her first fourteen years' service saw iron hulls and compound engines evolve to steel hulls, greater compartmentalization, and triple-expansion engines until she was converted from passenger liner to immigrant ship. Her barkentine rig was removed, two bunks added to each room, and small, four-bed bunk rooms created from cargo holds and steerage berthing. The reliable steam plant was left unchanged, crew spaces were not altered, and the captain's cabin retained its original elegance.

Her master, Captain Ian Smith, knew their best hope was a ship passing near enough to provide assistance since getting underway risked all. He first went to sea as a cabin boy on tea clippers then rose to command a four-masted cargo ship running between Chile and England; outbound with coal and inbound with copper. His Scottish wife, Janette, sailed with him until she passed two years earlier and *Portunus* offered a means to escape their empty cabin. Now, instead of cargo's known vicissitudes, he must control passengers weak from seasickness, physical battering, or both; with the possibility of panic once they recovered and realized the predicament. Except for the parsimonious, greedy fools who denuded the old lady's sails he could have reached the Mississippi's mouth where tugs waited to tow sailing ships upriver to New Orleans. Tapping their limited flare supply had been a desperate gamble but the payoff was two rescuers closing rapidly with bows cutting through blue-green water and stacks streaming smoke. Both had boats to the rail, despite *Portunus* flying a code pennant accompanied by the K, R, and

L flags requesting a tow. Paired-telescopes revealed two different American ensigns with the elegant black bark in sharp contrast of her white-hulled consort.

Watson boarded the liner through her forward entry port an hour later while *Vanguard* and *Calypso* loitered nearby, moving only to avoid being set down on the others. After returning he went directly to *Calypso*'s flying bridge, wiped sweat from his forehead, and reported, "She's *Portunus*, Captain, out of Palermo for New Orleans and crammed with Italians. Their plant's fine, so they've distilling water, lighting, and can power winches, but the shaft's fractured and their chief engineer says it cannot be repaired at sea. Lieutenant Buck says they could tow her to South Pass but the cutter's under your control."

Thinking aloud, Starke let slip, "She gets towed or one goes while the other stands by."

"Sir?"

Starke regretted musing aloud since towing was the only option; which is why Buck made the case without consulting Hunter. Anything else had too many variables, especially with passengers and crew speaking different languages.

"Well, Mr. Watson; what assistance does *Vanguard* require?"

"Lieutenant Buck believes his captain's only looking for agreement."

"Very well; come to my cabin and I'll provide a brief note."

Calypso lacked any real tow capability beyond a hawser, but *Vanguard*'s main-deck was arranged for emergency towing. She also possessed the required agility with a pair of 800 horsepower engines turning two shafts on a steel hull close to *Calypso*'s in width but seventy-four feet shorter and 600 tons lighter. Starke watched the cutter's boat make for the rolling liner, thinking that towing was demanding even for purpose-built tugs. Hunter must place his ship just ahead *Portunus* without being sucked in during the approach, send the messenger over, attach a larger line, and then bend on the unwieldy towing hawser; to be mated to an anchor chain on the liner's forecastle. Throughout, his engines must be worked to avoid being pulled astern or entangle a line in *Vanguard*'s screws. The hawser would be streamed by moving forward, since the cutter lacked a towing machine, then *Portunus* would use her windlass to adjust catenary and keep the ships in step; another difficult undertaking.

Calypso sailors on the main deck exchanged commentaries despite Watson's druthers. Starke believed it instructive, and they were far enough away to avoid creating a distraction. Hunter never mentioned his crew doing anything beyond practice tows on flat seas; and this was the real thing with a large ship and long swells. Exploiting her twin screws and power, *Vanguard* came from windward and astern at a slight angle then maneuvered to avoid being sucked into the larger ship. Once his cutter's stern would clear, Hunter cut in sharply off the liner's bow. They seemed only feet apart as the cutter's taffrail crossed *Portunus'* bow. Starke estimated something like 100 feet separated them when a .45-70 line-throwing gun's flat crack reached *Calypso* and shot-line lofted onto the liner's forecastle. *Vanguard* used engines and rudder to turn and stop just off *Portunus'* bow while her crew retrieved the thin line, threaded it and a messenger through her bow chock and ultimately hauled the large manila towing hawser aboard as *Vanguard* released it in bights to avoid fouling her slow-spinning screws. The risk increased once made up since sea and hawser would draw the hulls together; especially while paying out anchor chain for catenary.

Hunter jockeyed skillfully to avoid parting the rig by creating too much strain, or fouling a propeller with too little, as anchor chain slowly clattered out the liner's bow chock before being stopped off and shock lines bent to bitts. Once the hawser was secured, he eased forward with 1,600 horsepower pulling 3,500 tons on a fiber line that would part under a fraction of that tension. Hawser and anchor chain suddenly knifed up through the sea to break surface, but Hunter was already slowing. It did not part and the liner began moving, almost imperceptibly at first then clearly as the white cutter increased speed a knot or two, steadied, then repeated the process until reaching six knots with the appropriate catenary to remain in step.

With *Portunus* under tow, improving weather, and easy seas reflecting the afternoon sun, *Calypso* took station ahead and slightly off *Vanguard*'s bow where a casualty would not embarrass cutter and tow. Starke saw Watson speaking with Weaver as their at-sea routine resumed and knew the chief would like more involvement; then wondered if the *Portunus* passengers were aware of what awaited them. The Sicilian community that settled in New Orleans' old French Quarter to work docks and sugar plantations not only faced yellow fever but was often in conflict or competition with other factions fueled by politics, cultures, and wages; including a recent incident that saw several Italians lynched.

They steamed due west throughout the night, making for the Mississippi River's South Pass channel just below Port Eads. Starke retired to his sea cabin after signing night orders then awakened regularly as *Calypso* altered course and speed to remain a half mile off *Vanguard*'s port bow. The darkened cutter silhouetted by the large liner's lights blazing astern kept up communication with its tow through whistle signals as the hawser was shortened or lengthened tow to keep in step. Starke looked across the ink-black sea and knew Hunter was getting no sleep while his cutter maneuvered to maintain a steady pace, nurse the hawser, and avoid being overrun if way was lost.

Daylight revealed a disturbed and sediment-filled sea created by the river's broad plume flowing miles into the gulf then marshy green shoreline appeared as noon approached. Although the delta estuary's bays, peninsulas, and channels remained hidden, South Pass channel was quickly located by drifting ships waiting for a pilot but unable to anchor in the changing bottom's greasy, dark-gray mud. At another time there would have been a lightship as well but the station was vacant during hurricane and yellow fever seasons. A worn schooner closed the cutter then sheered off after hearing *Portunus* was the ship requesting a bar pilot take her to Port Eads where a river pilot would board to complete the 95-mile journey to New Orleans.

Starke's binoculars were briefly trained beyond these milling ships to the skeleton-like South Pass Lighthouse, forward range marker, and buoys while *Vanguard* gradually slowed and liner recovered chain. Breaking the tow required *Portunus'* anchor chain be retrieved slowly until the hawser's shackle was on deck and could be disconnected; while *Vanguard* avoided being pulled into the liner. *Portunus'* whistle finally blasted as the hawser ran free through her bow chock and the cutter increased speed to stream it astern and away from her screws. As *Vanguard* moved off, *Portunus* signaled three waiting tugs that were quickly made up; and *Calypso* turned due south for the thirty-fathom curve with the cutter moving to take station astern. The international code flaghoist, "Well done Vanguard," flew from *Calypso's* halyard. *Vanguard* deserved recognition but it also let ships waiting to go upriver, towboats, and pilots know the warship and cutter were off the delta. Once the gaggle of ships dropped below the horizon, *Calypso* came to a new course. By evening,

Yamashita had served supper and Starke was back to reviewing correspondence and reports; pausing only to tend his Meerschaum pipe.

CHAPTER TWENTY
TRANSITIONS

Captain Albert enjoyed walking home through a pleasant September evening in Washington. Theodore still acted for Long but went on a naval militia speaking tour then maneuvers off Fort Monroe; where the new gunboat *Wilmington* suffered a coal bunker fire that forced her to Jacksonville for repairs. Walking also provided a quiet interlude between the Building and nightly recounting of the Newport season. Olivia and Isabella now spoke of little but boating, balls, tennis, and other summer events; especially a violent August storm that washed away the Narragansett Pier Casino. The girls were treated like family during their stay and would never forget it, but their progressing metamorphosis to young women was proving even more pronounced and unsettling.

After the daughters retired, he told Abigail about Fitzhugh Lee's invitation to dinner at the Shoreham Hotel. Albert expected it involved his latest initiative to pressure the Junta's filibuster expeditions; which appeared successful despite court rulings hampering prosecution. The *Blanche Morgan* schooner was libeled in New London, the tug *Dauntless* placed under observation, and the press reporting *Wilmington*'s target practice as a filibuster taken. *Vanguard* and *Calypso* were cruising along the Gulf Coast and Vice Admiral Sir John Fisher would soon command British warships in the western Atlantic. Starke apparently knew of him from Alexandria where he was HMS *Inflexible*'s captain and led the British landing force. His reputation for energy and innovation had split the British navy into opposing camps regarding this storm petrel but no captain desiring to retain command under him would act lethargically; which probably encouraged the protected cruiser HMS *Intrepid* to take a filibuster off Fortune Island, board several other ships, enter Jamaica's Port Royal for coal, and immediately return to the hunt. Spain's caretaker prime minister, Lieutenant General Marcelo de Azcárraga Ugarte y Palmero-Versosa de Lizárraga, was constrained by an impoverished navy ordered to vigorously intercept Junta expeditions but avoid incidents. Even so, it managed to increase patrol activity near the Straits of Florida and in the Gulf of Mexico; including the torpedo gunboat *Nueva España*.

Around noon the following day, Albert sat in the well-appointed Shoreham Hotel's dining room across from the Virginia ex-governor, Confederate cavalry general, and consul-general in Havana. It was difficult to associate the portly, white-haired man with his war record except for the eyes. He reassured Albert that despite press claims he had resigned this return home through New York on the Ward Line's *Seguranca* was for thirty days leave and official calls. Two days were spent in the city, a courtesy call with Assistant Secretary Day at State occurred on the thirteenth, and he now returned to summarize the Cuban situation for President McKinley. Lunching with Albert was to understand the departments' coordination on filibuster expeditions, but once that was satisfied conversation shifted to Starke. He was slightly acquainted with the family, especially Jacob, but solicited Albert's thoughts on the lieutenant's availability for a detail in his Havana office to explore resuming port visits with *Calypso*. Lee noted his own father's attempt to resign brought dismissal by Secretary Welles, fighting for the Confederacy, and possibly death a few years later; so Starke's father expatriating to Brazil was as understandable as the uncle remaining loyal. Both men now enjoyed solid reputations in Havana, as did *Calypso*'s commander after *Rafael Riego*, which he felt could be put to use. Albert parried but Lee indicated they would speak again in October.

September 16, 1897, found Albert reflecting on this discussion, *Calypso* pushing further into the Gulf, and Katherine Louisa Ledford giving birth to Starke's son at Brydian Grange; the Curtis Estate near Bridport, England. In her large bedroom overlooking a well-tended park with the day's colors softened by dense, gray clouds; she took a last look outside, emphatically repeated earlier instructions to save the baby, and breathed chloroform. Katherine had grown increasingly stoical as what she feared since coming of age approached and her ungainly body was positioned with legs spread and knees up. The doctor worked by feel alone since births by midwives in the family's presence were out of fashion. When the amazed Katherine regained consciousness, she cradled the child Philip and their families long desired that was instead conceived during her only tryst. Later, still groggy and sore, with the nurse engaged for her laying-in month on an errand, she watched her brother Edward nap, with one leg dangling over his chair's arm, while a splotchy bundle with shut eyes and soft spot in his skull the size of a large coin snuggled against her ribcage, tiny pink fists clenching and unclenching, as soft sounds came from lips wet with breast milk.

Katherine dismissed family protests during her confinement and lived in the cottage she renovated on their estate. Upper-class women in the States removed themselves from public view once they began to show but, like Queen Victoria,

Katherine had no desire to sequester or corset to mask the condition. Since the child would be illegitimate, she kept to the estate but rode her bay hunter well into the pregnancy then took long walks until her body signaled the event that must surely end her life. She returned to the manor house in a changing mix of biliousness, depression, and elation that neared delirium while climbing the main staircase, belly stretched and breasts swollen. She felt the army captain study her progress from his painting with what seemed a slight smile. Her moral collapse in a Havana hotel was disgusting but she did not regret the baby and before entering the bedroom, confident it would be a boy, obtained her brother's assurance he would be Oliver Barrington Curtis.

She did not expect to survive and knew Starke was temporarily insulated from rumors, so he was not told and the family forbidden to act; except her brother was to obtain his agreement to add the Starke name later. The family acquiesced and her mother hinted Katherine was not the line's first instance where birth preceded marriage, or came soon after; while Philip's parents wished it was nearer their son's death so the baby might pass as a grandson. She was apprehensive about how the father's family would respond and dreaded his aunt's disapproval. Constance's mind, like her own, was open within church strictures; but upper-class Americans saw these events as a moral collapse rather than highly unfortunate and socially inconvenient. Her parents continued to urge writing the father since their grandson could not be announced as a late-in-life son. Edward, who got on with Jacob, was particularly persistent and frustrated when she continued corresponding without mentioning the birth. Katherine was unable to explain but suspected it was probably fear of rejection, manner of conception, a father's legal rights, and the potential proposal.

Illegitimate offspring were often more than a family embarrassment but her son posed no threat since the Curtis entailment passed through the lawfully born male line and the Starkes had no title encumbrances. English Poor Laws required women name the father to reduce those supported by the government and allowed illegitimate children to take the father's name even if the parents never married; should he consent in person. Workarounds, like declaring marriage had taken place, were available, but she felt these would abandon her last morals; and Americans were unpopular. Katherine, through her brother, controlled a large dowry and could establish a trust fund so shortly after discovering she survived found her desire for independence clashing with the need to ensure the father acknowledged their son. She delayed the decision using a short-form birth certificate that obscured the father's name.

Edward was shocked when his sister revealed her situation but changed after visiting the fashionable bordello where one of her school friends, unmarried and forbidden other employment, provided counsel while laying naked beside him. Sisters, she explained, had the same urges as brothers. He returned to Brydian Grange, offered to adopt the child, and pushed harder for Jacob to be told. This lack of candor also further complicated her tenuous relationship with *Calypso*'s captain since his discovering was likely to initiate a proposal and she had a plethora of reservations despite what he whispered in Havana. Still, watching Edward shift comfortably in the chair as sunlight struck his hair, she wondered.

CHAPTER TWENTY ONE
COMMAND DECISION

C hief Weaver felt water draining from his oilskins as he entered the chiefs' quarters. In semi-darkness behind a louvered wood door, the space was dominated by its large rectangular table anchored to the deck and surrounded by tethered chairs quivering from the storm. Eight bunks filled three walls, including one along *Calypso*'s hull, with the fourth dedicated to entrance and lockers. Tonight the close space possessed a surreal aura from incessant motion, uncoordinated snoring, groaning hull, constant engine noise, and intermittent rattling from gear drift; but still a welcome refuge with its own steward, customs, and ethos.

This sanctuary was shared with Chief Quartermaster Paul Owen, Chief Gunner's Mate Stefan Poniatowski, Chief Machinist Emery Baasch, and Chief Carpenter's Mate Cheney Lefebvre. Only their newest chief, Poniatowski, remained at the table; one foot braced against a leg to restrain the chair and upper body checked by a powerful hand grasping the edge. Their gunner's other hand maintained an equally firm grip on a stained, off-white mug; half-full of water boiled with coffee grounds. His body twisted as *Calypso* climbed a wave then half-rolled down through the trough, but these contortions failed to silence grunting taunts aimed at shipmates wedged in narrow bunks threatening to eject their occupants. Several unsecured items slid noisily to low points as he growled,

"Shut the door, Boats; or we'll be chasing that gear drift down the passageway."

Weaver looked at the Pole, "You're damn comfortable down here I see."

A sudden roll slammed the door shut as a genial voice came from Owen's upper bunk, "Can't you loafers climb in and shut up. Without my getting some shuteye we'll go ashore in Cuba while I'm catnapping tomorrow."

Poniatowski looked over his shoulder towards the dark rectangular opening, "Where're we now Owen?"

"Just cleared Yucatan Channel and heading for Cuba's north coast when this came up from the south; appears it's passing behind us."

The engine screamed then quieted as the sea lifted *Calypso*'s screw then retrieved it with a shudder from the overhanging fantail smashing down on frothed water. Weaver skidded towards his bunk as the next half-roll began, "Dark as Hell topside. Wind, rain, and spray. Forecastle and storm canvas are take'n a beating, and I'm for the rack."

He draped the soaked garments from a peg, grabbed an overhead beam, then levered his solid frame in place; thinking hammocks grew more challenging as years passed but still slept better. He glanced out to see Poniatowski's bulk twist as the Pole steadfastly maintained his charade of nonchalantly enjoying what coffee the cup still held. It felt days rather than hours since they gathered around the table as *Calypso* plowed easily though long, undulating swells nudging her starboard bow and beam. The topic, now washed away by the storm, was crew complaints about remaining in Veracruz only long enough to coal from a barge; after passing Galveston and Tampico. Owen was less concerned than Chief Machinist's Mate Baasch, from a north German state known for seafaring. His clear, accented, and direct English ensured black gang compliance. They also believed him less sympathetic than Osbourne and O'Leary, but Baasch argued privately for them to near insubordination then carried out whatever was decided without apology. The quartermaster chief had aligned with Weaver and Poniatowski on the complaints' validity while Chief Lefebvre focused on his pipe. French and slightly older, he seldom engaged, but if inclined proved as frugal with words as material. When their Creole steward, Michel Reynaud, was asked, he claimed to be more disappointed they did not go upriver to New Orleans.

Chief Owen had argued, "They'll survive. Gulf's riddled with yellow jack anyway. Melvin says *Portunus'* bar pilot told *Vanguard* there's quarantines along the Gulf coast and up the Mississippi past Natchez; Spain's even quarantined New Orleans and Mexico. A day in Norfolk or Port Royal and it'll be forgotten."

Weaver grinned, ". . . and some new injustice found."

Lefebvre knocked his battered pipe against their heavy ashtray fashioned from a brass 4-inch shell casing, "Saw yellow jack in Jamaica. You've had it when your vomit's a black paste looking like coffee too long over heat. Doc says northerners seem more likely to catch it, one in four die, and some never recover."

Poniatowski set down his coffee, "Coloreds are immune."

Lefebvre shook his head, "Doc says no and I've seen Black Africans catch it."

The present storm struck soon after Weaver ended debate by leaning back in his chair, "I'll pass on a run ashore in Veracruz to see my family again."

Poniatowski finally bowed to the storm and left the table when he judged the others asleep then undressed, turned off the bulkhead light, and climbed into his bunk across from Weaver. Only a muted glow from the passageway filtered through their louvered door. Owen, braced in the fetal position and shifting under his wool blanket, was kept awake by the engine's racing when stem, bowsprit, and jibboom burrowed down and her abused stern lifted clear.

He reflected on the ten days since leaving *Portunus*. Bark and cutter steamed south twenty miles, turned, and coasted to a halt for the captains to confer. Their decision was to bypass Mississippi Sound, since towing *Portunus* placed it far to the northeast, and begin the western Gulf sweep. A track west and north to Sabine Pass, Texas, was laid out then another past Galveston to Port Isabel; with *Calypso* offshore and *Vanguard* close in. Hurricane debris was plentiful for some distance and they stopped several times where enough detritus floated to suggest a lost ship. When this desolation was slowly replaced by ship traffic, any tugs and schooners they met were scrutinized or boarded. They loitered for a time off Port Isabel, since it was a blockade runner haven during the war with rail connections for exporting cotton. This was repeated for the Mexican port of Tampico; a small town where shipping kerosene now replaced slavers that became plentiful early in the century after the States outlawed importation. The first port entered was Veracruz where *Vanguard* led *Calypso* in and they anchored in sight of the low, gray and white silhouette of the prison-fortress, San Juan de Ulúa.

While Owen stood nearby, Starke told Watson the American consul reported that Díaz used *Rafael Riego* as justification to deport foreign anarchists but several American liners refused passage. Coaling was arranged through Sharett's firm, as in Tampa, and once complete they steamed northeast on the route *Vanguard* used to trail *Rafael Riego*. When clear of the track's small reefs and low islands, such as Triángulo Oeste, they turned southwest towards Puerto Progresso, passed through its anchorage, and steamed east along the coast. *Vanguard* turned before the Yucatan Channel to patrol the Straits of Florida's north boundary while *Calypso* continued east and was overtaken by this storm, thundering north past the Cayman Islands.

Owen finally drifted off, despite *Calypso*'s heaving, thrusting, groaning, half-rolls, and shrieking engine. Starke's sea cabin was higher with more severe motion but that proved irrelevant since he remained in the pilothouse. Heavy seas repeatedly submerged their stern with such brutality he spent much of the night searching for a less abusive heading without success. The tall bark crashed and scudded east until the northbound storm passed and by early Sunday morning, with the Pinar del Río coast just visible to starboard, there was a brilliant red sun emerging from the horizon ahead, calming seas, less wind, and no rain,

Seaman Cullen Flynn went reluctantly aloft when Blair and Timme's starboard section relieved since the sun seared his light reddish hair and fair skin. Once in the foretop, he pushed back his cap then swept the horizon with paired-telescopes. The surrounding sea was empty and shoreline to their south only a thicker boundary. The Caribbean was pestilent, sultry, and a long way from Brooklyn but his home was *Calypso* and he took life's full measure, enjoyed what was on offer, and let consequences be damned. His runs ashore were understandably infrequent and each opportunity embraced as though the next would not come soon; which invariably proved true. Although Catholic, he gave Paymaster Wiggs, a Baptist deacon, close to a priest's respect; especially after springing him for mass and confession in Pensacola. That unsuspecting priest was overwhelmed by the long-deferred, dramatic, and lengthy confession. However, the penitence that squared Flynn with Holy Mother Church proved inconsequential to that exacted by Chief Weaver over the Nassau debacle and a Tampa bar donnybrook; the latter resulting from two hard-cases taking his table then inviting him to move them, which he gladly did.

Flynn shifted to avoid the mast's metal fittings while keeping his paired-telescopes on a ship running inshore and nearly parallel to *Calypso*. When a rising sun separated her stack smoke from the shoreline he anticipated some coastal freighter but made out a schooner rig, black hull, then gun sponson. Only warships had such protrusions so he hailed the pilothouse. Blair and Timme came to the starboard bridge-wing then acknowledged with a wave. He continued sweeping, as Kearney taught, to discover a thin pole slightly off *Calypso*'s starboard bow, almost invisible in the morning sun. Further examination revealed a two-masted schooner with one stick overboard and no canvas up so he reported it and saw a messenger leave the pilothouse. The bow began swinging and quickly settled on the schooner's bearing. There was no hesitation with Blair. He may be a bucko, but Flynn preferred officers who let you know where they stood.

The schooner was *Astraea*; with her foremast down and pounding the rolling hull's starboard side while its fittings and rigging were stripped. She was bound for Pinar del Río's south coast near Cabo Corrientes with military goods and insurrectionists when the storm and a watch officer's misjudgment parted an already weakened foremast stay. Her single hold contained a crated Hotchkiss gun, shells, cartridges, dynamite gun rounds, machetes, and medicine; along with twenty-eight damning but less valuable insurrectos recruited in American cities and cigar factories to replenish losses from the guerilla war and disease. Weyler was committing fresh troops, General Maceo was dead, his successor had surrendered, and what remained of that army was isolated from the eastern provinces by Spain's western trocha so *Astraea* and similar ships emerged as a lifeline for what were now little more than isolated bands. Consequently, the Junta pushed these small schooners hard and this trip had proven one too much for *Astraea*.

Her master, Captain Buff, removed a battered hat to swipe sweat from his pate while scowling at the mate who was on the helm when *Astraea*'s foremast splintered above the boom. His neck compressed to three fleshy red rolls. Just south of their position was Cuba's north coast with its deep green border of tall palms and brush rising beyond the whitish sand and shell beach that slid gently under shimmering waters of blues and greens. The storm prevented them from reaching the island's southern coast then a broken foremast left *Astraea* adrift near the port of Mantua; about sixty miles north and slightly east of Cabo San Antonio on the north coast. Now, unless that foremast was jettisoned and mainmast jury-rigged, wind and seas would soon put them on some offshore reef, barrier island, or beach. *Astraea* carried four boats to land cargo, and only one was slightly damaged, but troops and guerrilleros patrolled those beaches. Moving ashore would also require two trips so launching boats could cause a panic, especially since this crew consisted of hard cases willing to touch a yellow fever coast. Besides, they might make Key West on a jury-rigged mainmast or get far enough off the coast to avoid patrolling river gunboats and hail a passing ship that was not Spanish.

Starke entered *Calypso*'s pilothouse, conversed with Blair, ensured both boilers were on line, obtained their estimated position from Chief Owen, and took his binoculars to the flying bridge. The dismasted schooner lay off the bow and a gunboat paralleled *Calypso* to starboard, steaming slightly faster. He expected both were Spanish so it was their show unless assistance was requested. The morning was pleasant and invigorating with the sea shedding its night gray for a deep blue, the sun climbing, and distant gray clouds to the west floating above a dispersing wake. The wind had also died away, leaving only the breeze created by *Calypso* passing through salt air. Blair already turned them towards the schooner, but kept to ten knots, so there was time and Starke's binoculars could just reveal shoreline features beyond the gunboat; confirming Owen holding them beyond Spain's territorial waters.

Starke watched as the gunboat revealed a pronounced ram bow, accentuated rake to her masts, schooner rig, and no canvas. Just forward of the pilothouse was a gun sponson and above it a single raked stack. He believed it was a *Temerario* class torpedo gunboat, possibly *Nueva España*. If so, her two 120mm/35 caliber Honotoria breech-loading rifles would match *Calypso*'s 4-inch guns in range, around six miles, but their short barrels and bag ammunition were disadvantages; and the few modified for fixed ammunition often malfunctioned if his research at the Building was accurate. Her secondary battery consisted of 57mm Nordenfelts that were not the equal of *Calypso*'s 3-pounder Hotchkiss guns; but there were twice as many. The class also mounted a small Nordenfelt that could not match *Calypso*'s four Gatlings; and there were two tubes for German Schwartzkopff mobile torpedoes with a low speed range of 450 yards. Her steel hull was around three-quarters *Calypso*'s length, with narrower beam, shallower draft, and half the displacement. The class had twice the bark's power and twin screws, with a design speed of nineteen knots, but the ragged black smoke plume streaking Pinar del Río's near cloudless skies indicated poor maintenance and worse coal reduced that to perhaps twelve.

Captain Buff looked over the schooner's taffrail. *Astraea* gained some notoriety with the Puerto Rico incident so he hoped both ships would pass by, perhaps after a brief exchange. The southern one would pass down the schooner's starboard side, two or three miles distant if it did not change course. The bark off his port quarter was traveling slower and would have remained six or seven miles north but apparently sighted *Astraea*, changed course, and was closing. Given time, the schooner's mainmast canvas might be raised and enough way achieved, aided by the current, to limp northwest towards the Keys. That was no longer possible so he called for the first mate, a tartar currently engaged in bullying an insurrecto, to hoist the United States ensign. He flew it only when forced since the flag rising through tangled rigging was but a few stars different from that carried by invaders who destroyed his family and home; but *Astraea* was wallowing just outside Spanish waters.

Blair saw it break from the remaining mast, shifted his binoculars to the gunboat, and watched her turn suddenly hard to port and go for the schooner; blossoming standards, flags, and immense red and yellow war ensign. Starke was down from the flying bridge, checking position with Dunbar and Owen at the chart table. Blair paused, to ensure he sounded calm, then turned, "Captain; the schooner's raised our flag and the gunboat went for her like he's going to war."

Starke straightened and looked through the open door, "I believe you're correct Mr. Blair," then walked to the window and raised his binoculars. Provoking a diplomatic incident, abandoning the schooner, losing his ship, or all three vanquished the pleasant morning. Ignored Spanish gunboats had fired across American merchant ships' bows, inspiring the press to clamor for war, but displaying battle flags before any boarding attempt was beyond provocative, especially after an American flag was raised; and could mean the two nations were at war.

Blair recognized the look from just before engaging *Rafael Riego* as Starke said quietly, "Mr. Blair. Please log the schooner's American flag, the gunboat's battle flags, and her course change; then set general quarters."

Bosun pipes' shrill blasts sounded throughout the ship as sailors moved rapidly up the starboard side of the deckhouse going forward and down the port side for those headed aft. Engineers aligned their plant for battle and gunner's mates stripped gun covers and muzzle bags from 4-inch rifles, uncased Hotchkiss guns, mounted Gatlings, unlocked magazines, and staged ready-use ammunition on deck. Watson went aft, in case Starke fell, to lead their fire and flooding detail. Osbourne left the engine room, climbed to the pilothouse, and assumed the conn; freeing Blair to race eagerly for his guns. Yeoman Pond took the stadimeter and began calling ranges as their largest American ensign rose steadily to the mainmast truck, followed by slightly smaller versions on the fore and mizzen.

All stations reported manned and ready within ten minutes, thanks to the executive officer's persistent drilling, but Starke would have preferred time after the storm to exercise the main battery. At that instant, two nearly simultaneous flat cracks followed an elongated flash and yellow-gray smoke spurting from the gunboat's port sponson. The first round produced a water column beyond the hapless schooner while the second fifty-five pound shell skipped across the surface then sank quietly. This pair of live rounds passed over the schooner, not across her bow, and was unnecessary since she was immobile. Starke watched the Spaniard come due north after firing, noted her ammunition was probably faulty or improperly fused, and calculated *Calypso* could likely shoot better. The gunboat would pass about a mile astern of the schooner, long but effective range for smaller caliber weapons, so Starke turned due east to converge at a right angle.

If the disabled schooner was in Spain's territorial waters, Starke could do little without violating Navy regulations but she was not so he must stand against an adversary with potential advantages. He felt confident this was a *Temerario* class torpedo gunboat so it could be *Nueva España* operating out of Cuba; that meant a steel hull with light armor. While some war veterans claimed shells ricocheted inside iron or steel hulls but passed through wood, the Spaniard was still better protected. She could also theoretically fire directly ahead and astern since her main battery was in sponsons, but this halved the broadside and seldom worked in practice. Her two breech-loading rifles matched *Calypso*'s 4-inch guns in range, around six miles, but would fire more slowly if using bag ammunition. The secondary battery numbered twice *Calypso*'s but there was only a single rapid-fire Nordenfelt to take on the bark's Gatlings. If mobile torpedoes were on board, they would be effective close-in where twin screws gave the gunboat a maneuvering advantage. *Calypso* was likely faster and enjoyed weapons superiority for most target angles so Starke calculated he could control the engagement initially then attempt to achieve a beam-to-beam position, avoid mid-range gun duels, and rely on crew performance to prevail with the least casualties possible. He also cleared his mind of courtesies received in Havana, legalities, and politics.

Captain Buff was considering how to play the cards dealt when two flashes appeared on the gunboat and before the accompanying smoke cleared shells screamed overhead like a short train racing past some country depot. One exploded a half mile beyond, creating a water column that paused before collapsing on itself, while the other grazed their mainmast, skipped over the water, and sank quietly. As the gunboat altered course to pass astern, with a growing white bow wave, Captain Buff realized the Spaniard intended to sink *Astraea* rather than risk ambush by boarding, and began lowering boats. While watching for the next flash, so everyone could be warned to drop, he stole a quick glance at the coming execution's sole witness; expecting the merchant bark to haul off for safety. She instead continued closing, turned east, increased speed, and three American battle flags broke at her mastheads. An iron fist struck the railing's hot wood as he realized the wooden bark was *Calypso*. That bastard Starke was closing to engage the modern steel gunboat on a Sunday morning off Cuba; emotions atrophied since before the war flashed, then vanished.

The commander of *Pedro Menéndez de Avilés*, a *Temerario* class torpedo gunboat, cursed the Yankee for not revealing himself before his own battle flags broke and *Astraea* fired on. American filibusters supported the last insurrection and the current fighting had not only nearly bankrupted Spain but left thousands dead, crippled, or recovering from disease; among them a young cousin whose right arm was lost to an American-made machete. Governor-general Weyler was winning when the government wanted to recall him and it seemed the same politicians might retry the *Competitor*'s crew sentenced to death a year before; something not possible for the dead and maimed. It seemed they also lacked the backbone to stand against American newspapers applauding attacks on small gunboat patrols. He was there when the battered *Francisco de Montejo* limped into Havana and before leaving for this mission was informed her assailant's master now captained *Astraea*. This probably explained why his orders were clear about compliance with international laws and conventions but delivered with the verbal suggestion a warning round accidentally striking this ammunition-laden schooner would be considered unfortunate and resulting explosion proof of filibustering.

His gunners were told to aim between wind and water because the storm left a battered canvas strip, intended to conceal *Astraea*'s name, hanging under the counter by a single nail. She was, by God's grace, the filibuster he was sent to intercept after their Washington legation alerted Weyler that *Astraea* was sailing for a secluded southern coast beach near Cabo Corrientes with insurrectos and military stores. The storm had driven him back from Cabo San Antonio and ended any chance of intercepting the filibuster so he was returning to Havana when the disabled schooner was spotted. As they approached to assist, the dangling canvas revealed storm and Providence had delivered *Astraea* on this pristine morning with no traffic besides an eastbound bark that just revealed she was a warship. He had slowed to approach the schooner but with the American working up to full speed and cutting through rolling blue water, now did the same.

Everything changed with that warship's appearance off the Cuban coast near *Astraea*; and he had not forgotten the last war's rumors that filibusters were shielded by the same navy. His one consolation was her resemblance to obsolete steam screw sloops with muzzleloading Dahlgren guns that were now mostly training ships. Even so, she was not behaving like one. A feathery white bow wave plowed out and back from her stem after the aligning masts confirmed a turn south and there was no request to parley so, when she steadied on a course that would bring her down his port side and mask the starboard 120mm gun, he countered with a hard port turn to place him astern of the black-hulled bark where her main batteries would be unable to train. He was also confident in any fight *Pedro Menéndez de Avilés* would benefit from a

Spanish crew rather than mix of merchant seamen and landsmen from numerous countries, regions, and races.

Starke turned port to maintain a reciprocal course that would take them within a thousand yards. He had not intended to come in this close but it prevented the gunboat from getting astern and shielded the schooner. As bark and gunboat tensely circled, both crews saw everything from colorful flags to gray scupper discharges; including their opposites on flying bridge, deckhouse, and gun mounts. Starke could see faces through his excellent Bausch & Lomb prismatic binoculars, more people on deck than a gunboat crewed to about ninety should carry, and an odd assortment of uniforms.

Captain Buff studied the ships warily circling, like opening parries in a fencing match, but it was quixotic to expect an obsolete wooden bark would take on a modern, steel-hulled gunboat. He expected her grim-faced bastard to break off, but their maneuvering bought time to abandon *Astraea*, still wallowing in the slight swells, before scuttling her in deep water. Without evidence, the gunboat might leave her boats to *Calypso*; if Starke remained close enough to dissuade the Don from firing on them. Without *Calypso*, anyone the gunboat failed to kill would be segregated into those claiming American, French, or British citizenship for trial then execution or prison; while the rest would make perfunctory appearances before a military court then pockmarked fortress wall.

Calypso's Gatlings gave Starke a temporary advantage at something like 1,000 yards since they could sweep the Spaniard's open mounts and smother her larger secondary battery; so he gambled her captain wished to parley and had turned to Dunbar about signaling when its small Nordenfelt's staccato unleashed a lead stream striking just below *Calypso*'s pilothouse before moving aft and down, leaving jagged holes through deckhouse then hull. Dust, splinters, and paint chips were still airborne when her port 120mm gun flashed with a deafening explosion. That round screamed over *Calypso* because the gunner fired on the up-roll. Starke released all batteries.

The incredulous Spanish commander briefly glimpsed his twenty-four kilogram round pass between the bark's fore and mainmast, skip several times, and climax with an explosion of white water against blue sky as *Calypso* erupted in gray and black smoke punctuated by bright yellow flashes. He dropped the paired-telescopes and died with several others as heavy .45-70 rounds struck steel, wood, and flesh with different sounds. Gatlings swept the gunboat's decks, concentrating momentarily on the gun sponson; followed by the port Hotchkiss 3-pounder walking her hull from bow to stern; and finally 4-inch, thirty-three pound common projectiles detonating against 13-millimeter armor with ear-shattering blasts. Although these large shells loosed showers of steel splinters, her armor miraculously shielded engineering from wounds that should have been mortal; and would have been with armor-piercing rounds.

Starke turned *Calypso* north, wreathed in gray gunsmoke from her steady fusillade, as *Pedro Menéndez de Avilés* continued west; placing the bark about 2,000 yards astern. *Calypso* had taken little damage because the Spanish gunboat commander died before releasing his powerful secondary battery; and her crew allowed no time to reply independently before they were overwhelmed by Gatling rounds, then subdued by the 3-pounder. Starke knew full well if the bark received similar punishment, she would be dead in the water, probably sinking, and few men topside would have survived.

Captain Buff on *Astraea* was beginning to lower the first boat when startled by a sharp staccato, flat crack of heavy ordnance, and deafening barrage. He could see the separation between warships fill with gray smoke and, from the flashes, it seemed *Calypso* was getting the best of the exchange, sending round after round into the gunboat's side then unprotected stern; before flag signals halted what emulated a painting of some old frigate action. It was the first American single-ship action against a European since Decatur and Hull.

Starke opened the range, uncertain whether his adversary was mortally wounded or merely infuriated, to prevent a mobile torpedo or her secondary battery coming into play; and gambling *Calypso*'s 4-inch gun captains and armor-piercing rounds would force their adversary's withdrawal. Instead, her battle ensign and other flags came down at the run, excluding a single flag at the maintop to uphold Spanish honor. This signaled the gunboat desired a cease-fire but refused to submit. *Calypso* continued her turn then slowed; leaving the bark equal distance between schooner and lacerated gunboat. Starke looked across the mile and a half then chanced it was no ruse.

Calypso's best defense was to continue shooting but Starke ordered firing checked, retrieved his battered pipe, placed it in his mouth, and noticed stains on his uniform collar he hoped would be attributed to the sun. The gunboat must have taken greater damage than its trim outboard profile suggested, since the code pennant jerked up her halyard followed by the B, M, and W flags asking to communicate. *Calypso* acknowledged and offered assistance using the commercial signal book; which was answered with a request for medical help. Starke brought *Calypso* within 200 yards then sent Watson, Conrad, and most of the medical department. Watching their whaleboats cross from the flying bridge, his hands grasping

266

the burning steel rail, Starke knew what Conrad would find could easily end the surgeon's desire to remain in the Navy; and his own career was probably over anyway. He felt strangely relieved as he ordered the steam pinnaces prepared.

CHAPTER TWENTY TWO
AFTERMATH

Captain Buff watched *Calypso* close the Spaniard then lower whaleboats that were quickly filled and away. Once they reached the gunboat, *Calypso* made for *Astraea*, slowed to bare steerageway just off her stern, and lowered two steam pinnaces. White-uniformed sailors with rifles and web harnesses began climbing into them as the code pennant and four multi-colored flags broke at her masthead. Captain Buff did not open his signal book to confirm the cloth fluttering fitfully above guns still hot from firing read, "I will board". He would survive but *Astraea* remained in extremis so lowering her four boats continued to reduce topside weight and be ready to abandon. She was severely wounded by storm damage, long hours of wallowing, and the round striking her mainmast. Looking up, he judged that mast nearly ready to join the fore alongside and unable to take canvas even if splinted. Both must now be eased overboard and the weather kind to make Key West, even under tow.

Coxswain Melvin threaded his pinnace past the partly submerged foremast to a gangway lowered by the spar's weight. Ensign Blair immediately boarded with a half-dozen armed seamen and formed his detail; rifles loaded, bayonets fixed, and cutlass scabbards filled. Neither *Astraea*'s crew nor her insurrectos had any means to resist since Captain Buff ensured only he was armed after *Rafael Riego*. Starke chose Blair with some apprehension but felt an aggressive nature would be required with Captain Buff; and the ensign's first words were an undiplomatic, "Your cargo and passengers?"

Captain Buff's neck compressed fully, his head became red, and he inadvertently stepped towards the ensign while cocking a massive fist. The move startled Blair but not the sailor beside him known for brawling and memorable, but infrequent, runs ashore. He smoothly brought his rifle up and thrust it butt-forward with a powerful right arm; striking the large head with a dull thud. After confirming the blow sufficient, he turned to his officer with a grin, "Wanted a piece of that big bastard for a while, sir."

The irritated, appreciative, and empathetic Blair growled, "I'll deal with you later," then called for crew and passengers. They were stripped of knives, whiskey, and other contraband then ferried to *Calypso* in the schooner's four boats towed by a steam pinnace. Blair and two sailors remained until Captain Buff could regain his wits, gather personal effects, and produce the ship's papers. The still-groggy master considered scuttling her but each glance towards the hatchway leading below brought an expectant grin from the sailor who brained him; and detonating the cargo was the only certain method. When passengers and crew were taken off and *Calypso* returned to *Pedro Menéndez de Avilés*, the schooner was left abandoned.

Captain Buff demanded to see Starke as he boarded *Calypso* and, still recovering, burst into the captain's day cabin with Watson in tow. As the door slammed shut, Starke saw a sailor known for causing havoc ashore in the passageway with a satisfied expression. Captain Buff's head reddened and snapping turtle neck contracted during a verbal assault composed of sulking, threats, and demands that climaxed with, "I demand my ship, crew, and passengers be returned and proper assistance rendered."

Watson instinctively stepped back as Starke passed instantly through red-hot anger to a white heat he had never seen. *Calypso's* commander carefully set the lightly browned meerschaum pipe on a steel ashtray; reminding Watson of a large diamondback that stood coiled on the ground in front of his horse without rattling. The low, controlled response was, "*Astraea* may not have anyone killed Captain, but I just received a first cut at Spanish casualties."

Watson shuffled back an inch or two more as Starke continued coldly, "*Pedro Menéndez de Avilés'* captain fell at his post but her acting commander has agreed to take *Astraea* in tow for Havana since *Calypso's* unable and the schooner's likely to founder before Key West. Your manifest declares agricultural machinery that can be sold off in Havana and the harbor has repair facilities. The authorities there can also address crew and passengers so anyone desiring to accompany her is free to do so; and this command will take the remainder to Key West. If no one remains, she'll be abandoned and claims may be filed with the Spanish consul."

"Bastard."

Watson then saw Starke's cold, blue-steel eyes impale Captain Buff. He was clearly no more concerned with the filibuster being shot, hanged, or garroted than putting down a rabid wolf. The battered knuckles of Captain Buff's paws turned white grasping the table as he pressed forward, "I demand immediate return of my ship, crew, cargo, and passengers."

Starke's response came in the cold, precise tone of a seasoned executioner, "*Astraea's* barely afloat, nearer Cuban ports, and this ship cannot enter Spanish waters uninvited."

"You're surrendering an American ship that was fired on."

"Her senior surviving officer claims two rounds were fired to gain your attention and formally apologized for any unintended damage."

"He's a liar; and *Calypso* was also attacked."

"They admit that and believe it was by accident or someone on *Pedro Menéndez de Avilés* acting without orders. The Spanish navy will investigate; although the executive officer was aft with their repair party and most eyewitnesses killed."

Captain Buff's riposte was cut off with a dismissive wave, "Far better men than you were killed and wounded today. I could do without your company but *Pedro Menéndez de Avilés'* acting commander assures me you are welcome there."

"Bastard."

"You brought this about but others paid, or will; so go to the gunboat or remain here under close arrest with the guards free to take whatever action necessary should you even contemplate an untoward move."

Captain Buff turned, bulled through the door, and headed down the passageway with the eager sailor two steps behind. Starke watched for a moment then turned to Watson, "Please remain, XO, and shut the door."

"Yes sir."

As the two sat, *Calypso*'s commander resumed his familiar demeanor, recharged the pipe, and passed a flame over center bowl. Through a light blue tobacco smoke cloud he began, "Pond is at your disposal for the battle report, XO. It must be especially detailed, clear, and accurate so get statements from both ships then gather whatever charts and logs are available from the gunboat and schooner."

"Yes sir."

"Also, prepare to assume temporary command again once we reach Key West."

"You think it will come to that, Captain?"

"Probably, but for now let's get underway."

Two *Calypso* sailors were wounded by splinters, a hot shell casing burned another's hands, and several suffered hearing loss; but *Pedro Menéndez de Avilés* butcher's bill was not so light since she carried artillerymen detailed as infantry to engage any insurgents ashore. Five sailors and seven soldiers already died. Fifteen were seriously wounded; with three amputations that might succumb to hemorrhage or shock. Conrad was told to report directly when he returned and did so; exhausted and still wearing his filthy white uniform smeared with blood. He looked unflinchingly into Starke's eyes, "Reporting as ordered, sir."

"Sit down, Sidney."

The surgeon half-collapsed into a chair as Starke continued, "Bad, I take it?"

"We took the first to arrive and each additional man in turn; just finished the last serious casualty before leaving. An officer thanked me as I removed his arm. There's blood all over the ship with pools where someone was struck down. A bayman went into shock so I sent him back for rest and medicinal brandy."

As the surgeon began, Starke could see his report was backing Watson's. Two 4-inch common rounds should have penetrated but instead burst against the light hull armor. If they had entered, or were armor-piercing, the gunboat's engineering and machinery spaces would have become the same bloody shambles as her main deck and unprotected areas. Once Conrad completed his verbal report, Starke told him to clean up and start the written one while events were fresh. He recognized the surgeon's emotional maelstrom from his own on a Montana bluff twenty years earlier and knew the best bridge was a task. As Conrad rose to leave, Starke added, "You've seen what defeat looks like but remember it could have been us and having to recover means you survived. I would prescribe a medicinal brandy."

"Thank-you Captain; but one would be too many and a dozen not enough."

Starke returned to the flying bridge while a blazing Caribbean sunset illuminated distant cumulus clouds in every imaginable color then extended this palette to the sea. *Calypso* came about beneath this spectacle in a wide turn that cleared the gunboat before steaming slowly north and east for Key West. The Spaniard was preparing to board the sluggishly rolling schooner and recover four whaleboats Coxswain Melvin left on a long painter. Starke felt his battle fever drain while considering a father in Rio de Janeiro, joining his uncle's firm, and Aunt Constant's perpetual quest to arrange a suitable consort who could bear children. Katherine was soon uppermost in his thoughts and the attraction that blossomed in an impetuous and contagious night of passion in Havana.

Calypso passed through Key West's shallows before noon to anchor off the ship channel; just west of the Marine Hospital and within sight of Fort Taylor, several small keys, the naval station, and city waterfront. Her sailors had been kept busy making repairs for the same reason Conrad concentrated on his medical report, but also to make their arrival seem routine. The same held for Starke's official call on Forsyth, although Naval Cadet Timme was already sending one telegram reporting their arrival and another in code.

Captain Albert's day at Washington's ornate State, War, and Navy Building was well into its last half when they crossed his desk. He read the plain language telegram reporting *Calypso*'s arrival in Key West when the cable from Veracruz should have her leaving the Straits of Florida for Port Royal; and immediately slit the second envelope. Any expectation she brought in a filibuster, perhaps even *Laurada*, vanished as he deciphered. Hand-printed on a stiff sheet of off-white writing paper was, "Engaged Spanish gunboat attacking disabled filibuster. Little damage Calypso. Few wounded. Gunboat damage heavy. Gave aid. Schooner under tow for Havana without crew. Report to follow. Starke."

Albert left to warn Crowninshield, the new Bureau of Navigation chief. Minutes later they interrupted Secretary Long's briefing about a trial post exchange for Marines at the Boston navy yard. As Crowninshield spoke, Albert thanked Providence the secretary returned to his Portland Hotel suite from vacation the previous afternoon and Theodore was no longer acting. Long read the short message twice then dispatched his private secretary, Lewis Finney, to locate Day; the assistant secretary of state who oversaw that department due to Sherman's health.

An unscheduled meeting convened soon after with participants seated on either side of a large table, glistening with polish, in the navy secretary's elaborately furnished office above the east entrance. While providing his understanding of the message to Long, Roosevelt, Day, and Crowninshield; Albert recalled the filibuster project's initiation and, equally odd, that the election swept Clarence Newcomb from his Diplomatic Bureau office.

Roosevelt was first off the mark, "Spain fired on the flag; it's war."

Day, a criminal and corporate lawyer, looked across the table into the pugnacious New Yorker's eyes, "Not based on this. Starke provides no location and says the schooner was a filibuster. It also appears some understanding was obtained if he sent medical help and permitted the tow."

Commodore Crowninshield's plain civilian attire contrasted with Albert's uniform as he tweaked his mustache then glanced towards Long, "I agree. Navy regulations are precise and I don't believe young Starke to be rash so this must have occurred beyond Spanish jurisdiction. The outcome is more puzzling. A river gunboat would not stray beyond protected waters or tow a schooner after being damaged and suffering casualties; but a large one should have damaged *Calypso*."

Day looked briefly at Roosevelt, Crowninshield, then Long, ". . . and who fired first."

Roosevelt's blood was up, "Bully for Starke if he bloodied their nose in a single-ship action!"

Day was equally grateful Long was back but anxious about Roosevelt's regular press indiscretion; and anticipating a diplomatic note before the day ended, followed by another Dupuy de Lôme meeting. Starke's telegrams also seemed to explain why Spain's minister visited the previous afternoon after returning early from vacation. He often avoided speaking with Secretary Sherman, who detested Spain, but must have received information from Havana and was reconnoitering. Day looked at the Bureau of Navigation chief, who controlled officer assignments, then Long, "Will Starke be summoned, sir?"

Albert anticipated the question but hoped it would not come up here. Crowninshield, unlike Ramsay, would discard protocols he objected to but castigate others for the same practice. While this made him unpredictable; it could work in Starke's favor since the two met when the commodore commanded *Maine*. Crowninshield's mustache moved slightly and his eyes locked on the assistant secretary, inspiring Roosevelt to speak first, "The American nation will not stomach removing *Calypso*'s commander for successfully engaging a Spanish warship attacking an American merchant vessel. It would be rightly viewed as failing to back our man and dishonorable; while Spain could argue it admits guilt."

Roosevelt was regularly patronized by a gaggle of reporters because his statements made lively copy and Long deferred to bureau chiefs so Albert thought it possible Crowninshield provoked the assistant secretary to make the case against removal because his opinion could easily surface in the press; especially if he thought it timid or spineless. Long turned to Crowninshield, who responded, "Mr. Roosevelt's correct. Removing or relieving *Calypso*'s commander without investigation paints him as culprit or scapegoat. We must also keep her crew together or the fleet will be infected with rumors. I suggest ordering *Calypso* to Norfolk for hull inspection and maintenance. Once there, Starke is available; and shifting work from Port Royal is expected since that channel is to be dredged for larger ships."

Day interjected, "I understand, but with Spain under a caretaker government we must put forward an unassailable account or it could precipitate war."

Albert touched Crowninshield's forearm, received a nod, and then added, "Executive officers compose the battle report and she can transit to Norfolk without Lieutenant Watson; who could be here within a week by train."

Long and Crowninshield nodded as Day added, "The president's due back so we could see him after he arrives. I'll inform Secretary Sherman and make discrete inquiries with the Spanish legation. Their current government may be more anxious than ours about this since it could upset any balance between liberals and conservatives and give Don Carlos an opening; besides, Minister Woodford's delivering a proposal in Madrid as we speak."

An agitated Roosevelt played briefly with his round glasses, considered the others, then addressed Long, "If war is near, why delay until more troops arrive, ships being bought become operational, and their torpedo boat squadron's in

Havana? They attacked and Starke met them. We must show grit and more backbone than an eclair."

The assistant secretary then amplified his torpedo boat concerns. Fed by Starke's analysis and others, he viewed them as a threat to the capital ships being pursued in Congress, constantly raised public interest in the type through statements to the press, and continued to argue that Spain sending a flotilla to Cuba was an act of war. Albert reached for a pipe, then recalled it leaned against his desk ashtray, as Long's smooth voice responded, "Theodore, I believe we can delay war a few days. Commodore, please prepare orders for my signature."

Albert suspected this abruptness with Roosevelt was partly due to his recent political scheming that gave the Asiatic Squadron to a favorite. Long looked directly at his bellicose assistant, "This goes no further until we learn what occurred and the president has been appraised."

As they passed through the broad wooden door, framed by an archway stenciled on the room's green walls, Albert was reminded everything and everyone moved too slowly for Roosevelt. His intelligence, energy, and naval promotion were valuable, but the unbridled enthusiasm made Albert uneasy; and Theodore misread *Calypso's* commander.

CHAPTER TWENTY THREE
THE INQUIRY

A lbert met separately with Commodore Crowninshield in the Bureau of Navigation office to consider options. Replacing Starke by an exchange with Commander Moore, assigned to deliver the old sloop *Yantic* to Michigan's naval militia, was considered but that officer was to command a more fitting ship at Boston's navy yard afterwards; and there was Roosevelt's point about removing Starke. Sending *Calypso* to patrol off Guatemala for filibusters supplying rebels there was weighed; as was sending the bark after seal poachers violating the Bering Sea Agreement. Another possibility was transfer to the European Squadron since *Calypso*'s capabilities would be welcome, Starke knew the eastern Mediterranean, and the missionary lobby would applaud it; although the long-legged bark would be equally valuable in the Asiatic or South Atlantic Squadron. Albert appreciated the opportunity to discuss and dispose of these alternatives since Crowninshield seldom changed positions and he anticipated an upsurge in filibuster expeditions.

Maximilian Falk, the Justice troubleshooter who worked Cuba, supported filibuster cases, and liaised with Congress had projected a surge to influence the unraveling Spanish and Cuban politics. Following the Spanish prime minister's assassination, Lieutenant General Azcárraga, whose mother was Filipino and wife Cuban, headed an interim government working with the queen regent to preserve political stability and the monarchy. Cuba was their primary impediment because the national consensus was it must remain with Spain and the insurrection would have ended except for expeditions from the States. Consequently, the Liberal Party's leader, Praxedes Mateo Sagasta, advocated autonomy while conservatives opposed negotiation until rebels stood down. Island politics were even more fractured according to Falk, although most held no political aspirations beyond survival. Business interests supported remaining with Spain, a minority argued annexation to the States, autonomists wanted home rule, most insurrectos would accept only independence, and others, like anarchists, had broader agendas. This political mélange rested on the fault line between Cubans of African and Spanish descent Martí had transcended. Since his death, the New York Junta claimed to speak for a popular front government representing everyone but African Cubans were uncompromising on independence, dominated the southern provinces, and constituted a large portion of the insurrecto army. Spanish Cubans were located in cities and northern provinces, more divided, and feared independence could resemble Haiti.

The prime minister's assassination coming when Weyler seemed about to end the insurrection shuffled this deck, suggested some climax was near, caused some factions to plan for fighting after Spain, and initiated maneuvers to strengthen positions. This struggle suggested expeditions would increase so Albert wanted *Calypso* at sea and the latest gunboat incident resolved before December. For October and part of November, he hoped to add filibuster patrols to winter exercises in the northern Caribbean and argued that increasing these patrols might damp Spanish protests against squadron training near Cuba. Rear Admiral Sicard's North Atlantic Squadron would contribute, as would America's first torpedo boat flotilla; five boats under Lieutenant Kimball. Crowninshield agreed to send *Calypso* from Key West to Norfolk but held these orders until Long returned from an extended cabinet meeting the following day. At that meeting, State announced they had been officially informed *Pedro Menéndez de Avilés* reached Havana where her senior surviving officer confirmed the gunboat fired in error and Cuba's governor-general saw no reason to exaggerate the incident. *Astraea* did not make port but a salvaged cargo sample confirmed she was a filibuster. Albert's day improved further when Theodore and a pregnant Edith departed for three weeks in Oyster Bay.

Commander Forsyth sensed ripe carrion for Key West press vultures who routinely embellished the slightest rumor or supposition then wired it to their papers. Rather than wait for Washington, he all but closed the Key West naval station under the guise of preparing for a North Atlantic Squadron visit. Her Veracruz port call provided a convenient excuse to delay liberty so coaling started soon after arrival. Standing on the steel pier watching tugs shift a battered barge alongside, he was confident it had been the best course; especially after Starke mentioned Chief Weaver overhearing some sailors comparing their skirmish to *Bon Homme Richard's* fight with HMS *Serapis*; and *Kearsarge* against *Alabama*. This would be harmless in their dotage and boosted morale, but coming from liquored up sailors mixing with reporters in local bars could prove disastrous.

Starke's resignation letter lay on his desk while the duty steam pinnace went to retrieve a Navy Department telegram and Thaddeus explored the day cabin for food or a likely nap spot. *Calypso's* commander took a comfortable chair near an open window, lit his best pipe, and enjoyed the early evening light breeze tinged with late summer sea smells. He expected

Watson would assume temporary command unless the executive officer was also held responsible. Should that occur, he would speak with his uncle or father about a position in one of their shipping firms. He was also sensing unexpected relief about the approaching estrangement with *Calypso* and considering a visit with his father in Rio de Janeiro then England. Softly scented pipe smoke lofted towards the ceiling as sounds of *Calypso*'s in-port routine were disrupted by the pinnace's steam engine announcing its return. Within minutes Timme brought a thin brown packet to his captain then left for the wardroom where Watson and Dunbar were listening to Conrad explain how a Dr. Charles Finlay believed one particular evening mosquito carried yellow fever.

Starke sent for Watson after reading the message; and his executive officer knocked on the door a few minutes later. The lieutenant entered to find his captain at the table and a paper sliding towards him, "Take a seat XO, you'll need it."

Watson picked up the deciphered telegram and read, "Watson report Crowninshield soonest. Travel authorized. Calypso transit Hampton Roads for upkeep."

Navy regulations required executive officers to complete the battle report so Watson had a final draft, and Washington wanting it yesterday was understandable, but the summons was perplexing. He read it again before responding, "I don't understand, Captain."

Starke smiled, "Olivia Albert will be surprised. *City of Key West* leaves for Miami in the morning and the new rail line from there should get you to Jacksonville for a fast mail to Washington. That's quicker than going through Port Tampa."

"Yes sir."

"Take your draft report and turn over to Dunbar. Have him arrange a meeting with the officers and chiefs once you've left. *Calypso* will follow on Saturday."

"Yes sir."

"I'll telegraph my aunt and uncle; you're welcome to stay with them, unless," Starke almost grinned, "you prefer more convenient lodgings."

He could only respond, "I'll get started, Captain; and thank you."

The steam pinnace left for city dock early next morning so Watson could board *City of Key West* before she left at seven o'clock. The veteran liner would paddle up the Keys to an expanding Miami where he would take a Florida East Coast train to Jacksonville then connect with The Southern Line's United States Fast Mail. He kept the same Pullman car after Jacksonville, despite a locomotive change in Columbia, so sleep would be possible before Washington. Starke watched the pinnace move off with Watson in its sternsheets beneath a white canvas awning and felt the night's gentle coolness succumb to a rising sun. Dunbar stood beside him after studying Navy regulations' detailed list of executive officer tasks late into the night; with a noticeable slump to his shoulders after discovering what the next rung up entailed. Starke checked a smile. Dunbar was an excellent officer and would have a writer to assist and provide continuity, but Osbourne, the chief engineer and next senior to Watson in relative rank, would have been his first choice. As a steam engineer, however, he was not in line for command; although whether officers should be competent in both disciplines or excel in one was debated from the *Proceedings* magazine to Congress. Starke slightly favored the generalist position but made a point of not discussing it since the bedrock issues were less philosophical: change, status, and power.

The white side-wheeler carrying Watson passed between *Calypso* and the Marine Hospital two hours later. Its boiler, engine, and paddle-wheels made it appear to sag amidship but the liner was considered solid and reliable. As she churned past the red-brick fort, around Whitehead Spit, and then entered Southeast Channel under a gray-black smoke plume, Starke recalled Forsyth observe she fit the Key's shallows and reefs, sip his brandy, then add the old lady allegedly did some filibustering before Flagler acquired her.

Calypso had four days grace, since the words "immediately" or "without delay" was not in the orders, but left later that morning. After taking the same channel as *City of Key West*, Starke planned to clear the shallows, reefs, and coral heads during daylight then remain far enough offshore to take advantage of a current funneling through the Straits of Florida. Riding that flow, they would turn almost due north beyond the straits into the Gulf Stream then stay with it past the Bahama Islands' shallows. Further on, Dunbar's track took them northeast to weather Cape Hatteras then began the last leg to Chesapeake Bay's mouth where they would pass between Capes Henry and Charles.

Since most of the voyage followed a major Atlantic sail route north established by prevailing winds, *Calypso* also spread her canvas beyond Matanilla Shoals. While this gave the black gang some relief, the crew was occupied with maintenance, inspections, drills, singlestick practice, and unannounced man-overboard exercises. Starke noticed gun drills had acquired even greater interest, intensity, attention to detail, and precision. Morale was high despite another weekend departure and it appeared Osbourne colluded with the chiefs to ease Dunbar's lot as navigator and executive officer.

Calypso plowed through various hues of blue waters threatening to turn gray during Saturday afternoon rope-yarn then doing so for Sunday morning's full dress monthly muster and weekly church service. Starke used his time to focus on an endless queue of Navy records, logs, and reports since he anticipated being relieved. The electrical journal, deck, and steam logs were approved; monthly uniform inspection completed and replacement requisitions signed; the ship's *Steaming & Sailing Qualities Report* readied; and their cadets' journals examined then endorsed. He also completed letters to his aunt, Katherine, and then Tyson; the last sent in care of *The Sun*. Osbourne, O'Leary, and Blair worked a consolidated shipyard worklist while Martyn assisted with navigator duties. This was possible because Timme and Caldwell stood pilothouse day watches alone for the first time, leading sections they were familiar with; freeing ensigns to prepare for the shipyard, fattening personal logs cadets needed to compete for commissions, and showing the command was attempting to follow Navy regulations' urging to assign officers three-section duty. Groups of sailors on the main deck "pounded an ear" while Paymaster Clerk Eberhardt worked his hurdy gurdy, fantail minstrels played *Annie Laurie*, and Yamashita trolled a baited hand-line.

The relaxed mood changed when a massive hammerhead shark's tall dorsal fin surfaced astern, ignored Yamashita's bait, then paralleled *Calypso* about twenty yards off. The creature steadily cleaved the ocean with water sliding over its brown back as though *Nautilus* had come. A gun captain requested permission to try a shot, but the powerful fish hauled off to starboard, dropped astern, then disappeared as though knowing what was coming. Not only was the creature's behavior odd, but ocean and sky were devoid of life, so word began circulating they were near where Matthew Parnell went over and some claimed their dead shipmate returned to haunt the ship that abandoned him. A respected Sandwich Islands sailor added credence by pointing out where he was from human spirits often inhabited sharks.

While this gained crew converts, *Calypso's* wardroom dismissed it until Wiggs recounted Jonah; and the chiefs quickly took to their two camps. Parnell's spectral return became irretrievably woven into the ship's lore.

Favorable winds, little traffic, and an unusually docile Cape Hatteras found *Calypso* raising Chesapeake Bay to her north and east the following Saturday morning. Cape Henry lighthouse was spotted first then its northern companion on Cape Charles; both easily confirmed by location and nearby predecessors. Cape Henry's lighthouse was just forward of a bald hill face, with woodlands above and beside, while its counterpart on Cape Charles' mosquito-plagued lowland was backed by trees and due east of a lightship moored southeast of Smith Island Shoal. *Calypso* passed slowly through Virginia and Maryland pilot boats loitering outside the bay, expecting a message from the U.S. Signal Service's seacoast telegraph station on Cape Henry directing them to Norfolk, Newport News, or a quarantine anchorage. The surrounding schooners closed to where homeports painted on stern, foresail, and mainsail could be read then hauled off when no pilot was requested. Navy ships were not required to use their services and Starke knew the lower bay well enough to let his navigation team work without a net; and throw a bone to the accountants.

Starke positioned *Calypso* nearly due west from Cape Henry to enter Chesapeake Bay between The Middle Ground and Lynnhaven Roads, Admiral de Grasse's anchorage before sailing to meet the British. Since she would continue west to Hampton Roads; the bark lined up on Thimble Shoal Lighthouse, a large octagonal structure on piles, then held course until sighting buoys marking the channel between Thimble Shoal and Willoughby's Banks. While passing Old Point Comfort and Fort Wool, Starke swept the Chamberlain then Hygeia Hotel with binoculars, recalling his evening at the second with Katherine; before shifting attention to a heavily laden collier outbound from Newport News. *Calypso* eased up to their anchorage, west of the channel off Sewall's Point and midway between Buoys 4 and 6; where her black anchor plunged through dark water into Hampton Roads mud, dragging its thundering chain under clouds of dust and rust. While the ship backed slowly to set it and lay a proper scope, those not directly involved rigged the accommodation ladder and readied steam pinnaces. Starke chose to anchor north of Craney Island instead of the Elizabeth River naval anchorage off the hospital because it was equally convenient whether they were sent to Newport News across Hampton Roads or ordered to the Norfolk yard. The quarantine official boarded immediately, examined the crew list, and would have detained them, since *Calypso* was arriving from a southern port, but Conrad's diplomacy, growing knowledge of yellow fever, and elapsed time since leaving Veracruz prevailed. Using the first steam pinnace lowered, Starke headed upriver to complete his courtesy visit to the commandant on Norfolk's receiving ship *Franklin*. Rear Admiral Brown had retired so respects would be paid to Commodore Norman von Heldreich Farquhar; *Trenton*'s captain during the Samoan hurricane that put her and other warships aground some eight years before, antislavery patrol veteran, assigned to the blockading squadron during the war, and commander of various other ships, including the cruiser *Newark*.

In Washington, Captain Albert began Monday with coffee at the window; looking past the Executive Mansion to Lafayette Square. A Metropolitan streetcar on its far side started for Dupont Circle then continued north to line's end near the Starke mansion while Capital Traction Company tracks on its south side remained unused since the firm's power house burned; and intermittent detonations told him crews were still blasting its remains. This did not disrupt his commute since the Albert row house was within easy, albeit mosquito plagued, walking distance; although travel to the Navy Yard and congressional offices was inconvenient. Temporary horse-drawn cars still operated on some sections and taxis were enjoying a boom since government workers and summer exiles returned.

Madrid was also adjusting to its summer refugees' reappearance; and liberal faction's win in a close election. Praxedes Mateo Sagasta's party assumed power but also possession of a near-bankrupt treasury, Cuban morass, and renewed Philippines fighting. Weyler seemed successful in Cuba but some soldiers deserted rather than board the West Indies transports and reconcentrados in squalid, makeshift camps or buildings were dying in droves. The loss of lives, capital, and prestige with no clear end and a public unwilling to abandon their colonies strengthened Sagasta's faith in autonomy over independence; so he would begin with the Philippines, move to Puerto Rico, and finish with Cuba.

Washington and Madrid viewed the *Calypso* and *Pedro Menéndez de Avilés* duel particularly alarming; which was why Dupuy de Lôme returned early to Washington from his summer vacation and the meeting with Day billed as routine discussion of their new legation building; despite no details released to the press. A silent Junta puzzled Albert until Falk explained most of its factions wanted American support and license, not the direct involvement war would bring. With Roosevelt away from the city and Senator Lodge strangely subdued, the jingoes' were similarly muted. Press coverage was confined to a Tampa paper stating Havana reported their *Nueva España* torpedo gunboat entered port from Pinar del Río with four whaleboats, a Hotchkiss gun, and Zalinsky dynamite rounds from a filibuster. Tampa readers were then reassured most of the Junta expedition's men and supplies reached insurgents since there was no mention of prisoners or any filibusters reported lost. Watson's draft report established *Astraea* was an American-flagged filibuster and it was *Pedro Menéndez de Avilés*, not *Nueva España*, that *Calypso* fought; although the damaged sister ship had been quietly sent to Spain. The story might have escalated except the overloaded wood steamer *Triton* sank off Pinar del Río on a trip to Cabanas. She tried to reach Mariel during the storm, went aground, and slid into deep water with 130 soldiers, families, army mules, and silver coin payroll. When the gunboat *Maria Christina* and a tug *Louisa* brought *Triton* survivors into Havana, American and Spanish correspondents shifted to this tragedy then the next; leaving the filibuster story behind.

Albert disliked Spain's military attaché, Capitán de Corbete Jose Sobral, whose caustic disposition was matched by his repeated boasts, claims, and articles that the American navy could not match Spain's. The press was less tolerant since they viewed his frequent trips to cities with navy facilities as spying. However, during a visit portrayed as discussion of possible Cuban port access for ships on filibuster patrol, Sobral was unusually candid. It seemed *Pedro Menéndez de Avilés* entered Havana for voyage repairs then expeditiously ordered to Spain's Arsenal de la Carraca under her executive officer; leaving seriously wounded to the San Ambrosio Military Hospital. A detail did board *Astraea* and found flooding through sprung planking was blocked by crated weapons, ammunition, and explosives. Moving cargo to reach its source only increased the flow, a fothering attempt using her mainsail failed, and it was decided to abandon. The senior officer felt obligated to salvage the schooner and made a good faith effort, but would not risk leaving anyone with her and wanted to get his wounded to hospital. *Astraea* went done by the head soon after and he delayed leaving for Havana a half hour to ensure she was not floating below the surface. Contra Almirante Navarro was unable to ascertain how the gunboat came to fire on *Calypso* but possessed enough physical evidence to establish *Astraea* as a filibuster and conclude that Starke committing the bark's entire medical department saved lives. Sobral anticipated the gunboat would complete repairs in Spain, a brief inquiry conducted, and she would sail for the Philippines.

Although Starke and *Calypso* were implicated in a third incident, Albert found everyone wanted it to slip quietly into oblivion. Calls to relieve Starke pending formal inquiry faded when instigators discovered their motives would be questioned after the old bark successfully fought a modern steel gunboat; especially with Long barely restraining Theodore's urge to go public. *Astraea*'s cargo lay deep off Pinar del Río so there could be no trial in the States, Spain had no one to bring before their courts, and both nations' diplomats were eager to avoid any issue that might catch fire with their publics. Captain Buff avoided drowning, trial, prison, and a Spanish firing squad.

Although American courts could do nothing unless the *Astraea* passengers admitted they were insurrectos, and proof her cargo was not what was manifested could only come through Spain, a formal Navy inquiry was required to establish facts and forward recommendations. Albert was concerned these were often unpredictable, even if their findings were favorable, so careers might end and reputations tarnished. *Calypso* and crew would be in the Newport News shipyard while it took place, to maintain their expertise and distance them from Norfolk bars and reporters, while Watson and Starke would travel by train between shipyard and Building; ensuring one was always with *Calypso*.

Lieutenant (j.g.) Benjamin Watson asked for Olivia's hand during his fourth visit to her family's row house. The couple desired to wed immediately but hurried ceremonies could be socially scandalous so a truncated six-month engagement was agreed, and Olivia gained a ruby ring. Albert allowed them several days to reconsider before contacting Watson's family in Colorado and sending announcements to friends. Their eldest daughter's wedding preparations then enveloped his seldom tranquil home and he began to appreciate elopement's positive aspects.

Calypso offloaded munitions at Norfolk's new armory, crossed to Newport News, and dry-docked just south of the battleships *Kearsarge* and *Kentucky*; resting on their building ways. The morning after, Starke boarded the Old Point Comfort train for Richmond then Washington; apprehensive over orders north for the inquiry and threatening skies to the southeast. Momentarily unable to address either, he dozed fitfully in a seat unsuited to that purpose, made the Richmond connection, and was greeted by his uncle on Washington's Baltimore & Potomac station platform. The family groom and retired trooper, Darius Sutton, waited outside with the black landau; watching its canopied entrance from his driver's seat. The well-sprung carriage stood apart with its glossy lower body, silver and ebony trim, half-doors, glass windows, oiled leather upper body, and red-leather bench seats. The bay geldings, Gemini and Castores, were encased in heavy black-leather harness and when Starke stroked Gemini's nose out of habit the large horse began to whinny and shake its head as though remembering Sunday morning rides a year before. Starke buckled the rear luggage rack straps then followed his uncle through its right-side center door with glass windows filling openings beneath a seam joining the upper body's oiled-leather clam sections. After taking a seat across from his uncle on red leather bench seats with coil springs, they left for Starke mansion, just off Florida Avenue. The immaculate landau's elliptical springs and rubber-rimmed wheels ensured a superb ride, disrupted only when crossing streetcar tracks.

Immanuel Starke remained a dominating figure as his sixtieth year approached but there was a hint of slowing, thinning hair supported a fashionable hat, and his beard had begun the transition to white or silver gray. The patriarch's authority, inclination to act, and innate kindness had not waned. He extracted a large cigar from his leather case while passing the Executive Mansion, snipped its end with a silver cutter, wet the tightly rolled tobacco with his lips, and lit up. Holding the glowing tip from his face, he studied it then warned, "Prepare for an interrogation by your aunt. Miss Barton's returned from Vienna and they spend a great deal of time on reconcentrados."

"Does she know Olivia Albert's engaged to my executive officer?"

His uncle exhaled blue smoke, chuckling, "We received a card which, I'm afraid, stoked your aunt's matrimonial interests closer to home. However, there's no candidate since it appears Mrs. Ledford won't be returning with her brother at year's end and Miss Evans leaves for Havana next week. She's left *The Evening Times* for a position with *The Sun* . . . ," then, flicking cigar ash through the lowered window with a rarely seen grin continued, ". . . to work for your aunt's favorite correspondent, Mr. Darwin Tyson."

Starke's aunt treated his longtime friend like a family black sheep since they first met and, unfairly, suspected he undermined several attempts to maneuver her nephew to the alter. It was as though Tyson evoked memories of someone shelved long ago because she seemed particularly cordial but slightly odd during his visits, pretended offense when their liquor cabinet went untapped, and referred to his surreptitious silver flask as private stock. Starke was considering whether Evans might carry his most recent letter to Tyson when his uncle interrupted, "Consul-General Lee's preparing his return to Havana. Spoke to the president, myself, and twice with Captain Albert."

Starke was nearly lulled to sleep as the ride progressed by comfortable red leather seats, rhythmic motion, and muffled tread of shod hooves striking different road surfaces but revived as they turned off Florida Avenue. The Romanesque mansion in one of the city's newer additions was unchanged despite a year's passing. Its red stone exterior reached four stories, counting the ground floor and gabled living areas. A tall turret, capped with cone-shaped roof and lightning rod, substituted for the fourth rounded corner while a smaller half-turret was grafted to the building's front face. Saplings along the street clung to what little fall colors remained as surrounding grass dulled for winter. Sutton brought them to a smooth halt in front of its gray stone porch, obscuring a ground floor service entrance below. Within minutes, Starke followed his uncle through thick, double doors and greeted their butler, Joshua Altman. Starke's Aunt Constance embraced him in the parlor.

The Navy inquiry took place in the Building conference room Albert regularly used; behind a pine door encased in a sculpted frame, inset slightly, and below a transom window. Its exterior matched others along long off-white corridors, but inside a large, rectangular oak table encircled by plain parlor chairs with cane inserts consumed most of the space. Above a dark pine floor, the ceiling, walls, door, and trim were covered by layers of off-white paint and the far wall almost completely given over to a large four-pane window. Except for that and the door, its only relief was framed ship pictures hung above an inconspicuous chair rail.

The inquiry was conducted by a senior commander nearing retirement. He was assisted by a Judge Advocate clerk, and other participants designated witnesses for the time being. Those conducting the affair sat below the window with anyone testifying seated near the entrance and responding to specific questions requiring precise answers; revealing the examiners' familiarity with details contained in books and documents spread across the table. Those summoned from Treasury, Justice, and State usually rotated through alone but Watson was allowed to submit a statement and Albert sometimes accompanied Starke. They met a Spanish lieutenant commander leaving in dress uniform one afternoon who barely acknowledged the pair before moving on. The Revenue Cutter Service's Captain Fischer, on the other hand, greeted them by nodding his weathered head conspiratorially, commented about a pleasant hour on the rack, and mentioned *Vanguard* boarded a small schooner off the Keys with an abnormal number of Cubans but no military goods. It seemed Hunter anticipated he lacked enough evidence to prosecute but remained with her until the master understood continuing would expose the larger expedition and returned to Key West. Since *Vanguard* was working the Gulf, Fischer submitted Hunter's report and favorable correspondence from the *Portunus* rescue but was unable to contribute additional details concerning the event in question. After speaking, he continued to the east wing's elegant marble staircase with his leather shoes echoing dully off the floor's checkerboard marble.

Albert approached Building politics like related chess games with the ultimate result overriding individual matches.

He could see Starke was uncomfortable with this and tried to ease his junior's apprehension by emphasizing *Astraea*'s nefarious status, the ships' location, and which warship fired first were not being challenged; so the contentious points were only *Calypso* not signaling before closing, removing *Astraea*'s crew, and abandoning the schooner.

Falk contributed significantly by his ability to accurately divine where the inquiry was headed each day. Starke enjoyed working with him but, while discussing Cuba over steamed oysters at Harvey's Restaurant one evening, realized he was less optimistic about the island's future. Starke believed exhaustion could reconcile the most implacable adversaries to rational discourse but Falk did not and, after quickly scanning the room, opined, "Madrid's liberals are being forced to recall Weyler. It's an understandable political decision to show good faith generally and assuage the States, but he's an effective military leader who's nearly cleared insurgents from provinces he proposed to pacify first. This will allow insurrectos to regroup and the Junta to reject autonomy; but the insurrectos cannot prevail. Spain and its leaders will not accept independence unless the army is defeated, which is unlikely. In one move, liberals weakened their position, crippled the proposed solution, and left abandoning Cuba the only option; which risks this Spanish government and the monarchy. Unless something changes, one side must eventually collapse and the other left unable to govern; which could see another Haiti but just off our coast, or a war with Spain that brings in other nations."

Each evening, a subdued Starke returned to the mansion, greeted Altman, reviewed the day's events, and found little sleep due to the inquiry and those memories he warned Surgeon Conrad to bury. He sometimes sat with Martella Young at her kitchen table, when not studying Navy regulations with a stiff brandy and pipe. Cynthia Jefferson sometimes passed by but seldom strayed far from his aunt and was meticulously proper. He also fenced and practiced singlestick at an athletic club, fired the civilian Remington-Lee rifle or his single-action Colt at a Washington range, and made several short bicycle excursions. Sunday mornings brought the most relief. After donning his unfashionable riding ensemble, he would go to the stable where Sutton had Gemini ready to saddle then spend a morning riding west of the mansion. It was not quite like their previous year since foundations of brick, block, or field stone set in thick, gray mortar were numerous along the route; signs that within a year or two he might be forced to use Rock Creek Park like the assistant secretary.

Starke's West Point plantation, Oxen Grove, provided another complication when its overseer, Newman Pearce, reported an offer to buy. The plantation income relied on Pearce's management and it was home to the man's family. There was also the Oakley burial ground containing his mother's family, Cynthia Jefferson's, and generations of servants and slaves. His uncle regularly pushed Starke to become more involved but now offered no advice while his nephew agonized. In the end Starke could never sell what his mother's family and others gave everything for.

Calypso was another matter. The lower Chesapeake Bay was pummeled by a hurricane's remnants on the day he left for Washington, followed a three-day blow that surged tides five feet above normal. Fortunately, preparations remained in place from the first assault, and Watson rigged additional shoring while the waters rose during the second, so only time was lost. Others fared worse. Ships were left port-bound, Norfolk was partly flooded, the Newport News breakwater collapsed, an arriving lumber schooner lost a mast and two seamen, and several rail sections to Old Point Comfort washed away.

CHAPTER TWENTY FOUR
DIVERSIONS

Watson found Newport News shipyard work predictably Sisyphean. The weather delayed several exterior jobs and the inevitable crew losses began. Besides yard injuries and expiring enlistments, three black gangers were condemned for lung maladies and other ships tried poaching *Calypso* sailors. However, most routine work fell to the executive officer when not at sea so little adjustment was called for.

Dunbar concentrated on replenishment and tasks put off. The charts, sailing directions, port guides, signal books, and light lists required review and updating. One chronometer was slightly inconsistent and the mechanical speed log broken so obtaining replacements meant hog-wrestling bureaucracy; and navigator's stores required inventory. The dynamo spaces, electrical apparatus, and steering gear were his responsibility as well, but Osbourne and O'Leary provided assistance to the extent their steam engineering bureau would overlook. Weaver performed the same service for anchor chain maintenance, another navigator responsibility. The ship's library was also a constant source of minor vexation because *Calypso*'s captain was more involved than most, wanted material the crew could learn from, and added his own funds to buy popular French, German, and Spanish novels. Dunbar also obtained *Harper's Readers* for every grade and the newer *Baldwin Readers*; then Watson wanted sheet music, although only one of their musicians read it, and Conrad lobbied persistently for the latest mystery novels.

The surgeon, apothecary, and baymen inventoried supplies for renewal or replacement and held sick call after breakfast when turn-to sounded. Only minor yard injuries and liberty mishaps augmented regular malingerers but two sailors had a lung disease common among miners and another was consumptive. They were transferred to the Navy Hospital for treatment, boarding, condemnation, and discharge with a small pension. The surgeon watched for signs of typhoid, pneumonia, malaria, scarlet fever, whooping cough, and other maladies while continuing to study yellow fever. Although the season had passed, this year's had been particularly malevolent and during any outbreak about fifteen percent of those afflicted would die and some survivors left severely crippled. There was no cure or vaccine, and diagnosis required an autopsy, so its arrival was often denied even as people fled. Not only nations but states, counties, cities, and towns instituted quarantines that were often enforced by threats, shootings, or lynchings; yet it still spread along the Gulf Coast, Atlantic seaboard, and up the Mississippi to Memphis where thousands died during a previous outbreak. Shipping from Mobile, Jackson, and Galveston was quarantined; along with the Cuba, Nicaragua, and Jamaica arrivals. Gulf Coast travel and business all but ended, the Alabama government fled to a safe location, and detention camps constructed. Mail arrived with fumigation punctures. Fire, lime, and steam chambers were enlisted to sanitize every item possible; with formaldehyde generators becoming commonplace. Ships jettisoned cargoes at sea when it appeared then gassed when they made port. Railroads that ignored local quarantines risked attack by mobs and rolling stock destroyed. State and local governments, Marine

Hospital Service, Revenue Cutter Service, and others worked to prevent its spread, but cause remained a mystery. Candidates included polluted oysters, poor drainage, unsanitary conditions, unusual ocean currents, and more. Evidence did exist that people not from yellow fever states were especially susceptible, locals were not immune, and the popular belief African blood offered protection was open to question.

Chief Weaver welcomed time with his family in Newport News but not Cullen Flynn's liberty. The seaman went ashore in Nassau with the deceased Landsman Parnell and would have backed the young New Yorker except being nearly unconsciousness from drink. Had they shared a cell he would have no doubt ended the young man's diatribe with a single punch. The sailor enjoyed many things but brawling, drunk or sober, topped the list. He even challenged Weaver once with, "You wanna make something of it," and returned to consciousness in sickbay from the fall. Even so, Flynn was the man to have your back in tight spots; like when he expeditiously felled Captain Buff during the *Astraea* boarding. In the end, Watson loosed Flynn on Newport News over Weaver's protests because the sailor was an excellent seaman and Navy regulations guaranteed individuals a minimum number of trips ashore. Both men expected the constabulary to return him and were not disappointed. The Black Maria, or Paddy Wagon, drawn by a worn mare with her coat matching its paint rolled up to the brow; then two helmeted men in blue uniforms with standing collars, double rows of buttons, large badges, and varnished oak nightsticks wasted no time delivering the mostly docile penitent.

Although Flynn staggered unaided across the brow to report his return, the police told the duty officer enough to ensure a sickbay visit, where his wounds were dressed and he was certified fit for confinement, then a waiting cell. The quixotic reveler told Conrad he went ashore alone to avoid trouble but fell in with four English sailors off a bark waiting to load coal. After exploring the entertainments and libations of Newport News' seamier eastern section, their well-lubricated dialogue grew increasingly philosophical then political. Flynn remarked at one point that a single Irishman was worth at least four Englishmen in a brawl due to their mothers' lack of any extended acquaintance with the fathers. A patrol was called to the alley where this hypothesis was being tested to find five pugilists too intoxicated or stunned to seriously resist. Flynn and another tried but were quickly clubbed unconscious with the sensitivity anglers might show fresh-caught bass. It had been a busy night and the jail beyond capacity so these miscreants were delivered to their ships. As Griffin's sobering took hold, he stoically contemplated punishment, liberty becoming an illusion for months, and his chief's notoriously creative retributions. Thaddeus passed between the bars to commiserate while he reflected. The tom's deck privileges were revoked after exchanging insults or invitations with a coal black cat of undetermined gender across the chasm separating deck edge and dry-dock wall. Their unearthly chant woke the crew, sent sailors searching for the source, and ended his main deck privileges.

In Washington, Starke joined his uncle at the Metropolitan Club, where Roosevelt was a member, and invited Cassandra Evans to dinner at the Ebbitt House. They met near a Corinthian column in its lobby, rising two stories above the marble floor, then went to the dining room. Under its frescoed ceiling they were taken to a small table draped with white-linen near tall windows overlooking F Street's horse, foot, and rail traffic. Starke felt physical attraction as he positioned a chair on the marble floor for Cassandra to sit; a feminine activity requiring some agility with the light corset, small bustle, and tight traveling dress. This warmth was perhaps due to the slight, well-distributed weight increase since New York; although the chestnut hair twisted and pinned in a pompadour caught his eye over a year before on a streetcar. He now wondered how it looked down and brushing the floor. Her face was still pleasantly lined about deep brown eyes beneath flawless eyebrows and the same intriguing scent present. She was clearly more confident and less ready to take offense, with stronger intellectual discipline, than when his aunt cornered him into escorting her to a mansion dinner party. Their conversation centered on the city, her profession, Dana's passing, and Tyson. Starke listened but, appreciative of her capability and persistence, avoided raising anything about the inquiry. She agreed to deliver his letter but appeared ambivalent about returning to Cuba. When the extremely pleasant and diverting evening finished, she parted with the clean break a soldier might make before campaigning or sailor facing a long voyage. Starke suspected his aunt might have hoped for more but would accept what came, as she had with others; then his thoughts drifted towards Katherine. The widow continued their correspondence but passages in the same letter often swung between staid propriety and nearly passionate. He suspected she reentered society and became involved with someone but decided to avoid pressing.

The inquiry ended with a summons to the Bureau of Navigation office where Albert and Crowninshield explained the report was complete except for administrative nits and would soon be forwarded for approval. The Spanish legation acknowledged without explanation that *Calypso* was fired on by *Pedro Menéndez de Avilés* outside Spain's territorial waters;

partly because its government's desire for the incident to pass without triggering a war equaled McKinley, Long, Day, and Reed's. The inquiry found *Calypso* acted according to Navy regulations, ceased firing to render aid, and properly left *Astraea* to the gunboat based on Starke's assessment and authority; but had failed to question the gunboat's intent with a flaghoist. Abandoning the schooner might have caused a press upheaval except the consul-general in Havana examined what cargo was taken off, interviewed the gunboat's officers, and concluded *Astraea*'s manifest was falsified. Since an illegal filibuster expedition nearly brought war, the press printed only that a damaged schooner driven off course by the storm was abandoned by her crew then sank while being prepared for tow by a Spanish gunboat.

Starke was returned to *Calypso*. This was due as much to the assistant secretary as the commodore and Albert. An attempt to replace him with a more favorable officer failed when Roosevelt emphatically promised an outraged public would not tolerate removal of the commander who fought a superior Spanish warship firing on the American flag; then intimated Senator Lodge agreed. The assistant secretary was confident war would come after the yellow fever and hurricane seasons, be decided at sea with a blockade, and include strikes against Spain; so the Navy's inferiority in gun and torpedo boats could only made up with men like Starke officering ships like *Calypso* and private yachts

Starke left for Newport News on Saturday, the last day of October. The five and a half hour rail journey began with steam whistles, a series of jerks as one car snatched the next, and increasing momentum once the train shed was left behind. In Richmond, his Old Point Comfort Special repeated this process as he looked back towards the red-brick station with surrounding street lamps flickering in late evening.

Rolling down the dark peninsula, light-black smoke drifted from the right-of-way, condensed steam dropped to creosoted ties buried in gravel, and the monotonous click of steel wheels crossing joints caused him to nod off. He woke around ten o'clock when they reversed into Newport News where *Calypso* waited pierside. He boarded late then resumed command the next morning by reviewing what was still required to get underway with Watson.

On the Spanish protected cruiser *Alfonso XIII* off Havana's gray-brown Morro, General Ramón Blanco y Erenas relieved Governor-general Weyler who, despite strong Spanish and Cuban support, would leave Cuba on the Compañía Trasatlántica steamer *Montserrat* without returning ashore. In Washington, Captain Albert left early that afternoon, relieved to face wedding preparations after two unexpected blows were visited on his filibuster project in a single day. *Vanguard* was returning to the Revenue Cutter Service because the Navy preferred spending money on its own and Treasury became uneasy about her working with *Calypso*, despite their accomplishments. Only Captain Fischer's influence averted the cutter's immediate assignment to a district. This made the bark even more critical at the same time she was tagged with an unrelated mission and despite assurances this was a one-time event Albert knew few things fenced off in the Building survived the smallest breach.

The new mission's genesis had nothing to do with the Junta but a murky civil dispute in Port au Prince, Haiti, that September. Emile Lüders allegedly struck a policeman during a petty thief's arrest or cab fare dispute, was fined, and given a month's jail time. Lüders was also a German citizen through his father since such marriages were convenient when only Haitians could own real estate. Germany was heavily invested on the island so her charge d'affaires, Count Graf von

Schwerin, became involved when Lüders' appeal brought additional charges and a year in jail. After approaching several ministries and believing he was being stonewalled, the count approached President Tirésias Simon Sam in a manner the public viewed as disrespectful. Haiti's large army was called up for service and Germany threatened to support their charge d'affaires with warships. The American consul, William Powell, intervened and orchestrated a pardon in October. Lüders, however, was forced to seek safety at the German legation with a lynch mob in close pursuit. Later, when it was discovered he had been sent to Germany through New York, the legation was besieged by mobs, its flag lowered, and records sent north. Demands were presented to Haiti's government in response but ignored because Lüders had been pardoned and the island expected United States' support under the Monroe Doctrine.

The Building response solidified during a morning meeting in State's Diplomatic Room to consider a recommendation for the president. After Ambassador Andrew White completed discrete inquiries in Berlin, State's position was that Haiti made no formal request for assistance and risking war inadvisable unless Germany intended annexation or exceptionally harsh measures. Everyone agreed they would similarly respond had it been an American legation so supporting the Haitian position would establish an untenable precedent and further embolden a nation viewed as poorly run, cursed with turbulent politics, and counting previous incidents with the United States, Britain, and Germany. Backing Haiti might also increase European monarchies' support for Spain and raise political questions at home about refusing to recognize Cuban insurgents while throwing the gauntlet down to a more powerful nation over a dubious incident. American voters with German ties would also be opposed, the extensive trading between the two nations damaged, and public resistance to foreign adventures excited. Those anticipated to support standing with Haiti were Colored Republicans who felt protective of the Black republic, interests that believed a firm response would dissuade European powers from viewing the Americas as a next China, and advocates of a Nicaraguan canal.

Long, Day, Roosevelt, and Crowninshield agreed the Navy was needed in Port au Prince to protect or evacuate American citizens. Roosevelt wanted a powerful ship or squadron because the German ships *Kaiserin Augusta*, *Gefion*, *Gneisenau*, and *Stein* were wintering in the Caribbean or coming. Albert observed three were training ships that already visited Port au Prince that month and the others unconfirmed. He also suggested any overt overmatch could drive German escalation leading to British or French involvement. Since the North Atlantic Squadron and fledgling torpedo boat flotilla were in the Caribbean for exercises, the consensus was to send a single ship to protect American citizens and interests while adding weight to Powell's diplomacy.

Albert kept silent during subsequent deliberations concerning the appropriate ship but his expertise was unnecessary for the group to conclude most were committed, fit poorly, or laid up for repairs; and *Maine* already standing by for Havana. The Revenue Cutter Service was put forward despite Treasury's absence but State argued a cutter could be viewed as a weak response and most lacked space for refugees. This discussion necessarily focused on *Vanguard*, the only cutter not assigned to a district, so *Calypso* soon slithered across the table and Albert was forced to respond to questions that slowly tightened the garrote. Yes, she was assigned to the Special Service Squadron. It was true Starke had shown initiative, displayed sound judgement, and spoke German,

Spanish, and rudimentary French. There was a well-trained crew on board. Yes, the ship was preparing for sea. The only hesitation came after Roosevelt's soliloquy that a man of action with a single ship could achieve more than an irresolute one with a squadron; then illustrating this using HMS *Lorraine*'s commander ending *Virginius* executions twenty years before by apprising Santiago's governor the nearest Spanish warship would be sunk if they resumed. Day paused to consider possible ramifications then added it might be useful to temporarily distance *Calypso* from filibuster patrols after having fired on both parties. Albert's ferret was snared. The president approved this new mission that afternoon and Long signed Starke's orders the next morning for hand delivery by a State Department clerk with additional verbal instructions.

Calypso completed most yard tasks during November, loaded ammunition and stores, then moored north of Craney Island Flats, west of Sewall's Point, and just outside the Norfolk channel between Buoys 4 and 6. The mooring assigned by the harbormaster was near where she anchored almost two months before in four fathoms with less than a knot current and a three-foot tide. Two anchors went deep into soft mud fixing her position in the broad anchorage amongst sail and steam shipping that was waiting to load, unload, or be repaired. The dredged channel east of *Calypso* was marked by a single strand of red buoys continuing past Craney Island Lighthouse. Near the Elizabeth River's mouth, south and a little east, was Lambert's Point with Norfolk & Western Railway's coal docks, wharfs, and terminals; and lighthouse at the end of a pier that was no longer lit or providing the wind and time signals now coming from the U.S. Signal Service Station on Norfolk's main street. Due west was the six-year-old caisson lighthouse for Newport News

Middle Ground with its concrete-filled iron base, black foundation, brown tower, and two white boats in davits. There were also can buoys marking each end of that shoal; waiting to be replaced by spar buoys for winter. The massive grain elevator west of Newport News Point and downriver from the shipyard was clearly visible. At night, however, this entire panorama was replaced by dark shadows with lights from flashing beams, windows, and portholes reflecting off the bay's glasslike black onyx surface.

The light frost dusting her rigging each morning rapidly gave way to southern winds bearing rain, drizzle, and temperatures flirting with sixty degrees. Extra food was laid on for Thanksgiving and that afternoon found officers in wardroom or cabin, chiefs gathered in their quarters, and sailors on the fantail enjoying two string instruments and a penny whistle. This relaxed mood was partly due to learning their captain was to meet with Commodore Farquhar on Monday afternoon; ensuring Saturday and Sunday would be spent in Hampton Roads.

On Monday afternoon, Coxswain Melvin left the boat docks extending out from the receiving ship *Franklin* then started down the Elizabeth River's Southern Branch with piers, tracks, and industrial buildings to port. The Norfolk & Southern terminal was on a short peninsula to starboard just before the turn into the Eastern Branch where Norfolk filled the shoreline to starboard. As he curved into the broader river, the stone and granite naval hospital dock, jutting from its manicured peninsula, were left behind to port. Starke was sitting in the sternsheets, enjoying what sun slipped under the awning, and reviewing his *Franklin* meeting.

Calypso was bound for Port au Prince to monitor foreign vessels and make periodic runs to Cap-Haïtien's submarine cable office. As senior navy officer, he would consult with the

American consul, William Powell, but answer to Washington. The State Department clerk delivering his orders also provided a news article with Powell's background and likeness. The consul served with the navy during the war, perhaps in sick bay as he later earned a pharmacy degree, and clerked in Treasury as an auditor; but was known for his education contributions. After teaching at one of Virginia's first state schools for Colored children, he oversaw two of the same type in Camden, New Jersey. His features were not markedly African, which was not unusual. Starke's own family was predominately German on his father's side while his mother's was less clear. Despite English ancestry there were stories of a female child pulled from the debris of a magazine explosion at Florida's Negro Fort. Starke considered himself American, which strengthened at sea where a man's worth rested on performance and whether he would stand. Powell sounded as though he cleared both hurdles since anyone with his opportunities who remained in the Haitian climates proved he would stand. The clerk emphasized Haiti must not be allowed to destabilize the Caribbean or any European nation obtain a sphere of influence.

Besides covering Haiti, the press constantly portrayed Weyler as butcher and solitary barrier to Cuban independence but lauded General Gómez, whose strategy was to create unsustainable costs and cripple the island economy. After crowing over Weyler's recall a month earlier, he was accused of a coup when mechanical problems developed on *Montserrat* and she entered Cuba's Puerto de Gibara for repairs before continuing to Puerto Rico. When this truth became undeniable, the press did not break stride but began predicting his arrest and trial when *Montserrat* docked in Spain. He was instead received as a hero by the public and most political parties when he landed in Corunna around mid-month. People turned out at every stop on his way to Palma with many seeing him as the loyal soldier liberals scapegoated rather than stand up to the United States; and most political factions courted him. Unrepentant New York papers then predicted he was about to overthrow the Spanish government; while the British press denounced their American cousins for unwarranted attacks and demands for trial. His farewell address laid blame for the lingering insurrection, with lost Spanish and Cuban lives, on American support of filibusters; then passed the speech off as normal press inaccuracy when hesitantly reproached by a government aware their army in Cuba was owed six months back pay and supported him.

Starke considered this while his gig chugged downriver because there was little conversation. Timme and Melvin kept to strictly professional topics, their forward bowhook said nothing, and both engineers concentrated on tending its small boiler with polished brass stack. After clearing Hospital Point, Melvin steered for Craney Island, beyond Lambert's Point, and they glided past coal piers, railroad terminals, wharfs, and then red-painted wood piles driven deep in the mud to mark shallows. After making a final turn, using the abandoned Lambert Point Lighthouse and massive piers, pinnace occupants felt open water's chill, the scent of burning coal strengthened, and *Calypso* appeared beyond a string of buoys leading north. Melvin began his approach several minutes later by paralleling the ship, putting his rudder over, and then shifting it while briefly reversing the engine. The pinnace eased gently alongside the port accommodation ladder platform, lines were passed, and Starke went aboard where Watson was waiting. While they spoke, Melvin took his pinnace to the boat boom for the night.

CHAPTER TWENTY FIVE
COLLISION

Saturday morning off Cape Henry was overcast and gray with a steady wind that meant easy sailing for the Virginia pilot boat eyeing *Doireann Bannan* approach the southern channel, just north of the cape. Her master tacked starboard then raced for the inbound liner to get alongside before she crossed the line freeing her from taking a pilot until Old Point Comfort. *Doireann Bannan's* master, Horace Blackburn, was equally set on not boarding a Chesapeake Bay pilot before Hampton Roads; where it became mandatory. He believed the expense unnecessary since the lower bay's intricacies and moods were second nature to him and heavy weather already delayed their passage. His arrival message, using the *International Code of Signals* relayed through Cape Henry's telegraph station to the terminal in Norfolk, projected the liner would be pierside before sunset.

Sunday would be spent unloading cargo and Monday traveling up the bay to one of Baltimore's shipyards since this completed her final New York City run. The charter to carry cargo and passengers on western Atlantic routes was ending and his last trip as master was delivering her to a yard that would convert the single-stack, iron-hulled *Doireann Bannan* for the European immigrant trade. The British-built liner with pronounced clipper bow ship was 250 feet long, a little over 1,400 tons, and boasted forty first-class cabins when she went to sea thirty-five years before. Since then, a triple-expansion engine replaced her compound one, the black hull lengthened seventy feet, her full ship rig cut down to a barkentine, and the jibboom truncated; but she still failed to compete with newer ships.

Blackburn evaded the schooner then boarded a pilot and a quarantine officer at Hampton Roads before making for Norfolk's ship channel. While *Doireann Bannan* approached, *Belliveau Pride*, a Nova Scotia-built schooner, was warped from Elizabeth River lumber piers and made up to the steam tug *Andreana* for towing through Hampton Roads. This 150-foot, three-masted workhorse was Havana-bound with a crew of seven and cargo of rough-cut pine filling her hold and secured on deck. The wooden schooner departed an hour later than planned, was passing the lightship to starboard and, after clearing the lighthouse, would follow a line of red nun buoys to port. As the tug eased its tow through a slight starboard turn, aligning both with the channel, the schooner's helmsman reported her steering felt strange; but had just been repaired and twice tested before leaving so it was attributed to riding the slight current under tow.

The Elizabeth River is more tidal estuary with three short branches than river. Its sources are Great Dismal Swamp, Chesapeake Bay, and rainwater runoff so submerged tree trunks created by bank erosion, or snags, were unusual. On rivers where these were common, most remained anchored to bank or bottom, creating natural weirs, but others floated into the channel and became deadly for ships, barges, and boats. These often settled on the riverbed with their roots downstream creating a natural abatis and called planters if single, or a raft when intertwined with others. Some let the river carry them away, like the large, barely awash specimen that drifted down the Elizabeth River or came through

Hampton Roads from the James River to find its way into the Norfolk channel between *Doireann Bannan* and *Andreana*.

Naval Cadet Caldwell stood near *Calypso's* gangway. He had the port section and Timme the starboard since Watson was allowing naval cadets to assume the more benign day watches. Their Hampton Roads mooring was away from the channel, visibility fair, a main boiler on line for security, and he was beyond Ensign Blair's reach until relieved by Timme's section just before dinner. Smithers and Chief Owen had been working Haiti charts in the pilothouse, but that petty officer just emerged to shoot a round of landmarks and confirm their anchors held. The navigator's report would soon reach the quarterdeck and remainder within an hour. He would ensure all had been submitted, entered in the log, and sent to the captain before noon. The redheaded Irish seaman Flynn stood nearby, but they spoke little since the watch began. In steam pinnace alongside the lower accommodation ladder platform, Melvin and his crew were busy; the coxswain adjusting its white-canvas canopy's lashings, his boathooks polishing brass, and the two engineers oiling their engine.

The atmosphere not only carried a fragrance of burning coal, escaping steam, and riparian scents but an impending rainstorm stalled over Willoughby's Bay, or just east of it. Once the southerly morning wind veered slightly east, Chief Owen intermittently left his work for the collapsible bridge-wing to examine ship traffic in the buoyed channel to their east and dark cloud bank beyond. Entering the channel's Norfolk end was a three-masted schooner under tow while a large liner did the same from the bay end; her dark smoke plume barely clearing the masts before settling on the bay. When the cloud bank began moving west to engulf ships in the channel then Hampton Roads, he sent a quartermaster aft to alert Caldwell. The cadet already passed the word to prepare for rain and was on his way to the pilothouse when a black curtain entered the bay and that shoreline vanished.

Doireann Bannan's master eyed the approaching squall line to port, line of red nun buoys to starboard, lightship near the channel's eastern terminus, and approaching schooner under tow. While his pilot mentioned the first telephone line was now operating between Washington and Norfolk, Blackburn considered possible options; since meeting a tug and tow in any channel warranted additional caution. The shoal water to port, north of Sewall's Point, ranged from one to seven feet, but Craney Island Flats beyond the buoy line to starboard was over twelve; with more than nineteen assured if forced to leave the channel between Buoys 4 and 6; where they would most likely meet. Hampton Roads anchorage presented no impediment since visibility was unlimited in that direction, so he concentrated on the approaching ships then agreed, using whistle signals, that tug and tow would pass down *Doireann Bannan*'s port side. Visibility under the liner's bow was restricted by high sides and pilothouse located nearly a third of her length aft so a lookout, separate from the anchor party, was stationed in the ship's eyes when near land. That sailor scoured astern of the schooner through paired-telescopes and intermittently checked on the seaport and closing tow while the thirty-foot, semi-submerged snag, with twisted, broken, and sodden roots floated unnoticed in the channel.

Andreana's master and pilot monitored liner, squall, channel buoys, and tow while their deck crew slowly payed out hawser so speed could be increased once clear. The tug's wood hull dropped sharply from the single bitt crowning its high stem to her flat fantail work area while a low bulwark encircled the main deck. Her single-level deckhouse extended aft from a half-round pilothouse with stubby stack and tall signaling mast. The meticulously maintained tug's solitary blemish was an off-white, black and tan canvas canopy rigged aft. Visibility was unobstructed forward of her beam since she was designed to work ships, barges, harbors, and coastal waters so her master, John Hackett, and pilot did not need a lookout to spot the snag floating placidly athwart the channel with its roots near the east side. Forced to turn starboard, Hackett cursed and spun the large brass helm while his pilot sounded the danger signal, a succession of whistle blasts, as the squall's leading edge entered the channel and visibility dropped to a few feet.

Because *Belliveau Pride* relied on sails, her helm was aft and towing ship almost totally obscured at short stay; but a mate and deckhands were on her forecastle operating the steam windlass that ran off a small donkey boiler. That mate raced for the bow when the tug's danger signal sounded; and saw a large snag bounce and scrape down *Andreana*'s port side as the tug maneuvered to clear stern and screw. He yelled aft and *Belliveau Pride* tried to accommodate the tug's starboard turn but her sluggish steering let the tow hawser submerge and the turn incomplete when this snag slammed against her stem; grappling it with roots that anchored the large tree for a century of violent storms. Tension returned to the hawser as the schooner's momentum died, causing it to knife up through opaque water, become rod-like, spray water from its fibers, and snap with a flat crack. *Belliveau Pride*'s helm spun counterclockwise and, with the snag dragging her bow to port, was quickly athwart the channel, bow pointed north.

The blind tug stopped, still sounding the danger signal, to retrieve the hawser's remnants before her screw sucked it in. *Doireann Bannan* went hard right into Hampton Roads with visibility dropping to zero as the red nun, Buoy 4, became a near miss. The 320-foot hull with 2,300 tons of wood, metal, coal, and flesh drove into the anchorage; whistle sounding and engine room struggling to meet the emergency full astern order. Valves spun shut; massive pistons, rods, and crankshaft were brought to a halt. Then, with different valves opened, engine and propeller shaft increased turns in reverse, water frothed below her counter, and yet the liner coasted forward.

Starke and Watson reached *Calypso*'s pilothouse while *Doireann Bannan*'s whistles still echoed *Andreana*'s and the thundering blanket rapidly enveloped Hampton Roads anchorage. As a cacophony of whistles, bells, and gongs erupted around the bark, Starke ordered the danger signal sounded, set general quarters, and aimed both powerful searchlights towards the channel and into the torrential rain. Their beams' penetration increased as downpour and squall passed by until one locked on *Doireann Bannan*'s approaching prow, masts, and superstructure. *Calypso* was firmly moored in a mud bottom by two anchors and no time to payout or cut cables so rigging for collision and sounding the warning signal was all that could be accomplished.

Alerted by searchlight beams, Captain Blackburn studied the three masts and black hull emerging from an indistinct gray haze then attempted to steer *Doireann Bannan* down the bark's port side to avoid striking hull or mooring. The large brass helm forced her steering mechanism to its stops in a hard port turn pitting rudder against hull while the bite was weakened by backing screws. Blackburn, clutching the bridge railing's damp wood, felt shuddering as his slowing liner closed *Calypso*'s port side at a walk. Meanwhile, Newport News Middle Ground lighthouse and buoys far beyond the liner's truncated bowsprit vanished in the retreating squall.

Starke calculated they would be struck forward near the port bow at a slight angle. He also noticed three sailors, ignorant of mass and speed but sharing these thoughts, were attempting to insert a large rope fender. After some hesitation in being warned off, *Calypso*'s taciturn commander tapped a rich reservoir of phrases from time spent as a mate. Their expressions changed, the fender was abandoned, and they sprinted aft as the liner's overhanging bow eased into the bark's main deck causing a dull explosion and spraying splinters above them in a huge arc. The iron prow continued inboard to the 4-inch mount with an amalgamation of grinding, splintering, and cracking. Restrained by her anchors, *Calypso* rolled starboard as the stem crushed and chewed through sheathing, frames, and shear strakes before *Doireann Bannan*'s backing screw began extracting her own mangled bow. As the liner pulled away, passengers emerged from public areas and cabins to line rails midship aft; startled and confused as they watched their ship extract itself from *Calypso*'s gaping wound.

Astern of the retreating liner, a red and black tug standing by her anchored tow flew the international signal asking if assistance was needed. *Calypso*'s rocking died quickly but she was down by the head and listing to port. With compartmentation limited to a collision bulkhead forward and one either side of engineering, Starke felt she should be settling faster. If their crew was ordered into the rigging and she sank evenly, most would be probably saved, but many would die if she capsized. He could see the untouched accommodation ladder and steam pinnace alongside but their other boats remained in skids under davits. Lowering would take time and the men might be better off keeping the ship afloat since their four boats could not take the full complement and neighboring ships were already swinging theirs outboard. In the end, he committed the crew on instinct more than logic. The ship had been fortunate to date and her crew resourceful so he retrieved his much abused and unlit pipe then turned to the engineer, "Mr. Osbourne, please get steam to the pumps."

The chief engineer left at an unnatural walk-run while Starke waited for Watson, with the repair party, to determine damage, set men to work, and report. Looking down from his position, *Calypso*'s commander saw the deep gash across her forecastle where the wet deck encircling deeper, reddish wood tints mixed with metal beams mimicked a compound fracture. The foremast backstays were clearly bruised and forestay slightly stretched. The forward 4-inch mount's barrel pointed skyward with base and stand deformed from halting the penetration.

Watson returned, "Captain; she's open nearly to the waterline with some planks below sprung or broken. We've started plugging and shoring. Hand pump's also being set up forward."

"That fits, XO. She settled slowly so the lower hull must have held."

"Yes sir, but barely. Osbourne and O'Leary have steam to the bilge pumps and can cut in a feedwater pump if ordered."

"Very well, your evaluation?"

"She may capsize if we lose more than a foot or two forward and fill."

"Recommendation?"

"Ground her on Craney Island Flats, Captain."

Starke's thoughts flashed to Katherine's husband dying when HMS *Victoria* capsized attempting the same maneuver, "We may have to, XO, but the weather's clearing."

"Yes sir; squall's moved out and wind's dying."

"Very well; drop the anchor chains under foot, that'll raise the bow and absorb shock, then set anyone not in engineering or working forward to lowering boats. Start forward." Starke then pointed the pipestem at their metal foremast, "Too bad we can't send them over."

Watson was considering how when Starke intruded, "Even if we could, XO, toppling a mast might finish her; but have Weaver look to that forestay or we may find ourselves testing that particular theory. There's no time to fother a sail but ask if he can put canvas over the sprung planking."

Surgeon Conrad was unable to list casualties before muster but they appeared light; probably due to the damage being forward with her crew at general quarters and not in berthing. Around a half dozen black gangers were thrown against hot surfaces or injured handling coal; one of three sailors with the fender took jagged wood splinters in the lower back and buttocks that would, unless infected, result only in a painful cutting-out and some weeks healing; and there were two simple fractures. Once Conrad finished, Starke asked him to bring his patients to the fantail in case they abandoned ship.

Chief Owen hoisted a code pennant, above the B, G, and R flags, advising nearby ships the extent of *Calypso*'s damage was unknown. Several of the closest had boats at the rail; including *Doireann Bannan* now anchored near Buoy 4. Starke asked them to stand by since many sailors were unable to swim and must be quickly retrieved from rigging or bay; and should *Calypso* founder they would be in shock from the cold bay.

Andreana retrieved her hawser's remnants and ensured *Belliveau Pride* was safely anchored with snag alongside then made for the stricken bark. Hackett recognized *Calypso* from frequent trips past the navy yard and using paired-telescopes judged her close to sinking. The V-shaped gouge midway between bow and superstructure left about two feet of planking above water; a margin easily overwhelmed by waves, wake, or prop-wash. Consequently, he coasted slowly towards the wound until a speaking trumpet from the bark requested he stand clear but pass over any staging on board for patching.

Hackett not only owned and operated *Andreana* but many lower Chesapeake mariners were in his debt; and *Belliveau Pride* carried deck load of planks. He replied something better was possible, eased *Andreana* back until safe to pivot then made for *Belliveau Pride*. Starke soon observed an animated debate between the two ships' masters followed by twenty-foot planks sliding from schooner to tug fantail. *Calypso's* carpenter and a working party were sent to the starboard quarter and stood ready when Hackett eased *Andreana* gently alongside. Once lines were passed, sailors dropped to the tug and heavy pine boards began moving across then forward.

Calypso's attitude forward improved slightly once both anchor chains were payed out to their ends, boats launched, pumps at work, and the heavy-weather canvas poultice secured to anything convenient was sucked against stove-in planking. Watson planned a temporary bulwark of paint stages along the base of the gash to gain a foot or two of tenuous freeboard, but two dozen long, wide planks would allow Chief Carpenter's Mate Lefebvre to span the chasm, add a tarred canvas skin, and shore the interior with whatever was available. A light gun tackle lowered the first plank in place for sailors working from inside and a float to begin its fastening with nails and screws. As planking rose, Starke dispatched Caldwell in the steam pinnace to alert Commodore Farquhar then send a telegram to the department and Albert reading, "Calypso struck while moored Hampton Roads. Extensive damage. Temporary repairs in progress. Immediate dry-docking required. Will attempt Norfolk. Starke."

The receiving ship *Franklin* was permanently moored opposite the shipyard boathouse at the timber basin entrance.

Steam launches that shuttled people across the river were tied to her finger piers and a pennant told Caldwell the commodore was not on board. He made for the boathouse, spent several minutes explaining their unexpected Saturday arrival, then declined an offer of the small locomotive idling nearby. Its tracks snaked through the yard's red-brick structures and never passed closer than two blocks from the administration building, which was only a half-dozen from where he landed. That long structure straddled the yard's main gate, with a bell tower above its entrance portal and yard workers passing between Marine guards. Caldwell entered its archway, turned left into the office area, and was immediately driven to the commandant's quarters in a light carriage.

Caldwell entered Farquhar's two-story residence through its front door at the top of curving staircases with black ironwork railings then ushered down an entrance hall to a parlor in the rear where Farquhar waited. The commodore seemed almost ancient at first; with a roundish, pudgy face topped by short, dark hair, clipped to eliminate any suggestion of sideburns, and white mustache. Years of command brushed that aside when he spoke and the cadet immediately understood Farquhar asked precise questions and demanded succinct answers. After learning Starke did not plan to ground *Calypso* on Craney Island Flats he instructed the Captain of the Yard to send a tug and barge for her ammunition, or crew if necessary, and prepare a dry-dock for Monday. Farquhar also took note Starke sent the cadet on watch during the collision which meant Caldwell could provide firsthand information, there was no attempt to conceal, and the cadet blameless. After the commodore was satisfied, Caldwell left to send Starke's telegram.

During his return, Caldwell surveyed Hampton Roads from the steam pinnace as it left the river. The schooner had been warped into the anchorage by *Andreana* and snag beached east of the channel. White-pine planks from *Belliveau Pride* were screwed or nailed across *Calypso*'s hull breach and stood out against the black. Navigation lights heralded sunset as they closed and lanterns illuminated her main deck along with the bow work. A whaleboat and float were alongside with two unused boats secured to the fantail and small buoys still bobbing gently over both anchors.

Caldwell arrived between rounds Starke was making with Watson to inform and bolster confidence of those below deck. The captain felt relieved a barge was on its way to offload ammunition and Drydock Number One being prepared. Empty magazines would further lighten the bark before getting underway and the old granite dock, next to a wooden one built eight years earlier for larger ships, suited *Calypso* perfectly.

Progress appeared slow and makeshift patch dubious so any panic could bring the end, especially in engineering spaces since *Calypso*'s survival depended on steam to operate pumps and machinery. Black gangs lived under constant threat of being crushed, scalded, and drowned in darkness without warning, unlike the sailors emptying storerooms, patching leaks, and shoring; but hysteria was contagious.

Few slept that night and those napping preferred near freezing temperatures topside over an uneasy confinement below. Riding to the boat boom, Melvin and his crew huddled around their steam pinnace's small boiler for warmth with one person on watch and others half-asleep while the bay gently brushed their hull. Starke made time to review the Elizabeth River charts with Dunbar and Chief Owen then dozed restlessly in a leather chair; rising intermittently to add a note in his personal log, revisit Navy regulations, or take reports from the deck officer, O'Leary, or Osbourne. Yamashita kept to his pantry, monitored by an unsettled Thaddeus, until early morning when he brought Starke hot coffee.

Watson formally dispensed with Sunday's dress uniforms and, since the morning cold was predicted to linger into the afternoon, allowed the officers' long, blue overcoat and its short enlisted version. Starke lifted his from a wall peg, fastened its seven plain black buttons in two rows, brushed lint from two pairs of black-braid sleeve stripes, and aligned the shoulder straps. Donning round cap and white kid gloves, he left for the pilothouse. Made up to their starboard side during the night was an empty barge for their morning offload of munitions that would require everyone not forward working the patch or preparing to get underway. The small, black-hulled yard tug with white superstructure that brought it was soon joined by another but Starke decided to take *Calypso* in under her own power. Excluding an emergency or need to substitute for anchors left in Hampton Roads, their makeshift patch did not need to be tested by a tug's prop-wash or grazed while it maneuvered.

Starke left the pilothouse for flying bridge when Watson reported ammunition offloaded and ship ready, then scanned coast, river, and shoreline. He did not ask for a pilot and would conn himself to ensure control. Caldwell stood quietly by, staring at the main deck and masts canted slightly to port. The chief engineer was below and Watson with their repair party on the fantail. Yeoman Pond prepared the deck log while Dunbar and Owen double-checked navigation details. In the foretop, grateful for his undress dark blue uniform with flat blue cap and five-button overcoat, Doran Kearney watched the light Sunday traffic closely; completely aware even wakes from ships observing the channel's four-mile an hour speed limit could threaten the patch.

Newport News Middle Ground lay to starboard and the channel to port was lined by red nun buoys that appeared black along its right-hand boundary. Nothing marked the left side except shoal water that became Willoughby's Bay beyond Sewall's Point. A warning flaghoist from the *International Code of Signals* broke from their signal halyards after the EOT bell and pointer reported engineering was standing by. Starke tested rudder and engine then began easing forward until the first anchor chain was up and down. The staple attaching it in the chain locker was removed earlier so once the stopper was released it raced madly overboard through a cloud of dirt and rust-laden dust until the bitter end vanished. This process was repeated when Weaver released the second chain stopper and once complete the ensign broke at their mainmast truck and *Calypso* was underway.

Manipulating sluggish current with backing bell and rudder, he let the ship's head fall off towards the channel, shifted his rudder, and then eased ahead at dead slow for Buoy 6; calculating the weak current would set him towards Buoy 4 and allow an easy turn into the channel. The ammunition barge was left anchored astern with two guards while the tugs trailed *Calypso*; prepared to come alongside. Sailors on the forecastle monitored their patch while others below watched for a change in leakage or vibration. Starke took them steadily towards the channel, ensuring the bow wave never reached the poultice's lower edge and shifting to the pilothouse after gaining the feel of his battered command and sensing rain.

Between Buoys 4 and 6, he eased *Calypso* starboard to gain the channel; heeling her slightly port. Although unavoidable, she was already listing to that side and free water remaining in bilges could shift and submerge the patch. If their pumps were overwhelmed by that maneuver, flooding would cause her to roll and sink while moving forward; taking the engineers and many others with her. The turn seemed unending as he balanced minimum heel with entering the narrow channel, but they finally steadied and looked ahead to Norfolk and the Elizabeth River. Newport News Middle Ground faded to starboard and Hampton Roads astern as they passed by red nun channel buoys marking the right boundary. Beyond them lay Craney Island Flats and a low island; while to the left was a lightship moored off Tanner's Creek, near birds landing in shallow water. Starke eased *Calypso* left then right as he swung wide and avoided sharp turns until past the Craney Island jetty and Lambert's Point coal piers, passing *Doireann Bannan* waiting for inspection and temporary repairs at a round-roofed terminal. He swung wide for the next leg, which passed a small terminal to starboard and cleared the Navy Hospital's pier. Keeping left, they went by Fort Norfolk's curving brick and earth ramparts before leaving the city astern; steering for Berkley's piers. Two starboard turns to make the navy yard were completed with no more than nervous comments; although Quartermaster Smithers quietly whispered to Chief Owen, "The captain's having a pipe and conning the ship like a yacht out for the afternoon, Chief."

Owen saw no reason to disabuse him but was well aware Starke preferred conning from the flying bridge and was in the pilothouse to eliminate delay receiving reports or warnings, and confirm the correct engine or rudder orders were executed. Even more telling, Starke lit the pipe cradled in his right hand so he was unknowingly violating his own standing orders and probably Navy regulations; but its pleasant aroma did add a calming air to the pilothouse. Owen replied, "Worry about a solid round of bearings; and none of your five-finger fixes today."

Calypso slipped up the Elizabeth River's Southern Branch towards the shipyard leaving many industrial piers and terminals to starboard; and significantly fewer to port along the Berkley shore. Shipyard line-handlers went to station as the bark approached the same quay where she commissioned and must now moor before dry-docking. Starke observed a dozen Franklin sailors spread along it to receive lines; not the normal hodgepodge of Sunday draftees. Although tugs usually made up alongside to ease ships against the quay then counter any current until mooring lines were over and secure, those with Calypso were signaled to standby. Starke intended to drive the ship alongside and eliminate the risk of tug damage to the patch. With a single screw and damaged hull, deft control of lines and engine would make the difference. Besides an inherent delay between engine order and response, wind, current, and line handling must all be considered. River current was thankfully negligible and the wind, although increasing with the smell of an approaching storm, was on-setting. Against these, there could be only one attempt before resorting to tugs and risking the patch. Using the bowsprit base rather than jibboom, due to Calypso's list, Starke adjusted his approach angle; aiming three-quarters down the quay, just past the timber basin's mouth. Weaver pointed out the landing spot to a petty officer on the stone quay while Starke, employing a command voice, unnecessarily reminded the chief their fore and aft spring lines would go over first; to alert quay line-handlers.

Commodore Farquhar surveilled this from his carriage; parked where a shipyard street along the waterfront turned from the quay. He would own Calypso once moored, but Starke retained absolute responsibility until then; and he was well aware flag officers mixing with line-handlers invited catastrophe. Besides, the physical separation prevented his tours as Commandant of Cadets and captain of the training ship *Portsmouth* from getting the better of him. He judged Starke's angle too much at first but just before the jibboom passed over the quay, *Calypso*'s commander backed and put his rudder hard left. The bark slowed and swung her stern in, twisting the bow away, and the engine stopped. She was alongside and nearly parallel when heaving lines sailed across the gap and Starke, through his speaking trumpet, ensured fore and aft spring lines had been taken to cleats along the quay then ordered them held so the momentum against them, aided by the rudder, warped her hull in. When current eased *Calypso* slowly aft, the remaining lines tightened, and her hull snugged in. Once settled, the EOT signaled the engine room they were finished.

The commodore drove around the broad open area facing the ship and left his carriage to cross the brow while it was being secured. Watson spotted the waiting coach and pawing bay start for the ship, so Farquhar received regulation honors as Starke left the pilothouse. In Washington, a meeting between Long, Day, Crowninshield, and Albert sent *Marblehead*, in Annapolis for torpedo boat testing, to Port au Prince. The protected cruiser was known in the Caribbean and her new commander, Captain Bowman McCalla, thrived on independent operations.

CHAPTER TWENTY SIX
THE LADIES

Shipyard trades began trickling aboard at the same time Captain of the Yard, William Wise, sent naval constructors, steam engineers, and line officers to survey damage. They concluded the patch was holding, which allowed time for a better planned dry-docking, but Watson still permitted sailors to sleep topside since some feared being below deck. Day or night, crew anxiety invariably spiked when a passing ship's wake struck the patch, gently rolling the bark, and this was simultaneously aggravated and assuaged by grunting bilge pumps sending pulsating water streams overboard through scuppers and a main boiler kept on line for beaching.

Calypso had been fully fitted out so she required stripping to reduce weight for docking and allow space inspection. Its most disagreeable part began with the battered coal barge brought alongside and moored safely aft of the patch. For two days, while it gently compressed rope fenders protecting the black wood hull, this miserable work was only slightly mitigated by cool weather. A small amount of coal was held back for the boiler but tons of black, dusty lumps were extracted from bunkers using the same chutes that filled them. Once broken free and manhandled to the barge, coal was sorted by type, source, and age before transfer to yard boilers and kilns. *Calypso*'s exhausted crew then swept the ship, washed down, cleaned empty bunkers, removed a layer of fine black dust from their person, and started unloading storeroom contents for the surveys required before disposal or return to the owning bureau.

Control of *Calypso*'s daily life shifted to outsiders while Starke waited to learn whether he faced a board of inquiry, or three-officer panel; since Navy regulations required one or the other to establish what occurred, *Calypso*'s condition, and her crew's actions. Farquhar avoided the topic so Starke suspected he was waiting for department direction. Albert and Crowninshield supported him in the past but he just survived a different inquiry and the department had other perturbations with press interest. The battleship *Indiana* was sent to Nova Scotia for hull work because Brooklyn Navy Yard's new Dry-dock 3 required repair, the venerable sloop *Yantic*'s transit to Michigan's naval militia in Detroit generated a trail of incidents, and there were several lesser embarrassments. In addition, Congress' first session predictably ignited the perennial line and staff officer debates with vehemence since pay and medical corps proponents were pressing harder than usual; and the antagonism between line officers and steam engineers intensified with amalgamation gaining popularity. Starke anticipated this climate would press for expediency regarding *Calypso*, but not any specific outcome, so he prepared for the worst.

Starke and Albert also monitored Haiti out of curiosity. Their minister traveled from New York to the capital and requested support while *Marblehead* was steaming for Port au Prince. The two German training ships conducting their annual Caribbean cruise unexpectedly left Jamaica on December 6, 1897, for the Haiti where they allowed its government eight hours to meet Count Graf von Schwerin's demands or have the port shelled. French and German citizens were fleeing to their respective national ships and the unprotected cruiser *Geier* departed Kiel.

Meanwhile, *Calypso*'s bow cautiously inched over the dry-dock sill; shifting responsibility for most of what was not already controlled by Navy bureaus to the dock master, and transforming the elegant bark into an industrial site. This process began when the ship moored and Starke started reporting to Farquhar as commandant rather than through the Special Service Squadron to Albert. Consequently, an apprehensive Starke climbed *Franklin*'s enclosed stairwell to her main deck from the floating platform where *Calypso*'s pinnace delivered him. He was greeted on the quarterdeck by her commander, Captain Silas W. Terry, and then walked to a well-furnished cabin opening on a screened stern-walk.

Farquhar wasted little time on preliminaries. *Franklin*'s captain would head a three-officer board that included Commander George Pigman, recently assigned to Newport News, and Commander Willard Brownson, en route to the Board of Inspection and Survey after two years at the Academy and commanding *Detroit* during the Brazilian Naval Revolt. They would be supported by naval constructors, a representative sent from the judge advocate general's chief clerk, Edwin Hanna, and several administrative personnel. While ship condition, documented events, and related aspects were examined, *Calypso*'s minimal crew would be reduced to man new ships and supply replacements. Starke's single surprise was orders to Washington on detached duty; temporarily leaving *Calypso* with Watson. He was astounded Albert possessed such influence since achieving this easily equaled Roosevelt's manipulations to give Commodore Dewey the Asiatic Squadron over a slightly senior Commodore John Howell, the prolific inventor and respected officer.

Starke's unlikely guardian angel returned from the Building that evening to his row house aligned with a half-dozen similar red-brick structures along a sidewalk contrasting pleasantly with the asphalt street. Above its basement servants' quarters, occupied by a single Irish housekeeper, the first floor's large bay window shared frontage with three regular upstairs windows and entrance door flanked by a carved stone casing and lintel. He later half-listened to Abigail and daughters plan Olivia's wedding from his favorite stuffed chair while gazing through a first floor window overlooking the street. Under a cloudless night beyond those panes, stars were emerging, a full moon would soon follow, fall's smell of burning coal replaced that of window boxes and saplings in sidewalk tree wells, and flickering gaslights confirmed six o'clock had passed. On the small table beside him was a snifter of bourbon, *The Evening Times*, and *The Evening Star*. Both announced Congress would convene Tuesday despite a proposed delay for the president to remain with his dying mother. It appeared McKinley felt compelled to open the session. This also initiated the social season's events, visitations, and other activities so hotels and boarding houses were filling with entourages, supplicants, correspondents, lobbyists, officials, clerks, and more. One paper contained the president's speech to Congress arguing Spain deserved an opportunity to implement autonomy; although Roosevelt and other jingoes would rail at this and his not calling for Hawaii's annexation. The latter omission was no doubt because a treaty was under Senate debate, with the Hawaiian, or Sandwich Islander, delegation squaring off against groups supporting planters who overthrew the queen and those fearing another nation would annex the islands.

Albert was aware, as *The Evening Star* predicted, *Marblehead* arrived in Port au Prince after the German school ships left and Haiti's government acquiesced despite popular demand for war. Although *Calypso* was no longer involved, he continued attending meetings and learned that State, in contrast to their consul, held Haiti responsible for its plight and viewed German demands less onerous than Great Britain's in Nicaragua that went unchallenged. Domestic politics aside, they were equally concerned a confrontation with Germany would be unpredictable and might spark a European war. It was also anticipated the Haitian president, Simon Sam, would see repercussions in a nation known for explosive instability. In any case, *Marblehead* was no match for *Charlotte* and *Stein* since the ship-rigged steam frigate and corvette were well-armed before conversion to training ships, with around 900 sailors between them; while Haiti's navy possessed only one modern gunboat, *Crête-à-Pierrot*, and three inferior ones. Albert was charging a pipe and about to continue reading when Abigail reentered. After speaking for a few minutes, she smiled, gently took his hand in her warm one, and they climbed the narrow stairs to retire. The day's tribulations were soon forgotten.

Constance Starke visited Clarissa Barton at Glen Echo that week; a trip requiring a full day. The American Red Cross headquarters and storehouse that also served as Barton's home was in what was to be a well-off area before the panic left scattered homes, vacant lots, and an abandoned Chautauqua site. Immanuel refused to let Constance go alone, but she would only agree to take Cynthia Jefferson. He agreed since the formidable twenty-seven-year-old resembled her father, who oversaw Oxen Grove and saved it from Federal cavalry. She was intelligent and dignified with a manner that turned unyielding and assertive when necessary. Cynthia possessed a firm figure that was neither short nor tall and complimented an attractive countenance. Her distinctive oval face was composed of translucent cinnamon-brown lips below slightly hooded almond eyes, dark eyebrows, and rich black hair piled over and around her head. Although their senior maid, she was more housekeeper and family; especially after her father's passing. Immanuel often wondered why she never married since he knew her to be caring, open, and sociable despite contrary affectations.

The excursion was mostly by train, so Immanuel watched them board at the New Jersey Avenue station in spring-like December weather then returned to the landau thinking he was blessed with Constance. She was gliding towards sixty with long, silvering hair gathered above her head that accentuated a figure and carriage surpassing younger women; even without corset and bustle. Over time, her poise, speech, and confidence were sculpted into flawless elegance that was undiminished by raising Jacob; perhaps because he substituted for their lack of children. She was unnaturally quiet after returning that evening, so something clearly disturbed her, but their long marriage taught him to let his wife decide when to speak. When he joined her in the parlor later, the traveling suit was replaced by a flowing robin-egg blue tea gown, an oval broach fastened to a wide ribbon encircling her throat, one plain gold bracelet, and the wedding band she never removed.

There were rumors Miss Barton, in her seventy-seventh year, was in poor health despite retaining control of the American Red Cross and attending an overseas conference two months earlier, so he ventured, "How did you find Clara?"

"Under the weather and frustrated but nothing more; says she must get out and about to dispel rumors of her imminent passing and, as she puts it, efforts to put her on the shelf."

Constance slowly sipped some coffee, with a teaspoon of brown sugar adding luxury to the mild winter's eve, then continued, "They've been ten months in the building but its waiting rooms, closets, and storerooms still require attention. She insists the Red Cross runs itself but someone on the staff resigned and that seems more troubling for her than she lets on. Says she's thankful for every day God grants and works late into the night to make the most of it; but we mostly spoke about Cuba."

"Then she read Miss Evans' Havana letter?"

"Yes; and was grateful for reliable information."

"Even though Miss Evans works for Darwin Tyson?"

Mentioning the nephew's longtime friend usually got a rise, but she briefly smiled, lifted the china cup and saucer, and continued, "Cassandra says Governor-general Blanco is trying to feed reconcentrados or allow their return home, but those leaving fortified areas face insurrectionists and guerrilleros. Most won't or can't so they're condemned to squalor, starvation, and disease. Old people, women, and the young are skeletons; children with bloated bellies are begging everywhere; coffins have become a luxury; and the dead left beside those barely alive."

"So newspapers are accurate for once."

"She says many correspondents can't, or won't, go to the source it's so depressing. Besides, there's typhoid, cholera, and typhus; even if the dengue and yellow fever season's past."

Immanuel thought best with a cigar, and unconsciously pulled one from his leather case before remembering he was in the parlor. Constance knew the tightly rolled tobacco would be worried until lit, "Congress appropriated funds for Americans there and Clara's been asked to lead a relief effort. She'll not ignore anyone, of course, but needs both governments and the insurgents to allow it. Blanco wants help but not another country caring for those under his charge; and no one's sure of the insurrectos."

"You can't mean Clara intends to go to Cuba?"

"Yes."

"It's dangerous for Miss Evans but Clara's seventy-seven."

"They're aware, Immanuel."

"How is Miss Evans faring?"

"She's at the Inglaterra with Darwin because our consul-general and most diplomats live there. Says he's a tartar who demands facts; but overly protective, which seems out of character."

Constance paused, then resumed, "She'll miss the annual Women's Press Association convention at the Willard Hotel this week; and asked about Jacob."

Immanuel rolled his cigar, pawed his pockets for the oval cutter, caught himself, and stifled the urge, "You once had some thoughts in that direction, I believe?"

Setting cup and saucer on the table with feigned indignation, she responded, "Jacob's of an age and must consider eligible women. She lacks Katherine's connections but is intelligent, strong, of an independent mind, and, judging from your reaction, attractive."

Immanuel found the description also fit the woman just across the table he constantly found had more to love as years passed. Constance's thoughts were now solicited on most actions, the firm benefited from her Washington connections, and their lack of offspring was ameliorated by raising Jacob after his mother died during the war; and Cynthia when her mother passed.

Since she raised the subject, he asked, "Anything from Katherine?"

His wife's face clouded, "No. Her mother and I rarely correspond but Katherine stopped writing after August and the last letter sounded as though she was ill."

"You once thought she'd suit Jacob?"

Constance reached over the table, looked into her husband's eyes, smiled, and softly squeezed his right hand, "She's a Christian woman who mostly knows her mind but learned too late how much she loved her husband."

Immanuel smiled, "Not like us."

Constance's forehead and corners of her mouth wrinkled, "Not like us; and I believe you mentioned other news."

Continuing to fondle the cigar, he replied, "Edward's returning before the month ends so you'll learn about Katherine then. He's exploring the feasibility of reopening the mill and plantation since Spain's implementing autonomy. Jacob also telegrammed he'll be on the train from Newport News this week. Albert expects the inquiry will exonerate him but can't predict if he'll still command *Calypso* or what happens to her."

Constance was silent for a moment; then her eyes twinkled, "Cassandra's not here for the conference and Katherine's unavailable, but I've others in mind."

After letting her perplexed husband struggle several seconds, she smiled, "For heaven's sake. Take that poor cigar to the library and once you've done for it and your whiskey, come to bed. I'll be waiting."

Immanuel went to the library, poured a whiskey, found his customary soft leather chair, lit the cigar, and released a gray cloud of smoke. He wished his nephew a marriage as fulfilling as his own. The half-smoked cigar and nearly full whiskey snifter was found instead of the usual ash and empty glass during morning cleaning.

Starke left for Washington around seven when a Captain of the Yard's carriage conveyed him to the Portsmouth ferry landing. Preparing to depart was the side-wheel paddle steamer *Louise* with its white hull supporting a three-deck superstructure, pilothouse, walking-beam, tall stack, and ventilators. The cool, clear morning's promise of afternoon showers and river's scent were all but overcome by the bouquet of burning coal and steam as she paddled down Elizabeth River's Southern Branch past piers and warehouses. The Union Depot slid astern to port; across the river from a small Berkley shipyard separated by marsh from the Norfolk & Southern Railroad facility. She soon turned left to thrash along Norfolk's waterfront before stopping at the Chesapeake & Ohio's rail and dock complex to board additional Newport News and Old Point Comfort passengers. From there, *Louise* crossed Hampton Roads, skirted Newport News Middle Ground, and made her approach on the Newport News combined ferry pier and train shed. Its red, open sides and gable roof jutted into the river from a light-yellow Chesapeake & Ohio railroad station dwarfed by the mammoth grain elevator and massive coal piers. A panting black steam locomotive waited in the train shed; already coupled to several coaches. He immediately boarded one and found a tolerably comfortable seat. Several noisy jolts later, they left the rail station; and its bouquet of coal dust, river shore, grain, and fish. He wore civilian clothes so the only person showing interest was a slightly older woman who glanced furtively at his sword's canvas sock until he locked eyes on her. She departed in Richmond when his car was coupled to the Washington train that rolled north leaving steam and smoke drifting out and away from the right-of-way. The last weeks' tension dissipated as he drifted off to clicking steel wheels crossing rail joints. He visited the dining car a half hour later then returned to watch towns, forests, and fields pass.

Their approach to Washington's Baltimore & Potomac station was announced as they descended from high ground west of the city, just before starting over a wooden trestle to a small island. After crossing the Potomac River's Long Bridge his train entered the city just north of the port where *Newport News* took him to *Calypso* over a year and a half earlier. The rebuilt buildings and piers replacing those damaged during the recent hurricane were servicing scows, barges, and schooners; alongside or in the stream. As they eased up Maryland Avenue with the locomotive dusting buildings and streets with steam, smoke, and soot; Starke saw the Building still dominated surrounding red-brick, wood, and stone structures from its elevated location. They cleared the wye just after crossing a spur to the station's switches and sidings near the Fish Commission building, halted briefly, and then backed to the train shed. The gently rolling mall to their east, encircled by buildings and containing less trees since the hurricane, soon gave way to a plethora of windows and freight docks sheltered under a massive barrel roof. After a lurching halt jumbled impatient passengers in the aisle, Starke rose from his seat, reclaimed baggage, and left through the station's B Street entrance. He was not met since there was no reason for Sutton to subject their carriage to the disruption from Capital Traction Company rebuilding its street car line so an unenthusiastic coal-black gelding drew his Herdic cab past Center Market and away from Baltimore & Potomac's red-brick and stone station with its black-mortar, single tall clock tower surrounded by subordinates, gables, and long train shed extending south. Further on, they passed by Pennsylvania Avenue's torn up rails and horse-drawn street cars.

He reached the mansion just before Saturday supper and climbed its front steps, leaving his small trunk, Gladstone bag, and sword at the curb. His cab returned to the city with a driver reflecting on the day's best fare and tip; obviously from someone familiar with Washington since his passenger expertly handled the walking stick gentleman carried to prevent or disable assailants in a city that controlled firearms and edged weapons. Starke was greeted by their butler, Joshua Altman, with unusual informality as he took the coat, cane, and hat; then sent a servant to retrieve what remained curbside. Butlers and second men were rapidly being displaced by a head maid and female subordinates; creating enough demand to open a school in New York to train aspiring women. Most justified this by claiming females were less inclined to drink or fight but his uncle maintained the true reason was cost. He chose carefully, often trusted people from the firm, and paid well so Altman, Jefferson, and Young ran an efficient staff. Starke also went downstairs to visit Martella, who interrupted supper preparations to crush him in a firm embrace while Cynthia nodded a greeting.

After arranging a Sunday morning ride, he passed an evening with his aunt and uncle in the parlor then retired. Starke considered taking his Yellow Boy bicycle instead of Gemini since wheeling was immensely popular, covered extensively in newspapers, undergoing Army trials consisting of a cycle troop, and encouraged for recreation in both services. Some *Calypso* sailors already joined a local navy club in Norfolk and O'Leary was an early devotee of the machines; but Starke still preferred the bay gelding.

Gemini whinnied a greeting the next morning when Starke entered their stable wearing the inelegant and unfashionable riding attire that meant an outing. Sutton often spoke of bonding with cavalry mounts and Starke felt something like that with Gemini; who ignored Castores' frantic stamping and head shakes as they left. The clear, bright, and warm morning added a cathartic quality to a ride spent mostly at the walk, but cantering on good dirt or grass, and a final gallop home.

Sunday evening was spent in the library with his uncle where they enjoyed a snifter and cigar while discussing news from Saturday's *The Evening Star* and Sunday's *The Times*. The American stillborn Haitian intervention apparently inspired a Spanish paper to call for naval expansion by national subscription and demand an end to all Cuba interference. A congressman advocated exterminating Bering Sea seals as the best way to end that international issue and cost. Cabinet members and others would limit holiday festivities with the president's mother near death and the same society pages offered sufficient debutants to encourage his aunt's matrimonial endeavors. *The Times* claimed Hawaiian treaty ratification was doubtful. Spanish troops in Cuba continued to lose engagements as three separate commissions arrived in Havana to study yellow fever when it was least active. Reading that China was pressured by Great Britain, France, Germany, and Russia after the recent war, Starke recalled Philo McGiffin describing how Li Hongzhang's efforts to modernize and expand the Beiyang Fleet were sabotaged by a corrupt bureaucracy and Dowager Empress skilled in preserving the status quo. His friend paid the price along with Chinese sailors who fired sand-filled practice shells at Japanese cruisers. A German ship reported discovering two partly submerged wrecks far into the Atlantic that probably resulted from a collision since they were floating within a few miles of each other. There was no sign of either crew; reminding him that *Calypso* could not have recovered at sea and her boats would not hold everyone.

Starke passed an unsettled Sunday night then donned the blue service dress uniform, overcoat, and cap he wore coaxing *Calypso* into the navy yard. Less mild weather was forecast but still clear and unseasonably warm so it was a pleasant after-breakfast walk to St. Margaret's Episcopal Church where he took the Metropolitan Company streetcar line south; the same route where Evans and her Brussels carpet bag first attracted his attention. He gazed through a window as the slightly rocking car clattered past Grafton Hotel, churches, embassies, and homes. When The Cairo, a twelve-story Romanesque apartment building with roof garden sanctuary, flashed past down a side street, he wondered if Queen Liliuokalani was there preparing for another day opposing treaty ratification. He disembarked above Lafayette Square, near the corner shared by Arlington Hotel, St. John's Episcopal Church, and duplex mansion shared by Washington society's Hays and Adams families. Walking across the square towards the Building, Starke passed behind a Capital Traction Company horse-drawn car then skirted construction work near the Executive Mansion's greenhouse and stable. Once inside the Building's wrought iron gates, he climbed two flights of marble steps to enter though the State, War, and Navy Building's East Wing entrance; below double-fluted columns, windows, and porticoes. It was over a year since he worked there so few people remembered or greeted him as he eschewed the elevator to rapidly climb fitted granite stairs with brass balusters beneath the rotunda's colored glass skylight. He turned left twice for the next staircase before reaching the fourth floor then walked down the familiar off-white corridor with checkerboard marble floors running between black borders. After knocking on Albert's recessed pine and mahogany door below its partially opened transom window, Starke twisted the polished brass knob with embossed anchor and entered. The captain pushed back his chair, rose, and offered a firm hand, "Welcome back, lieutenant."

His sincere greeting lacked the courtesy title of captain so Starke told himself there would be other ships, perhaps outside the Navy. Captain Albert, his uncle, and *Eveleth's* master Stede Schumacher often claimed overlong in command created an unnatural attachment. He felt its effects as Albert grinned, "The secretary agrees with Captain Terry's finding there's no justification for a formal board of inquiry and Crowninshield's observation that going to sea's inherently dangerous. Unless something new surfaces their consensus is no action on your part could have prevented the collision; and *Calypso* was saved by those taken.

"What about *Calypso*, sir?"

Starke was motioned to a small leather settee as Albert retreated behind the desk in his rolling gait then slowly sat. The captain shifted desktop items using solid arms jutting out from a short and stocky torso. Other than a slightly increased paunch, he had changed little. The round head was clean-shaven and retreating, close-cropped hair graying; while his immaculate service dress blue uniform showed the slight regulations changes just implemented. Like always, his shoes were polished black calfskin, not patent leather. Albert retrieved a favored pipe, charged it, and lit up, "I believe you meant the two of you?"

"Yes sir; I suppose so."

"Terry's board will determine *Calypso's* physical state and we need gunboats so her future turns on cost to repair. Even your last ship, *Detroit*, just back from Asia, is to be immediately overhauled then returned to sea." Converting *Calypso* to an Academy practice ship was discussed but her steam plant would require removal and the contract for a new school ship's already let. Bering Sea patrols were another proposal, but she's not strengthened for the arctic service."

When Albert's pipe went out, he scraped its burnt contents into the ashtray, "Your future depends on the final board report. I've asked for you in the meantime, but so has Consul-General Lee; and your torpedo boat paper has two bureaus requesting you visit England, France, and Germany. They're following Spain's lead with Villaamil's *Destructor* and building torpedo boat destroyers. Roosevelt's pushing the department on this because he's convinced these will threaten battleships. We have sixteen approved but not designed so Crowninshield wants a line officer to explore what's happening overseas. At the moment he's less enamored with our London attaché than Simms in Paris and Germany's developing torpedo boat tactics. Since you speak both languages . . . ."

"That means leaving *Calypso*?"

"You'll lose *Calypso* if she's decommissioned but not if she can be repaired without. Watson would take her through the yard. It's Roosevelt's scheme."

Starke leaned back into the leather settee and was about to speak when Albert raised his hand, still grasping the pipe, "Let this play out before you say or do anything."

He then grinned conspiratorially, "It seems officers cannot be ordered from any ship until every item signed for is reconciled; which requires your presence."

Albert ended the interview by rising from his desk, adding, "You'll need to officially report your arrival," then, grinning broadly, "On a more pleasant note, Abigail and the girls are looking forward to your family's Christmas ball since it won't conflict with the Seaman Gunners Ball on the twenty-third."

CHAPTER TWENTY SEVEN
FATHERS AND SONS

C aptain Albert walked to the window and prepared his pipe while studying Executive Avenue's pedestrians and carriages. Years of throttling commissions and stagnated promotions dulled or drove out officers, a point Roosevelt argued relentlessly, yet the Bureau of Navigation expected their experienced line officer surplus would vanish as war veterans retired and fleet mushroomed. For that reason and Starke's performance to date, he did not anticipate the lieutenant's relief if *Calypso* remained in commission. Farquhar already sensed Starke did not see this and might resign rather than risk dismissal; so he related his experiences after *Trenton* was lost during the Samoan hurricane but failed to reach him. Albert was not surprised since Starke seemed always on the cusp of resigning; and it was a quality he sought for *Calypso*'s commander since the ferret scheme required an officer who was innovative, energetic, and expendable. He observed the first two qualities at Alexandria when Starke was a cadet serving under him on *Apalachicola* and the officer's subsequent career. As for the third, Albert was aware opportunities outside the service were easing Starke towards resignation before offering *Calypso*. The odds of Starke now remaining in the Navy or his steam bark returning to sea seemed roughly even, but Albert hoped to improve the officer's by speaking to the Bureau of Navigation chief about proposed orders for the interim assignment.

Starke spent that week and part of the next responding to bureaus or the board while Watson worked Norfolk. Both men addressed numerous inquiries and derailed ill-advised initiatives before bureaucratic mortar set. Starke was also updating a torpedo boat analysis created before accepting *Calypso* since the assistant secretary believed these threatened battleships and the department should buy Holland's submersible version. This revision included Britain's construction surge, improving French and German tactics, *Turbinia*'s sprint through the Spithead Naval Review, and additional information on Spain's *Peral* and France's *Gymnote*.

Preserving *Calypso*'s hand-picked, experienced crew meant constant skirmishing to fend off the bureaucracy's raids and other ships' poaching but a third or more could be lost so it was critical to retain a solid nucleus. Their naval cadets transferred immediately to a departing ship where they would remain competitive for commissioning. Fleet demand for steam engineers cost another cadet and Osbourne; leaving the unsuspecting O'Leary as interim chief engineer. *Maine* wanted Grier and Kirby for her 6-inch battery but they preferred a ship with 4-inch mounts so Watson placed them aboard the fifth and last *Annapolis* class gunboat being built; before the battleship returned from Tompkinsville in late December.

The Starke Christmas ball was one of a decreasing number of private events on the social calendar so nearly 150 were invited with 130 anticipated; but Starke was surprised to find his aunt enlisted Albert and Falk to assist with the guest list. It seemed her visit with Clara Barton at Glen Echo resulted in using the event to negotiate reconcentrado relief. With thousands dying from disease and starvation in Cuba, McKinley started a New York committee to solicit donations, and Congress appropriated $50,000 in May; but this caused a conundrum since Havana's consul-general office was not appropriately staffed and Spain or the Junta taking it on clearly unacceptable. The Red Cross was approached but Barton refused to commit until everyone agreed and provided assurances that efforts and supplies would not be blocked, taxed, stolen, or disrupted. Sensitive negotiations were sometimes conducted under the cover of private balls and the Starke's was especially convenient with the usual social events sponsored by the Executive Mansion, cabinet, and others curtailed or cancelled due to the president's mother passing.

The ball began on the Tuesday evening before Christmas in the mansion's Louis XVII off-white ballroom with its parquet floor newly waxed for dancing. Three cut-crystal chandeliers, the exterior wall pierced by tall windows, and large mirrors on the interior achieved a grand ballroom illusion. A raised band dais was at the rear and large half-round alcove incorporated in the front. Pocket doors opened from the entrance hall's right side, opposite the parlor. The formal dining room was directly above with a smaller salon at the rear and dumb waiter to the ground floor kitchen area for supplying early evening refreshments and more substantial fare during the midnight dancing break.

Cabs and carriages lining the curb outside dropped off passengers then rolled behind the house where Darius Sutton offered drivers a hot toddy and food. Guests arrived through the large oak doors then, before entering the entrance hall, left overcoats, shawls, and top hats between butler office and cloak room. Immanuel and Constance Starke welcomed guests in the two-story hall dividing the house; with its curved staircases rising under Tiffany stained glass windows at the far end. As with the ballroom and formal dining room it was trimmed with fresh flowers from their greenhouse. The receiving line formed at the time invitations stated but arrivals increased later as arriving just fashionably late was customary. Most passing through were couples, with the occasional single male, but no unchaperoned women, single or married, would attend. Constance greeted each, spoke briefly, and passed them to her husband who, unlike dinner parties, was titular host; with planning and execution still falling to the wife, supporting ladies, and household staff. Custom and courtesy limited remarks to a sentence or two, although a few invariably stretched that courtesy.

Immanuel Starke wore a formal black tail-coat and trousers requiring only a change of trappings to match any fashion; and tonight these included a heavily starched white shirt with diamond studs above a low-cut vest of fine, light wool; accompanied by a small off-white bow-tie, white cotton gloves, thin pocket-watch with chain, and black-bowed leather pump shoes. Beside him, Constance stood, confident and gracious, possessing the classic charm of a firm, well-formed face, and trim figure. Unlike Clara Barton, she did not dye her hair when it began graying but let it alter naturally to a dark silver-gray that enhanced her other attributes. It was in the Grecian style tonight, a perfect match for her pale burnt-orange gown of layered silk. Mature ladies traditionally choose rich, dark colors but her youthful figure carried it off. The bustled skirt eschewed overt decoration above a scalloped hemline, dropped smoothly, and continued to a train flowing lightly over the floor. Most modern gowns dispensed with these or made them detachable because they demanded dancing proficiency. A fitted bodice to accentuate her figure was cut straight over the breast tops then anchored with embroidery; and the same extremely fine, light-gray lace rising above it to her neck also lightly screened bare shoulders, back, and upper breast. It also formed the drop sleeves that fell below her elbows and over a pair of long, white-silk gloves. The five-strand pearl choker around the throat matched her earrings and single-strand necklace swung down loosely over her bust then nearly to the waist.

Jacob Starke stood near his uncle wearing the latest style black tail-coat suit with trousers and waistcoat; despite tuxedos' increasing popularity. Like his uncle, diamond shirt studs closed a starched cotton shirt with wingtip collar and white silk tie. His father's plain gold Patek Philippe & Cie pocket watch, retrieved from a drawer, was in the vest pocket at the end of a fob chain. His evening dress uniform contributed white gloves and he chose low-cut shoes with flexible soles for dancing.

Captain Albert led Abigail, Olivia, and Isabella through the line wearing an evening dress uniform with cocked hat, epaulets, and parade sword suspended from slings. Its double-breasted, navy-blue coat was close-fitting with two rows of five gilt buttons in front, two identical ones in the back, and each sleeve encircled by four gold-lace stripes under a star. The coat was worn open over a white shirt with standing collar and navy-blue waistcoat with four small, gold buttons above gold-striped trousers. The ensemble was completed with white lisle thread gloves, a black bow-tie, and his seldom worn patent leather shoes. Constance's two summer guests wore new gowns so she suspected those from Mary Dickerson's Newport dress shop no longer fit the sisters' figures. All three Albert gowns were in the classic style, with the mother's a dark fabric; recently engaged daughter, perhaps under duress, in less opaque but light-colored silk; and youngest in the same material but finer and more revealing.

Isabella was escorted by Passed Assistant Engineer Osbourne; in Washington for promotion examination and dressed like her father except there was no star over his two gold stripes separated by red cloth. *Calypso*'s executive officer or commander was required to remain on board so Starke agreed to escort Watson's fiancée Olivia; which conveniently avoided his aunt's matrimonial initiatives and conveying a lady to and from home.

Maximilian Falk y Machado, the Machiavellian Justice clerk, brought a Spanish beauty of near boyish figure and mesmerizing countenance with dark brown eyes that were striking and intense. Aron Sharett, his uncle's friend and chandler, attended; as did Lieutenant Alexander Sharp, Assistant Secretary Roosevelt's aide. Captain Gibson Fischer arrived, in obvious discomfort wearing the Revenue Service's evening dress uniform, accompanied by his formidable but sociable wife with similar shape and countenance. Clara Barton passed through with Dr. Julian Hubbell, her alter ego; then Spain's Naval attaché Capitán de Corbete Jose G. Sobral in a resplendent evening dress uniform. Arliss Spencer, from Justice and a senior clerk from Assistant Secretary Day's office were also guests. Herminio Gonzales y Ochoa, the Cuban Club president *Calypso* rescued when *John Gwinn Williams* sank off the Florida Keys, attended and seemed genuinely pleased to see Starke; who guessed he was a proxy for Gonzalo Quesada since Gonzales could justify his attendance as reciprocation for Starke attending a San Carlos Club dinner in Key West. Edward Curtis, Katherine's brother and patron, entered alone and appeared unusually ill-at-ease.

Most guests circulated through the large entrance hall, waiting for the horn to summon them, but some women drifted to the parlor and men the library. Starke went from one cluster to the next, pausing for brief conversation. Most were mundane and repetitive but some were tête-à-têtes conducted with diplomatic language's subtle thrust and parry expected in the volatile and eclectic concoction created by

Falk's discrete finesse, his aunt's practiced societal skills, and Barton's tact.

Summoned by notes from a horn, married women escorted by husbands entered the ballroom, unmarried ladies with their chaperones, and then single men. Starke and Olivia led the unmarried contingent; astern of Captain Albert and Abigail but ahead of Osbourne and Isabella. Playing a warm-up tune from the raised dais were two violinists, a flutist, and female pianist; the last being unusual but increasingly common in professional quartets and quadrille bands. Each lady held one of the dance cards distributed when roughly half the expected guests were through the receiving line. These fan-shaped mementoes regulated male behavior and ensured all ladies received dance invitations. The host, with help from his wife or lady delegated the role, enforced this and other customs by ensuring those ignoring them received few future invitations. Married and engaged couples dancing together, especially when obvious, was considered bad taste and exceeding four dances with the same partner unacceptable. Every male made, and no female refused, a proper invitation unless ill or the dance taken. Although Starke's aunt often called on him to fill a breach, he willingly obliged since balls were to promote dancing, it was improper to speak on the floor, introductions were for the evening only, white gloves eliminated suggestive touching, and taking a seat beside your last partner was thought rude.

An evening included twenty-four dances beginning with a quadrille then several waltzes, a schottische, two marches, and a lancers; ending the next morning with a gallop. Two sorties with Olivia and one with her sister convinced Starke they were exuberant and skilled novices whose talents came from Abigail. The mother was accomplished with natural agility and movement while Albert proved the epitome of technical exactness. Starke spent the evening inviting ladies that lacked attention using formal, contrived phrases communicating intent without offense. He considered approaching Barton before recalling she never learned once her family had forbid it; which he thought odd since they apparently encouraged every other endeavor.

Dancing slowed near midnight when carved beef and pork, vegetables, tea, iced sherbet, and cakes were laid out on the second floor dining room table. Ladies were then served by their standing escort while sitting along the wall. Starke passed through the entrance hall on his way to the library and observed several women congregating by the first floor powder room and Isabella energetically questioning the stolid Dr. Anita Newcomb McGee; a lady in private practice before turning to research and Daughters of the American Revolution medical endeavors. Clara Barton was nearby with Dr. Hubbell, Spain's naval attaché, and his wife. Her petite frame displayed a reputed tactful intensity so Starke stood clear to avoid becoming a disruption since Sobral regularly supplied Spanish papers with caustic and dismissive articles on the American navy.

Small clusters of men found refuge amidst the library's bookshelves, oriental rugs, floor globe, chairs, and large wooden desk with brass lamp and high-backed leather chair. His uncle and Sharett were just inside, debating some potential or ongoing business venture, while the normally affable Edward Curtis stood apart at the window nursing a half-consumed cigar and brandy. He was staring outside, appeared subdued, and failed to notice Starke's approach. They had no real opportunity to speak since his arrival from Britain since he politely declined an invitation to lodge at the mansion; claiming business required staying at the Arlington Hotel. Curtis turned with a weak smile when he saw Starke approaching from the window's reflection, "Good evening, Jacob. We've not spoken for some time; dammed unfortunate about *Calypso*."

Starke diverted, "You're back for business?"

"For the syndicate; we need to know if it's time to start rebuilding the Cuban properties. Fighting in the Philippines appears over and Blanco wants to restart Cuban businesses now that the Queen Regent's proclaimed autonomy; but we're undecided."

Starke's eyes locked on Curtis, "Someone I trust predicts it will get worse and insurrectionists will reject autonomy. They apparently won't trust Spain after Zanjón and believe it shows they're winning; while loyalists, especially guerrilleros, have no illusion regarding their fate. Many in Spain believe liberals caved and did not stand up to the States when Weyler was within months of a victory. Our press wants intervention on behalf of the reconcentrados, for the moment anyway, and Tyson wrote from Havana that the starvation and disease is not exaggerated. My other source is a guest so I can introduce you tonight."

"That would be useful. Europe's convinced autonomy is the solution and Americans are promoting colonial insurrections."

Starke thought Europe should consider its activities in Africa, India, and China, but instead asked, "Is Katherine in good health? She still writes but seems different."

Curtis' gaze returned to the dark yard beyond the window, quickly downed the drink, then turned back nervously, rolled a half-smoked cigar between his fingers, sighed deeply, and acquired an odd expression, "No way to avoid it, I suppose."

Starke braced himself. She would have stopped writing if engaged or about to be, and the normally expansive brother was clearly uncomfortable. He immediately backed off, certain she was sick or dying and chose not to tell him, "You're uneasy and I understand."

Curtis returned to the window, "She made me swear and I agreed; since you and *Calypso* were to be in the Caribbean."

"That would true if not for the collision."

"However, you are here and have every right to know."

Deliberately lowering his cigar to the ashtray, Curtis stiffened, "Katherine's never been disingenuous or dishonest. She could even be described as dauntless until a few years before marrying Philip then grew more reserved after he died. I had hoped bringing her here, then Havana, would change that."

Starke's expression unintentionally shifted to one familiar to his officers when they struggled with bad or embarrassing news, "Yes?"

"You've a son, Jacob; Oliver Barrington Curtis. She chose a short-form birth certificate to leave the father obscured so I believe she intended to tell you at some point."

Starke was stunned and engulfed with conflicting emotions, but it explained the odd tension in her letters after their night in Havana; and what she told her brother was undoubtedly true. Even more unsettling, that Katherine had borne his son felt unexpectedly agreeable, so he pointed to a leather chair facing the fireplace, "Let's sit, Edward. We've time before dancing resumes."

Curtis sat then leaned forward, "She did not want anyone thinking you were deceived into marriage and feared losing your aunt's respect."

"I've shamed her, Edward."

"She blames herself for Havana but loves the boy; and I've taken to him as well."

Starke immediately responded, "Edward, I wish to marry your sister."

"I will certainly act for you, Jacob; but she asked that I not tell and expects no offer. She's also changed and now seems impervious to notoriety, or being excluded from society, and has the resources to do so with some impunity. She may not accept and our father might oppose the match since his opinion of your countrymen is never high at the best of times."

Before the mantel clock summoned them to the ballroom Starke said he hoped to propose in person but ventured nothing about the possibility he would soon be in Europe; whether ordered there to study torpedo boats or after his resignation. He also agreed that Curtis would write first to explain how he learned of the birth and his intentions. Her brother was also asked to explore what marriage negotiations were necessary since he was unfamiliar with English customs. Before returning to the dance, they agreed to meet later that week, discuss what came next, provide for Oliver Barrington Curtis if she refused, and determine what was needed to add Starke to his son's name. The ball finished in a blur and he spent what remained considering how to best approach his aunt and uncle.

He doubted the uncle would say more than strike out from where he was, but his aunt held unshakable religious convictions and he now had an illegitimate son. Starke told her in the same parlor she first announced Katherine's visit and suggested he favorably consider her distant relative. In the event, Constance accepted Starke's revelation as God's gift and overstimulation caused by natural forces rather than moral depravity. She attributed no ulterior motives to Katherine, but took pains to emphasize his son's mother possessed a quality, depth, and passion he must not fail to explore and treasure. Marriage was not mentioned but assumed. His uncle, as anticipated, considered it a decision made and immediately turned to addressing the illegitimacy and an international marriage. In neither conversation did Starke see fit to reveal Katherine had not received or accepted his proposal; nor the impediments her brother mentioned.

Albert began the cold and bleak day before Christmas anticipating Starke's nine o'clock interview and enjoying a second coffee. He shivered and slowly swirled the cup's grainy remains as he looked beyond the Building's panes. A cold, windy night ended their unusually temperate weather but denied any holiday snow. Still, coffee tasted best on such days and its aroma always lingered. He went to the oak desk and set the worn china cup on one corner before extracting its rolling chair. Arthritic knee pain, another sign of the season, added a sharp electric shock as he settled in then scooted forward over a Persian rug. He was reviewing a report when the clamor of arriving government clerks, stenographers, and staff in the interior hall caused him to glance up at the clock.

There was good news for Starke. Preliminary findings recommended *Calypso* for repair and retaining crew. This included Starke after the assistant secretary threw his considerable energy behind Albert's maneuvering; and frustrated perhaps a half-dozen hopefuls. His ferret would survive even as the filibuster project acquired renewed support from the president's message to Congress and Treasury secretary's clear declaration the American effort to prevent filibuster expeditions far exceeded Spain's. Albert's current anxiety lay with Starke, who seemed destined to straddle the service and some private life; a point the lieutenant entering Albert's office emphasized by the civilian attire. Even so, the captain pushed from the desk, rose, and greeted him with a grin. After settling his visitor in a small settee with worn leather upholstery, Albert retreated to his chair, reached forward for a meerschaum pipe, dredged its cinnamon brown bowl through a leather pouch, carefully charged it, and then carefully passed a match over center.

"*Calypso* will be repaired. Our lack of gunboats for the next year or so was the deciding factor. There's even talk of converting larger yachts."

"Good news then, Captain."

Starke noticed his status was not immediately addressed, but pressure from his uncle to join Starke Shipping & Shipbuilding had increased with the assumed marriage to Katherine and a son. Albert re-lit his pipe, shook the match until its flame vanished in blue smoke then dropped it to the ashtray, "Roosevelt believes officers like you are needed to command and convinced Long despite their recent Dewey imbroglio; so you won't be exiled to Europe."

Since learning about Katherine and his son, Starke welcomed the potential European assignment and ending his career even seemed palatable, but it appeared *Calypso* was not finished with him. He heard Albert begin, "She'll be at least two months in the yards . . . ." Starke was about to press for leave when the captain continued, ". . . but you'll not be returning to Norfolk. Consul-General Lee's request for your services in Havana's been approved."

Misreading Starke's hesitancy, he added, "Lee's pushing the Department to resume Cuban port visits through Day and State feels a German training ship's presence there makes it difficult for Spain to deny *Calypso*."

Sensing little change, Albert pressed on, "He praised your last trip and says you've a useful reputation with Armada Española officers despite pummeling one of their gunboats."

Albert set his pipe aside, "Sending a naval attaché to a consular post like Havana could provoke Madrid so you retain command while *Calypso*'s repaired. They'll be unable object and you have your father and uncle's connections."

Observing Starke's mind shift from apparent reticence, Albert allowed him an opening by relighting his pipe.

"I'll not spy or compromise either firm's people."

"You'll be asked to do nothing more than a naval attaché; plus explore their willingness to resume courtesy visits. Although, anything you discover about gunboat operations and plans for the large dry-dock they just towed across the Atlantic might prove useful. Roosevelt thinks they plan to make Havana a Caribbean Gibraltar."

"The assistant secretary's involved?"

"Yes. In confidence, he's an odd bird. Likes Long, but envies Day's role at State and feels cramped here. Roosevelt's done well but is inexperienced, unpredictable, and intent on war. He's convinced it's inevitable with Spain but I doubt he'd forego the opportunity with Germany, France, Britain, or any other country."

"And your thoughts on a Spanish war, sir?"

"I've discussed it with Falk. Everything turns on autonomy and whether insurrectos are agreeable. Governor-general Blanco will announce it next month but opposition's growing in Spain and Cuba. Their government knows the island cannot be held if forced to fight the States and deal with an insurrection; but their public blames us so it cannot accept anything compromising national honor without falling. Instability's already growing, Lee thinks loyalist partisans left a small bomb near our consulate but the candidates include every group from anarchists to the *New York Journal*."

Darwin Tyson and Cassandra Evans entered Starke's thoughts as Albert moved on, "Anyway, Commander Clover relieved Wainwright as chief intelligence officer last month and focused the office on Germany because of Haiti. Roosevelt's convinced they should concentrate on Spain so he sided with State and arranged your assignment with Crowninshield."

Albert relit his pipe, "Roosevelt makes the better case about Spain but State's concerned Europe might take sides if it's war. In the meantime, *Maine* is standing by and Lee has authority to summon her should our nationals or consulate require support; which raises another subject. Wainwright's her executive officer for now but I've received a definite commitment to relieve Sigsbee and want you with me. It's a lieutenant commander billet; but if you're not promoted by then we'll see what can be done."

Albert studied the lieutenant through rising pipe smoke while Starke struggled. He could not abandon *Calypso* or her crew; and felt the rising, irresistible attraction that drew him to Montana, Alexandria, and Far East. With Katherine and a son, he understood his father's susceptibilities and inability to ignore obligations. Later, after returning to the mansion, Lieutenant Jacob Starke spoke with his aunt and uncle, wrote to Katherine offering whatever she would allow for their son, and completed instructions to the family's lawyer for revising his will. Captain Albert spent the same evening with his family preparing for Christmas Day and grateful *Calypso* would be in the Caribbean flushing filibusters before summer.

About the Author

Born in Lapeer, Michigan, and raised on farms near Davison, Michael T. Ribble received a Bachelor's Degree in journalism after attending the University of Colorado in Boulder and Central Michigan University. During high school and college he worked road construction, farmed in Colorado, helped construct a feedlot, harvested sugar beets, and spent one summer as a camp counselor/rifle instructor. Enlisting as a seaman recruit, he attended basic training in San Diego, served on two minesweepers, a guided missile cruiser, destroyer, and frigate, before retiring from active and reserve service as captain. After obtaining a Master of Business Administration degree from Florida State University, he held integrated logistics, program analyst, and cost estimating positions at Naval Sea Systems Command and the Department of Homeland Security. Besides a year in Guantanamo Bay, he participated in towing de-fueled nuclear submarines and early *Virginia* class development, taught naval science at Northwestern University, facilitated the National Naval Reserve Policy Board, and completed the United States Naval War College's continuing education program. He has served on steam and diesel ships as a Surface Warfare Officer and crewed in annual sail races down Chesapeake Bay. Besides two previous Starke novels, he has been published in university publications, newspapers, and U.S. Naval Institute *Proceedings*.